Burgundy

BURGUNDY

ANTHONY HANSON

faber and faber
LONDON · BOSTON

First published in 1982
by Faber and Faber Limited
3 Queen Square London WC1N 3AU
Reprinted 1983 and 1985
Filmset by Latimer Trend & Company Ltd, Plymouth
Printed and bound in Great Britain by
Redwood Burn Limited, Trowbridge, Wiltshire
All rights reserved

British Library Cataloguing in Publication Data

Hanson, Anthony
Burgundy
1. Wine and wine making—France—Burgundy
I. Title
641.2′223′09444   TP553

ISBN 0-571-11797-X
ISBN 0-571-11798-8 Pbk

TO ROSI
with love

Contents

9

APPENDIXES

Illustrations

MAPS

TABLES AND FIGURES

Acknowledgements

So many people have helped me while writing this book that it would not be possible to name them all. I hope they will accept my thanks for the time they gave, the books they lent, the corks they drew, the information and advice which they passed on so generously.

I would particularly like to thank three Burgundian brokers: Henri Meurgey, Tim Marshall and Maurice Vollot; and Messrs Robert, Georges and Paul Bouchard, who most hospitably first gave me a job in Burgundy. Dr P. Wallace, Patrick Saulnier Blache and Tim Marshall respectively checked the geology, *appellation contrôlée* and vinification sections, and Robert Joseph brought to light several errors. I am most grateful to them all, as to the many readers who have written in with queries or findings. Any remaining inaccuracies are, of course, entirely my responsibility.

Amongst many friends in Burgundy who encouraged me and gave me practical help I would especially like to mention Bart and Becky Wasserman. How Julian Jeffs recognized something worthwhile in the first draft of 1969, and how he had the patience to wait for the book's completion in 1980 I shall never understand, but I am much indebted to him for his help.

To my wife Rosi, who has lived with the writing of this book through all its ups and downs, who has read and re-read it, determinedly encouraging me to complete it, my thanks are immeasurable. I cannot imagine how it would have been written without her.

For permission to quote from published sources my thanks are due to: Editions Montalba, for extracts from the section by Raymond Bernard in *Le Vin de Bourgogne*; Société Française

ACKNOWLEDGEMENTS

d'Editions Vinicoles for a quotation from *Les Vins de Bourgogne* by Pierre Bréjoux; Mitchell Beazley Publishers for a quotation from Hugh Johnson's *Pocket Book of Wine*; Madame Rolande Gadille for much material drawn from *Le Vignoble de la Côte Bourguignonne* published by the Université de Dijon; the estate of the late Professor Roger Dion, author of *Histoire de la Vigne et du Vin en France des Origines au XIX Siècle*; Les Presses Universitaires de France for a quotation from *Origines du Vignoble Bourguignon* by the late Pierre Forgeot; Flammarion for an extract from *La Bouillie Bordelaise* by Bernard Ginestet; Dunod for a quotation from *Connaissance et Travail du Vin* by Emile Peynaud; Penguin Books for a quotation from *Valois Burgundy* by Richard Vaughan and for permission to reproduce the geological time scale in *The Penguin Dictionary of Geology* by D. G. A. Whitten and J. R. V. Brooks; Madame Françoise Grivot for an extract from *Le Commerce des Vins de Bourgogne*; Justin Dutraive for a quotation from *Jadis en Beaujolais*; Pierre Poupon for quotations from *Nouvelles Pensées d'un Dégustateur*, published by the Confrérie des Chevaliers du Tastevin; the Comité National des Appellations d'Origine des Vins et Eaux de Vie and Louis Larmat for quotations from *L'Evolution de la Législation sur les Appellations d'Origine—Genèse des Appellations Contrôlées*; Jonathan Cape for a quotation from *A Book of French Wines* by P. Morton Shand (revised and edited by Cyril Ray); A. P. Watt Ltd for a quotation from *Champagne, the Wine, the Land, and the People* by Patrick Forbes; Christie Manson and Woods for a quotation from a sale memorandum by Michael Broadbent of June 1969; Masson for permission to reproduce the diagram showing rock strata of the Côtes de Beaune and Nuits from *Bourgogne Morvan* by Pierre Rat; Horizons de France for a quotation from *La Bourgogne, Tastevin en Main* by Georges Rozet; and Editions de Seuil for several quotations from *Les Bons Vins et les Autres* by P. M. Doutrelant.

A. H.
July 1983

PART ONE

1

Burgundy and its Wines: an Introduction

For centuries Burgundy has produced some of the finest wines in the world, wines steeped in tradition and praised wherever wine is drunk. They are mainly dry white and red wines, though some rosé and sparkling wines of various colours are also made.

A glance at the map on page 154 will show that the Burgundy area is found in central-eastern France, on the right bank of the Saône river, which runs into the Rhône at Lyon. It is divided into six main regions, which will be considered individually; from north to south they are: Chablis and the Auxerrois, the Côte de Nuits, the Côte de Beaune, the Côte Chalonnaise, the Mâconnais and the Beaujolais.

Before looking at the regions one by one, let us note that the wines of Burgundy are classified into four levels of quality:

REGIONAL WINES
These are the least prestigious and carry names like Bourgogne, Beaujolais or Mâcon, being made on certain soils from specified grape-types within a large area.

VILLAGE WINES
These carry the name of their own commune, such as Beaune, Meursault, or Saint-Amour and the yield from the vineyard is restricted to a greater extent than with regional wines.

FIRST GROWTH WINES (*Premiers Crus*)
These come from superior vineyards within a commune, such as Beaune Les Grèves or Meursault Les Charmes.

GREAT GROWTHS (*Grands Crus*)
These are in theory the finest wines of all and are labelled simply

with the name of the vineyard, for instance, Chambertin or Montrachet,[1] without mention of the commune, and output is further restricted.

Understanding Burgundian wine-labels is made more difficult by the fact that certain villages added the name of their most famous vineyard to their own, in order to benefit from its fame. The village of Gevrey became Gevrey-Chambertin; Morey became Morey-Saint-Denis; Chambolle became Chambolle-Musigny; Aloxe became Aloxe-Corton; and Puligny and Chassagne both tacked on Montrachet, the world-famous white wine vineyard approximately half of which is in each commune. So one should not imagine one is drinking Chambertin when one buys a bottle of Gevrey-Chambertin.

The best vineyards are very small indeed when compared with their peers in Bordeaux and they are usually split up between many wine-growers. Each grower cultivates his vines and makes his wine differently, and much of the wine is then sold in barrels and bottled by local shippers, so varying qualities appear on the market with the same wine-name on the label. The names of the wine-maker and bottler are more important in Burgundy than in any other wine-producing area—indeed they are more important than the name of the wine. That is why a significant part of this book is devoted to an examination of who is responsible for what.

Chablis is an isolated pocket of vineyards in the Yonne *département*, two hours' drive down the motorway from Paris. Here we first meet the Chardonnay vine, whose grapes are responsible for all of Burgundy's best white wines. The vineyards are planted on limestone hillsides and produce dry white wines which vary in character from light and appetizing to rich (though without sweetness) and long-flavoured. In a neighbouring valley near Auxerre, a little-known wine-producing area offers a variety of white wines from other grapes (Aligoté and Sauvignon), some red wines which are mostly consumed locally and sparkling Crémant de Bourgogne. In the wake of the world success of Champagne, many French vineyards have increased their productions of sparkling wine. Burgundy has four main centres for the industry: the Auxerrois, Nuits Saint-Georges, Savigny-les-

---

[1] There is an exception in the Yonne where the Great Growths carry the word Chablis as well as the individual vineyard name such as Les Clos or Vaudésir.

Beaune and Rully, and Champagne methods are used in the production, as we shall see.

The greatest Burgundy vineyards are to be found in the *département* to the south-east of the Yonne, the Côte d'Or. It takes its name from the narrow golden slope of vineyards thirty miles long, running approximately north–south from Dijon to Santenay. In the autumn, the leaves of its vines turn gold before they fall, which may have given it its name; or perhaps it came from the fact that this is some of the most valuable agricultural land in the world. The hillside is divided into two vineyard areas, the Côte de Nuits centred on Nuits Saint-Georges, and the Côte de Beaune on Beaune. The vineyards form an east-facing strip approximately 1,500 metres wide, but the slope is at varying angles, as is the orientation. The bedrock, soil and drainage change repeatedly, for the Alpine upheavals 35 million years ago caused faults in the many-layered limestone and marlstone. The wines of the villages along the hillside taste different, and there are major variations within each commune.

Almost all the wines of the Côte de Nuits are red and are produced from the Pinot Noir vine. The best are highly individual and their detailed origins can be identified to within a few hundred yards by people who are familiar with them. No other wine-producing area in the world has yet succeeded in planting Pinot Noir vines and producing wines of the complexity and fascination of the best Côte d'Or bottles—but there is a catch. It requires long hot summers for the red pigments in the Pinot Noir grape-skins to develop satisfactorily, and these summers are only seen about once every three years in Burgundy. The wines from these vintages have made the reputation of the region. Two years out of three, however, the wines produced bear famous names but little resemblance to fine Burgundy.

We shall return to the problem of the off-vintages later, but for the moment, let us look at a glass of red Burgundy from a good vintage—wherein lies its fascination and complexity?

Maximum enjoyment is to be had from wine-drinking if one looks at a wine before smelling it, and smells it carefully before tasting it. One will look at it for purple tones which signify youth or the red-brown colour which comes (often all too rapidly) with age. Burgundy is not normally as deeply coloured as a fine claret or northern Rhône wine, but it should be limpid. Whether young or

19

old, wines from the Pinot Noir have a perfume about them which is hard to describe but wholly their own. They are often slightly mouth-watering, because of the presence of natural acids in the grapes. The perfume is not straightforwardly grapey, or plummy, or floral; it is as if the smell of a recently-shot game bird had mingled with that of the leaf-mould on which it fell. The result is neither animal nor vegetable, but both appetizing and intriguing.

Only four things are perceived by the sense of taste: sweetness, acidity, bitterness and saltiness; the last being of little significance in wine-tasting. A really fine wine has sufficient acidity (coming from natural grape acids) and astringency (from the tannins of the grape-skins) to balance the sweetness of the grape-sugar, the latter having been completely or partially transformed into alcohol (which itself has a sweet taste) when the wine was made. The palate also notices the weight of the wine—its wateriness or richness. At the same time, the sense of smell continues to register the intensity and variety of its perfumes. Some wines make an immediate impact when tasted which may or may not persist while they are in the mouth. The very best coat the inside of the mouth with a layer of lingering flavour which is still noticeable half a minute or more after the wine has been swallowed.

One of the reasons Burgundy's fame has spread so far is that the Côte d'Or is easily accessible. A railway line, a *route nationale* and now an *autoroute* run along the foot of the slope in full view of the vineyards. The slope is mostly wood-capped, with villages in the combes formed where streams run down. To the east, the flat plain of the Saône runs into the far distance where the Jura mountains rise. The Côte d'Or is scenically unremarkable (indeed marred between the Côte de Nuits and Côte de Beaune by pyramids of broken stones from the marble quarries) but its village names, nevertheless, bring one to a halt: Gevrey-Chambertin, Vougeot, Volnay, Puligny-Montrachet—these and their neighbours are capable of producing exceptional wines. Sadly today they mostly do *not*, for too much praise has gone to the Burgundians' heads. The fabled quality has almost ceased to exist, even at outrageous prices.

But one should not be deterred from trying to find it, if one is out there, and the Burgundians are extremely generous at allowing one to taste. You may notice that, broadly speaking, the red wines of the Côte de Nuits have more richness and length than those of the Côte de Beaune and that they take longer to mature. And you may find the white wines at the southern end of the Côte de Beaune (in the communes of Meursault, Puligny-Montrachet and Chassagne-Montrachet) more rewarding than you have found the reds. The Chardonnay grape from which they are pressed is usually sweeter at vintage time than the Pinot Noir, and fine white Burgundy can be made virtually every year. It is a beautifully balanced dry white wine which acquires honeyed and buttery aromas with age, and accompanies the first half of many fine meals to perfection.

In the hills to the west of the Côte d'Or, wine is produced in the Hautes Côtes de Nuits and Hautes Côtes de Beaune. The grapes ripen later than on the Côte, because of the altitude, and many vineyard-owners also grow raspberries and blackcurrants, and keep sheep or other animals. Pinot Noir and Chardonnay grapes are grown, along with the white Aligoté (its wine has higher acidity and less length, flavour and roundness than that of the Chardonnay).

The last wine-making village of the Côte de Beaune is Santenay. If one continues southwards, one crosses into the Saône-et-Loire *département* and a different wine region, the Côte Chalonnaise, otherwise known as the Région de Mercurey from its best-known red wine. There are three other wine villages: Rully, Givry and Montagny.

Rully is a centre for sparkling wine manufacture, which in the past has been the best way of rendering saleable large quantities of Burgundies from the Aligoté and Gamay grapes which were too acid for sale as such. Improved wine-making methods and replanting in Rully with the noble Pinot and Chardonnay grapes have recently changed the village's main activity and one can now find good bottles of Burgundy there, in the style of light Côte de Beaune wines. Mercurey has a large production of longer-lasting reds, Montagny specializes in whites and Givry makes a bit of both.

We are now approaching the Mâconnais, which supplies much of Burgundy's regional *appellations*, the Bourgogne *blanc* and *rouge*, the Bourgogne Aligoté and both red and white Mâcons. The vines are planted on chains of small hills, interspersed with meadows and fields of vegetables. Many of the growers have grouped themselves into co-operatives, and these produce large quantities of Mâcon Villages from Chardonnay vines. It is a prime source of fine white Burgundy which in 1980 was still reasonably priced.

The countryside changes to the south of Mâcon, where the Beaujolais begins, for the rounded eroded forms of ancient granites are found at the surface, where previously we have travelled through still jagged limestone hillsides. The Gamay grape is here in its element, and its grapes give mouth-wateringly fresh red wine if picked just before complete ripeness, and vinified without being squashed. One hundred million bottles of authentic Beaujolais are produced every year, varying in style from light quaffing wine such as Beaujolais Nouveau to deep purply-red, strongly constituted wines from single communes such as Fleurie or Saint-Amour. The region is highly prosperous, for it makes France's most immediately attractive red wine, and one which requires the minimum of ageing.

Something must be said of the characteristics of recent vintages, and details will be found in Appendix B on page 343. One should be cautious with generalizations about Burgundy vintages, for several reasons. Human brilliance or error produce successes or disasters from similar raw materials, and wines are often quite altered in character after they have sojourned in the cellars of *négociants*, as will be explained in Chapter 8. Following bottling, the conditions in which wines are stored are of vital importance. Fine whites or light elegant reds can turn brown and oxidize irrevocably if stored at ground level without temperature control, or if exposed to light, or kept standing upright for long in a shop window or on a shelf. *There is absolutely no substitute for tasting what is in the bottle,* and no purchase of Burgundy should ever be made unless you have tried the wine or are buying from a properly qualified and trusted supplier.

I have not transcribed many of my tasting notes, for wines develop unexpectedly according to how they are kept, and tasting notes are almost immediately out of date. Because of the enormous number of different wines produced each year by the many owners of Burgundy's vineyards they would be unlikely to have much relevance. Tasting notes on Burgundies belong, it seems to me, in wine articles and merchants' lists, followed by a price, so that the reader may track down what appeals to him. Instead, having lived behind the scenes in Burgundy and watched some of its best actors at work, I have tried to describe how they practise their art. We shall also meet ham actors and charlatans who stage-manage pretentious and expensive illusions. But if you read on to the end you will know, I hope, how to tell the one from the other, and, more important, feel confident about tasting all Burgundies in critical spirit.

2

The History of
Burgundy Wines

'Beginning this work, I would like to have written on the opening
page the name of the man who first tried to cultivate the vine in
the Côte d'Or; he who, divining the perfume beneath the rock of
our hillsides which the plant knows how to extract, installed the
first vine and ran off the first wine.' Thus Dr Lavalle, writing in
1855, opened his *Histoire et Statistique de la Vigne et des Grands
Vins de la Côte d'Or*. Since then there has been much research, but
we are no closer to knowing for certain who began it all.

FROM EARLY TIMES TO THE BARBARIANS

Popular tradition in Dr Lavalle's time had it that the Gaulish
conqueror Brennus was responsible for importing the first vine
into Burgundy. The story went that he brought it back with him
after his invading exploits against the Romans. In recent times the
theory has been picked up by the late Pierre Forgeot in his
Origines du Vignoble Bourguignon, published in 1972.

The Iron-Age Celtic tribes living in the region we now know as
Burgundy may have got their first taste of wine from the
Phoenicians. Legend has it that around 1300 B.C. the latter
travelled to England after tin. Their route lay up the Rhône valley
and then down the Seine and they would have carried gifts with
them, for instance wine, for the tribes likely to bar their passage.

The discovery in January 1953 of a burial-ground dating from
about 500 B.C. at Vix near Châtillon-sur-Seine in northern
Burgundy has supplied some evidence. Vix is situated on the Mont
Lassois, commanding the Seine Valley (near where it becomes
navigable) and the tin route from Italy to the Cornish mines. Here

the Celts had an encampment in the sixth, fifth and fourth centuries B.C. and they may have exacted payment from travellers along the route.

Although the magnificent shoulder-high Vix vase, capable of holding 1,250 litres, could equally have been used for carrying olive oil or wine, an Etruscan wine jar and a complete Greek wine service were also discovered at the same time. It seems reasonable to assume from these objects that first the Phoenicians, and then the Phocaeans[1] around 500 B.C., were paying for their passage with money, presents and wine. Imported wine was therefore known in Burgundy by this time.

The next important fact is the invasion of Italy by the Celts. There were minor invasions between 590 and 550 B.C., but the main movement took place around 400 B.C. Authors such as Plutarch and Pliny, the Naturalist, attribute the motive for the invasion to the Celts' passion for Italian wine. Titus Livius wrote in the first century B.C. 'The Gauls penetrated the rich plains of Lombardy, installed themselves, then summoned their brothers who came in compact masses to invade the wine country.' As many as 300,000 are thought to have made the march. The Celtic tribes settled in different parts of Italy, the Aedui between Milan and Lake Como. The Aedui are the ancestors of today's Burgundians. Courtépée describes how the Aedui (*Eduens* in French), based on their capital Bibracte, were first amongst the independent peoples. They were to earn the description of brothers, friends and allies of the Roman people, and to be the first Gauls to be admitted to the Senate.

Diodorus, a Greek historian of the first century B.C. relates that, once arrived in Italy, the Celts started cultivating the land and abandoned their nomadic instincts. There was plenty to learn on the subject of viticulture, as the Italians practised propagation by cuttings, layering (known as *provignage* in French, and indeed in use until the nineteenth century) and grafting, even on to vines already in production. If young vine plants were to be transported, roots and soil were established in a basket, buried in a ditch. At a given moment, the young vine was severed from its parent, and the basket lifted without the roots being disturbed. Around 280 B.C. the Gauls attempted to invade Greece and Macedonia but

---

[1] From Phocaea, an Ionian city of Asia Minor.

were driven back, and from 238 the Aedui began to lose ground in Lombardy to the Romans. This lasted for a century and during this period it seems likely that certain tribes began their way back over the Alps to their old homelands.

P. Forgeot concludes from this story as follows: 'It seems unthinkable and illogical that a people liking wine, who to a large extent invaded Italy because of it, who were reputed for their intelligence and manual skill, who lived for several generations in a land of famous vineyards, who became farmers and *vignerons*, who were able to learn everything on the subject of vines and wine, should not have started producing it in Gaul, immediately they returned home there from Italy. . . . ' The plantation of vineyards from 200 B.C. onwards is therefore possible. Sadly, Monsieur Forgeot can provide no evidence. And what happened, one wonders, to his wine-making Aedui for the five centuries from 200 B.C. onwards? Initially there was relative peace in the region, but soon they were invaded by the *Séquanes*, then the *Helvètes*, then enemies from Germany. They then allied themselves with the Romans to fight the Bretons and, finally, there was the revolt of the Gauls under Vercingétorix, which resulted in Caesar's victory at Alésia in 52 B.C. and the Roman subjugation of Gaul. The development of a wine-growing area at this time seems unlikely, and in the absence of evidence can only be considered hypothetical.

As Professor R. Dion has shown, the origins of French viticulture go back to the establishment of a Greek colony at Marseilles around 600 B.C. The wine trade was one of the principal means used by Mediterranean societies to acquire slaves before the times when their armies were large enough to carry off whole nations into bondage. The Gauls would exchange a slave for a measure of wine, indeed sell themselves as a last resort. If the wine could be provided on the doorstep of the people who were prepared to pay so high a price for it, all the better. Much Greek colonization was done with this aim, he says. Tradition has it that the hostility of the Celts prevented the extension of the vineyard area by the first Greek colony. But as the centuries passed, there was a gradual extension along the trade routes.

There is a first-century-B.C. mention in Cicero of the vines of central Gaul, and Columella at the beginning of the first century A.D. was writing that the vine was tended in almost every climate and area of Gaul. Caesar's *Commentaries* have been variously interpreted. On the one hand they do not specifically mention viticulture in Burgundy, on the other they seem to imply that it was present in most areas.

Towards the end of the first century (A.D. 92) the Emperor Domitian issued an edict which prohibited the extension of vineyards in Italy, and ordered the uprooting of half the vineyards in the provinces. Many texts show that the reason for Domitian's edict was economic. There was overproduction of cheap wine in the Roman Empire, indeed in Ravenna it was cheaper than water. One motive was probably to favour Italian wine-growers by cutting competition, and another to encourage the growing of corn. It would seem that Domitian did not put his edict into effect. It was rescinded by the Emperor Probus in A.D. 281, and there is no evidence that it had the slightest effect in Burgundy.

From the second century A.D. we at last begin to get the archaeological finds pointing to the existence of a commercial vineyard area which have previously been lacking. A gravestone found at Corgoloin shows a Celtic god whose right hand holds what may be a vine; other gravestones have reliefs featuring grapes and the god of wine. More important, as E. Thevenot has shown, from around A.D. 150 wine amphoras disappear from Burgundy. True, the distinction between amphoras used for wine and those used for oil or fish sauce is a delicate one; true also that it is possible that the amphoras were replaced by wooden casks;[1] nevertheless the disappearance of wine amphoras indicates that local production was now enough to satisfy demand.

Between A.D. 253 and 277 however, barbarians (Franks, Alamans and the Vandals under Crocus) returned to the area. Many Roman villas were destroyed, and fortified camps were built to shelter the local population, like the one whose remains can be found on the Mont Saint-Désiré, above the vineyards of Beaune.

There is also at last some written evidence: a document of A.D. 312 known as the Panegyric to Constantine, which was spoken by the orator Eumenius. R. Dion explains that the Emperor had recently reduced the taxes of the Autun citizens, and that the

---

[1] The Gauls can take credit for the invention of the first receptacles made of assembled wood, the first barrels. The earliest mention is at the 51 B.C. siege of Uxellodunum (now Vayrac in the Lot), when barrels were used for defence, filled with inflammable matter.

object of the Panegyric was to thank Constantine while showing that the tax exemptions were well-deserved by the impoverished citizens.

Mention is made of the *Pagus Arebrignus*, the area around Beaune and Nuits, where the vine was cultivated. A convincing picture is painted of abandoned vineyards and age-old vine-stocks whose roots have become confusingly interlaced. But it appears that these vineyards were once an object of admiration, surely evidence of an established wine-growing area. Burgundy's renown dates from this time: A.D. 312.

The fall of the Roman Empire and the invasions of the barbarians had seemingly little effect on viticulture. The area under vines stayed much the same, and Gregory of Tours was announcing in the sixth century that the land round Dijon produced a considerable amount of quality wine.

Les Burgondes, the people who have given their name to this region, originated in Scandinavia. Their traces can be found in Norwegian, Swedish and Danish place names.[1] They made their way south through Germany at the beginning of the Christian era, and founded a kingdom along the Rhône valley in A.D. 456, taking advantage of the decline of the Roman Empire to establish themselves in Lyon and then Dijon. They reigned until 534, when their kingdom was split up and shared by the Franks after a defeat in battle.

THE MONASTERIES

Soon afterwards the first large gift of land including vines was made to a Burgundian abbey—by Gontran, King of Burgundy, to the Abbey of Saint-Bénigne in Dijon in 587. At the beginning of the sixth century, Amalgaire, Duke of Lower Burgundy, founded the Abbey of Bèze, which was to give its name to one of the region's greatest wines. Dr Lavalle tells us that he endowed it with vines situated at Chenôve, Marsannay, Couchey, Gevrey, Vosne and around the Beaune, along with the *vignerons* needed to exploit them. Charlemagne gave a large area of vines between Aloxe and

---

[1] Perhaps I may be forgiven for not going any deeper into this, for, as the Abbé Courtépée warned: '*L'etymologie du mot de Bourgignons est une de ces vaines recherches qu'il faut abandonner à l'oisiveté et à la fiction de ceux qui s'en occupent.*'

Pernand (it still bears his name) to the Abbey of Saulieu in 775. Church records of donations from now on serve to announce that, one after another, celebrated growths were producing wine. Aloxe had appeared in 696, then Fixey (733), Santenay (858), Chassagne (886), Savigny (930) and Pommard (1005). The oldest mention of the fame of Beaune's wines is in a book by Guillaume le Breton at the beginning of the thirteenth century.[1]

Two religious orders played large parts in the plantation and development of vineyards. The first was Cluny, founded in 910 in the Mâconnais, which at its height controlled 1,450 monasteries and 10,000 monks; and then Cîteaux, founded in 1098 in the plain opposite the Côte de Nuits by Robert, Abbot of Molesme. Both received donations of land and vineyard at the time of the crusades. The Cistercians created the Clos de Vougeot, planting vines for the first time on a hillside dotted with scrub, and building the famous wall, the château and its presses; they also owned vines on the Côte de Beaune.

One of Burgundy's most brilliant public-relations coups was the gift of thirty barrels of Beaune and Chambertin by Jean de Bussière, Abbot of Cîteaux, to Pope Gregory XI in Avignon. Some years later Jean de Bussière was made a cardinal, but better still the Papal Court got a taste for the wines. Petrarch was to write that the Cardinals did not want to quit France and return to Rome because Beaune wine would no longer be available to them.

The Cistercians and then the Valois Dukes (to whom we shall come in a moment) made Burgundy the first wine of Europe; the coronations of both Charles VI in 1321 and Philippe VI in 1328 were celebrated at Rheims with Beaune wine. It was made to spout from a stag's nostrils.

THE VALOIS DUKES

Although the fame of the wines was spreading, Burgundians had problems at home. In 1349 the Plague struck the region. It caused many deaths including that of all Beaune's *curés*. Because of the decreased work-force, the vineyards suffered neglect, and for

---

[1] Two Beaune wine-growers, both established in 1270 (Clerget-Buffet et Fils and Raoul Clerget et Fils), are the sixth and seventh oldest businesses in the world according to the *Guinness Book of the Business World* (1976).

fourteen years there were virtually no harvests. Then it was noted that a vine in the village of Gamay not only withstood disease but was also producing sizeable crops. It was propagated and, under its village's name, planted along the Côte. But it failed to give quality wines as the Pinot had done, and soon was attacked. The first of many instructions to uproot the '*très-mauvaiz et très-desloyaul plant, nommez Gaamez, du quel mauvaiz plant vient très-grant habondance de vins*' was issued by Duke Philip the Bold in 1395. His vineyards had the reputation of producing the best, most precious and proper wines of the Kingdom of France for the nourishment and sustaining of human creatures. So that they should recover their lost renown, the use in the vines of manure from cows, goats, horses and other beasts, animal's horns, or bone-scrapings was forbidden.

In France at this time the King was confronted by great fiefs which were nominally subject to the French crown but in fact independent: Normandy, Guienne, Gascony, Toulouse, Burgundy. The French kings had the habit of allotting great territorial domains to princes of the blood, and Burgundy was granted to his fourth son Philip by John II 'the Bountiful' in 1363. Under the reign of Duke Philip and his successors John the Fearless (1404–19), Philip the Good (1419–67), and Charles the Bold (1467–77) Burgundy enjoyed its period of greatest glory and pre-eminence. The four royal Valois Dukes were ambitious, able, flamboyant rulers, whose lands (covering an area the size of England and Wales) straddled the border between France and the Holy Roman Empire. In a century they came close to hiving off an independent kingdom for themselves.

The first Duke Philip had earned himself the title of 'the Bold' by his courage on the battlefield of Poitiers at the age of fourteen. He was to marry the heiress of Flanders, and through his wife also became ruler of Franche Comté, Artois, Nevers and Rethel. He laid the foundations of the Burgundian state to which would later be added Tonnerre and the Mâconnais, Hainault, Brabant, Holland, Limbourg, Luxembourg, Picardy and, briefly, Lorraine. By 1392 he also had his hand on the French Treasury. An unfortunate king was on the throne, Charles VI, who 'during his protracted fits of madness, capered about the corridors of the royal palace howling like a wolf; or else, believing he was made of glass, proceeded with the utmost caution, for fear of breaking himself.'[1] Thanks to economic upsurge in the Low Countries (Brussels and Antwerp were expanding, Bruges was the busiest port in Europe), Philip the Bold had the finances to maintain his position as regent over Brittany, Savoy and Luxembourg; he was the undisputed master of France, and even laid plans in 1386 to invade England. But he never crossed the Channel.

His son John the Fearless helped Henry V of England to victory by his absence from the French army at the battle of Agincourt. He led the Burgundians in bloody civil war against the Armagnacs, and spent most of his reign trying to keep control of the French government. He resorted to the assassination of his rival Louis of Orléans in a Paris street in 1407, openly admitting it, but was himself murdered by his political opponents twelve years later, having been lured to a 'diplomatic parley' with the Dauphin.

The next Great Duke of the Occident, Philip the Good, allied himself with the English in 1420, and handed over Joan of Arc (in exchange for 10,000 gold crowns), who had fallen into his hands beneath the ramparts of Compiègne. Under his rule Burgundy remained hostile to France, and there was a more or less permanent Anglo-Burgundian alliance. Philip had simple tastes in food, according to Bishop Guillaume Fillastre, who wrote that frequently he left partridges on one side for a Mainz ham or a piece of salt beef. This did not prevent him entertaining visitors, as in 1450 when some Scottish knights and squires travelling with William Earl of Douglas partook of this banquet: 2 hares, 10 pheasants, a heron, 4 bitterns, 156 rabbits, 72 partridges, 10 geese, 12 water-birds, 34 dozen larks, 231 chickens and 56 brace of pigeons. Philip the Good founded the Chivalric Order of the Golden Fleece, including among its members noblemen from throughout his territories as well as foreign rulers, such as the Kings of Aragon and Naples, and Prince John of Portugal. A resident agent was maintained at the Papal Court, and gifts of wine or tapestries despatched to Rome from time to time. Thus he hoped to widen his influence and strengthen his alliances.

He was in no doubt about the Duchy's wines, declaring that the Dukes of Burgundy were immediate lords of the best wines of Christendom. In 1441 he forbade the planting of vines in

[1] From *Valois Burgundy*, by Richard Vaughan, Allen Lane, 1975, to which this account owes much.

31

unsuitable land around Dijon, which noble town was described by its mayor and corporation in 1452 as being based on the culture of vines, with wine its chief merchandise. R. Vaughan has shown that the main commercial and agricultural activity of the Duchy was the export of fine wines, mainly to Paris and the Low Countries.

Duke Philip the Good appointed an Autun burgess, Nicolas Rolin, to be his chancellor—the most important, influential and best-paid Burgundian official. Rolin amassed a fortune while serving the Duke, and in 1443 endowed a poorhouse and hospital, the Hôtel-Dieu in Beaune. He donated no vines to it, but one of its finest red Beaune wines always bears his name.

The next Duke, Charles the Bold, saw himself as a new Alexander—had not his father carried the same name as Philip of Macedon? A German cleric, Conrad Stolle, reported 'that the Duke of Burgundy claimed there were only three lords in the world, one in Heaven, that is God; one in Hell, the devil Lucifer; and one on earth, who will be he himself.' He had a passion for military campaigning,[1] and fought to consolidate and unify the Burgundian state. He temporarily acquired Upper Alsace, and for a year Lorraine, thus almost joining his northern and southern possessions. He dressed even more ostentatiously than his predecessors, in jewelled hats—were they ducal, archducal or regal?— his robes, and even armour, glittering with rubies, pearls and sapphires. When he visited the emperor he wore a floor-length ermine-lined open-fronted cloth-of-gold mantle, with underneath a pearl-bordered coat, studded with diamonds. One of his plumed and jewelled hats cost nearly £500, so the ducal accounts record.

Burgundian power reached its zenith under Charles, whose allies were listed by one of his officials as the pope, the emperor, the kings of England, Aragon, Scotland, Denmark, Portugal, the dukes of Brittany and Austria, the house of Savoy, the doge and signory of Venice, the elector-palatine of the Rhine, the dukes of Bavaria, Cleves and Guelders and my lords the archbishop-electors of Mainz, Trier and Cologne. But it was not to last.

The kings of France and the emperors resented and feared the upstart state on their borders. The dukes had failed to impose centralized administration, or centralized justice, on their scat-

---

[1] Some claim he was the inventor of military drill.

tered territories. The energetic, violent Charles alarmed his neighbours, not without reason, and they proved formidable, determined enemies.

He was brought down by an alliance between Austria, Lorraine, the confederate cantons of Switzerland, and the towns of Strasbourg, Basel, Sélestat and Colmar. Twice he allowed his army to be taken by surprise and defeated while campaigning against the Swiss. He then shifted the theatre of war northwards, in an attempt to reconquer Lorraine which was slipping from his grasp. Against the advice of his captains he laid siege to Nancy during the bitter winter of 1476–7. Four hundred of his soldiers froze to death on Christmas Eve, and on 5 January his army was routed by the enemy. Valois Burgundy collapsed with the death of Charles the Bold before the walls of Nancy. He had only one child, a girl promised in marriage to Maximilian of Austria, son of the emperor. There was no-one to carry on the fight, and Louis XI, King of France, rapidly annexed the Duchy.

Charles's body lay undiscovered in a frozen stream for two days. He had been felled by a battle-axe; when found his corpse was half-devoured by wolves, so legend has it. Many believed that he had survived, and would return after seven years, and bills of exchange in Burgundy were held until that time had elapsed.

Valois Burgundy was broadly contemporary with the Italian Renaissance, but unheedful of it. The Dukes looked to the north for their artists and craftsmen. Philip the Good employed Jan van Eyck, sending him to Portugal to paint Henry the Navigator's sister, the Infanta Elizabeth, before he married her. He appointed van Eyck official court painter, and stood godfather to his son, believing that he would never find his equal in artistic skill. Roger van der Weyden (whose 'Last Judgement' can be seen at the Hôtel-Dieu in Beaune) may also have been employed by the dukes. The outstanding name in sculpture is that of the Dutchman Claus Sluter, employed by Philip the Bold at the Charterhouse of Champmol just outside Dijon. R. Vaughan describes him as the greatest sculptor then living outside Italy; at the very moment when Donatello and Ghiberti were competing to produce the bronze doors of the Baptistry in Florence, Sluter was at work on the statues of a monumental Crucifixion for the Valois Duke, parts of which can still be seen in Dijon.

The Dukes commissioned illuminated manuscripts, and built

up one of the best princely libraries of their day, over 200 of these books being now preserved in the Royal Library of Belgium in Brussels. Their court was of great splendour, and a cause of admiration throughout Europe, as was its feasting. 'We went to see my lord of Burgundy at dinner, and we saw all the majesty and all the triumph which occurred when he dined,' declared some deputies from the city of Metz, obviously impressed, at the court of Charles the Bold.

The Valois Dukes were not great builders, and little of their architecture survives except part of the ducal palace in Dijon, and the Tower of Duke John in the Rue Étienne-Marcel in Paris. (Here the 'Fearless' Duke locked himself up, under bodyguard, in a sort of fortified bedroom with bathroom beneath it.) In music however R. Vaughan considers that the Burgundian impact was important and long-term. The court chapel employed some of the foremost musicians of the day, and a Netherlandish tradition was built up which under Maximilian was to influence German music-making significantly.

The vineyard enactments of the two Valois Philips were well-meaning but ineffective. A multiplicity of complaints against vines planted in land more suitable for crops caused an investigation under King Charles VIII in 1486, and further regulations in 1567. In 1590 there were calls for vineyards to be uprooted, in 1627 and 1731 new plantations were forbidden. Just before the French Revolution the Abbé Courtépée was writing that a new order like that of Philip the Bold was much needed, for the *gamet* (Gamay) had been planted in land more suitable for wheat. In 1855 Dr Lavalle exclaimed: 'God knows with what terrifying activity the vulgar plant has driven out the noble one, and what progress it makes each day. Our ancestors would have been appalled!'

Nevertheless the popularity of the wines had continued to grow, and under Louis XIV they had received two useful puffs. The first occurred when the King's doctor Fagon examined some wine (presumably Romanée) sent by the monks of Saint-Vivant. He declared that it produced '*des effets merveilleux*', and recommended it for his Majesty's robust temperament. The second was thanks to a Mâcon *vigneron* named Claude Brosse who drove a cart laden with barrels from Chasselas near Juliénas to Versailles. During Mass the Sun King noticed Brosse, who seemed to remain standing while everyone else knelt. But Brosse was a giant, and he seized the opportunity of speaking to Louis to ask him to taste his wine. The King approved of it, and the court followed suit.

THE EXPORT OF BURGUNDY WINES

The earliest shipments of Burgundy across the Channel, according to A. L. Simon's *The History of the Wine Trade in England*,[1] took place during the reign of Henry II (1154–89). Rouen had an important trade in the wines of Normandy and the Seine Valley, though A. L. Simon describes them as very inferior compared to the produce of the Burgundy vineyards. Burgundy merchants used to bring their wines to Rouen, where they sold them to the local traders, who had a monopoly on navigation from their city to the Channel. In 1212 King John purchased 348 casks of wine for £507.11s, of which twenty-six came from Auxerre (three came from Germany, eight from Anjou, fifty-four from the Orléanais and Île de France, 267 from Gascony). During the same reign the Abbot of Fécamp paid two barrels of Auxerre wine for letters patent enabling him to bring a shipload of wine to England before the feast of Saint Peter in Chains. King John stocked his cellar in part by imposing fines on his subjects, the Bishop of Winchester being relieved of a cask of good wine for not reminding the King to give a girdle to the Countess of Albemarle.

A. L. Simon declared that the fame of the wines of Auxerre in England is more ancient than that of Bordeaux wines, even if their consumption during the Middle Ages was always less; this of course because Gascony was English for the 300 years after Henry II had married Eleanor of Aquitaine.

Those Burgundies that reached Britain came sometimes via Rouen, sometimes via Flanders. In 1512 Louis XII sent thirty-six puncheons of *Vin de Beaune cléret* to James IV of Scotland; in 1537 Auxerre wine was sent from Rouen direct to Cromwell in London; in 1538 an advice from Brussels referred to wines of Burgundy (*Borgoyn*) sent to Henry VIII.

A. L. Simon goes on to describe that Burgundy was greatly appreciated in England during the seventeenth century, but never common; its scarcity and consequent high price being due to the

---

[1] Reprinted by the Holland Press, 1964.

difficulties of bringing it over, usually down the Yonne and the Seine, via Paris and Rouen. Louis XIV made a present of 200 *muids* of very good Champagne, Burgundy and Hermitage wines to the King of England in 1666.

Julian Jeffs in *The Wines of Europe*[1] writes that only wealthy connoisseurs could afford to import Burgundy. He instances John Harvey, first Earl of Bristol, who imported red and white Burgundies between 1700 and 1739, though in very small quantities as compared with claret. A century later English cellar-books still feature it rarely.

The Burgundy wine trade began to organize itself during the eighteenth century, and a number of the companies established at that time are still in business. Champy was founded in 1720, Bouchard Père in 1731, Poulet in 1747, Chanson in 1750. Until then most exports of Burgundy went to Belgium, indeed the Belgians came regularly after the harvest to visit growers' cellars with a Beaune commission-agent. The wines travelled north on vast carts; risk of robbery was high, as was the chance that wine would be tapped on the way.

AFTER THE FRENCH REVOLUTION

The multiple ownership of most of Burgundy's vineyards dates from the French Revolution. Following the suppression of religious orders and the flight or guillotining of the nobility, their lands were dispersed and broken up. The Clos de Vougeot was to be reunited under one owner in the nineteenth century, but the majority of famous sites were irrevocably split. Today individual holdings are sometimes so small that it is impossible or impractical to vinify the wines separately. So not infrequently the Clos de Vougeot grapes go into the same vat as the Chambolle Charmes, or the Vosne *Premier Cru*. Identical wines will then be sold under two separate and very specific names of origin, neither of which corresponds to the truth.

The second important repercussion of 1789 was increased consumption of wine. The Gamay was again widely planted.

In common with France's other vineyard areas, Burgundy had to fight two deadly threats in the nineteenth century. The first was

[1] Faber and Faber, 1971.

a disease called Oidium, or powdery mildew, which attacks the green organs of the vine. It was first discovered in Margate, Kent in 1845 and may have come to Britain on an ornamental plant, perhaps from America. By 1852 it was endemic in all France's vineyards, reducing the crop substantially. Fortunately a remedy was at hand, for it was discovered that dusting with finely-ground sulphur was effective in combating the disease. Tens of thousands of tons of sulphur are used in vineyards to this day in the fight against Oidium.

The second threat was to appear in a Hammersmith greenhouse in 1863 and soon after in the south of France. A burrowing vine louse had been imported into Europe on vines sent from the United States. Small yellow insects were to be seen on the roots of dying vines, sometimes so numerous that the roots appeared to be varnished yellow. In 1868 the insect was identified as 'phylloxera', and named *vastatrix*, the devastator. 'Gentlemen, it is disastrous: it goes forward like an army, laying waste all before it,' declared a vineyard manager to a scientific commission. Over the next fifteen years it was to invade every vineyard area in France, costing the country more than twice the indemnity (5,000 million francs) paid to the Germans after the Franco-Prussian War.

The cure was not so rapidly discovered as had been that for Oidium. The Government offered a 300,000-franc prize, and was deluged by crazy suggestions: burying a live toad under each vine; watering the vineyards with white wine, or sea-water; applying hot sealing wax to the pruning cuts. Five years of experiments failed to provide the answer, but two processes seemed promising. The first was flooding, which killed the insects but was impractical on hillside sites; the second, injection of the soil with carbon bisulphide (CS_2), a heavy liquid with an unpleasant smell. It is an effective fumigant but dangerous, since its vapour is toxic, and it is liable to catch fire or explode when being manipulated. Although it killed the phylloxera, the vineyard was immediately open to infection again. The first process was used in the flat plains of the Midi, indeed flooded vineyards can still today be seen from the Marseilles–Toulouse autoroute; the second had its adherents in Burgundy until 1945, the last vineyard to be so treated being Romanée-Conti.

The solution to the problem proved to be grafting on to resistant American root-stocks. According to G. Ordish, to whose book *The*

Great Wine Blight[1] I am much indebted, the suggestion was first made in 1869 by Gaston Bazille at a Congress in Beaune, but neither he nor Léo Laliman (who claimed to have been the first to indicate that certain American vines were resistant to phylloxera) ever saw the prize-money.

It was many years before the solution was universally adopted, the interval seeing fierce disputes between proponents of carbon bisulphide and grafting. The pest reached the Côte d'Or officially in July 1878, though Burgundians believed their vineyards would be immune from harm. They claimed that it only attacked poorly-tended vines, or those pushed to give enormous yields. A year later thirty-four infected centres were to be found in Beaune, and the local government was forced to take action.

Searches and treatments with carbon bisulphide became compulsory. They were unpopular, as the first treatments had killed the vines as well as the phylloxera. G. Ordish describes how 160 growers in Chenôve chased the treatment team out of the area, saying they were more to be feared than the aphid itself. A decree of 1874 had prohibited the introduction of American vines into Burgundy, for it was feared that growers would replant and produce directly from them, causing deterioration of quality and increased yields. The realization that resistant vines were invaluable as root-stocks, on to which the traditional varieties could be grafted, was not widespread until the mid-1880s.

The *Société Vigneronne de Beaune* brought in three skilled craftsmen-grafters in 1886, though a decree permitting the introduction of foreign vines into the Côte d'Or was not passed until June 1887. That year free grafting courses were set up in thirteen communes. It was evident that if complete reconstitution of the vineyards was necessary, a vast quantity of plants would be needed. Skill at the grafting table was to become a necessary accomplishment for the wine-grower.

By 1890 the chemists, advocating treatment with carbon bisulphide, were in retreat before the Americanists; it was estimated that 1,000 hectares (ha.) had been replanted with transatlantic vines. 1893 was the critical harvest, when wines from grafted vines could be tasted and compared. A Meursault Goutte d'Or was awarded a Paris Gold Medal the following

[1] Dent, 1972.

spring, and its owner decorated with the medal and cross of the *Mérite Agricole*. After so many years of wondering whether the vineyards were doomed, the relief must have been tremendous.

From now on the search began for the most suitable stocks to use in the alkaline soils of the Côte. Equally the door was open to experimentation with high-yielding types of Pinot, with sometimes disastrous effects on quality, as will be seen. The worst consequence of the destruction of Burgundy's vineyards by the phylloxera was not the modification of the style of wine, but the opportunity it gave to vineyard-owners to replant with Pinots known for their high yields.

A subsidy was paid to growers for reconstitution, as it had been for treatment; however, it represented only 18 per cent of the cost in the case of a grower doing his own grafting, 8 per cent for those who bought the plants. Many small growers had chosen emigration to Algeria or the United States, become Burgundian farmers as well as wine-growers, or gone to work for large estates who needed labour for chemical treatments, or to organize flooding. The vineyards lost about 6,000 people through emigration, and the area under vines was never remotely the same again.

It is the cheap-table-wine areas in the plain which have never been replanted—no great surprise, and no great loss, for table wine can be produced more economically in southern France. The completion of the Paris–Lyon–Marseilles railway line in 1856 had brought Midi wines easily and cheaply on to the Burgundian and Paris markets. Against 31,000 ha. of *vin ordinaire* vineyard in the Côte d'Or in 1882 there were 1,152 ha. left in 1976. The area planted with fine varieties in 1882 was just over 3,000 ha. In 1976 there were 6,594 ha. producing *appellation contrôlée* (AC) wines. So great an area under fine vines has never previously been known in Burgundy.

3

The Development of
AC Legislation *or*
The Buyer is Still Deceived

When the phylloxera destroyed France's vineyards towards the end of the nineteenth century, an artificial wine industry soon appeared to take their place so that the demand might continue to be satisfied. Concentrated must (grape-juice) was imported from abroad, water, sugar and colouring matter were added, and the result sold as wine.

But then other ingredients like animal blood, chemicals and industrial alcohol appeared. According to J. Capus, who was to become Minister of Agriculture, by 1905 fraud was more and more frequent and dangerous because of the advances of science. As the vineyards were replanted, natural wine (which, being from young vines, was not of exactly marvellous quality) found itself in competition with the artificial product. M. Charles Quittanson[1] has written that it was after pressure from producers with their backs against the wall, and consumers whose well-founded interests were wronged, that the law of 1 August 1905 was born.

The French claim that this was the first major legislation in the world to govern the naming of wine by its geographical origin. It was certainly pre-dated by an enactment of Charles VI in February 1416, confirmed by François I in August 1527, which stated that 'all sorts of wines harvested above the bridge at Sens, as much those of the Auxerrois as those of the Beaunois . . . which travel on the Yonne river shall be called Vins de Bourgogne.'

[1] He is *Inspecteur Divisionnaire du Service de la Répression des Fraudes et du Contrôle de la Qualité* as well as *Chef de la Brigade Nationale de Surveillance des Vins et Eaux-de-Vie à Appellations d'Origine.*

Philippe-le-Hardi, Duke of Burgundy, was much ahead of his time when he ordered the uprooting of the Gamay vine from the vineyards of Dijon, Beaune and Chalon on 31 July 1395, as were the consular deliberations of Saint-Georges d'Orques in the Midi on 31 May 1744. These ordained that the wines of the nearby communes of Laverune and Saint-Jean de Vedas should neither be blended with Saint-Georges d'Orques, nor allowed to use its name. None of these, however, can be called major legislation.

The 1905 Act was mainly concerned with protecting the consumer from fraudulent *vins ordinaires* and in this was extremely successful. The law made it necessary for a vineyard-owner to make a declaration of the amount of wine produced each year, and at the same time the *Service de la Répression des Fraudes* was set up. It stated that a wine might only bear an *appellation d'origine*[1] if it came from the usual zone where such wines were produced. In addition, it limited chaptalization (the addition of sugar at the vintage), for there had been abuses.

In 1906 the *Société des Viticulteurs de France* organized a sort of Congress of Names of Origin. Representatives from the great fine-wine regions were asked to describe their local wines, for the 1905 law had declared its intention of mapping out the regions. J. Capus reported from the Gironde, and issued a warning: 'Now that names of origin are protected, it would be possible for certain proprietors, one must admit it, to plant in unsuitable soils of a famous region vine-types which produce large quantities of mediocre wine; in this way they would have wines of absolute authenticity, but of an inferior quality, capable of disqualifying the region.' Sad to relate, this is exactly what happened, and it took thirty years to put it right.

The law-makers of the time had failed to understand that the soil and the vine are both vital influences on a wine's character, and many proprietors compounded this misunderstanding. They claimed that, just as a son carries his father's name simply because he is the son, so any wine produced in, say, the Gironde, might call itself Bordeaux. They missed the point that a consumer does not order a Bordeaux solely in order to drink a wine from this region— he wants a wine with the smell and taste he is used to, or which made the region famous.

---

[1] *Appellation d'origine contrôlée* came later, as will be seen.

41

The decree of 1905 established that the wine-producing regions should be delimited by administrative order. This soon led to trouble, for a Paris-based body can have little understanding of the delicate questions of soil-types, climatic conditions, vine species, or vinification methods, and the parts they all play in a region's wine-making. The new powers were first put to the test in the Champagne district, where there was much dissatisfaction. Large quantities of grapes were being brought into the district from outside, there to be vinified and christened Champagne. There were two rival factions in the Champagne province: the *vignerons* from the Marne and the *vignerons* from the Aube *départements*. Both *départements* form part of the historic province of Champagne and both claimed the right to the name Champagne for their sparkling wine. However, the soil and grapes, as well as the climate, were different. It was hoped that a government order would settle the dispute. By the decree of 17 December 1908 the Aubois were denied the right to the *appellation d'origine Champagne*. One might imagine that the *vignerons* of the Marne would have been satisfied but they were not, for part of the Aisne *département* was included, and the latter's wines, according to the Marnais, resembled '*la purée des haricots*'.

The vintages of 1907, 1908, 1909 and 1910 had been appalling; many vineyards were mortgaged and the *vignerons* faced with bankruptcy. Again the Government acted, by legislating that the production of Champagne and that of sparkling wine made from grapes grown outside the Champagne area must take place in two different buildings. The new decree did nothing to help the Aube *département*, however, and its *vignerons* turned militant.

Patrick Forbes[1] describes the scene: 'In Troyes there were processions, huge demonstrations and disorders of a grave nature, including the burning of tax papers; Bar-sur-Aube, in the heart of the vineyard district, hung out red flags and chanted the Internationale. Thoroughly alarmed, the Government prepared to give in; on 11 April, the Senate was persuaded to pass a resolution recommending that the law of 17 December 1908, which had delimited the Champagne district, should be annulled forthwith.' When the Marne *vignerons* heard of this intention, *they* rioted. Merchants' houses were sacked and wine ran in the streets.

---

[1] *Champagne, the Wine, the Land and the People*, Gollancz, 1967.

By June 1911, although certain regions like Cognac, Armagnac and Banyuls had been successfully delimited, the Government had come to realize the foolishness of imposing solutions from Paris. It was agreed that the local courts should be given the power to map out an *appellation d'origine*. However, legislation was slow to come, and the war then provided an interruption. It was not until 6 May 1919 that power was finally given to the local courts to decide in the event of conflicts, upon intervention of the persons concerned. In addition, it was declared that every vintager who intended to give a name of origin to his product must indicate this in his harvest declaration. The declarations were made public for anyone's inspection. *Appellation d'origine* wines were to be made in accordance with the established, honest, local customs (*'les usages locaux, loyaux et constants'*). Wine merchants were to keep a record of all *appellation d'origine* wines entering and leaving their premises.

The law of 1905 had made it clear that, for instance, wine produced in Languedoc could not be called Bourgogne; that of 1919 enabled court cases to be brought to establish just how far down the hillside and into the plain one might produce wine and call it Bourgogne. Between 1920 and 1934, many legal de-limitations of villages and vineyards took place.

These were heroic times when men like the Marquis d'Angerville and Henri Gouges (the latter succeeded the former as President of *l'Union Générale des Syndicats pour la Défence des Producteurs de Grands Vins de Bourgogne*) led the fight against malpractices. Because local merchants were among the first to be taken to court, d'Angerville of Volnay and Gouges of Nuits Saint-Georges found that their traditional market closed its ranks against them. They were forced to tend and bottle their wines themselves, and sell them direct to the public. It is from this moment that the domaine-bottling movement begins to gather strength.

Although the Service for the Repression of Frauds had been created in 1905, merchants were not effectively controlled until after 1919, and even in 1925 one could buy a good wine in Beaune called Beaune—but it might have come from anywhere. Things are a bit better nowadays.

The 1919 Act was bad law because of its omissions. It gave no lead on permitted grape varieties and failed to state the maximum amounts of wine which any vineyard might produce. The result was that many proprietors bought *ordinaire* from merchants, declared a large production of *appellation d'origine* wine, and received certificates for what they had declared. In the 1920s it was as simple as that.

As Capus had predicted, unsuitable soils of a famous region were soon being planted with vines. One such was the palus-land of Barsac, in the Bordeaux area, which is close to the river and made up of alluvial soils which had hitherto produced cheap red *ordinaires*. They were now turned over to producing white wines simply because these would have the right to the famous commune name.

All sorts of grape-types came to be planted in famous villages, often giving vast productions of strange-tasting wines. Some of the greatest abuses were due to hybrid Franco-American vines. The American vines had of course originally been introduced to combat phylloxera, for their roots were resistant to the louse and the French vines could be grafted on to the transatlantic stocks. The hybrids were crossings between the two nationalities; they were sometimes known as *producteurs directs* because they produced wine directly, without grafting. They yielded an inferior-quality wine, but nothing prevented their being planted in France's most famous vineyards. 'The new legislation, far from protecting buyers, thus exposed them to a fraud which it authorized.' (Capus)

During the 1920s, the importance of listing permitted grape varieties thus came to be realized. So on 22 July 1927 a new Act was passed to allow local tribunals to decide which vines might produce *appellation d'origine* wines, and hybrid, direct vines were denied this right. It was in 1930 that the Pinot Noir was legally defined as Burgundy's noble grape, with the Gamay and others being permitted in certain circumstances.

The new law of 1927 had two main disadvantages. Firstly, it was optional, which meant that in many famous regions where the tribunals had not regulated the names of origin, large-yielding vines were still being planted in totally unsuitable soils. Secondly, it did not enable tribunals to fix a minimum alcoholic degree for an *appellation*. (A few, however, went beyond the strict text of the law to do so.) The result of the second omission was that *appellation d'origine* wines of a mere 7° were produced at a rate of

120 to 200 hectolitres per hectare, or four times the normal yield.

At this time, the words *appellation d'origine* on a label offered one of four different types of guarantee:

1. In a few rare cases, judgements by tribunals had laid down area, vines and minimum degree. Châteauneuf du Pape was one of these, thanks to the leadership of the Baron Le Roy.
2. A few rare regions had applied the law of 1927 strictly. Minimum degree was left to the conscience of the producer.
3. In two famous Bordeaux districts, the law of 1927 was misunderstood and ill-applied. The palus-land of Saint-Emilion, often under water, was confirmed in 1934 as part of the Saint-Emilion *appellation* and in 1932 the tribunal of Bordeaux judged that the palus-land of Barsac and Sauternes had a right to these famous names. The Bordeaux Court of Appeal scandalously confirmed this in 1934.
4. In most regions, however, the law had not come into operation and all sorts of wines and soils were producing *appellation d'origine* wines.

Different names of origin thus offered some or no guarantees to the consumer, and the whole system risked falling into discredit, to say the least. The confusion was now further aggravated by the producers of *vins ordinaires*. These wines were obliged by law to display their alcoholic degree on the label, where *appellation d'origine* wines were not. Unfortunately, however, the latter had no legal definition, so quantities of wines which had never been anything but ordinary were declared with a name of origin.

A multiplicity of names resulted for other reasons as well. The law which forbade merchants to launch fictitious '*Crus*' or '*Châteaux*' applied only to *vins ordinaires*. So the *Châteaux* were launched with an *appellation d'origine*, and if there were no traditions for using one, this did not prevent a court case being brought so that a new region could be legally mapped out. Local court decisions tended to favour local interest.

From 1927, there was a mounting crisis due to overproduction of *ordinaire* in France and Algeria, which resulted in the *Statut Viticole* of 1931. This statute forbade the plantation of vineyards for a ten-year period by properties larger than ten hectares; taxed high yields and big harvests; blocked a percentage of a large estate's wines at the property, and obliged proprietors to have

45

their wines distilled if total production exceeded a fixed maximum. The producers of *appellation d'origine* wines were exempt from these measures; so again many improvised names of origin were created in areas which had traditionally produced *vins ordinaires*. The importance of the *scandale des appellations d'origine*, as it came to be called, can be seen from the following figures:

Quantity of wine declared with an appellation d'origine
1923   less than 5 million hectolitres
1931   over 9¾ million hectolitres
1934   over 15½ million hectolitres

The law of 1927 had been known as the *Loi Capus*, and it was again Capus who prepared the new law, which was passed on 20 July 1935. He was aided by, amongst others, the Marquis de Lur Saluces of Château d'Yquem; Baron Le Roy de Boiseaumarié of Château Fortia, Châteauneuf du Pape; and from Burgundy, the Marquis d'Angerville and Henri Gouges. The memory of the last two is preserved not at the foot of statues but more appropriately (and with distinction) by their heirs on wine-labels, every good vintage. Futher details can be found in the Volnay and Nuits Saint-Georges chapters of Part Two.

The new law had two objects: firstly, to enable the consumer to tell the difference between the name of origin given to a *vin ordinaire* and that given to a fine wine, and secondly, to discipline the production, and control and guarantee the quality of fine wines. This was to be achieved by eliminating ignoble vines and unsuitable soils, establishing a minimum degree and a maximum yield and laying down procedures for viticulture and vinification. On the subject of differentiating between fine wine and others, Capus wrote: 'We cannot forbid wine-growers to give their wines, whatever they are, a name of origin. But we can let the consumer know that certain names correspond to prime-quality wines. These *appellations d'origine* will be known as *contrôlées* (AOC—or AC for short). This qualification will be applied to them in price-lists and will be shown on labels. By this fact alone, a selection will be established amongst *appellations*.' Ordinary wines carrying a name of origin were to be described as having an *appellation d'origine simple* (AOS).

After the failure of the Administration's efforts to delimit the Champagne area, there was no question of it controlling the

46

factors of production. The state and the wine-growers had to combine and work together, and the *Comité National des Appellations d'Origine des Vins et Eaux-de-Vie*[1] was founded to co-ordinate them, financed by a tax of two francs per hectolitre on AC wine. The decisions of the *Comité*, issued in the form of decrees in its official bulletin, were to become law. The members of the *Comité* were to be chosen by the state: two-thirds from the presidents of those viticultural associations in AC areas, which had been at least ten years in existence; the other third from representatives of the Ministries of Agriculture, Finance and Justice.

The INAO was re-organized in 1967. It is responsible to the Ministry of Agriculture, which nominates its Director. It is composed of a National Committee of 64 members—a President, 25 producers, 16 *négociants*, 9 'qualified people' (oenologists etc.), 8 people representing the various Ministries, and 5 'commercially qualified' people, including *négociants*. There was no-one to represent foreign customers' interests (in spite of the fact that we are the principal market for many of the greatest AC names), and above all no-one to represent consumers' interests.

The National Committee has a subsidiary executive board and a permanent commission of ten people to deal with current affairs. There is a total administrative staff of about 140, in twenty centres throughout France as well as Paris. Part of the INAO's job is to make technical, practical and legal studies of all the problems related to AC (which extends to cheese, pottery etc.), including production and composition, and the ways in which products are presented and sold. Its activity is thus not simply limited to the definition of *appellations contrôlées*. It is charged with studying and proposing any measure which may favour the improvement of quality or regulate the market and must contribute to the defence of the *appellation* system. This is enforced by two bodies, the *Service de la Répression des Fraudes et du Contrôle de la Qualité* (the Fraud Squad) and the *Direction Générale des Impôts*—the latter being involved because of the fiscal element covered by the transport documentation.

Capus comments that the 1935 legislation provoked sharp

[1] Later the name was changed to *Institut National des Appellations d'Origine des Vins et Eaux-de-Vie* (INAO).

47

hostility among a large number of merchants. A Bordeaux daily paper wrote that the new law would bring ruin to merchants and growers alike. Fearing that this opposition might reach the *Chambre des Deputés* and the law perhaps be repealed, a transitional period was allowed when both AOS and AOC existed in the same region, the latter being applicable only after a request from a grower that his wine should be submitted to the controls. This transitional period ended on 3 April 1942. In the next four years the average production of AC wine was $4\frac{3}{4}$ million hectolitres, where in 1934 we have seen that it was $15\frac{1}{2}$ million hectolitres. The new law thus removed over a thousand million litres per annum of unjustifiable *appellation* wine from the market.

But abuses still existed, for although the grower was now controlled, and the wholesaler obliged to keep records of the amount of AC wine bought and sold, the retailer and bar-keeper were not affected. *Vin ordinaire* was sold as AC wine simply by refilling empty bottles bearing AC labels. This fraud attained prodigious proportions, said Capus. It is the basis for the often-heard claim that Lyons and Paris each consume the whole annual Beaujolais production.

It is an interesting fact that under the terms of the *Ordonnance Mondifiée* No. 1483 of 30 June 1945, producers of wines are not obliged to make out sales invoices. Instead, they must go to the local tax office (*la Régie*) to ask for a 'movement entitlement'. If the wines are travelling under bond, they require an *acquit* certificate—green for AC wines, buff for *vins de consommation courante*. If the wines are for sale within France, local taxes must be paid and they will travel with a *congé* certificate, or dressed in capsules which incorporate an official tax receipt disc.

When large quantities of wine are being moved, these movement entitlements are always obtained. But small quantities—three or four dozen, collected from a grower unlabelled—frequently bypass the systems. Consumers have become most adept at escaping detection by the police. Only a novice would drive down the Dijon–Chalon road at a weekend with unlabelled uncapsuled wine in his car-boot without supporting paperwork, as there are police officers stopping and searching at regular intervals. But during the week and late in the evenings the roads through the Hautes Côtes which lead back from virtually every Côte d'Or village carry large quantities of undetected bottles.

Both grower and consumer are delighted in this way to be depriving the state not only of local taxes but also of Value Added Tax (VAT). When the grower is asked to justify the difference between his declared stocks and the amount of wine which the movement entitlements show to have left his premises he can attribute the difference to family consumption and sampling by customers.

The perpetuation of this practice does much to encourage overproduction, for if bottles can leave the producer without labels or paperwork, it is in the grower's interest to have plenty of wine around produced outside the law, or he would be left with paper and nothing in the cellar.

A law of 18 December 1949, completed by a decree of 30 November 1960, established a group of *appellations* known as *Vins Délimités de Qualité Supérieur* (VDQS). These wines are often described as being halfway in quality between *vins ordinaires* and AC wines. In fact this is unfairly derogatory, for many of them are of greater quality than AC wines. From the beginning all VDQS wines have had to be approved by a tasting panel before reaching the market. (Only with the 1979 vintage have most AC wines had to submit to this stringent control, and not even then in Burgundy, because of the success of Burgundian pressure groups—as we shall soon see.) There is only one VDQS in Burgundy, Sauvignon de Saint-Bris, discussed in the chapter on wines of the Yonne (Chapter 11).

This is not the place to go into the reasons why France has saddled herself with three separate, complex, but almost identical categories for describing wines by their geographical origin. Not only are there AC and VDQS, but also *Vins de Pays*. The latter appeared with the abolition of *Appellations d'Origine Simples* (which, as we have seen, were names of origin given to ordinary wines) by the law of 12 December 1973. They are mainly from the Midi: attempts to produce individual wines of quality to be sold as such, in contrast to the mass of Midi plonk which is good only for assembly in vast vats, where the grossest defects are merged together to form the Frenchman's palatable though mediocre staff of life. *Vins de Pays* can be excellent, and like VDQS many are better than some AC wines. Countless are the bottles of fruity, purple-coloured *Vins de Pays de l'Aude* I have drunk in preference to pricey, unbalanced Beaujolais!

Historical and selfish reasons probably account for there being three frameworks in France for naming wines by their geographical origin. Certain wine regions, particularly in the south, were slow to adopt a policy of quality. The National Committee of the INAO is made up of representatives from existing AC areas, and it would seem that there has been a policy of excluding new areas from joining the club, particularly if they were likely to bring large productions of reasonably-priced fine wine in with them. At the same time the lucky members of the club had extended where possible their production areas and selected special strains of noble vines with the object of increasing yields. These initiatives bore their greatest fruit in 1973, when 13·6 million hectolitres of AC wine were produced, the VDQS contribution taking the total to over 17 million hectolitres. Over 20 per cent of the French harvest masquerading as quality wine! We were back to 1934.

It was time for new legislation, and the problems to be tackled were those of excessive yields and poor quality. There had already been straws in the wind, for instance the AC Châteauneuf du Pape took a most interesting initiative by its decree of 2 November 1966. A basic figure for the yield was fixed, which could be lowered but not raised. The total yield for a vineyard could not be more than 20 per cent above the basic figure, otherwise the whole quantity produced lost its right to the AC. The same system applied to the Rhône AC Tavel and the Corsican Patrimonio.

The trouble with the AC system until 1974 was that it set a limit on the amount of wine which could be bought and sold under each famous *appellation*. But there was *no limit* on the amount of wine that a vineyard could produce. A 'cascade' system of naming was in force which allowed a grower in Pommard, for instance, to produce 80 hectolitres per hectare (hl/ha.) of wine from a vineyard. Of this one identical wine, 35 hl were called Pommard, 15 hl Bourgogne, and the rest was *Vin rouge*. And there were several markets (Holland, Germany and particularly the UK) which were delighted to purchase these overproductions, baptizing them Pommard as soon as they had crossed the frontier. 'Where's the harm in that?' I hear you cry. Were these wines not harvested on Pommard soil, had not the advent of fertilizers, the advances in grafting techniques, the better use of sprays caused a genuine increase in the yield of good wine beyond the out-of-date legal maxima? Well, yes and no. First of all, there were many years when poor weather at the flowering in June was responsible for containing a vineyard's yield naturally within the legal limits. It was the case in 1969 and 1971, and in those years overproduction scarcely existed. Secondly, years of plenty such as 1970 and 1973 produced thin wines which often lacked colour and substance. One London buyer cannot forget attempting to find genuine overproductions of Nuits Saint-Georges 1970 for shipment as Bourgogne, and labelling as Nuits Saint-Georges in the United Kingdom (legal at the time). Sample after sample, from grower after grower, had to be rejected; indeed he could not find an overproduction wine from the commune of Nuits Saint-Georges of that vintage with sufficient fruit and length to stand on its own under the famous name. He ended by buying overproductions of First Growth Nuits Saint-Georges vineyards: Procès and Richemonnes. What happened to the rejected samples? They were bought by merchants prepared to strengthen them with 10 per cent, 20 per cent or more of other wine. Perhaps a full-bodied Pinot from the previous vintage; perhaps a proportion of Gamay; more likely Rhône or Roussillon, Corsican or Italian. Maybe they were sold in their natural state in markets which love light and fruitless Burgundies; but I am afraid that London buyer does not believe it.

There are many who mourn the passing of the days before 1 September 1973 when AC legislation came into force in the UK. The British wine trade was delighted to purchase, and the Burgundians to supply, what they called overproductions of Côte d'Or communes. This is what Michael Broadbent was referring to when, as Chairman of the Institute of Masters of Wine in 1969, he wrote of 'the cynical devaluation of well-known Burgundy commune and vineyard names over a long period by the trade on both sides of the Channel.' These wines were not genuine Burgundies at all, or only very, very rarely. They were weakbodied Pinots, strengthened from the south to produce drinkable blends which were easy to sell under famous names. This style of wine completely falsified the consumer's ideas about the taste of Burgundy.

New legislation to control vineyard yields (Decree 74/872) was introduced on 19 October 1974, and made immediately applicable to the 1974 vintage. One cannot help wishing that a simpler solution had been found—the one adopted is extremely complicated. The old law had established a maximum-yield figure for each AC. This figure was retained in Burgundy, and named as the 'basic yield' (*rendement de base*) of the *appellation*. The old law had also permitted the maximum-yield figure to be reviewed annually to take account of bounteous or niggardly years, and this concept too was retained. Each wine-growers' syndicate might propose its idea of a suitable annual yield (*rendement annuel*) to the regional committee of the INAO, who would pass it up to the National Committee for a decision. New ground was broken with the introduction of an absolute maximum for each vineyard, known as 'the classification ceiling' (tautology has crept into the French *plafond limite de classement*, which is abbreviated to PLC). This absolute-maximum figure is arrived at by adding a percentage (typically in Burgundy 20 per cent) to the annual-yield figure. The cascade system which allowed a given AC vineyard to produce an unlimited quantity of wine, perhaps 90 hectolitres per hectare, with imaginary lines being drawn through the vat specifying that 35 hectolitres of this one identical wine could be called Vosne-Romanée, 15 hectolitres Bourgogne and 40 hectolitres *Vin rouge*, was finally abolished. Henceforth the produce of a vineyard could only be sold under one name.

So far so good. In 1975, a year of grey rot on the Côte d'Or, growers' syndicates suggested annual yields in line with the damage suffered in the vineyards. In Gevrey-Chambertin, Fixin, Morey-Saint-Denis and Vosne-Romanée the basic yields held good at 35 hl/ha. Nuits Saint-Georges and Chambolle-Musigny (apparently worse hit by rot than Vosne-Romanée, or else setting their sights higher) dropped their annual yield to 28 hl/ha. Aloxe-Corton went to 20 hl/ha., being particularly affected by rot.

What is not so splendid, however, is the action taken when the annual yield plus the agreed percentage is exceeded. In this case a grower has only to send the excess over the limit to the distillery or vinegar factory to be allowed his certificate for the rest—so once again an imaginary line is being drawn through a vat of wine, with the two sections being given a different name. Above the line it's vinegar, below it's Pommard, but Pommard from a vineyard which has grossly overcropped. To do the law-maker justice, he was at the same time insisting that a wine produced in excess of the annual yield must be tasted before being granted its certificate.

Another decree was published in 1974 (No. 74/871), which laid down that all wines to be offered with an AC must be subject to analysis and tasting. There are possibilities for re-assessment of wines which are not approved at the first examination. A five-year introductory period was allowed in Burgundy, which meant that the legislation would come into force for wines of the 1979 vintage.

Burgundian growers still resist this control. They say that there are too many small *cuvées* (vats) of wine on the Côte d'Or for them all to be tasted, and that the inspectors would surely be hoodwinked by the growers. The growers would manage to submit samples of a good wine twice, and then attribute the second certificate to a poor *cuvée* which would thus escape analysis. In any case, should not the tasting take place further down the line in the merchants' cellars? Why should growers be controlled if merchants can go on blending as before? They question whether there are enough qualified people to form tasting panels, and whether these are capable of judging the wines when young, which would appear necessary given that much wine changes hands in the three months after the vintage.

The growers are making some valid points, but all are a smoke-screen to divert attention from the real problem. For at last, seventy-five years after the first legislation, it would appear that the transition is being made from quantitative to qualitative control. We know how much Burgundy is made each year, and the INAO have, for some time now, been effective in ensuring that no more should be sold than has been harvested. That is what the Marquis d'Angerville cried out for in the 1920s, and that is the position today. But not everything sold as Burgundy *is* Burgundy. To put it another way, the AC system does *not* guarantee the authenticity of the wines bearing AC names. Decree 74/871 is an attempt to draw the net tighter, and it is opposed by Burgundian growers because they know their wines will lose their right to famous names in the off-vintages, as indeed they should.

They have successfully had the decree watered down for Burgundy so that only occasional wines are sampled from each grower's cellar. The sample is collected by a local man and tasted by a team mainly composed of locals. The Burgundians are the first to admit that very little is achieved. The good old, bad old days when any rosé can call itself Clos de Vougeot, Chambertin or Corton so long as it comes from the right soil and vines and fulfils a few conditions are still with us.

I shall close this chapter with two quotations from Capus, as he concluded his description of '*L'Evolution de la Législation sur les Appellations d'Origine: Genèse des Appellations Contrôlées*', to which I am much indebted:

We think that this exposé will have enlightened those who, with good reason, are amazed that abuses still exist at the production and in the commercialization of wines with names of origin. It is necessary to realize, or not forget, the extraordinary anarchy which reigned before 1935. . . .

And finally:

Thus by reading the preceding pages one will gain the conviction that the question of *appellation d'origine* is inseparable from the notion of quality and that of integrity. These two things hold together, for if the wine does not correspond to the quality promised by its *appellation*, the buyer is deceived.

4

Climate, Rock and Soil

CLIMATE

Unless the local climatic conditions are favourable to the vegetative cycle of the vine and the maturing of its fruit, good wine cannot be made. So before looking at soil, type of vine or working methods, we must examine the climate: rainfall, wind, temperature, hours of sun and relative humidity. Nowhere has this been studied in greater detail than by R. Gadille in *Le Vignoble de la Côte Bourguignonne*,[1] to which I am greatly indebted.

Rainfall

Rain falls in Burgundy on about 155 days of the year, totalling 700–750 mm per annum. The months of February and March tend to be dry (less than 25 mm per month in twelve years, during the period 1945–63), those of May and June wet (often over 100 mm). It is difficult to generalize about rainfall during July, August and September, but the first month is normally dry, the second very wet and the third begins a phase of lesser rainfall which is accentuated in October. Regular light rains are more characteristic than heavy storms, but the latter do occur, particularly in June, the record being 52 mm in less than an hour on 16 July 1947.

Vineyard development is favoured by dryness at the end of the winter, which allows the soil to warm up, but often compromised by rain during June, when the vine is in flower. If the rains are heavy and persistent, either the flowers can be destroyed, or their fertilization can be hampered by low temperatures, both causing *coulure* or a reduction in the size of the harvest. A dry July is favourable since it brings the growth period to a halt and advances

[1] Les Belles Lettres, Publications de l'Université de Dijon, Paris, 1967.

the date of the *véraison* when the grapes turn colour. This process is helped by rain in early August, but if the month is persistently wet, an attack of grey rot can be unleashed.

Many vintages have been saved by the diminishing rainfall of September and particularly early October, for this dryness is sometimes enough to halt the development of grey rot, and bring the grapes to a late maturity.

There are considerable local differences in rainfall in Burgundy—Saint-Romain for instance in the Hautes Côtes regularly receives more rain than Dijon. The plateaux of the Hautes Côtes are wetter than the Côte d'Or throughout the year, as is the plain during the summer. As one progresses south, through Chagny and Mâcon to Lyon, the rainfall increases, particularly in July and August. In spite of the disadvantages of a wet May/June and an uncertain summer, the vineyards of the Côte d'Or benefit from two favourable factors as regards rain. Protection is afforded by their sheltered position halfway up hillsides, and also by their very northerliness—for rain-bearing clouds from the south have often shed their moisture by the time they reach the Côte d'Or.

The prevailing winds of Burgundy are those from the west (which often brings rain), south-west, north-east and north. The last, known as *la bise*, is the coldest, but has the merit of often drying out the vegetation after rain.

Graph A shows the average monthly rainfall in five major French vineyard areas: Alsace (Colmar), Champagne (Reims), Burgundy (Dijon), Bordeaux and the Midi (Montpellier).

In both Champagne and Alsace the flowering normally takes place in better weather conditions than in Burgundy, but in all three areas a dry autumn can be looked for. In Bordeaux the rainfall seems very well balanced; even the increase in September is not excessive, and can favour the development of noble rot, a fungus which grows on vines. Montpellier is quite different, being characterized by a very dry July. If this fails, the autumn is unlikely to save the quality of the crop.

The northerly vineyards seem the more likely to suffer hail damage. In the period 1926–35, the most frequent hailstorms were in April and May in Reims, Dijon and Colmar (in descending order). Burgundy and Bordeaux are less at risk in the summer than Champagne and Alsace; the Midi rarely suffers.

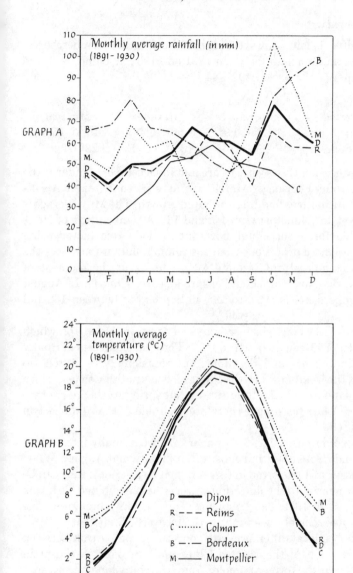

GRAPH A

GRAPH B

D —— Dijon
R - - - Reims
C ········ Colmar
B -·-·- Bordeaux
M —— Montpellier

From R. Gadille, *Le Vignoble de la Côte Bourguignonne*, 1967.

57

Temperature

The table below shows the average centigrade temperatures, minima and maxima, between 1851 and 1962 at Dijon, with the exception of the period 1931–44:

Period	Average temperatures	Minima	Maxima
Annual	10·7°–10·9°	5·9°–6·4°	15·3°–15·5°
April–Sept.	16·18°–16·74°	10·5°–11·25°	22°–22·25°

The lowest monthly averages are met in December, January (the lowest) and February. March averages 6° to 7°, then April's 10–11° encourages budding and rapid growth. The May average is just over 14°, June between 17° and 18°. A temperature of 16° is desirable for a successful flowering period—this factor being therefore more propitious than the rainfall. July usually sees the highest temperatures (around 20°), coming at the moment of lightest rain, and this should ensure an early *véraison*. In August the temperature is close to 19°, in September between 16° and 16·6°, in October scarcely 11°.

There are about sixty-six days of frost in Dijon, of which fourteen or fifteen go down to − 5°. These strong frosts normally occur in January and February, but occasionally in March. So long as the weather is dry the Pinot vine has nothing to fear, since it can support − 17° without harm, but spring frosts are another matter. A late budding is therefore desirable so that damage can be limited.

Days of intense heat (30° or over) are occasionally met with in May and September, but most often in July and August. When they occur in June, often in three- to five-day periods, they can be most beneficial to the flowering. Intense heat combined with lack of rain, as in 1952, can delay the *véraison*, but scorching of the grapes has scarcely been met with since 1727 and 1819.

As far as local differences are concerned, comparison between Saint-Romain in the Hautes Côtes and Auxonne in the plain reveals that the former is cooler from March to June but warmer from July to October. From July to September the temperatures on the Côte Chalonnaise are notably lower than those at Dijon.

The vineyards of Champagne, being somewhat closer to the ocean, are cooler than those of Burgundy, those of Alsace warmer, though in both cases the differences lessen in the autumn. Bordeaux's monthly average temperatures are always higher than Burgundy's, and it has a decidedly warmer August and September (see Graph B above).

Sunshine

There is a heliograph at Dijon which records the hours, though not the intensity, of the sunlight. On average, Dijon receives about 2,000 hours of sun during a theoretical total of 4,476 hours of daylight. During 1959 the sun shone for 2,532 hours, in 1960 only 1,741 hours—56·6 per cent and 39 per cent respectively of the hours of light. Although July stands out as the sunniest month, August and June are not far behind, and May on average beat August during the period 1946–63.

This table shows the hours of sunlight in the main vineyard areas:

Areas	Average hours of sunlight
Montpellier	over 2,600
Bordeaux	1,990 to 2,052
Dijon	1,938 to 2,044
Reims	1,746 to 1,780
Strasbourg	1,653 to 1,688

Hours of sunshine in Bordeaux and Burgundy are thus extremely similar, and this is particularly so in July, August and September. Montpellier of course heads the league, but certain months in Dijon approach Montpellier's averages. This occurred from May to September inclusive in 1949 and from May to July in 1952. It happened in 1959 (May and September), in 1947 (August and September), in 1962 (June and August) and 1953 (May and August). One cannot help noting that all these years produced famous vintages. Certain great wines are made without the year having seen concentrated Mediterranean-type sunshine however—for instance 1948 and 1961.

The long hours of sunshine in Burgundy are tied to two factors—the latitude, giving more daylight, and the area's Continental position, which causes it to be affected during the summer by anti-cyclones. Sunshine goes a long way to compensate for less happy rainfall and temperature averages.

59

Relative humidity

A study of rainfall alone is not enough to give an idea of the dampness or dryness of Burgundy.

The annual average relative humidity of the air at 13.00 hours shows the following figures for the period 1926–35:

Marseilles	58 per cent
Bordeaux and Dijon	65 per cent
Reims	66 per cent
Strasbourg	68 per cent

There is a remarkable similarity in humidity between Bordeaux and Dijon throughout the vine's vegetative cycle. The Bordelais starts the day damper (and often foggier) because of the closeness of the ocean, but the air dries out to Dijon's level by 13.00 hours, then further by the evening. Reims and Strasbourg are damper than Dijon throughout the day.

During April and May Marseilles is more often than not damper than Dijon, and on six occasions between 1945 and 1963 the Côte d'Or has enjoyed a relative humidity during July, August and September comparable to that of the Mediterranean region.

If all four factors are considered together it is to be noted that Burgundy's climate is remarkably like that of Bordeaux, although its average temperature is lower and its rainfall less favourably spread over the months. Burgundy's weather, however, is most irregular from year to year and this is one of its fundamental characteristics. The region owes its fame to the wines produced after good summers.

It would be possible to take the study of climate much further. Statistics collected at Marsannay, Vosne, Beaune, Meursault, Saint-Romain and elsewhere show subtle local differences which go some way to explaining the varied successes of the villages. These local climates are influenced by depressions in the hillsides, by the orientation of slopes, by the opening up of combes leading back through the Côte, by the altitude, by the closeness of woods. One could go into the detail of micro-climate. Six thermometers buried 15 cm below the soil of the south-east-and south-west-facing sections of the hill of Corton, on different contours, surmounted by instruments for measuring relative humidity, with maximum-minimum thermometers just above the level of the foliage, again display that subtle differences exist. But micro-climate cannot be divorced from the differences in soil and subsoil. It would be fruitless to search for the origin of the diversity of Burgundy's *crus* solely in the distribution of micro-climates. The answer lies partly in the soil.

FISH-ROES, SEA-LILIES AND BABY OYSTERS: BURGUNDY'S ROCK FORMATIONS

Some knowledge of how Burgundy's rocks and soil were formed is necessary, I think, if one is to understand the wines. So prepare yourself, please, for a rapid 400-million-year survey of the Burgundian scene.

Europe's geological history is long and complicated. The heart of the Continent is known as the Baltic shield (which roughly approximates to present-day Sweden and Finland), continuing eastwards as the Russian platform. Around this shield various mountain ranges have been formed at different times.

There were three main periods of mountain-building. The first affected Northern Scandinavia, Scotland, Wales and much of Ireland. It was first studied in Scotland and because of this christened Caledonian. It took place during the Silurian period, about 400 million years ago (see the Geological Time-Scale table on page 62). The seas were inhabited by trilobites, sea-lilies and brachiopods; the first animals, such as millipedes, were gaining a foothold on land, as were the first seedless plants.

About a hundred million years later a second folding of mountains took place, called Hercynian, from the Latin name for Harz Mountains. The Harz form only a small part of this fragmented range, which stretches from the west coast of Europe (Cornwall, Brittany and Portugal) to Poland. The Massif Central and Morvan, on whose eastern edge the vineyards of Burgundy are to be found, was formed at this period. Sharks dominated the seas, while on land amphibians (evolved from fish) became an important group, and giant tree ferns grew.

Millions of years passed, while the jagged outlines of the Massif Central mountains were ground down by the erosive action of water, wind and sun. Near Autun a great lake existed, the home of fish, microscopic algae and giant frogs. During the Jurassic period

61

TABLE 1. THE GEOLOGICAL TIME-SCALE
(IN MILLIONS OF YEARS)

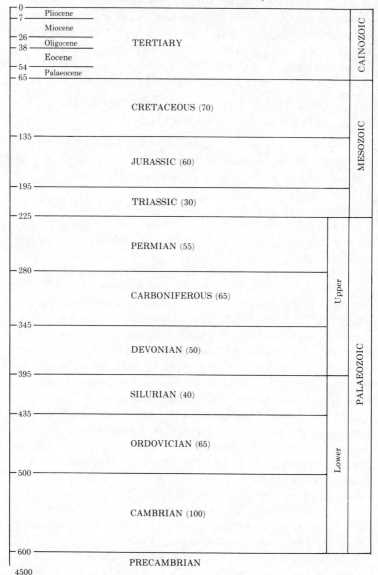

Taken from D. G. A. Whitten and J. R. V. Brooks, *The Penguin Dictionary of Geology*, Penguin Books, 1972.

(135–195 million years ago) the whole of Burgundy sank beneath shallow seas. The ancestral bird Archaeopteryx took wing, great dinosaurs roamed the land, while on the ocean-floor marine sediments were slowly laid down. The shells of myriads of baby oysters piled one on another, while the skeletons of countless crinoids or sea-lilies were compacted together; from such petrified remains limestone rock is formed. Jurassic limestone rocks, interspersed with marlstones, are fundamental keys to the excellence and variety of Burgundy's wines. We will come across their outcrops on hillsides from Chablis down to Mâcon.

The sedimentary rocks formed at this period have three origins. That just described is biological and, as well as baby oysters and sea-lilies, there were molluscs and sea-urchins, brachiopods and corals, foraminifera (protozoa with a calcite skeleton) and calcareous sea-weeds. Such rocks consist almost entirely of fossils. A second type results from the erosion of nearby land-masses above sea-level—in this case not the Morvan, Massif Central or Jura, as these were also submerged, but the Ardennes and the schistous mountain-mass of the Rhineland. These rocks are composed of fine particles of clay and sand, gravel and marl (itself a calcareous mudstone). They form the marlstones which outcrop on both Côte de Beaune and Côte de Nuits. The third type of rock is caused by the precipitation of carbonate of lime from sea-water and its subsequent accretion around a nucleus, for instance skeletal debris. Millions of such tiny grains packed together form oolitic limestone (so named from its distant resemblance to fish-roes)— the same rock which forms the Cotswolds, and stretches in a great swathe of wonderful building material from Dorset up to Yorkshire.

The Jurassic period was followed by the Cretaceous, then the Tertiary. The seas finally withdrew from Burgundy about seventy million years ago, when dinosaurs and pterodactyls were dying out. During the Tertiary period, flowering plants like magnolia were appearing alongside ferns, conifers and ginkgoes, and mammals were evolving rapidly; many fish and reptiles resembled those of today.

At this time the third great phase of European mountain-building took place, a mere thirty-five million years ago. The Pyrenees, the Apennines, the Atlas and the Alps all date from then. A depression began to form south of Dijon, which was to sink further during the Miocene period, to become the rift-valley of Bresse. Palms and Judas-trees flourished at its edges. The great Alpine upheaval caused faults to form on the Côte in a north–south direction, and many of the old Hercynian rifts moved again. This is the moment when Burgundy acquired the geological structure we can see when we visit it today, its Jurassic bedding-planes dipping towards the Saône.

The figure opposite shows the Côte between Dijon and Meursault, viewed from the plain.

The outcrop of Liassic marls north of Gevrey is the same rock which is responsible for the rich pastures of the Auxois, the finest grazing ground for white Charollais cattle. Above it is Bajocian (so-called because first studied at Bayeux) crinoidal limestone. This is most characteristically formed from the accumulation of the broken stalks of crinoids or sea-lilies; it is a powerful rock, resistant to erosion, from which were cut the dark stones of the Vézelay basilica. Next comes a layer just eight to ten metres thick, of softer marly limestone. It is characterized by the presence of innumerable tiny oysters, steely-blue on extraction, turning yellow after contact with the air. They outcrop in the lower third of the Côte between Gevrey and Nuits and have an undoubted influence on the wines. The oyster is a coastal animal; these lived and died at the edge of a shallow Jurassic sea.

Above these marls comes Bathonian limestone, again compact and resistant, laid down by deeper seas. First ten metres of pink Prémeaux stone with flints, then twenty metres of white oolite, easily broken down by frost. Above this comes Comblanchien 'marble', one of the hardest limestones, frost-resistant and taking a good polish. It forms the precipitous picturesque walls of many of the combes or dales which lead back from the Côte, and old Dijon is largely built of it. The next Callovian layer was formed when the seas became shallower again, 155 million years ago. Large oysters in banks of oolitic limestone alternate with marl. Above it is a thin layer of ferruginous oolitic marls (exploited in the Chatillonnais during the Iron Age). Then comes a 100-metre layer of marly limestone, known as the Argovian, of great importance on the Côte de Beaune; finally compact coralline limestone containing fossilized sea-urchins, the Rauracian. This is resistant to erosion and caps many of the hills of the Côte de Beaune and both Hautes Côtes.

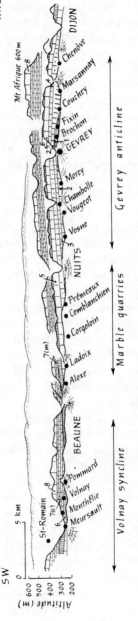

SW

Altitude (m)
600
500
400
300
200

0   5 km

Mt Afrique 600 m

St-Romain · 7(c) 8 · Pommard
· Volnay
· Monthélie
· Meursault 6

BEAUNE

7(m) · Ladoix
· Aloxe

· Corgoloin
· Comblanchien
· Prémeaux

NUITS

· Vosne 3
· Vougeot
· Chambolle 2
· Morey

GEVREY 2 5 6

· Brochon
· Fixin
· Couchey
· Marsannay 4

· Chenôve 8

DIJON

Mt Afrique 600 m

Volnay syncline — Marble quarries — Gevrey anticline

NNE

FIGURE 1. THE ROCK STRATA OF THE CÔTE DE BEAUNE AND THE CÔTE DE NUITS
(Adapted from Pierre Rat, *Bourgogne-Morvan*, Masson & Cie, Paris, 1972.)

In the foreground: the front has the form of an 'S' due to two transversal movements. Where the combes open out, old sedimentary cones can be seen, which the Dijon–Beaune road climbs or cuts through.
In the middle ground: hillocks and slabs of Rauracian limestone in the Arrière-Côte, which also follow the 'S' design.
On the horizon: line of the Montagne, eroded to 600 m. Comblanchien limestone, which is quarried on the Côte at around 260 m, can be found at a height of 640 m in the Montagne section.

Types of Rock Outcrop
1. Summit of Liassic marls, outcropping in the vineyards in the heart of the Gevrey anticline.
2. Crinoidal limestone (Bajocian).
3. Upper Bajocian (marls with *acuminata* oysters).
4. White oolite (Middle Bathonian).
5. Comblanchien limestone (Middle and Upper Bathonian).
6. Callovian limestone (pearly slabs).
7. (m) Argovian marly-limestone (slopes of Mont Afrique, hill and vineyard of Corton).
   (c) Argovian limestone (south of Beaune).
8. Compact Rauracian limestones, forming the caps of the hills.

Figure 1 (p. 65) shows that the layers of rock form a shallow ridge, known as an anticline, at Gevrey, and a basin, or syncline, at Volnay—so different sediments outcrop at different levels all along the two Côtes.

To complicate matters further, the Alpine upheavals caused faults in the bedding planes so that not all of the Côte de Nuits hillsides have a regular succession of rocks. Chenôve, Nuits-south, Prémeaux and Comblanchien are straightforward Bathonian; but Gevrey-south has a double outcrop of Callovian. The maximum of complexity is to be found, according to R. Gadille, on the Echézeaux hillside, where lower Bathonian and upper Bajocian interplay the length of the slope.

On the Côte de Beaune there are fewer faults, but more variations in the characteristics of the rocks. Between Ladoix and Savigny, and between Pommard and Saint-Aubin, the Argovian sediments are mainly gritty marl; yet between Savigny and Pommard they contain thick layers of oolitic and crinoidal limestone. By contrast the normally limestone Rauracian includes marly layers ... it is very confusing!

Geologists would divide the southern section of the Côte de Beaune into a separate Côte de Santenay, as here the rock formations of the Côtes of both Nuits and Beaune are found, from Liassic up to Rauracian. There are many dislocations due to tectonic faults, caused at the time when the Alps were thrown up.

The vineyards of Mercurey are established on Liassic slopes of marl and limestone debris, with the higher sections on middle-Jurassic Bathonian. Buxy-Montagny's bedrock dates from the period between these two, the Bajocian. The limestone strata end in the southern Mâconnais, giving way to the granite of the Beaujolais. We shall look more closely at these in the chapters on each region.

Far to the north in the Yonne *département*, we still find Chardonnay grapes growing on Jurassic strata, though they are younger deposits than we have so far met. Bitter quarrels have developed over whether Chablis vines may rightfully be planted on Portlandian as well as Kimmeridgian limestone—we shall return to the problem in the Chablis chapter.

The role of the underlying rock is four-fold. Its disintegration partly forms the topsoil, as we shall see in a moment; it permits the penetration of vine roots to varying degrees; helps or hinders the draining of rainwater, and may or may not prove a reserve of moisture during dry spells.

Upper Bathonian or Comblanchien stone is hard, with few fissures, limiting root penetration. Callovian and Bajocian marly limestones on the other hand are often split, containing pockets of red silt which permit the roots to descend. Excessive water retention after rain is not normally a problem on the slopes of the Côte. Trouble comes however from the fact that many of the Jurassic strata are relatively impermeable—Liassic marls, Bajocian, Argovian, Comblanchien, sometimes Rauracian—and this causes soil erosion in heavy rain. Land where the slope is shallow, such as the Gevrey vineyards between the road and the railway, or the lower part of the Clos de Vougeot, depend on their subsoil for drainage. In Gevrey this is satisfactory, for the vines are on accumulated banks of Tertiary or Quaternary pebbles. Lower Clos de Vougeot is planted on Pliocene and alluvial deposits, and heavy rains are harmful to quality.

During dry periods most of the Côte's limestones and marlstones provide some reserves of water, the vine's ability to benefit depending on the depth of its roots. Vineyards on banks of pebbles (situated opposite the openings in the Côte where streams have washed sediments down into cone-shaped deposits in the valley), inevitably suffer from their excellent drainage.

The Côte de Nuits and the Côte de Beaune are orientated differently, the former facing almost due east,[1] the latter southeast. Certain vineyards are exceptions to this rule however—for instance Les Varoilles in Gevrey which faces south.

Vines generally grow on the Côte at altitudes between 200 and 300 metres, but most of the best growths are located between 250 and 300 metres, in the hillside's navel. The width of the band of vines is variable, with extremes on the Côte de Nuits at Prémeaux (750 metres) and Gevrey-Chambertin (2,000 metres). Meursault presents the broadest swathe on the Côte de Beaune (2,500 metres).

The angle of the slope, with its influence over drainage and the amount of sun available to the vine is a vital factor in determining

---

[1] There is advantage in an eastern orientation, as P. Pacottet noted in *Viticulture* (Paris, 1905), for the sun dries the dew or the humidity of the soil from the first hour of the day: 'It touches the skin of the grape, still damp from the night, and colours it without scorching it.'

quality wine production. R. Gadille goes so far as to say that quality is more bound up with the angle of slope than with the bedrock. She classifies slopes of less than 3 per cent as plateau or plain, and it is only exceptionally that quality vineyards are to be found on them.

THE SOIL

Approximately 80 per cent of a vine's root system is to be found in the topsoil at a depth of between 20 cm and 40 cm. The exact constitution and structure of the soil are, not unsurprisingly, of considerable importance.

Broadly speaking, the soil of the Côte is a complex and extremely varied mixture of particles from the different rocks which have outcropped and decomposed on the upper parts of the slope. There is a long-standing tradition however of bringing earth artificially, to ensure the depth necessary for root development and tilling the soil, and to achieve the most favourable mixture of soil particles and different minerals.[1] Also, the centuries-old practice of carrying back uphill soil which has been washed down by heavy rains has contributed to diversifying the naturally-evolved soils. We shall return to the subject in the chapter on vineyard cultivation.

You can grow a vine virtually anywhere, so long as it is not in standing water. Good drainage is the first essential, so the fact that Burgundy's best vineyards are on slopes is not surprising. Pebbles and small broken stones also help the rapid evacuation of water.

The most detailed recent soil classifications in Burgundy are those of R. Gadille, in *Le Vignoble de la Côte Bourguignonne*. Madame Gadille took ninety soil samples from plateau, hillside and plain[2] from Chenôve down to Dezize-les-Maranges. She covered Chambertin, Clos de Vougeot and the Montrachets;

---

[1] In 1829 a report by the Préfecture in Dijon on the state of viticulture in France since the Revolution gave three causes of the success of new vineyard plantings: the transport of earth, the choice of vine, and persistent work. There was no mention of the natural virtues of the site.

[2] Mostly at a depth of 30–40 cm, the principal nutrition level of vines. On the skeletal plateau soils samples were taken at 5–10 cm, in the plain a second sample at 60 cm.

Marsannay, Corgoloin, Saint-Romain and Meloisey; Beaune Les Grèves, Pommard Les Rugiens, Meursault Les Perrières; Corton, Musigny, Magny-les-Villers, and many others. The angles of slope were recorded, and the soils analyzed for alkalinity, texture, presence of stones and pebbles larger than 2 mm in diameter, active lime, organic nitrogen, phosphoric acid, presence of magnesium, potassium, sodium and trace elements.

On the hillsides one finds moderately alkaline[1] soils: rendzinas brown chalky soils and brown chalky clays. The first are usually high up the slope, stony and particularly suitable for white wines. The second are by far the most common, medium-textured with a higher proportion of silts and clays. They often occupy the whole of the vineyard area, almost always the lower third of the slope, and produce most of Burgundy's finest wines. The third group is normally found at the foot of the hillside, and is composed of over 70 per cent fine silt and clay.

The varying quantities of active lime, organic nitrogen, phosphoric acid and magnesium in the soil do not appear to have a determining influence on the quality or diversity of the wines produced. Nor are sodium levels particularly significant, though it is curious to note the relatively high levels in the great white vineyards Meursault Les Perrières and Montrachet. The importance of potassium as a factor for growth and fruit development is well known, potash fertilizers being widely used.

Many trace elements are found in the soil, including manganese, chromium and cobalt. These are held, when sprayed in pulverized form on to the vines, to be beneficial by encouraging the accumulation of sugar (manganese), favouring fertilization (chrome), and speeding the maturity (cobalt). The relationship between their presence in the soil and viticultural success is, however, unknown. Other trace elements present are lead, gallium, beryllium, molybdenum, tin, vanadium, copper, nickel, strontium, barium, lithium, rubidium. The slopes of Marsannay and Dezize have higher than average levels of strontium, barium and lithium; those of Puligny and Meursault a little more beryllium; Fixin and Beaune seem relatively poor in manganese; Gevrey, Vosne, Flagey, Vougeot, Beaune, Pommard have lower than average traces of tin. It is tempting to conjecture that the

[1] pH 7·9–8·3.

presence of some of these elements is a negative influence on quality, but one must be cautious, for the vine does not always assimilate the elements available to it. No pattern emerges to link particular types or qualities of wine with specific trace elements.

More interesting conclusions can be drawn from looking at the texture and structure of the soil. The proportion of pebbles and small broken stones influences the drainage; that of fine clay particles the fertility.

Pebbles of over 1 cm diameter are often a major part of vineyard soils, particularly at the middle and top of the slopes. They absorb heat during the day, liberating it at night, but their presence in a vineyard is irregular and difficult to chart. Small broken stones (2 mm–1 cm in diameter) are more widespread. R. Gadille records their incidence (as a percentage of the total weight of the sample), feeling that they play an undoubted role in obtaining quality wines.

In a rendzina soil such as Morey Saint-Denis Les Monts Luisants, they represent 30–35 per cent, in normal brown chalky soils between 10 and 30 per cent, in chalky clays as little as 5 per cent. On a famous vineyard slope the proportions can vary considerably. The top section of Chambertin has about 30 per cent, the middle and bottom 8–12 per cent. Over the road in Charmes-Chambertin the figures are 15–20 per cent, further downhill 5 per cent, then 10 per cent. The superiority of clay-rich Bâtard-Montrachet over vineyards below it can be partially explained by the 10 per cent of small stones, compared to less than 5 per cent downhill.

Soil particles are graded by size into sand, fine sand, silt, fine silt and clay. The proportion of clay particles is capital, for they retain water and form the soil solution in which the roots of the vine develop and draw nourishment. R. Gadille shows that fine wines are made on soils with contrasting proportions of clay particles:

	Percentage of clay particles in soil sample
Bâtard-Montrachet	approx. 50
Musigny	44–49
Chenôve, Clos du Roi (bottom)	approx. 45
Fixin	approx. 45
Corgoloin	approx. 45

Pommard Les Rugiens	37–40·5
Clos de la Roche	36–40
Clos Saint-Denis	36–40
Chambertin	30–40
Corton	approx. 30
Blagny-Meursault	28–40
Montrachet	32–36
Chevalier-Montrachet (top)	approx. 20

She feels that a high proportion of clay particles contributes to a wine's staying power, but if this is not counterbalanced by adequate small stones to ensure good drainage (the case in Chenôve, Clos du Roi (bottom), Fixin and Corgoloin) then the necessary texture is not achieved, with consequently less successful wines.

'In northern wine-regions, more than elsewhere, it is impossible to dissociate the soil from the micro-climate which envelops it'— so maintains R. Bernard, and he goes on to mention the many natural factors which contribute to making Burgundy's wines fine: aspect, drainage, hours of sun, soil structure and so on. It is a complex pattern, as we have seen.

No one factor accounts for quality, variety or character, for there are as many factors as there are cards in a pack. Each vineyard is dealt a different hand, and every year the cards are shuffled. Nor have we yet discussed the Joker in the deck, man. The part he plays will make or mar the game.

5

Vines and Viticulture

VINE-TYPES OF BURGUNDY

The Pinot Noir

The most illustrious vine of Burgundy is the Pinot Noir, the same variety of vine that is grown in Champagne on the Montagne de Rheims, in Alsace, Germany and Switzerland. Its wine is first mentioned in the accounts of Philippe le Hardi, Duc de Bourgogne, in 1375, for he sent before him to Bruges a consignment of *vin de pinot vermeil* for his entertaining. The records show that various notables drank it with him, including the 'conte de Sallebrucke, Elion de Granson, Othes de Granson et autres Anglois . . . le duc de Lancastre, le conte de Salabery'. The English got to taste Pinot wine the very first year of its recorded existence.

The Pinot Noir has thick dark-green leaves of medium size and small compact bunches (7–10 cm), shaped, so it is said, like a pinecone, whence its name. The grapes are egg-shaped, blue-black and thick-skinned. All the red colouring matter is contained in the skins, the juice and the pulp being colourless. It buds and ripens early, and can withstand winter frosts down to − 17°C. According to P. Galet[1] its wines reach their highest qualities in dry calcareous soils in a temperate climate, such as the Côte d'Or. In hot dry areas the wines have no *cachet*. He lists many synonyms: Pineau, Franc Pineau, Noirien; Savagnin noir, Salvagnin (Jura), Morillon, Auvergnat, Plant doré, Vert doré (Champagne), Burgunder (Germany), Plant de Cumières; Cortaillod (Switzerland), Blauer Klevner, Schwartz Klevner (Alsace), Chiavenese (Tyrol), and others.

---

[1] *Cépages et Vignobles de France, Tome II*, Paul Dehan, Montpellier, 1958.

The Pinot Noir is a very large family, with over 1,000 individual types or clones, their productivity varying from almost total sterility to yields of over 100 hectolitres per hectare. We shall come back to individual types and clonal selection in a moment.

Chardonnay

There is a village called Chardonnay in the Mâconnais, but whether it gave its name to the vine or vice-versa is not known for certain. The Chardonnay is responsible for all the great white Burgundies. It is a handsome vine with large thin leaves and bunches of grapes which are less tightly packed together than the Pinot Noir, beautifully golden at vintage time. It is a smaller family than the Pinot Noir, but P. Galet lists even more synonyms: Chardennet, Chardenai, Chardonnet, Chaudenay, Pinot Blanc (Cramant), Pinot blanc Chardonnay (Marne), Arnaison blanc, Arnoison (Touraine), Aubaine, Auvernat blanc; Auxois blanc, Auxerrois blanc (Lorraine), Beaunois (Chablis), Epinette blanche (Champagne), Morillon blanc (Yonne), Arboisier (Aube), Blanc de Cramant (Marne), Rousseau or Roussot (Val de Saône), Gamay blanc (Lons-le-Saunier), Moulon (Poligny), Melon blanc (Arbois), Luisant (Besançon), Noirien blanc and Chaudenet (Côte Chalonnaise), Plant de Tonnerre (Yonne), Mâconnais (Isère), Petite Sainte-Marie (Savoie), Petit Chatey (Jura), Weisser Clevner or Klawner (Germany, Alsace). This vine buds a little after the Pinot Noir and also ripens later. Its yield can vary from fifteen to a hundred hectolitres per hectare depending on the richness of the soil.

Gamay

The Gamay grape may have originated in the Côte d'Or, for there is a hamlet of that name just behind Chassagne-Montrachet. It produces its best wine further south on the light soils of the Beaujolais and we shall look at it in detail in the Beaujolais chapter in Part Two. In northern Burgundy it forms, with the Pinot Noir, a part of the blend of Bourgogne Passe-Tout-Grains, and also Bourgogne Mousseux. In the nineteenth century it invaded many fine vineyards on the Côte Dijonnaise, its yield being greater than that of the Pinot Noir. No mention of this grape would be complete without reference to Philippe le Hardi's Edict of 1395 ordaining the rooting-up of this '*mauvaiz plant*' from

Burgundy's vineyards. The Gamay managed to hang on, and now, no longer '*desloyaul*', has gained respect south of Mâcon.

Aligoté

The fourth vine of importance in Burgundy is the Aligoté. Its wine is white, higher in acidity than that of the Chardonnay, refreshing and clean when young and at its best. Its yield is regular, higher than the Chardonnay's, and it is planted on less favoured slopes. One of the minor delights of the Burgundian wine business is finding an excellent Aligoté. Certain villages have a reputation for this wine, P. Bréjoux mentioning: Pernand-Vergelesses, Villers-la-Faye, Saint-Aubin, Bouzeron, Chagny and Rully.

Pinot Blanc and Pinot Gris

The Pinot Blanc was for long confused with the Chardonnay; it is a permitted vine variety for white Burgundies. It is said to be a mutation of the Pinot Noir, and not widely planted, its wine being, according to R. Bernard 'common and bereft of seductiveness'.[1] The White Pinot Beurot on the other hand is much praised, yet even more rarely planted. This is the Pinot Gris, known as Ruländer in Germany, and Tokay in Alsace. Its wine is richer in natural alcohol than that of the Pinot Noir. It used to be found interplanted with Pinot Noir on the Côte, as was the Chardonnay, and together they represented 5–7 per cent of red vineyards, adding perfume and finesse to the wine. The practice has been abandoned and the vines grubbed up, for the consumer does not look for these qualities in red Burgundy.

In the chapter on wines of the Auxerrois, mention will be made of four vines special to that region, the red César and Tressot, and the white Sacy and Sauvignon.

The survey of Burgundian grapes is completed by reference to the white Melon de Bourgogne, still permitted in the legislation for the lowest AC of the area, Bourgogne Grand Ordinaire. I have never come across its wine in Burgundy—it is important however in the Loire, where it produces Muscadet, and has indeed been renamed the Muscadet vine.

[1] There have been other mutations: P. Galet records that a certain Camuzet of Vosne-Romanée discovered a Pinot Noir in 1899 bearing black, grey and white grapes, and that some years previously the three colours had been seen on the same grape, like segments of melon.

74

Origins of the vines

One cannot help wondering at the diversity and number of
France's vine-types, and at the affinity that some seem to have
with certain geographical areas, soils or climates. It would be too
long a story to go into the origins and history of all Burgundy's
vines, but of one, the Pinot Noir, something of interest may be
said.

Deciding the ancestry of French vines is a difficult problem,
complicated by the fact that the phylloxera wiped out much of the
evidence a hundred years ago. Did the vine spring from the land of
France itself, or was it imported, there to be acclimatized? A great
stir was caused in 1879 by the discovery near Sézanne in
Champagne of the fossil remains in tertiary deposits of the leaves
and branches of a vine. This was immediately named *Vitis
sezannensis*, and proclaimed the ancestor of the Pinots of Epernay
and Rheims. Unfortunately, a glance at the other fossilized flora
on the site revealed that *Vitis sezannensis* was growing in a humid
sub-tropical climate which has long since moved on from Western
Europe. Professor Dion dismisses it, saying that its fruit would
have been quite unsuitable for making into wine.

Fossil remains of *Vitis vinifera*, the wine-maker's vine, have
been found in northern Italy, in Tuscany, and near Montpellier in
quaternary deposits. During the Ice Age it would seem that the
wild vine was driven back to two warm areas, one around the
Mediterranean, the other south of the Caspian between the Black
Sea and the Indus. As the last glaciers retreated the vine advanced
northwards, and fossils of the neolithic period have been found in
several parts of the Neckar valley, near Heilbronn. The climate
has since cooled, and now the northern limit of the wild vine in
France is just south of this. Before the phylloxera destroyed them,
wild vines were common along the banks of streams in the
Languedoc, on the hills of the Vivarais and in the alluvial soils of
the Rhine in Alsace.

The wild vine in France appears to thrive in moist soils, and
gives fruit which is too small and acid to produce wine. In addition
it rebels against pruning, and many botanists have sought to show
that the cultivated vine could not have descended from such a
stock. However, between the Black Sea and the Caspian in one of
the two areas to which the vines retreated in the Ice Ages, Russian

botanists have identified over sixty forms of wild vine, certain of them able to produce wine. Armenia and Azerbaijan, south of the Caucasus mountains, are the regions whence might originally have come the plants which have developed into Pinot, Cabernet, Riesling and so many others. But there is no evidence to prove this actually happened. Indeed, the difference in the climate forces Professor Dion to the conclusion that such a transplantation is most unlikely.

Studies of vine genetics indicate that certain of the vines producing today's famous French wines are not far removed from wild vines. Professor Dion writes: 'The original savour of the great wines made from . . . the Pinot of the Côte d'Or is, to a large extent, an effect of the still close relationship which this vine has with the wild species. The botanist Louis Levadoux classes the Burgundian Pinot . . . in a group of archaic vine-types which, he says, one could also call wild-vine vines. "They are characterized by a high vinous value and often by a savour of the grapes which resembles that of the wild vine." ' The thought, I must admit, delights me, for there is something untamed and ferocious about the smell and taste of top Pinot wines, particularly when they are young or still maturing.

The French appear to have satisfied themselves that the Pinot was not imported from the eastern Mediterranean. They do not deny, however, that the know-how to cultivate it was originally brought by the Greeks. It happened in the sixth century B.C. with the founding of the Greek colony at Marseilles, as we have seen in the chapter on Burgundy's history. Mention was also made in that chapter of the phylloxera (first discovered in Burgundy in July 1878) and it will be remembered that the most effective method of combating the root-sucking louse was to graft French *Vitis vinifera* on to louse-resistant root-stocks.

Vine grafting

Initially these were pure American vines, *Vitis riparia*, *Vitis rupestris* and *Vitis berlandieri*. The first two do not thrive in lime-rich soil, and the third (originating in the hot and dry southern states of the USA) does not adapt well to the Burgundian climate. The affinity between root-stock and graft is also of major importance. One root-stock will prove too vigorous, causing the flowers to abort; another will fail to bring the grapes to maturity on time; a third will be responsible for low production of sugar; a fourth will encourage foliage rather than fruit. For a hundred years crossings have been made between the different American vines and between French and American vines to produce the ideal root-stocks for various combinations of soil, climate and graft. These are generally known by numbers—3309, for instance, a *Riparia × rupestris* crossing realized in 1880 by G. Couderc which has for long been the most widely-used Côte d'Or root-stock, both for Pinot and Chardonnay. In lime-rich soil, however—such as most hillside vineyards of the Côte—it develops a disease known as Chlorosis, and in the 1930s its popularity waned in favour of another Couderc hybrid, this time *Riparia × berlandieri*, No. 161–49. I find it difficult to take an interest in root-stock crossings. How much pleasanter would it not be to evoke the lost vines of the Côte, with their intriguing names: *Tinevache* and *Amandelle, Machuzé, Enfariné*. But to hurry past 3309 and 161–49, not to mention SO4, 5BB and 41B, would be to neglect vital pieces of the Burgundian jigsaw.

Hybrid No. 161–49 is of medium vigour and can withstand up to 25 per cent of active lime in the soil. It is popular with wine-growers, as it favours grape production and advances maturity. But it is sensitive to disease, and because of this it is now being replaced by SO4 (introduced in 1959), also a *Riparia × berlandieri* crossing. This was developed in Germany and has many of the qualities sought: good resistance to Chlorosis and other diseases; sufficient vigour; good fruit production at an early date, and the ability to withstand periods of drought as well as to tolerate humid subsoils. It also takes well at the moment of grafting. A third *Riparia × berlandieri* called 5BB, can be used in the thin soils high up on a hillside; planted anywhere else its great vigour produces abundant foliage at the expense of the crop. All of these have been crossings of two American vines. There is one Franco-American hybrid, a *Vinifera × berlandieri*, No. 41B, with the highest known tolerance of active lime. We will come across it in the chapter on wines of the Yonne *département*. Its major fault is its heavy cost, the union of stock and graft being difficult to achieve.

'It is agreed that wines from grafted vines must be as good as those from ungrafted. Whoever would affirm the contrary would unleash the self-interested thunderbolts of trade and producers,' declared a director of Burgundy's Oenological Institute in 1907.

At that time, when pre- and post-phylloxera Burgundies were available for direct comparison, judgements were contradictory and inconclusive. Whether or not the quality has suffered can never be established, but it is certain that the wines have been modified. The root-systems of the old French vines explored quite different soil horizons to those now used by louse-resistant stocks. The old French vines had thicker roots which went deeper. Today's more superficial root-systems cause vineyards to be more quickly influenced by sudden rains or periods of drought. A. Gerbeaut, G. Constant and L.-N. Latour report with regret that the risks inherent in late harvesting, which generates quality, have been somewhat increased.

The other side of the coin is very positive, however, for several root-stocks advance the maturity of the grapes, and also increase natural sugar production. R. Bernard concludes that there has been an improvement rather than a drop in quality since grafting was introduced.

Monsieur Raymond Bernard is one of the most respected experts in Burgundy. He heads the Dijon Regional Centre of ONIVIT (*Office National Interprofessionnel des Vins de Table*), having been posted to Dijon in 1956 after four years under Professor Branas at Montpellier researching into vine virus diseases and the selection of vine-types. ONIVIT is concerned with the organization of the table-wine market, which might seem to exclude R. Bernard from concern with Burgundy's AC wines. Fortunately his brief covers viticulture throughout the region, and the research recently carried out under his leadership, and that of H. Biol of the *Institut Technique du Vin* in Beaune, will have the profoundest effect on Burgundy's wines for decades to come.

VITICULTURE

Before looking at this research and the future, let us first examine how a vineyard is planted and cultivated, and how the vine is tended throughout the year so that its fruit may be brought to maturity in perfect health. For recent developments in this field I am much indebted to R. Bernard's chapter '*le Bourgogne: technique et qualité*.[1]

[1] *Le Vin de Bourgogne*, Éditions Montalba, 1976.

For its root-system to develop well, a vine demands that the land be well prepared before plantation takes place. It is apparently during the first seven or eight years that the roots lengthen; thereafter they thicken. The land must be well broken-up (to a depth of about 60cm), and the soil finely divided for the vine to establish itself. Reclaiming land for cultivation and initial heavy ploughing are often done by an outside contractor who will disinfect the soil at the same time, rendering it at least temporarily free from virus diseases. Before the phylloxera Burgundian vines were planted higgledy-piggledy, and since it was impossible to get a plough into the vineyard, all cultivation was done by hand. As many as 24,000 vines were found per hectare, the vegetation in each case being attached in a bundle to a wooden vine-prop.[1] Plantation density was an important quality factor, for the closer the vines are one to another the more their individual vigour is limited, and their root-systems forced to develop. Rejuvenation of the vineyard took place by layering (*provignage* or *marcottage*), a shoot from an old vine being led beneath the surface of the soil so that it rooted independently. Today, vines are no longer planted 'in a crowd' as it was known, but in lines, where the distance between the rows and between each vine is approximately equal (varying from 1m to 1·25m) and giving densities per hectare of 8,000 to 10,000 vines.

Certain slopes suffer more than others from erosion. R. Gadille mentions particularly those of Aloxe, Beaune, Pommard and Volnay where the factors of steep slopes, relatively impermeable soil and subsoil, and the whole hillside being under mono-culture, can sometimes have catastrophic effects. Before and after planting a minimum level of topsoil must be maintained—now, thanks to tractors, a lighter job than when soil was carried up painfully by the backload, as it was in Burgundy for centuries. One might think that the composition of this replacement topsoil was of fundamental importance; and that a grower would be obliged by law to scour the Côte d'Or for the exact combination of brown chalky soil with 45 per cent clay and 5 per cent fine pebbles which corresponds, for instance, to his Enseignères vineyard in Puligny.

---

[1] These were made from oak, chestnut or acacia. This was not always easy to acquire, and in the centre and east of France one can still see acacia copses which were planted to furnish vine-props.

But it is not the case. It is recorded that in 1749 the Croonembourg family spread 150 cartloads of 'new turfed soil', brought from the mountain, on to their Romanée vineyard, and at the end of the nineteenth century one could see numerous holes up in the hills, dug for the same purpose, so Danguy et Aubertin affirm. Today soil is often brought in from the plain, and this must have made its contribution to increased productivity.

For centuries the spreading of manure in a vineyard was strictly prohibited. In 1395 Philippe le Hardi's Edict declared that it gave a bad taste to the wine. In 1732 the preamble to a decree of the *Parlement de Bourgogne* ran as follows: 'Burgundy is renowned for the excellence of the wines it produces and this reputation is beginning to decline; it is not that our precious vineyards have lost anything of their quality, but people are corrupting them by making them too fertile.' Those who had taken manure into their vines would have to remove it or pay a fine of twenty *livres*. In 1845 the Congress of French *Vignerons* in Dijon continued to forbid the use of manure.

It was after the phylloxera disaster that the use of manure became common. Growers were understandably anxious that the reconstitution of the vineyards should be successful. It had long been accepted that young plants should receive a moderate allowance of manure to help them to take, and this was now continued through the life of the vineyard, as it encouraged vigorous growth. After the Second World War, with the replacement of horses by tractors, and the specialization of wine estates (which had often previously kept a cow or two), organic manure became rare and expensive. The chemical industry, however, was on hand to supply fertilizers, and phosphorus, potassium, nitrogen and trace elements can now be returned to the soil from which the growing vine and man (by his operations of pruning, clipping and grape-harvesting) have removed them. That is fine, so long as the quantities of fertilizer used are not exaggerated. Too much nitrogen, for example, will lead to excessive leaf growth with a consequent increased risk of grey rot. More seriously, as R. Bernard stresses, the cost of fertilizers is recouped with interest by increased yields and abuses inevitably take place when wines are selling well—and when, may one ask, in the last twenty years, have the famous wines of Burgundy *not* been selling well?

Starting a vineyard

Acquiring and planting fine vineyard land from scratch today is about as daunting a financial prospect as starting to breed thoroughbred racehorses. It is an even more longterm investment, for four years must elapse before a newly-planted vineyard yields its first harvest of *appellation contrôlée* wine. We have seen that the soil of a vineyard must be thoroughly broken up before planting. Prior to this the grafting of fruit-bearing vine to phylloxera-resistant root-stock will have taken place, and the successful grafts planted out in a nursery for a year's carefully-tended growth. In February 1977 the *Association des Viticulteurs de la Côte d'Or* calculated the costs of bringing one hectare of new vineyard to the end of its third year as follows:

PREPARATORY WORK (grubbing up old vines, breaking up the ground, levelling and earth-moving, disinfection of soil, organic and mineral fertilizing, labour etc.)   *F.21,705.00*

FIRST YEAR (10,000 grafts and stakes, 1,700 posts, anchorages, wire, anti-pest and -disease products, labour etc.)   *F.41,790.00*

SECOND YEAR (5 per cent replacement of failed grafts, wire, anti-pest and -disease products, mineral fertilizer, labour etc.)
F.10,440.00

THIRD YEAR (anti-pest and -disease products, mineral fertilizer, labour etc.)   *F.6,557.00*

Total   F.80,497.00
Conversion @ F.8.50 = £1   £ 9,469.65

This does not mention, of course, the largest cost of all—the acquisition of the vineyard land in the first place.

There will be further costs in the fourth year, which, calculated by the same body in respect of six hectares of AC Volnay during 1975 were as follows:

	French francs per hectare
Labour for cultivation of vineyard (2,736 hours)	5,131.85
Labour for grape-picking (1,224 hours)	2,206.40

81

	French francs per hectare
Anti-pest and -disease products	1,417.24
Mineral and organic fertilizers	921.00
Oenological products (sugar for chaptalization, finings, tannins, sulphur sticks)	305.87
Replacement grafts for dead vines	170.00
Miscellaneous items (posts, wires, fasteners etc.)	108.33
Maintenance, fuel, oil, insurance, in respect of one petrol and one diesel vine-straddling tractor used for 540 hours normal work and 50 hours additional work, taking soil back uphill after 1975 summer storms	1,120.12
Social Security charges	648.94
Repair to implements, vat-house cellar etc.	1,233.33
Various charges (water, electricity, tools, office expenses, travel, union dues, anti-hail kitty, subscriptions, analyses, insurance, interest charges)	986.17
Depreciation (tractors, cultivation and harvest implements, vehicle and trailers, vinification materials, vats and barrels, small tools)	2,957.00
Renewal of 1974 tenancy	4,200.00
Total per hectare	F.21,899.59

These figures were in fact not accepted by the local tax officers who proposed the figure of F.19,500.00 per hectare. The growers' association pleaded that the poor 1975 summer had necessitated additional anti-grey-rot treatments and special personnel to hand-pick the healthy from the rotten grapes in the vat-house (would that all growers had actually taken the trouble). A figure of F.20,000.00 (or, @ F.8.50 = £1, £2,352.94) per hectare was finally agreed.

By the end of October in the fourth year there is actually some wine to draw off from the vats and offer for sale in bulk to the local trade with the possibility of part-payment in cash. If the grower opts to tend and bottle the wine himself, he must incur costs for a further year or two before he sees any income.

82

But we are rushing on ahead. It is time to look in detail at the cultivation of a vineyard, month by month. Certain vineyards look like a garden, '*elle a de la gueule*' as the saying goes. They have an allure about them, a certain air. How is it done, and is it sometimes overdone?

Round-the-year cultivation

The *Service de la Protection des Végétaux* in Beaune records three weather statistics for each month: the temperature under cover at 1·5 m, the rainfall and the hours of sun. The figures below have all been averaged out over the period 1941–72.

JANUARY

Temperature: 1·3°C
Rainfall: 64·4 mm
Hours of sun: 61

This is the quietest month for the vineyard-worker. The weather is capricious, with often a north wind and frozen, snow-covered ground. Traditionally, no pruning takes place before St Vincent's Day on 22 January, and even that would be early. At the turn of the century a grower might choose a dry, sunny day with the wind in the north (with no atmospheric disturbances to raise the lees in the barrel), to bottle his old wines. Now he is more likely to rely on finings and filters to ensure clear wine; and if he is a successful man, this month he may trade in the Mercedes for a new one, so as to set off light-heartedly for his skiing in the Alps.

FEBRUARY

Temperature: 3·2°C
Rainfall: 48·6 mm
Hours of sun: 94

This month and the next, before the plant begins to shoot, is the time for the *vigneron* to complete the pruning of his vine begun the previous autumn. It is the most important and skilful job of the year, apart from the wine-making itself.

Tradition has it that the usefulness of pruning was discovered accidentally, when an animal cropped the vine shoots and the resulting harvest proved exceptional. There are Egyptian wall paintings which show goats and kids being allowed to browse on the vines. In Greece, Pausanias came across the statue of a donkey near Nauplia said to represent the accidental inventor of pruning. In Touraine St Martin's donkey similarly lays claim to immortality; in Burgundy the animal belongs to St Vincent.

Ancient Greece considered pruning the very expression of viticulture. It has been described as a mutilation which exhausts the plant, the effect being to force it to improve its fruit in order to guarantee the perpetuation of the race. Regular pruning shortens the plant's life to around thirty years.[1]

Various types of pruning have developed in Burgundy, due to differences in soil, vine and climate. Two principles may be borne in mind: (1) A luxuriantly leaved vine will be a poor fruit-bearer. However, the sugar in the grapes being produced by photosynthesis, an adequate quantity of healthy leaves, well spread out to catch the sun, is essential. (2) The number of bunches of grapes which can be brought to maturity by a given vine is related to its vigour, and the soil's richness. R. Bernard states that it has been proved time and again that quality and quantity are incompatible.

Three types of pruning are used in Burgundy. The first is principally found in the Beaujolais:

Goblet pruning
The vine is free-standing, its head consisting of three or four horns of mature wood from each of which a fruit-bearing cane is cut back to two buds. The young vegetation is tied up around a post, or sometimes trained between wires, in this case the horns being encouraged to form a more fan-like shape (in one plane) than the traditional inverted goblet.

Cordon-de-Royat pruning
This is found principally in the south of the Côte de Beaune, in Santenay and Chassagne-Montrachet. The vine is trained horizontally, with spurs every fifteen centimetres or so, whence grow fruit-bearing canes cut back to one or two buds. This method spreads the vegetation out effectively and evenly between wires over a large area, but it is difficult to achieve the initial horizontal training.

---

[1] A vine which is allowed to develop freely, as at Hampton Court for instance, can live for several centuries.

Guyot pruning

Different forms of this are common in the Yonne (as will be seen in a later chapter), Côte d'Or and Saône et Loire. A long fruit-bearing cane, called the *baguette*, is attached to the lowest of the three levels of wire installed to support the shoots and foliage. In addition a short cane, the *courson*, is left to produce some fruit but particularly the shoots which will become the following year's *baguette* and *courson*. A double-Guyot form is known, and in southern Burgundy, where the soil is richer than the Côte d'Or, the *baguettes* are curved through 180 degrees to achieve an even distribution of the sap along their length.

In the past the pruned shoots were burnt at the end of the rows (a proportion perhaps being taken home for the cooking of *entrecôte sur les sarments*). Frequently today the *vigneron* will push before him down the row a metal wheelbarrow brazier into which the prunings are fed. It keeps him warm, and the mineral-rich ashes fall back on to the soil.

Vines are generally trained low in Burgundy, approximately 30 cm from the soil, the grapes benefiting during the night from the warmth acquired by the soil during the day. Experiments with

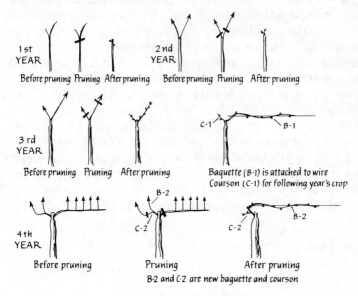

FIGURE 2. GUYOT PRUNING

85

high-trained vines (Hautes Vignes) are being carried out at certain estates in collaboration with the INAO (see Domaine René Roy, page 283, Domaine Clair-Daü, page 179 and the Mâconnais chapter).

MARCH

Temperature: 6·9°C
Rainfall: 46·2 mm
Hours of sun: 168

The pruning must be finished this month before the vine starts to shoot, and then begins the bending of the fruit-bearing canes under the lower wires. During the last days great care is needed to avoid dislodging the precious, swelling buds.

Now, around Easter, is the time when the few remaining peach trees flower, in amongst the vines. Their fruit, small, pink-fleshed and perfumed was once quite common on the Côte, but most of the little trees have been cut down to allow the passage of tractors.

It is time for the first ploughing, when those who piled the soil up around the vines the previous autumn will unbank it again. The object is to protect the vine from severe winter frosts, while aerating the soil. However, as 1956 showed, it is no great protection, and R. Bernard declares the operation to be actually harmful. Modern ploughs go too deep and destroy those roots developing in the top section of soil. He recommends a return to superficial scratchings of the surface in order to keep down weeds, the use of weed-killers or the cultivation of grasses between the rows. On steep slopes the last two help to prevent erosion. The mechanization of ploughing really spread from 1957, as J. Colombier has shown. Between that date and 1970, 870 vine-straddling tractors were sold in the Côte d'Or by the company which has approximately 60 per cent of the market. The splendid new machines were used to excess, ploughing deeply and more often than ever before in Burgundy.

Fertilizers may be spread this month, and grafting will start.

APRIL

Temperature: 10·6°C
Rainfall: 46·5 mm
Hours of sun: 196

The grower prefers a late to an early spring, hoping that any frosts will come before the vegetation is much developed. Grafting will continue during the first fortnight of the month, the new grafts being laid in damp sawdust or sand and kept at a temperature of around 20°C to take.

In the vineyard the twin wires which compose the second level of support for the leaves and shoots are detached from their posts and laid on the earth. They will be lifted up again in June, neatly enclosing the new growth.

New vineyards will be planted this month. Successful grafts from the previous year will be dug up from the nursery, the join tested, and the roots trimmed for planting out. They will give no grapes the first, nor the second year; in the third some wine can perhaps be made, though without right to the *appellation contrôlée*.

MAY

Temperature: 14·1°C
Rainfall: 65·5 mm
Hours of sun: 231

Late frosts are much feared this month, particularly in Chablis and the Auxerrois where we shall see that special preventive measures can be taken.

Successful grafts will be planted out in the nursery.

A second ploughing at this time is perhaps replaced by selective weed-killing. Towards the end of the month it is necessary to remove unwanted new shoots sprouting directly from the old wood; they would not bear fruit, for this only appears on shoots coming from the previous year's growth.

In the 1890s May was the time for cockchafer-hunting in fruit trees and hedges. They appeared on the Côte every three years, causing much damage. Today insecticides solve such problems, the principal enemies being red spiders and the caterpillars of cochylis and eudemis moths. The first treatments are made early after the appearance of the foliage, and usually combined with treatments against mildew and Oidium. When wet weather prevents tractors getting into the vineyards, the job is done by helicopter.

We have seen that in 1975 the necessary chemicals would cost a Volnay grower F.1,417·24 per hectare. The list of products and quantities used to combat various threats to his six hectares of vineyard is as follows:

Mildew (7 treatments)   210 kg Cuprosan S.D.

Oidium (7 treatments)   210 kg Thiovit

Tordeuses (leaf-roller-moth—2 treatments)   12 litres Methyl Ekatox

Acarians (red and yellow spiders—3 treatments)   18 litres Oleoparathion   12 litres Metasystemox

Pyrale (meal-moth—1 treatment)   4·8 kg Orthène

Esca ('Apoplexy'—1 treatment)   72 litres Double Pyralumnol

Botrytis (grey rot—4 treatments on 3 hectares)   24 kg Bavistine

Weeds (½ hectare)   40 kg Préfixe

None of these products is released on to the market without having first received the blessing of the *Service de la Protection des Végétaux* (which also has in mind, one gathers, the protection of the people).

JUNE

Temperature: 17·4°C
Rainfall: 73·3 mm
Hours of sun: 248

June is a critical month, when it is hoped that the flowering of the vine will take place in calm, warm weather. Rain and winds cause the flowers to abort (*coulure*), reducing the size of the harvest.

Before the flowering, some growers will take a plough through the vines, as they will after it (*griffage*). The double wires will be raised into position and the foliage spread out between each vine. Treatments must continue, recommendations on their frequency being made by the agricultural warning stations. The new shoots are attached to the upper wire by plastic ties or metal clasps, no longer the piece of rye-straw, osier or reed as in the past.

The participation of the grower's wife is important at this time, for more than one pair of hands is needed. R. Bernard records that aprons and hooded bonnets have now been replaced in the vineyards by blue jeans and beach wear. (The old hooded bonnets were known in Aquitaine as *quichenottes*, originally kissnots, from their ability to discourage the gallant enterprises of the English invader.)

Temperature: 19·7°C
Rainfall: 47·5 mm
Hours of sun: 266

By now sufficient foliage will have been produced for the first clipping back of vigorous shoots to take place, either by hand or by revolving blades mounted on a tractor. Treatments will continue, and aircraft go on the alert to seed the clouds with chemicals in the hope of turning hailstorms into rain storms.

This is the hottest month, and particular care must be taken of young grafts in nurseries, by hoeing, spraying and watering.

Binage or hoeing may be done by tractor, this month and the next. In the old days this was done by hand, using the *fessou* or *meille*, two types of short-handled pick. North Burgundians will explain that as you travel south the handles get longer, reflecting the southerner's unwillingness to get down to the job.

Towards the end of the month, Durand and Guicherd[1] permit the *vigneron* some rest if the season is favourable. He can watch the grapes fattening and his vine pushing out green fronds under the ardent rays of a beneficent sun. If all goes well he may even hum the old verse:

On this hillside sheltered from the wind
Who warms himself in the rising sun
like a green lizard? ... it's my vine!

(P. DUPONT)

Temperature: 18·9°C
Rainfall: 73·9mm
Hours of sun: 233

Further clipping will be necessary so that nutritive elements of use to the bunches of grapes are not wasted in producing foliage. In the nursery rootlets will be removed from the French grafts if these have appeared.

[1] *Culture de la Vigne en Côte d'Or*, Arthur Batault, Beaune, 1896.

On average fifty-seven days after the middle of the flowering the grapes soften and change colour. This *véraison* takes place just over halfway between flowering and maturity.

Preparations for the harvest may begin. Baskets, hods, fermentation vats, pipes, crushers, de-stalkers and presses must be thoroughly cleaned, seasoned with water (in the case of wooden vessels), and inspected.

SEPTEMBER

Temperature: 16·2°C
Rainfall: 70·1 mm
Hours of sun: 200

The *Service de la Protection des Végétaux* in Beaune gives the following dates as marking the maturity of Pinot Noir grapes:

1960 : 28 September
1961 : 3 October
1962 : 15 October
1963 : 12 October
1964 : 21 September
1965 : 11 October
1966 : 26 September
1967 : beginning October
1968 : 10 October
1969 : 8 October
1970 : 28 September
1971 : 16 September
1972 : 6 October
1973 : 23 September
1974 : 2 October
1975 : 23 September
1976 : 5 September
1977 : 5 October
1978 : 5 October
1979 : 27 September
1980 : 6 October
1981 : 28 September

Maturity varies of course from vineyard to vineyard according to the age of the vine, the care with which it has been tended, its

90

exact position and many other factors. There is a natural desire on the part of the grower to gather his harvest early, safe from last-minute weather mishaps. There are frequent occasions in Burgundy when the minimum natural alcoholic degrees laid down by the AC laws are not attained, due to early harvesting of vineyards which are carrying too high a yield of grapes. The difference is made up by illegal additions of sugar, the local fraud inspectors turning a blind eye. It is no wonder that so many wines are ill-balanced.

OCTOBER

Temperature: 11·2°C
Rainfall: 51 mm
Hours of sun: 139

Unless the harvest is very early the grower's place is in the vat-house during October, and we shall see exactly what he does in the next chapter.

The end of the vintage sees the beginning of another year's cycle of work in the vineyard. The grubbing-up of an old vineyard and deep-ploughing are the activities for this month, along with the spreading of manure. The distillation of the pressed skins and pips will also begin, yielding a clear *eau-de-vie* known as *marc*, perhaps to be kept, as Durand and Guicherd urge, in a small new barrel, there to take on colour while it improves.

NOVEMBER

Temperature: 5·7°C
Rainfall: 71·1 mm
Hours of sun: 64

Tasting the new wine and establishing opening prices are matters of concern this month. A watchful eye will be kept on prices in other vineyard areas, the sale of Beaujolais Nouveau and the Hospices de Beaune auction results.

In the vineyard, earth will be carried back up the hillsides and pre-pruning will begin. The fruit-bearing *baguette* will be cut away, leaving only two shoots on the *courson* for the spring pruning. In this way time is gained. Those growers still practising *buttage*, the ploughing of a furrow of earth around the feet of the vines (theoretically to protect the sensitive graft area from damage by winter frosts), will carry out this work. As we have seen, R. Bernard sees no merit in the practice. He states that it destroys those roots of the vine which must develop near the surface, drops the average level of the root-system and throws the plant into confusion.

DECEMBER

Temperature: 2·4°C
Rainfall: 55·7 mm
Hours of sun: 49

The autumn activities of preparing new vineyard-land, pre-pruning, ploughing and earth-moving continue, when weather permits. In the cellar barrels must be topped up, and last pre-Christmas deliveries prepared.

There is a saying which goes: '*Mieux vaut saison que labouraison*', meaning that however hard one works, the weather has the final word. But a vine only produces well when the grower has spared it neither tilling nor care nor treatments. A fine sense of sequence must guide his continuous labour, so that shoots, flowers, grapes and wine are uninterruptedly tended. The vine thrives in the shadow of the *vigneron*.

Combating diseases

'Viticulture has become a business for specialists . . . the *vigneron* has an unpleasing, difficult task which requires care and competence'—so R. Bernard sums it up. Science has provided the means to fight most of the diseases and pests which threaten the vine, with two principal exceptions, grey rot and virus diseases. And the end is perhaps in sight for these, as we shall see by looking at the research now being carried out, and the likely future for Burgundian viticulture.

Grey rot is a cryptogamic[1] disease, the fungus responsible for it being the famous *botrytis cinerea*. In parts of Bordeaux and Germany, given the right weather conditions, this fungus causes noble rotting of the grapes and makes possible the production of unctuous dessert wines. But in Burgundy it is feared and fought,

---

[1] A cryptogam is a plant with no stamens or pistils, and therefore no proper flowers.

92

particularly by red-wine-makers, for it destroys the colour cells.

Wet weather is the determining factor. Fifteen hours of rain, with a temperature of 15–20°C, are enough to allow contamination by the fungus. If cochylis caterpillars have attacked the grapes, scarring and splitting the skins, the rot can establish itself even more easily. Once it has a hold, the size of the harvest becomes seriously reduced. It might be hoped that there could be a corresponding gain in sugar content, as with Trockenbeerenauslesen or Bordeaux's dessert wines, but this is rarely the case. Instead there is destruction of the red colour cells once the grapes are affected. The fungus attacks the natural sugars in the grape, forming secondary products which can make later clarification of the wine difficult. Volatile acidity will be raised, and enzymes produced which will provoke a brown turbidity (*casse oxydasique*). The 1975 experience in Burgundy showed that once more than 15 per cent of the crop is affected by grey rot, the taste qualities of the wine are adversely affected. Grey rot was a major problem in 1965, 1967, 1968 and 1975. We have seen that wet weather is the determining factor; September is the crucial month. The average September rainfall in the Côte d'Or is 70 mm; in 1967 for instance it was 130 mm, in 1968 178 mm. However, there are other causes than rain, for the problem is of recent development. Many factors are thought to contribute.

Firstly, certain types of Pinot Noir seem genetically susceptible to the disease, as was seen in 1976. This was a year when grey rot generally caused little damage, but nevertheless certain clones in the experimental station at Echevronne (which we will come to in a moment), rotted extensively. Secondly, Pinot Noir grapes are more fragile than in the past, due to increased yields. The widespread use of fertilizers, particularly nitrogen, ensures healthier vegetation, but more and bigger leaves prevent some sun reaching the bunches. Increased yields following over-fertilization give thinner-skinned, so less rot-resistant, grapes; these are fatter and bigger, so touch each other, thus facilitating the spread of mould.

With the spread of tractors, vineyards have been more cultivated. Ploughing, which used to stop around 15 July, sometimes goes on for a further month or so. This late ploughing may liberate moisture from the soil, thus encouraging grey rot attacks. It has been noted that vineyards where ploughing is skimped are sometimes rot-free. Finally, the synthesized fungicides now used against mildew and Oidium do not harden the grape-skins as copper sulphate solution used to. This received the nickname 'vitriol' from *vignerons* whose hands it frequently burned.

In order to investigate the causes of grey rot and if possible prescribe a cure, a Grey Rot Study Group was formed in Beaune in 1969 under the auspices of the *Institut Technique du Vin*. The 1975 harvest was of particular use to the Group, which is now able to recommend various preventative steps which should be taken with respect to Pinot, Chardonnay, Aligoté or Gamay. Caterpillars are to be destroyed by spraying and four specific anti-rot treatments are recommended, beginning at the end of the flowering and finishing three weeks before the harvest. Various products have been recommended: Ronilan, Rovral, Eurapène and Sumisclex. Applications of a combination of these products have more or less controlled grey rot attacks since the 1977 harvest. For the time being the authorities must be content with treating the disease, rather than preventing it, but the means to prevent it, through clonal selection, may soon be known.

Plant selection

Since cultivation of the vine began one can imagine that there have been attempts to improve the plant, with the objects of increasing productivity, enhancing quality or selecting strains which will be resistant to a certain disease. This can be done in two ways: selection in the mass, or selection by clones.

The first consists of marking individual vines within a vineyard just before the harvest so that wood for grafting (or in the old days for layering) is taken only from healthy, vigorous specimens. The method is insufficient however to combat certain virus diseases, and here clonal selection is the answer. A clone is the whole family of direct descendants of a single mother-vine. There are different stages in the process, the first being the selection of the mother-vine or head of the clone, based on its healthy looks and the abundance, regularity and quality of its production. It will take some years for this vine to yield enough shoots for grafting and planting to take place to establish a sizeable collection of identical plants, whose performance can be watched, and whose grapes vinified and wine tested.

Clonal selection is a relatively new phenomenon in Burgundy, and one of exceptional interest. It began around 1960 because of the spread of infectious degeneration or fan-leaf (known in French as *court-noué*) amongst Chardonnay vines.

This disease is caused by a virus which is carried from vine to vine by a microscopic root-sucking worm known as *xiphenima index*. The phylloxera louse was at first suspected as the carrier but has now been acquitted. Deformed, asymmetric, nettle-like leaves appear, turning a variegated green-yellow. The vine takes on a stunted aspect, its yield falls off, and it dies within ten or fifteen years of plantation. The disease has been a major problem, particularly on the Côte de Meursault, since 1947. For a decade the only advice given was to allow the soil to lie fallow for ten to twelve years between plantings, but now it can be disinfected by the injection of chemicals. Re-contamination rapidly takes place, however, for mud-laden boots, tractors or implements can carry the worm back between the vines.

The worms usually seem to spread out from one vine to attack others, and since they do not climb uphill for choice the disease can be identified in hillside vineyards by yellow-green half-moon shapes. In 1970 two of these could be seen in the Puligny section of Montrachet, where it was estimated that 20 per cent of the production of Montrachet was being lost through the disease, which, as well as reducing yields, obliges a vineyard-owner to replant every twenty-five to thirty instead of every thirty-five to forty years. Clonal selection over fifteen years has now enabled the local viticultural research stations to identify Chardonnays which are apparently resistant to fan-leaf. By 1980 enough certified vines were available to plant 28 hectares of virus-resistant Chardonnay annually in the Côte d'Or.

Let us now turn to the Pinot Noir, looking first at the past. Before the phylloxera, the system of layering virtually guaranteed that the same type of Pinot Noir was perpetuated in any one vineyard. The complete reconstitution with grafted vines which became necessary gave growers the opportunity to choose higher-yielding varieties, and it is hardly surprising, given the losses they had recently suffered, that many chose this path. R. Gadille describes the conditions of the reconstitution as being '*assez anarchiques*', and the consequences are still with us.

There are many different types of Pinot Noir in Burgundy. Some are named after villages—Pinot de Pernand, de Pommard, de Santenay—others after growers—Pinot d'Angerville, Pansiot, Gouges, Crépet, Liebault.

The most infamous of the various types are probably the *Pinots droits* or straight-growing Pinots. Legend has it that the first *Pinot droit* was discovered in Richebourg around the turn of the century by a *vigneron* named Thomas. Where surrounding Pinots trailed along the ground, the easy preys to mildew, this one grew straight and healthy up its post. Cuttings were therefore taken and propagated.

Although mildew has now been beaten, the traditional Pinot whose shoots grow sideways (known as *Pinot fin*, *Pinot classique*, or *Pinot tordu* (twisted) when compared to *Pinot droit*) is still unpopular with *vignerons*. For if a clear way for tractors is to be maintained through the vines, three passages on foot are required during the summer to lift its young shoots up between the wires. The shoots of the *Pinot droit* grow vertically, but what endears it most to the *vigneron*'s heart is that its yield is larger and more regular than that of the classic Pinot.

In the hands of a man who is prepared, immediately after the flowering, to thin out the young bunches of grapes if the crop looks excessive, this reliable, time-saving vine can produce good quality. Such a man is hardly the rule, however. The old *vigneron* expressions '*Il faut faire cracher la vigne*' or '*Il faut faire pisser la vigne*' exaggerate, I think, most growers' attitudes. However '*On n'enlève pas ce que le Bon Dieu donne*' sums things up fairly well, with growers conveniently ignoring the possibility that other factors than the Almighty are responsible.

Some brokers and merchants believe that, even in careful hands, *Pinots droits* give inferior quality; that the generally big grapes produce wines lacking in character and short in life span. The issue is confused by there being different types, some bigger yielders than others. The spread of *Pinots droits* over the last fifty years, particularly on the Côte de Nuits in Vosne-Romanée and Vougeot, illuminates an amazing fact—that there is some legislation, but *no effective control* over the type of Pinot Noir which may be planted in Burgundy.

It is therefore most welcome news (though very overdue) that research is currently taking place. Those responsible are the Beaune Experimental Technical Centre of the *Institut Technique de la Vigne et du Vin* (CETEX-ITV), working in conjunction with the *Association Nationale Technique pour l'Amélioration de la Viticulture* (ANTAV) based at the Domaine de L'Espiguette, Le Grau du Roi, in the Gard. On the estate of Lucien Jacob at Echevronne in the Hautes Côtes and at three other centres, they have collected nearly 160 different varieties of Pinot Noir. There are *Pinots fins, moyens* and *gros* and many *Pinots droits*. There are Pinots from the Jura, the Côte Chalonnaise, Champagne and Switzerland. Pinots with cylindrical bunches, pine-cone bunches, bunches with ears and bunches with shoulders. They are planted on the same root-stock, in identical ground, and all trained, pruned and treated similarly. Their growth and development are charted, particularly with regard to their resistance to grey rot and virus diseases,[1] as are the yields per hectare, the natural alcoholic degrees and other important characteristics of the grapes.

The results are just becoming known, and they are fascinating. The first plot of vineyard was planted in 1971, and contains at least ten examples each of seventy different clones, whose grapes have been vinified for three vintages, 1974, 1975 and 1976. In 1976 the yields of these Pinot Noir vines varied between 26 and 90 hectolitres per hectare. The natural alcoholic degrees varied over almost 3°, between 8·8° and 11·7° (the basic permitted yield for AC Bourgogne is 50 hl/ha., the minimum degree 10°). The high productions were not *necessarily* connected with the low alcoholic degrees, nor did vines with moderate or low yields necessarily give good wines. It appears likely that respectable alcoholic degrees can be produced by Pinots yielding 40 hectolitres per hectare. But will their quality really correspond to what the consumer expects great Burgundy to taste like? Grey rot seems to depend on a genetic factor, since it attacks certain clones every year, and others are resistant to it, even in 1975. An interesting connection has appeared between good results in the blind tastings which take place, and an early *véraison*.

The experiments continue. In 1976 three plots were established on the Côte itself for successful clones to be tested further, and the wine made in larger quantities; two more plots were planned for

---

[1] *Court-noué*, described on page 95, is the principal virus disease, but *enroulement* is also serious. In the latter case, the leaves of the Pinot become thick, and roll up underneath. Sugar production is impeded with a loss of 1°–1·5° natural alcoholic degree in the wine.

1978. Progress is slow for obvious reasons, but there is a clear prospect that in the 1980s Pinot Noir vines will become available which are resistant to virus diseases and grey rot. A question-mark remains over whether productivity should be maintained at its current levels, increased or decreased.

The INAO has the power to pass laws compelling growers to replant with certain types of vine, and, if it stirred itself sufficiently, to enforce such legislation. Before a list of successful Pinot Noir clones is published, it is to be hoped that the authorities will consider very carefully how they define quality in Burgundy. Will the results of the clonal selection experiments be used primarily to increase quality or to increase yields?

6

Wine-Making

All farmers have worries about the weather, but if there is one period when *vignerons* might be expected to reach for the tranquillizers, it is during the two or three weeks of the vintage. To one who has never done either, making wine appears almost as nerve-racking an experience as being present at the birth of one's child. Wine is only made once a year, the raw materials and the ambient temperature being different each time. How tremendous it must be thus to bring twelve months' work to completion!

The choice of the best date for picking is a vital one. In the eighteenth century, so the Abbé Tainturier tells us, even the behaviour of the wasps around the bunches had to be taken into account when arriving at the decision. He felt that one needed cooked, roasted and green grapes ('*du cuyt, du roty, du verd*'), to produce fine, balanced wine. In the nineteenth century, when demand for deeper-coloured, fuller wines made itself felt, there was a tendency to harvest late, and in 1822, for instance, the result was wines which failed to last in bottle.

Nowadays the *Stations Oenologiques* in different wine-growing regions follow the evolution of sugar and acidity in the grapes throughout the summer and can forecast some weeks in advance a propitious starting date for picking. They must of course take into account that the vintage can sometimes last three to four weeks on a big property. Occasionally a marvellous autumn such as 1959, 1966 or 1971 can produce over-ripe grapes, whose acidity has fallen sharply; such wines are often difficult to clarify. The health of the grapes at vintage time is of almost equal importance to their maturity, and here the problem of grey rot looms large, as we have seen in the previous chapter.

Many red harvests in the Côte d'Or have not reached maturity when they are picked, if one takes as maturity the official natural grape-sugar level laid down by the AC laws. Growers immediately make up the deficit by massive additions of sugar, breaching the law when the crop is finally declared under the chosen AC, while the Fraud Squad turns a blind eye. I am thinking of 1967, 1968, 1970, 1972, 1973, 1974, 1975 and 1977.

In poor years it is basically the over-laden vines which fail to reach the minimum degree. A 35–40 hl/ha yield will reach the minimum, even in 1972 or 1975. The Chardonnay produces sweeter grapes than the Pinot or Gamay, and it is fair to say that the minimum is practically always reached with white wines. The problem is the reds.

Fermentation is the process by which sugar is decomposed into ethyl alcohol and carbon dioxide, by the action of enzymes in yeasts. Thus grape-juice becomes wine. There are various side-products and the process is extremely complex—fortunately beyond the scope of this book, since it is beyond my comprehension. There are various types of yeast, the most important in wine-making being *saccharomyces ellipsoideus* and *saccharomyces oviformis*, the latter working well in the later stages of fermentation. In order for yeasts to develop and perform their work, various phosphates and nitrogenous compounds must be present, and the temperature needs to reach around 20°C. Over 35°C they suffer, and stop multiplying, which will bring about a halt in fermentation. Lack of oxygen also prevents multiplication of the yeasts, and for this reason aeration of the must is strongly recommended early on in the fermentation. The antiseptic sulphur dioxide (SO_2) is vital to modern wine-making. It eliminates non-productive yeasts, destroys harmful bacteria, and protects the must from oxidation in the early stages.

There are differences in the making of red, rosé and white wines, the most obvious being that red wines are completely fermented with their skins, and rosés partly fermented with their skins, while white must is first removed from the skins by pressing. I will deal briefly with the different methods (leaving Beaujolais wine-making to its own chapter).

100

RED WINES

Red grapes are brought whole and uncrushed to the vat-house, whose vats, pipes, presses, pumps and implements have previously been carefully cleaned. They are fed into a mechanical crusher, which at the same time normally removes some of the stalks. Certain *vignerons* sprinkle the sides of their oak vats before fermentation with four or five litres of *marc* or *fine de Bourgogne*. The alcohol presumably serves as a disinfectant, though one suspects that an equally powerful reason is the wish to eliminate any lingering taste of water—for water has to be used for rinsing purposes. So far as I know there is no perceptible influence on the strength or taste of the wine. At least one man goes so far as to flambé his vat before putting in the grapes—or so the story goes.

It is often said that Burgundies these days mature too fast and do not hold up in bottle, and one of the causes is said to be the practice of removing the stalks before vinification. There are many advantages in de-stalking, which Bréjoux in *Les Vins de Bourgogne* (Société Française d'Éditions Vinicoles, Paris, 1967) has summarized as follows: more wine can be put into a vat; there is less *marc*[1] to press at the end of fermentation; the alcoholic degree is slightly increased because the stalks bring a little water; colour is increased for the same reason; tannin content in the wine is minimized, for the stalks will contribute not a little if given the chance. In years of imperfect maturity, he says, mellowness, finesse and quality are improved. However certain wine-makers continue to add a proportion of the stalks. Some feel that fermentation is more satisfactory if stalks are present to discourage a jam-like consistency in the must; others that the ratio of solids (skins, pips and stalks) to liquid (the juice) has been unbalanced by modern treatments which produce healthier, bigger grapes. They feel that at least some stalks are necessary to redress the balance.

Vats in Burgundy are traditionally of cylindrical shape, made of iron-hooped wood, open at the top. In very hot years there can be an advantage in placing some of the grapes uncrushed in the vat. Their cool juice is only liberated during pumpings or manipulations later on, resulting in a slowly progressive fermentation, and

---

[1] The mass of skins, pips and stalks left behind in the vat after the wine has been run off. This is later distilled to produce the spirit known as *marc*.

helping to keep down the temperature in the vat. Sulphur dioxide is now added, for the reasons already mentioned, by doses of between 50 and 150 g per metric ton of grapes. The density and temperature of the must are taken, and plotted on a graph.

It is important that fermentation should begin within twenty-four hours or at most two days, to avoid the risk of oxidation of the must. The Côte d'Or being northerly, it is not unusual to have to heat the must. There are various methods, the most common being the plunging of *drapeaux* (which look like portable wall-radiators) into the juice. Hot water or steam is run through them until 20–22°C is achieved, at least in a section of the vat. Pod-shaped electrical plungers are also effective. Alternatively, part of the must can be heated in a cauldron, then returned to the mass; and fires can be lit to increase the temperature of the vat-room. The first vats filled are always the tricky ones, and many growers prepare a *pied de cuve* to help start them off. A few rows of vines are picked some days before the main harvest, and the must warmed until fermentation starts, and a great quantity of yeasts have developed. The addition of this fermenting must to the first vats is usually enough to start them off. Cultivated yeasts are rarely required in red-wine-making.

If the picking takes place in hot weather it is sometimes necessary to cool the must, and here again the *drapeaux* can be used.

The object of macerating the grape-skins in the juice is to extract the colouring matter, aromas and tannins. Twice a day it is necessary to push the floating *chapeau* of skins and stalks beneath the surface of the wine, and to break it up so that dissolution of the skins be encouraged. At the same time the must can be pumped over from the bottom of the vat, to encourage the multiplication of the yeasts, which is essential if total transformation of sugar into alcohol is to take place. Some proprietors, even those with oenological degrees and modern installations, remain convinced that human bodies play an important part in successful vinific-ation. Well-washed feet or gum-boots will squash the grapes, and *pigeage* (the mingling of fermenting must with the grape-skins which tend to rise above it) will be done by the legs of men clinging to the side of a vat. Finally, in a large vat there is a danger that portions of must will start fermenting too fast. Only a swimming man, some believe, can discover these overheated pockets and mix them back into the mass. But if a century ago there was truth in the saying that this constituted a *vigneron*'s annual bath, today the need for total cleanliness is widely understood.

The *Station Oenologique* in Beaune recommends that the fermentation of Pinot Noir grapes should take place at around 30°C to achieve maximum colour extraction. This temperature is not easy to maintain. For Gamay grapes, a more interesting fruitiness and greater finesse can be had from low-temperature fermentation.

The practice of adding sugar to grape-must when sunless summers have failed to ripen the fruit completely is very old. The monks of Cîteaux, for instance, were adding small pieces of white sugar to light wines in the late eighteenth century. Unfortunately chaptalization (as it is called after Chaptal, Napoleon's Minister of Agriculture) is often overdone, for growers, brokers and merchants know that alcoholic strength goes a long way towards making up for a lack of real flavour.

The law in France states that a declaration of intent to chaptalize must be made. Careful vinifiers often do not add the sugar all at once, for a tempestuous fermentation might be unleashed, taking the temperature above the 30°C danger-level. They add it little by little during the vatting time. A very few find that small doses added throughout the winter produce the maximum bouquet—however, this is a dangerous game to play, for if once the fermentation stops while a little sugar remains unconverted into alcohol it is very difficult to get it started again. One man I know finds that neutral, non-aromatic honey gives to wine a special velvet roundness unobtainable from sugar. Heather or lavender honey would be disastrously over-scented, but acacia or wild alpine flower honeys are ideal. Of course, it is strictly illegal.

If the removal of the stalks is normally given as one reason for the precociousness of today's Burgundies, another is short vatting times—five or six days, compared to a fortnight in the old days. Leading oenologists appear to differ over the importance of vatting times. M. Léglise, Director of the *Station Oenologique* in Beaune, states: 'This question, which in the past caused great discussions, is a false problem ... one has recently been able to prove by simple experiment that an excessive length of vatting time for a harvest where the stalks have been removed brings no extra enrichment to the wine in the way of body or colour.'

But if one turns to Dr Émile Peynaud (admittedly a Bordeaux man, but one respected far beyond the borders of the Gironde) one learns something different. In his book on wine-making for the layman, *Connaissance et Travail du Vin*,[1] he explains that the colour of red wines, and a large part of their savour, comes from the class of aromatic organic substances known as phenolic compounds, which are found in the skins, pips and stalks of the grape. There are two main types—the anthocyans (or red colouring matter) and the tannins. The former pass from the skins into the must rapidly during the first three or four days of vatting if the grapes are squashed and the must is agitated. Thereafter the intensity of colour of the wine can actually diminish as the anthocyans fix themselves to the pips or stalks. The tannins are dissolved into the liquid at a regular rate throughout the maceration, and it is they which constitute the colouring matter in a fine wine when the anthocyans have virtually disappeared after two or three years' aging.

M. Peynaud concludes:

> The maturation, good conservation and colour intensity of *vins de garde* require sufficient concentrations of tannins. For, after several months or years, the colour of a wine no longer corresponds to the presence of anthocyans found in the grape— they have for the most part disappeared—but to that of tannins. In addition, the anthocyans have little savour. The quantity of tannins decides the sapidity and the longevity. For all wines which get their qualities from a certain degree of aging, the success of a vinification is based on a compromise between the necessity of guaranteeing them a good richness in tannins and the contrary necessity of assuring them a certain suppleness when they are young at the moment when habitually they are judged.

It is perhaps regrettable that Burgundy's *Station Oenologique* should be located on the Boulevards in Beaune, so much a part of the commercial life of the town. Under pressure from local merchants in need of Côte d'Or wines which can be turned over quickly, it has often, since the 1930s, advocated methods which

[1] Dunod, Paris, 1971.

are at odds with the region's destiny to produce great red *vins de garde*. A little academic isolation as part of the University of Dijon might not be a bad thing.

One cannot help feeling sympathy for M. Léglise. His thankless task is to advise a rough-hewn, hidebound band of Burgundian individualists who, if they cannot rip off a passing tourist, can usually dump unwanted wines on the local trade. They seem years ago to have given up listening to him. Perhaps it was because, after sunless summers, he expected them to plunge their bunches of rotting Pinots into 80°C heated must as easily as if they were dipping pieces of bread into cheese fondue. They pictured the grapes falling to the bottom of the boiling liquid, themselves holding the denuded stalk. And then there was the vintage, 1974, when he prepared his instructions for vinification a week before the harvest. While they were being typed and printed, enough rain fell per square metre to double the quantity of water in the grapes, had the vines been able to absorb it all. It washed out both harvest and advice.

For the 1975 vintage, he recommended a vigorous elimination of rotten grapes in the vineyard, and would have liked to have suggested a drawing-off of part of the juice from the vats to bring the ratio of solids to liquids to a more reasonable level. His is a frustrating job, for demand for Burgundy's famous names around the world has never ceased to grow. Fortunately it has not prevented him from writing a magnificent book on wine-tasting, technical yet readable: *Une Initiation à la Dégustation des Grands Vins,*[1] which is currently being translated into English.

The final stages of red-wine-making are the running-off of the wine and the pressing of the skins and pips. The most unpleasant and tiresome activity of the harvest—the forking out of grape-skins from a vat laden with CO_2 and alcohol fumes—is now being done on the larger estates by modern pumps which can handle solids and liquids together. The first pressing is almost always included with the *vin de goutte* (wine which has run off of its own accord). Subsequent pressings should be kept apart if they have unpleasant characteristics—often the case in 1975, when grey rot was common.

The malolactic fermentation (transformation, by the action of

---

[1] Max Léglise, DIVO, Lansanne, 1976.

bacteria, of malic acid into lactic acid) is now encouraged by maintaining the temperature of the new-wine cellar near to 18°C and not racking the wine off its lees. This means that it is left on the deposit of dead yeast cells, bacteria and particles of grape-skin which form the sediment at the bottom of barrel or vat. The transformation of malic acid into lactic acid is positively sought, as it brings about a softening of the wine; also, if not encouraged when the wine is young, there is a danger it will take place after bottling, making the wine gassy and out of condition. However, it is capricious, and some wines take a year or more to complete it, or indeed never do.

WHITE WINES

In white-wine-making complete cleanliness and isolation of all metal parts is even more important than with red wines. The whites generally have a higher acidity and are more corrosive, particularly after the addition of SO_2. The grapes are brought whole to the vat-house, and there pressed rapidly, all care being taken to minimize oxidation of grapes and juice. In years when grey rot has attacked, the different pressings should be kept separate, as the second and third are likely to contaminate otherwise clean-tasting must. Sulphur dioxide is added, particularly to prevent browning. In years of rot, or when the vintage takes place in muddy conditions, it is often wise to allow a twelve-hour settling or *débourbage* in vat, before the must begins to ferment. This permits mineral impurities and particles of grape-skin or dirt to sink to the bottom of the vat, whence the must is racked off. The addition of selected yeasts may then be advisable.

The greatest freshness and fruit in white wines is achieved when fermentation takes place at a low temperature, around 18–20°C. The ideal unit to achieve this temperature is the hogshead, as a large quantity of must in vat or tank quickly heats up, the resultant wine being often light. A happy medium must be found for filling the hogshead—too full, and the yeast will not develop; too empty, and the must may oxidize. Many of the best growers rouse their casks periodically with sticks or brushes, to mix up yeasts which have fallen to the bottom. One might add a line to the old verse:

A dog, a woman and a walnut tree
—as also a hogshead of Puligny—
The more you beat them the better they be.

White wines can go on fermenting throughout the winter, and often take a year to finish their malolactic fermentations. They should be left on the lees until the process is complete.

Proprietors owning both red and white vineyards tend not to make an equal success of both wines, for the two demand somewhat different temperaments. White grapes need lightning pressing, red a carefully-controlled long vatting time.

ROSÉ WINES

There are two types of rosé wine, the less common being *vin gris*. This is made from red grapes which are pressed immediately and give a pale grey-pink wine, when vinified away from the skins. True rosés are also made from red grapes, the skins being allowed to macerate a day or two in the must before this is drawn and they are pressed. Choosing the moment to draw off the vat to give the exact rosé tint required is a delicate decision. Vinification then proceeds as for a white wine.

SPARKLING WINES

The sparkle is obtained by adding a dose of sugar and yeast to the wine when it is bottled. A secondary fermentation takes place in bottle, and since the carbon dioxide gas cannot escape, it dissolves into the wine. The Champagne process of *remuage* and *dégorgement* is then needed to eliminate the sediment of dead yeast cells which have formed during the fermentation. Over a period of two to three months, the bottles are tipped upside down into a vertical position, being shaken every other day, so that the sediment slips down onto the cork. The necks of the bottles are then passed through a bath of brine at lower than freezing temperature, so that a bullet of frozen wine forms in the bottle-neck. When the cork is removed, the pressure inside the bottle expels bullet and sediment. The bottles are then topped up, their sweetness is adjusted, and they are re-corked. After a period of rest they are ready to be drunk.

The base wines for Sparkling Burgundy are the regional appellations, Bourgogne Aligoté and Bourgogne Grand Ordinaire, the latter being mainly made from Côte d'Or Gamays and Sacy grapes from the Yonne. Thirty per cent of more noble grapes (Chardonnay, Pinot) must be used in the *cuvée*, but it has to be said that these have traditionally often been low-quality examples, the sparkling process serving to disguise wine-making faults and excessive acidity. A new appellation, Crémant de Bourgogne, was created in 1975, imposing higher standards than previously on the base wines to be used. Grape maturity, methods of transport, pressing and vinification are now more strictly controlled; so it is likely that bottles bearing the AC Crémant de Bourgogne will be of higher average quality than those which bore the old name, Bourgogne Mousseux.

DEALING WITH A POOR HARVEST

There are at least four schools of thought about the way to deal with red grapes when a poor summer has failed to develop their colour cells fully, or when grey rot has attacked them. A large proportion of *vignerons* believe that producing acceptable wine from rotten or unripe grapes is impossible: '*On ne peut pas faire du vin vivant avec des raisins morts.*' All one can do is to chaptalize strongly and vat for a brief period so that the taste of rot does not get into the wine. If the result lacks colour, at least one's neighbour's is no better. And what is a merchant for anyway?

In the early 1970s Monsieur Léglise recommended a more positive approach. He suggested that the rotten bunches be dipped for three minutes into grape-must pre-heated to 80°C, so that colour extraction from the skins be accelerated. Taken to extremes, this could involve the installation of costly heating and cooling apparatus as at the Domaines Drouhin-Laroze or Charles Noëllat (q.v.); however, many estates and merchants economize by using double-wall, steam-heated copper basins to heat part or all of the must.

In January 1966 a blind-tasting took place at the *Station Oenologique* in Beaune of traditionally made wine against wine half-made from normal grapes and half from steam-heated grapes, where the temperature of the interior of the grape did not exceed 60°C. Both wines came from the same place. The traditionally made wine was said to be young, light and fruity, the part-treated wine full-bodied, round, maturer, showing a more aged bouquet, with no oxidization or cooked taste. 'According to their respective tastes, the members of the jury preferred either the freshness and youth (*primeur*) of the check sample or the more marked consistency of the trial sample.' Initially Monsieur Léglise's system encountered problems of clarification and partial loss of the acquired colour; but these are said to have been resolved. However many Burgundians (including not a few oenologists) are prepared to argue till the Charollais come home that must-heating is virtually unmanageable and prohibitively expensive; that what is suitable for Châteauneuf du Pape (it was pioneered by Monsieur Perrin at the Domaine de Beaucastel) is out of place in Burgundy where the wines have greater finesse; and that anyway fully treated wines come out common, their individuality destroyed. '*Ça tue certaines arabesques, certains dessins dans le vin*,' said a Pommard grower.

It seems likely that the use of copper basins will spread. Many wine-makers with high ideals believe that they can be used with moderation on, say, one-third of the harvest in an off-year; and that colour is gained without undue loss of character. However, there are at least a couple of successful approaches to off-vintage wine-making which do not involve must-heating.

One works on the principle that rotten grapes should be removed by careful sorting, either to be left in the vineyard or vinified apart. The Pousse d'Or estate in Volnay, for instance, extracts mouldy red grapes, presses them, sulphurs and fines the resultant must and then adds back small portions later. It has made many successful off-vintage *cuvées* since 1965, which have sold happily under *Premier Cru* labels.

Another system is that practised by Domaine Senard in Aloxe-Corton. Here the problem is approached not by extraction of mouldy grapes (which is often impossible when the whole bunch is attacked) but by carefully controlled *long* fermentations. Its off-vintages spend fifteen to seventeen days in the vats. Rotten grapes are never added after fermentation has started; nor is the debris which falls to the bottom of the vat ever mixed back in or pumped over. Mongeard-Mugneret in Vosne-Romanée makes some success of combining both methods.

The *Station Oenologique* now seems less committed to must-

109

heating than it was five years ago, which is welcome since cheaper and at least equally successful alternative methods exist. Somewhat wistfully Monsieur Léglise tells one that a couple of merchants, Louis Latour and Bouchard Père, are experimenting with various heating systems, but apparently without involving him.

Another way of attacking the off-vintage problem is by a blending of vintages, and many merchants market VSR or non-vintage wines. The *Syndicat des Négociants* in Beaune will tell you that VSR stands for 'Very Special Reserve' or '*Vin Spécialement Recommandé*', but the description is ironical. Most VSR wines are simply off-vintages which have been fortified by wines from the Mediterranean, for it is an expensive business to use your famous years to improve the others. Nevertheless some of the best merchants do so.

Thirty per cent of 1978 added to the 1977 works wonders for the latter's colour, and produces a reasonably priced VSR wine. If the same merchant sells another wine as 1978 and it proves to be not quite the greatest on the Côte, the reason may be that 30 per cent of 1977 found its way into it. The 'vintage' wine will still be better than the VSR though. Several merchants generally thought of as respectable operate this sort of solera[1] system.

Several domaines (particularly those bottling all their wine every year) operate in a similar way, though they would tend to call the lesser wine in this case 1977, rather than VSR, which smacks too much of the merchant's blending vat.

Many people, including myself, feel that the consumer is well served by such a system, and that the grower is making a better investment by keeping a small stock of fine wine for blending purposes than, for instance, by installing expensive must-heating-and-cooling equipment. Current legislation which forbids a mixing of vintages is misguided and unenforceable. It should have been brought into line with reality. To give an example: it should be legal to blend up to 15 or 20 per cent of 1976 Musigny with the 1975 and sell it as 1975. Equally, up to 15 or 20 per cent of 1975 or 1977 into the 1976, and sell it as 1976 Musigny. No doubt this sounds heresy to many. If one cuts off the mountain-tops to fill in

---

[1] The solera system is a method of fractional blending invented by and largely used by sherry shippers.

the valleys, they will say, the result will be a flat, uninteresting landscape. How will the distinctive characteristics of top vintages, whose fascinating variety constitutes Burgundy's greatness, not become blurred?

I am not suggesting that all wines *must* be a blend of vintages. Freedom should be left to the grower and merchant to offer wines which are exclusively of one year if they choose to do so. Those who can make balanced wines in a vintage such as 1975 will prefer not to sacrifice some of their great 1976s by blending them with the 1975s. But the law should permit it. After all, growers, shippers and merchants are in the business of making and supplying wines which will give pleasure to those who drink them. Pretty few unadulterated 1975s can do that, and it will take at least a generation before the use of improved wine-making techniques enables the majority to make balanced wines in poor years.

If a mixing of vintages is to take place, the best time for it to happen is at the moment of vinification. The reason is that certain yeasts are inefficient alcohol-producers (they are excellent carbon-dioxide producers, but this is not wanted), and these yeasts are prevented from working when the alcoholic content of the vat reaches 4°G.L. (Gay-Lussac is the percentage of alcohol by volume). If one can rapidly raise the alcoholic content by adding wine, only desirable yeasts will be given a chance of getting to work on the sugar in the must. Some growers believe in using the previous year's *vin de presse* in this context; of course, it must be a healthy one.

When a poor year is followed by a good one, as 1975 was by 1976, the wine of the poor year can sometimes be improved by putting it on to the recently-pressed skins and pips of the good year. Enough sugar is then added for fermentation to start again. Quite a few 1975s picked up colour in this way, but often it resulted in unfermented sugar remaining in the wine, or wines unbalanced by excessive alcohol.

And there is another danger, that the 1975 wine (which had probably finished its malolactic fermentation) would pick up malic acid from the 1976 skins. It would be extremely difficult to have this safely transformed into lactic and carbonic acid before bottling, leaving the grower with a nagging worry about secondary fermentation in bottle.

111

The difficulty of making an acceptable wine in off-years and the present loose laws which allow any rosé to call itself Chambertin, if it comes from the right vines and fulfils a few conditions, land the honest grower in a tricky position. The honourable course of declassing would cut his income into shreds (nobody does it); if he sells to the merchants he knows what must happen to his wine; if he blends his own vintages he will never sell them if he calls them VSR. The problems are formidable, but perhaps not insoluble.

7

Tending the Wines

Wine-making is a round-the-clock job. The well-equipped vat-room which is run by someone who combines understanding of the processes involved with adaptability to the differing conditions of each vintage will regularly produce acceptable wine. But the story does not end there. For a further six to twenty-four months the wine must be surveyed and tended before it can be bottled. This *élevage* requires common sense and sustained attention to detail, more than technical know-how and flair.

Wine deteriorates from contact with the air and from microbe attacks. The first is prevented by regular topping-up of containers, the second by decanting or racking clean wine off from the lees which fall to the bottom of barrel or vat, and by control of cellar temperatures.

The ideal temperature for the storage of wine is 12°C, a variation of 2°C in either direction being tolerable. Underground cellars supply such conditions, and when wines are stored above ground (as for instance at Puligny where the water-table is high) great care must be taken to avoid temperature fluctuations. Where wines are kept in wood, the humidity of the air should be near to saturation point if evaporation is to be minimized. The humidity of Burgundy's cellars, cut into the limestone, is usually satisfactory.

The most elementary danger to wine is *piqure*, vinegariness. A whiff of vinegar as one enters is a sure sign of a badly-run cellar, that somewhere will be found a leaking stave or barrel-head, an unrinsed pipe, or a small stagnant pool of wine left over from a racking operation. '*Pour faire du bon vin, il faut utiliser beaucoup d'eau*' goes the old saying, and every cellar should have running water. Evaporation of wine stored in cask varies (depending on the temperature, humidity, quality and thickness of the wood, and alcoholic degree) from half a glass to a bottle per week. It is 1 per cent per year in a humid cellar, 4–5 per cent above ground. E. Peynaud[1] affirms that out of a hundred litres of new wine, only ninety litres are left at the moment of bottling.

The law states that topping-up should be done with the same wine or one of a superior *appellation*. It is a law which is neither respected nor enforced. I know of one Burgundy merchant (ECVF Selection Jean Germain in Meursault) who goes to the trouble of topping up barrels with identical wine, involving himself in the expense of half-barrels, quarter-casks and glass *bonbonnes* in which the balance of the cask from which the topping-up was done is stored. There must be more than one, I suppose. Most merchants top up with the cheapest wine in the cellar, and often this is not even an *appellation contrôlée* wine. It is a powerful, deep-coloured *vin de consommation courante*, whose influence on the *cuvée* may or may not be perceptible when the wine is finally bottled. Many growers top up with the cheapest *appellation* they have, thereby diluting their single vineyard or commune wines as the months pass. I have never dared to do it, but whenever one buys from a Burgundian one's first request ought to be 'May I taste your topping-up wine?' He would not like it (indeed he would probably throw one out of the cellar secure in the knowledge that there are plenty of other buyers about), but if enough of us did it . . .

Racking is a less frequent operation in Burgundy, where it may be done two or three times, than in Bordeaux, where half a dozen rackings are not uncommon. The purpose is to draw the wine off from the dead yeast cells, bacteria, organic acid crystals, and any other solid particles which collect at the bottom of the barrel or storage tank. Some growers rack their wines too often, simply to avoid boredom on rainy days. Excessive rackings cause a wine to dry up and loose fruit. In a light year, there is good reason to leave well alone, storing wine in a tank rather than a barrel, touching it as little as possible.

We have seen that the malolactic fermentation is to be encouraged after vinification. To achieve this, the grower raises the temperature of the cellar to between 15°C and 18°C, and

[1] *Connaissance et Travail du Vin*, Dunod, Paris, 1971.

ensures that his white wines are left on their original fermentation lees, for this encourages the development of the bacteria which will transform the malic into lactic acid. He will avoid using the antiseptic sulphur dioxide, which inhibits them. In certain years the transformation takes place rapidly and easily, in others it is most troublesome.

It is not unusual for Burgundies to be bottled with the malolactic fermentation uncompleted, for oenologists have not yet mastered this period of a wine's development. Sometimes no harm comes of it, but occasionally an increase in temperature will provoke a fermentation in bottle. There will be a noticeable prickle on the tongue, due to the carbon-dioxide gas being produced, and a loss of bouquet.[1]

A not-infrequent complaint about white Burgundy is that it contains a deposit of crystals. These are identified by the customer as particles of broken glass, undissolved sugar, or, correctly, as a precipitation of tartaric acid. This organic acid is found naturally in the grape, a proportion of it crystallizing out during the aging process before bottling. To encourage it, the cellar doors can be left open to allow freezing winter air to penetrate, or the wine can be refrigerated if the right equipment is available. It tartrate crystals are found in a bottled wine they should never cause dismay, for their appearance will have brought about a natural softening of the wine. If the bottle is handled carefully, the wine can be poured out perfectly clear, and not a drop need be lost.

Before a wine is bottled it should be brought to a stage where it is biologically and chemically stable. The first is achieved when all the sugar and malic acid have been fermented, the second is verified by a number of tests. A wine may have picked up unwanted traces of copper or iron during vintage or cellar manipulations, or may rapidly deteriorate on contact with air due to the presence of *oxydase* (a secretion common in years of grey rot). The protein found in white wines can make them susceptible to hazing.

[1] Gas in a bottled wine may also be caused by two other factors. If the wine was bottled at cold cellar temperature there may have been some carbon dioxide still dissolved in it, which will become perceptible on warming up. Alternatively, it may have had some unfermented sugar upon which live yeasts have got to work, with consequent production of alcohol and carbon dioxide. Such wines should be decanted before serving and left to stand in a warm place. After several hours they may taste in good condition. If they do not, they should be returned to the supplier.

Analyses by a professional laboratory reveal such likelihoods, and will be accompanied by instructions for treatment, preventive or curative. Many products may be used: citric acid, gum arabic, potassium ferrocyanide, calcium phytate, bentonite and others.

A fining of one sort or another is recommended for fine wines, both red and white, before bottling. Whites of egg, gelatine, isinglass, caseine and bentonite are the most common agents, bringing about a coagulation of solid particles in suspension within the wine, which fall to the bottom of barrel or tank, there to be left after racking. Wines are stabilized by fining, and then usually receive a light filtration to clarify them before bottling. Some estates refuse to use filters, feeling that every manipulation removes something of the natural qualities of a wine, and that the customer's insistence on clarity has gone too far. It is natural for fine wines to throw a deposit. A slight haze is indeed as harmless in one's Bâtard as in one's bitter.

When looking at the roles of grower, broker and shipper we shall see the part played by the latter in correcting the faults so often found in red Burgundies. The blending-in of powerful southern wine takes place as soon as possible after receipt of wines by the merchant from the property, so that the maximum time may be allowed before bottling for the blend to marry. This is the _négociant's_ most significant act of _élevage_. While Algeria was still French, its wines were extensively used for the purpose. There are dozens of Burgundians who can rhapsodize over the natural affinity the one seemed to have for the other. The Algerian wine was smooth and rich and not so _typé_ that the Pinot Noir perfume and finesse were attenuated—or so one gathers.[1] Today the blending wines come from Roussillon and Sardinia, from Corsica, Sicily and southern Italy. Inoffensiveness is sought, along with depth of colour and alcoholic strength.

The activity is of course illegal, which is not true of pasteurization, a stabilizing process which one is amazed to find in common use for Burgundy's greatest _appellations_. P. Morton Shand wrote about it thus in 1928:[2]

[1] The _Confrérie des Chevaliers du Tastevin_ even once held a special Chapter when Burgundy's links with Algeria were honoured.

[2] _A Book of French Wines_, revised and edited by Cyril Ray, Penguin Books, 1968.

The claim is often made that this is a useful means of sterilizing common blending wines, arresting incipient or suspected disorders in poorly-made ones, and stabilizing those of low strength in difficult vintage years. At the same time it of course arrests the possibility of any further improvement. As a living organism the wine has been killed outright: what is left is the mummy of a wine, stone dead but artificially preserved ... there is nothing whatever to recommend this treatment and every reason to condemn it. As Mr Warner Allen has written, 'it is ruinous to any fine wine and unquestionably impairs the subtlest qualities ... '.

E. Peynaud[1] described it in 1971 as 'a brutal action entailing the destruction of certain fragile constituents, and a loss of quality in delicate wines.'

The Beaune shippers Louis Latour have been pasteurizing their red wines for over half a century: the Romanée Saint-Vivant, the Château Corton-Grancey, the Beaune Vignes Franches. The company thereby acquires a house-style for itself, as well as security from customer complaints. Such bottles are irrevocably stabilized. It would not be true to say that their wines do not change as they age; however they are different animals to naturally-handled Pinot Noir wines, and not everyone's idea of fine Burgundy. The largest shippers of Nuits Saint-Georges, Moillard-Grivot, also use the process.

That Louis Latour pasteurize their red wines is known in Burgundy, but no more talked about than if the King were walking about with no clothes on.

[1] *Connaissance et Travail du Vin*, Dunod, Paris, 1971.

8

Magician's Hands

Burgundy has a secret. It is the extent to which its reputation as a producer of great red wines is founded on occasional splendid vintages. Let us look at what happens after the not-so-splendid ones.

Approximately two years out of three there is insufficient sun for the colour cells in the skins of the grapes to develop fully, and for the natural grape-sugar to reach the minimum legal levels. Since the wine-making is left mostly in the hands of untrained small-holders, the result is that rosé-coloured wines are produced instead of red, and these are unbalanced because of massive additions of sugar. Yet in spite of their poor colour and lack of harmony such wines bear famous names like Pommard, Beaune or Clos de Vougeot, for they were produced on the right hillsides, from the recommended vines. In order that they may give satisfaction to wine-lovers who buy these famous names, a proportion of deep-coloured wine from Mediterranean shores is added to the Burgundies. It has been going on for centuries.

A letter of 3 May 1786 from Margue, Steward of the Prince de Conti, to the latter's *régisseur* in Beaune, runs as follows: 'I send you two samples of 1781 wine, one of Vosne and the other of Richebourg ... you will be able to judge for yourself. Gourmets and connoisseurs all say that it has more connection with the wine of Roussillon than the wine of Richebourg and Vosne, for myself I find it has a detestable after-taste.' On many occasions attempts have been made to forbid the blending of wines from outside the area with Burgundies. In 1622, for instance, the wines of Languedoc, Dauphiné, Vivarais, Provence, Lyonnais, even Beaujolais were only to be admitted to the province if in transit, and after being issued with a certificate. Penalties against wrong-doers were very high: confiscation and a fine of 1,500 *livres*.[1] If we return to the twentieth century, we find the Mayor of Auxey-Duresses, Armand Veau, writing as follows in a request to the Minister of the Interior for an Administrative Inquiry in January 1930: 'It is easy, while keeping the *appellation* Bourgogne of the certificates, to substitute exotic wines, or in fact Algerian wines, and to sell under the name of Bourgogne a product in which there is no, or practically no, fine wine. It is a fraud.' In *The Wines of Europe*,[2] Julian Jeffs gives two examples of blends used by 'a well-known shipper'. The first was sold as Clos de Vougeot 1961, and made up as follows:

Clos de Vougeot, first supplier	7 parts
Clos de Vougeot, second supplier	3 parts
Savigny	1 part
Châteauneuf du Pape	1 part
	12

The second was sold as Vosne-Romanée Les Malconsorts, and consisted of two-thirds just that, one-third Châteauneuf du Pape.

A certain amount of blending is legitimate in Burgundy and always has been. The Hospices de Beaune *cuvées* are made up of grapes from different Burgundian vineyards; most big merchants need to buy, say, their Gevrey-Chambertin from several growers, and blend the different wines together; the legal make-up of Côte de Beaune Villages was for many years a blend of wines from two or more specified villages. Thus a balanced wine is obtained, and made available in reasonable quantity. However, fortifying Burgundies with wines foreign to the area is a different matter.

The principal reason that the practice continues is that the general public appreciates a full-bodied, deep-coloured wine more readily than a fine delicate one. And it expects Burgundy to be full-bodied and deep-coloured. Cyrus Redding, writing in 1833 in *A History and Description of Modern Wines*,[3] had this to say: 'There is an infinite variety in the wines of Burgundy which an Englishman can hardly comprehend. Accustomed to wines less

[1] *L'Action Tutelaire du Parlement de Bourgogne vis-à-vis des vignes et des vins de notre Province*, by Albert Colombet.
[2] Faber and Faber, 1971.
[3] Published in London by Whittaker, Treaches & Arnot.

delicate than intoxicating, and regardful rather of the quantity than the quality of what he takes, his favourite beverage is chosen rather for strength than perfection of flavour.' Have we English advanced at all since 1833? I fear not, and that the wine trade is responsible.

I cannot forget seeing an impeccable example of authentic Nuits Saint-Georges returned in the early 1970s by the Managing Director of a London wine merchant, who complained there was something wrong with it. It emerged that he had been thrown by the individual character of the wine, for he had never tasted anything like it. Like most of us, he had been brought up on commercial blends.

They have the same problem in Burgundy. Here is Pierre Poupon, looking forward to the day when quality will triumph: 'How many merchants would be obliged to relearn how to taste, how many growers to relearn how to vinify?'[1] Merchants who need to relearn how to taste? How can that be?

There is a well-known story about a *vigneron* who drinks a litre a day from a quarter-cask for fifty-seven days without filling it up. So slowly does the wine turn to vinegar that he finds it as good on the fifty-seventh as on the first day; a visitor is needed to tell him it is *piqué*. The story fits many merchants too. Years of tasting and drinking Burgundies to which a percentage of Mediterranean wine has been added leave them convinced that such wines are best.

Blending with wines from the south is like using some drugs. Once a merchant has tried it he is hooked for good. Even good vintages have to be fortified, for otherwise they will seem to lack the richness of the off-years, indeed will not display his characteristic house-style. And once he is hooked the merchant can be heard to say: 'This is the style the public wants.' Newcomers to wine are much attracted by it; but wine enthusiasts move on to finer things when they can lay hands on them.

Such blending simplifies matters enormously for the Burgundians. Mistakes in vinification or tending are corrected without great trouble, the famous names can be sold every year, indeed a lot of poor wine got rid of at a reasonable profit.

[1] *Nouvelles Pensées d'un Dégustateur, Confrérie des Chevaliers du Tasterin*, Nuits Saint-Georges, 1975.

Perhaps I should add a word about the white wines, and the small amount of rosé produced in Burgundy. The same problem does not arise for these wines. Obtaining the correct colour for a rosé is not difficult, and under-ripe grapes can produce an attractive pink wine with refreshing acidity. The Chardonnay produces sweeter grapes than the Pinot, and nearly always reaches the minimum alcoholic degree. Indeed year in, year out, splendid white Burgundies can be made. This does not mean, however, that everything sold as white Burgundy is authentic.

In Chapter 3 we have seen that the *appellation contrôlée* legislation is successful in ensuring that no more Burgundy should be sold than is harvested, but that it falls down nevertheless, for not everything sold as Burgundy is exactly that. The actual mechanics of Burgundian blending were brilliantly exposed by a *Le Monde* journalist, Pierre-Marie Doutrelant, in 1976.[1] In a chapter entitled 'French Connection' he takes as his example a *cuvée* of 200 hectolitres of bad Pommard, bought from a careless *vigneron*. Here is how the *négociant*, in the darkness of his cellars, restores it to health:

He acquires 100 hectolitres of bone-setter red wine, a mixture of Roussillon, Côtes du Rhone and Sardinian, at F.2·00 per litre. He has only one formal obligation: that when he despatches these wines the authorities must always see 200 hectolitres of Pommard, and 100 hectolitres of *vin ordinaire*. He would be immediately nabbed if he sold 210 hectolitres of the first. But, unless he is caught in the act, there is nothing to stop him decanting 40 hectolitres of the bone-setter into the Pommard and vice versa. Thus will he give more body, vigour, colour and *je ne sais quoi* to the Pommard. . . . After which, he will sell it with profit at F.20–25 per bottle, for the wine has a famous name. . . .

But the *cuvée* of *vin ordinaire* enriched with Pommard (costly procedure), how better to sell it than as a simple *vin de table*? The *négociant* creates a brand *Cuvée du Pape* or *Réserve des Benedictins*. He launches it with much publicity. The wine, so he has one believe, while not Burgundy is not far from it, since it was tended in the Côte d'Or and aged in the heart of the vineyard area in oak casks by an eminent local merchant. After seasoning

[1] *Les Bons Vins et les Autres*, Éditions du Seuil, Paris.

with Pommard the *gros rouge* bought for F.2·00 per litre is resold at F.5–6 per bottle of 75 centilitres.

The authorities know what is going on, but they more or less turn a blind eye to it. This silence dates back, so Bernard Ginestet informs us,[1] to summit meetings between growers' and shippers' leaders which took place in Bordeaux on 17 and 18 September 1913, preparing the way for the *appellation d'origine* legislation of 6 May 1919. B. Ginestet quotes from a contemporary report: 'The representatives of the growers and the trade sought out the principal points where an agreement was possible. The growers' representatives pointed out that it would be dangerous, for all, to allude to the question of blends in the draft bill: they consider that with control being exercised quantitatively on *appellation d'origine* wines, the question is resolved by the very silence of the law, and the growers give their word of honour not to create difficulties with the trade on this subject.' Comments B. Ginestet: 'This is how and why the silence of the law became the law of silence,'—one which was widely observed until the events which led to the Bordeaux fraud trial of October 1974, when the leading actors in the play found themselves in front of a world audience.

Burgundy has not, so far, found itself spotlighted at the centre of a major scandal, and I hope it never does. But it is lucky to have escaped. For every *barrique* of Saint-Estèphe to benefit from 10 per cent medicine-wine there is a *pièce* of Côte de Beaune Villages unsaleable as such; for every bottle of arranged Bordeaux, another of arranged Bourgogne. And why should one be surprised at that? Burgundy is more northerly than Bordeaux, and often the Pinot Noir grape produces light wines without great depth of colour. The public now expects its Burgundies to be full-bodied, rich, velvety wines.

What is the solution to this problem? Various reactions may be heard, falling into three categories:

THE SITUATION IS NOT REMOTELY AS SERIOUS AS YOU HAVE DESCRIBED

Burgundy's off-vintages are assembled together and offered as VSR—*Vin Spécialement Recommandé*. There will always be a few black sheep in a flock, what they get up to is their business, by the

---

[1] *La Bouillie Bordelaise*, Flammarion, Paris, 1975.

way I happen to have a spare ticket for the Tastevin's Spring Chapter, I might be able to fit you in, what do you say?

THE TIME HAS COME TO END THE HYPOCRISY

This is Pierre-Marie Doutrelant's standpoint. He rightly points out that *négociants* would not become involved in blending, in breach of the law, if there were no poorly-made wines in need of improvement. He goes on: 'It is unrealistic to think of destroying all the second-rate wines produced, for growers would rise in revolution. . . . The trade should acknowledge that it is guilty and competent. *Quel art, messieurs du commerce! Allons*, let's tell the truth: a Pommard . . . having passed through your magician's hands is often better than it was in the grower's cellar.'

It is a solution which would appeal to many *négociants*. There are those who by no means relish the undercover nature of their work, with the risks involved; and there are many who indeed see judicious assembling of complementary wines as the veritable art of the wine man, the result of patient apprenticeship, fine analysis, just decision-taking and sincerity. The fact that the general run of medicine-wine is along the lines of the bone-setter described by P.-M. Doutrelant should not obscure the fact that one of the finest of Burgundy's merchants uses between 7 and 10 per cent of Gamay wine, from a commune such as Chénas in the Beaujolais; another a top Côtes du Rhône from Rasteau.

A limited amount of blending is permitted by both Germany and Italy for certain of their wines. A quantity of foreign wine not exceeding 25 per cent of the total volume was allowed to be added to German red wine, until 1979. It has been said that, with the exception of Baden and Württemberg, practically no region producing German red wines would otherwise be able to produce a wine suitable for ready sale.[1] One wonders what is going to happen in the 1980s.

The most famous DOC wines of Tuscany may be cut with a proportion of wine from outside the area without loss of their *denominazione d'origine controllata*. Brunello di Montalcino and Vin Nobile di Montepulciano may contain up to 10 per cent, Chianti and Chianti Classico up to 15 per cent of the total. Thus a long-standing practice was legalized. Of Brunello, B. Roncarati

---

[1] S. F. Hallgarten, *German Wines*, Faber and Faber, 1976.

has written: 'It is comparable to the very best *crus* of Burgundy.'[1]
If Chianti Classico is not too proud to acknowledge the help it
needs from southern Italy, what about Burgundy?

Perhaps Burgundians would just as soon their best *crus* were
spared comparisons with Tuscany. In which case the problem
could be tackled by saying:

THE TIME HAS COME TO ENFORCE THE LAWS

This can only start in one place, the beginning of the production
line, the vineyard itself. It must start before the picking, before
any blendings or substitutions are possible, when the grapes are
still hanging on the vines, and analysis of grape-juice can reveal if
the minimum natural degrees of sweetness, as set out in the AC
legislation, are being attained. Degrees of sweetness in the grape
are intimately linked to the yield. If an owner of Gevrey-
Chambertin *Premier Cru* vineyard has planted productive Pinots
and so fertilized and pruned them that, when he wishes to harvest,
his natural alcoholic degree will be 10·3° he should automatically
forfeit his right to the qualification *Premier Cru* (minimum degree
11°), as also to the commune name Gevrey-Chambertin (minimum degree 10·5°). The law is perfectly clear on the point; but it
is not enforced.

For this first example I have taken a First Growth. In fact the
most pressing need for stricter enforcement of the law is amongst
Great Growths, the *crème de la crème*. That over-chaptalized,
Mediterraneanized blends should continue to carry the great
names of Charmes-Chambertin, Musigny, Clos de Vougeot,
Corton-Bressandes etc., fetching £6, £12, £18 per bottle is, well, a
disgrace to every Burgundian. Twenty years ago there were
perhaps excuses for it; now, with the spread of wine-making skills,
and given Burgundy's new prosperity, I can see none. R. Bernard
concluded his chapter in *Le Vin de Bourgogne*[2] as follows:

> To resume, Burgundy has now at its disposal the appropriate
> technical means, both in the viticultural and in the oenological
> field. Barring climatic accident, it is possible for the *vigneron* to
> produce, good or bad year, a wine of good quality by bringing
> together healthy grapes and the appropriate technology. The

---

[1] *Viva Vino, D.O.C. Wines of Italy*, Wine and Spirit Publications, 1976.
[2] Éditions Montalba, 1976.

experience acquired by preceding generations, allied to the popularization of technical progress, shelter him from the gravest accidents. So quality seems to depend only on his willingness, and his conscience.

There are only a limited number of law enforcement officers in Burgundy, so, unless the band can be strengthened, it would be unrealistic to suggest that control could be extended across the whole range of *Grand Cru*, *Premier Cru*, commune and regional *appellations*. It should begin at the top; and when the limited number of Grand Cru owners have fallen into line, the inspectors should extend their attentions to the *Premier Cru* owners (very often they will be visiting the same establishments, but this time there will be larger areas of vineyard to survey). And so on down the line.

It goes without saying that the time has come for chaptalization levels to be observed (musts may be increased by 2°, no more); and for *Grand Crus* to be topped up only with *Grand Crus*.

If all this results in price increases for our Bonnes Mares, our Vosne-Romanée Les Malconsorts, our Beaune Grèves, as surely it will do (for growers will have less of these famous names to sell, and as sure as eggs is eggs, will increase their prices to maintain their incomes), then so be it. Great bottles of Burgundy lift the heart, they spread before the senses a variety of complex perfumes, tastes and textures which astonish us. By definition they are rare. And there is only one way to buy them, as Dr Lavalle set out in 1855: '*Soyez très-sévère sur la qualité, soyez très-facile sur le prix.*' ('Be very strict over quality, be very easy over price.')

9

Growers, Brokers, Merchants and Customers

THE GROWERS

Traditionally in Burgundy the grower has two functions: he cultivates the vineyard and he makes the wine, as we have seen in Chapters 5 and 6.

Pierre Poupon has compared the two activities:[1] 'There are many good *vignerons*, but few skilful wine-makers. The work is not the same. One takes place the whole length of the year, the other in a few days. A person can reflect while tilling, can think while pruning, but when wine-making there is no time left. One must act, and fast.'

A man only makes wine thirty or forty times in his life, the conditions and raw materials being different each time, so it is not surprising that many mistakes are made. Grapes get thrown into a vat or press with as little forethought as precedes the roasting of the English Christmas turkey. The turkey gets stuffed, the vat gets sugared, but how often are care and imagination brought to bear? It is a hit-and-miss affair, and many of us sit down to dried-up turkey breast, and talk ourselves into believing it's a feast. In Burgundy, vintage after vintage, the fruits of eleven and a half months of patient labour are spoiled through lack of training, lack of application, and the knowledge that mistakes can be painlessly corrected by blending.

Over-sugaring is the order of the day at vintage-time, for the alcoholic strength thus acquired goes some way to compensating

[1] *Nouvelles Pensées d'un Dégustateur, Confrérie des Chevaliers du Tasterin*, Nuits Saint-Georges, 1975.

for lack of real quality. The result, in P.-M. Doutrelant's phrase, can be Molotov cocktails which perforate the stomach. He goes on:

A wine which has been over-sugared lacks that balance which distinguishes great bottles. Often also, over-chaptalization leads to an abusive use of chemical stabilizers, especially sulphur dioxide, for the *vigneron* dreads a delayed-action fermentation. The wine then gives you a headache and stomach-ache. If, as the story goes, there was once a time when the juices of the vine set royal stomachs to rights, today's ulcer victims will take care to choose their sources of supply with care before following the august treatment.

They will have difficulty finding a source of supply. Heavy sugaring is a policy which has been adopted from one end of Burgundy to the other, by great estates and lowly—but particularly on the Côte de Nuits. I suppose it is the domaine-bottling grower's answer to the rich, velvety Mediterranean blends sold as Burgundy which have formed the public's palate. But do they honestly call these things fine wine? I am thinking of certain wines from the Domaine de la Romanée-Conti, of some of Armand Rousseau's 1972s, of Clair-Daü's Gevrey-Chambertin Clos Saint-Jacques 1971, of Georges Roumier's Bonnes Mares 1969, and of many more.

Given the example that is being set by prestigious estates, it is not surprising that the practice is so widespread. There have always been merchants to advocate it, who see it as perfectly logical and justifiable. Françoise Grivot spoke for many in *Le Commerce des Vins de Bourgogne*[1] (which she dedicated to her father, 'doyen of the *négociants-éleveurs* of the region of Beaune who worked with enthusiasm for sixty years and carried his profession to the level of art'), when she admitted that increased yields had brought about a certain reduction in quality. She went on:

Nevertheless one must note that the loss in quality relates essentially to the components giving strength and long life to a wine—components which correspond, if you like, to the figure of alcoholic degree. Apart from the fact that they are the easiest to

[1] *'Publié avec le Concours du Centre National de la Recherche Scientifique, SABRI'*, Paris, 1962.

remedy (sugaring the harvest, strengthening of the wines by adding well-chosen medicine-wines), these deficiencies do not harm the essential character of Burgundies, in no way change their taste, their finesse. Less rich if you like, less lasting certainly, great Burgundies continue nonetheless to be in 1962 what they were in the time of Stendhal, the most complete wines, those with the most nuances, the most generous wines which can be conceived, and nothing has changed in the characteristics which cause them to be sought out everywhere as the first of the great wines.

I cannot help feeling that if you believe that you will believe anything.

The Burgundy of Stendhal is the Burgundy of Dr M. J. Lavalle, as described in his 1855 *Histoire et Statistique de la Vigne et des Grands Vins de la Côte d'Or*. At that time the average yield could not be reckoned at more than 18 hectolitres per hectare. Increased yields had brought about a certain reduction in quality by 1962, she admits. Well, the situation has continued to deteriorate, as the table below shows.

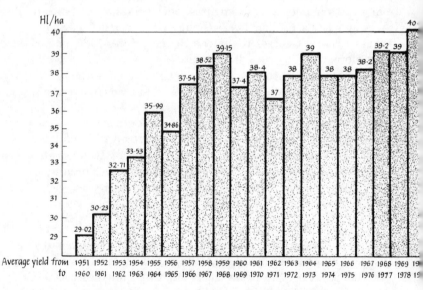

TABLE 2. EVOLUTION OF THE TEN-YEAR-AVERAGE
YIELD OF AC WINES IN THE CÔTE D'OR, 1951–79 (Source: INAO, Dijon)

Those who seek to justify this deterioration by reference to advances in cultivation methods, the advent of fertilizers, sophisticated sprays etc. may be interested in three quotations. The first is from Pliny, on the subject of Falernian, the most famous wine of the Roman world: 'The reputation of this district ... is passing out of vogue through the fault of paying more attention to quantity than to quality.'[1] The second is from a letter of 3 May 1786 by Margue, Steward of the Prince de Conti, to the latter's *régisseur* in Beaune: 'Besides, his Serene Highness in no way wishes that one should lean towards producing a large quantity of wine, but towards quality; you know that a vine too loaded with fruit produces only mediocre wine without quality. I beg you, sir, to tell the *vigneron* to prune the vineyard accordingly. Such are the last wishes of Monseigneur.' Finally, here is R. Bernard: 'One must therefore find the balance between a vine's possibilities and the pursuit of the best product, bearing in mind the rule which proclaims the incompatibility of quantity and quality, time and again confirmed.'[2]

One regrets having to say it, but most red Burgundies today (I am talking of the Côte Chalonnaise, the Côte de Beaune and the Côte de Nuits) are mediocre wines without quality, and poor value for money. Briefly, a rip-off. The Burgundians are coasting along on their reputation.

It would not be fair to hold the growers solely responsible for this state of affairs, and in a moment we will be examining the role played by the brokers, the merchants, and the customers. Before we do so however, let us look in more detail at a special group of growers, those who bottle their own wines at the domaine. For there are many who believe that to buy domaine-bottled wines is the only sure way of getting top quality in Burgundy, indeed that a wine so labelled will be the *crème de la crème*. It is not as simple as that.

Domaine-bottling

It is difficult for a *vigneron* to adapt himself to successful tending and bottling. Many fail to have their wine analyzed, or else disregard the advice given by the laboratory, with the result that

---

[1] Quoted in William Younger, *Gods, Men and Wine*, The Wine and Food Society & Michael Joseph, 1966.
[2] *Le Vin de Bourgogne*, Editions Montalba, 1976.

bottlings take place before all sugar has been converted into alcohol, or before the malolactic fermentation has finished. The result is popping corks and gassy wine when it eventually reaches the customer. In the 1960s many estates wishing to bottle lacked the equipment (not to mention the know-how) to carry it out. They relied on mobile bottling plants, installed on the back of a lorry, which moved from courtyard to courtyard on the Côte. Since the bottler had no idea how the wines had been tended before his arrival he often took care to stabilize the wines irrevocably, by pasteurizing as he bottled. This may be an acceptable way of treating cheap wines, or bringing on young Beaujolais which is destined to be drunk young, but it undoubtedly changes the character of *Grand Cru* Burgundy.

Although many estates are now equipped to do their own bottling, the correct procedures are not always followed (for instance the unifying of hogsheads in a vat, or the bottling of that vat in one uninterrupted operation). As a result, irregularities in quality are sometimes found from bottle to bottle when growers' wines are served.

Great wine is not made by chance, and almost never by growers under financial pressure. Not only must yield be restricted, but new casks may need to be bought, and a fine wine used for topping up. Money must be purposely tied up, by making wines of such a style that they need considerable aging. Many families have other priorities.

As more and more private customers and foreign buyers go direct to the growers, so their stocks drop, they are tempted to extend their yields, to pull up the old vines, to bottle the off-vintages and make wines which mature quickly. The result is that the quality of many domaine-bottling growers' wines is low, and the words 'domaine-bottled' by no means a magic guarantee of perfection.

Sometimes growers play funny games with the different wines and names in their cellars. A proprietor's vines might be divided up as follows: 15 per cent *Grand Cru* vineyard, 20 per cent *Premier Cru* vineyard, 40 per cent Village vineyard, 25 per cent Bourgogne vineyard. If by chance a portion of *Grand Cru* is lost through frost or hail or other mishap, there is a hard-to-resist temptation to baptize part of the *Premier Cru* wine with the name of the *Grand Cru*, and to upgrade part of the Village wine to *Premier Cru*, while declaring that some of one's Bourgogne has been decimated by the weather.

It is quite possible for a grower to play the merchant with his own wines, though it rarely happens. If it's no good, he washes his hands of it, gets rid of it, lets someone else do the dirty work. But if a grower wishes to 'arrange' his own wines, an order can be placed with a local *vin ordinaire* merchant for a delivery of table wine. Ostensibly this is for the vineyard-workers or pickers, but by telephone the merchant can be told that a deep-coloured 13° Mediterranean blend is required. When it is delivered, twenty-five litres or so (about 10 per cent) can be added to every hogshead. Provided that the twenty-five litres drawn off to make room for the Mediterranean are distributed as *vin ordinaire*, the books will be in order. Alternatively, if it has been a poor year on the Côte de Nuits, but decent red wines have been made in Santenay, Chassagne-Montrachet and Mercurey one might find a big grower of Gevrey-Chambertin phoning a friendly estate in Santenay with an order for two or three hogsheads. There is nothing to prevent one buying wine for one's personal consumption, it is interesting to compare wines of different communes with one's own. No, thank you, it is not required in bottle, delivery will be taken in bulk. No prizes for guessing what happens to the Santenay.

That is the seamy side of domaine-bottling but, I repeat, it rarely happens. The growth of the domaine-bottling movement dates back to the 1920s and early 1930s, and came about in reaction to the widespread frauds of the time. Men like D'Angerville and Gouges (whom we met in the chapter on *appellation contrôlée*) were forced to sell direct because they were involved in lawsuits against local merchants, and their traditional market had closed against them. The roles of grower and merchant were thrown into separate relief, with the merchant cast as sole villain of the piece.

Domaine-bottling has seen a big expansion in the last twenty-five years. The *vigneron* has discovered that his empty winters can be usefully filled, and that much satisfaction, as well as excellent profits, are to be had.

Very few have ever sent out a price-list, taken a stand at a country fair, or rung a doorbell to sell their wines. Demand from American importers and the home market created the supply, and then the Belgians, the Swiss, and the British joined in. The

131

Americans began to realize back in the 1930s that they could obtain top-quality wines and eliminate a middle-man by buying direct from growers. Initially unpopular because they only bought in famous years, they nevertheless paid well. But a high proportion of estate-bottled wines are sold to passing Frenchmen, on the road to and from Italy, the Alps and the Côte d'Azur. Not only is the Frenchman convinced that he gets a finer wine (just as chickens collected from the farm are automatically superior to the town-sold article), he also gets it cheaper while having the satisfaction of doing the government out of several francs in Value Added Tax, for many transactions between private client and *vigneron* are in cash. At present the *vigneron* is legally permitted to ascribe any discrepancies between his declared sales and his stocks as due to family consumption. There are indications, however, that the authorities may soon try to enforce some sobriety around the hearth.

Ask a proprietor how he got his clientèle and he will reply '*La boule de neige*' (the snowball). He had a friend, who told his relations, who brought their friends. Over the years countless snowballs have been dislodged from the Golden Slope, to begin their rollings up and down and around America and Europe. Each year they get bigger, and each year fresh ones get dislodged.

It is difficult to gauge the importance of the domaine-bottling movement. In 1969 a leading Côte d'Or broker estimated that a quarter of the *Premier* and *Grand Cru* production, in a good year, was being bottled at the estate. He now estimates that, in respect of the excellent 1978 vintage, 60 per cent of the total production was retained by the growers for their own bottlings. A high proportion of the very best estates practise it extensively.

There has been a startling transformation in the balance of power in the Burgundian wine trade over the last twenty years. As P.-M. Doutrelant says: 'In the Burgundian economy, the *vigneron* wears the trousers. The merchant follows.' Unlike their Bordeaux equivalents (who commercialize the vast majority of château-bottlings), the Burgundian merchants seem to have let the estate-bottling business pass them by. But if the merchants feel uneasy about the domaine-bottling growers, most are putting a brave face on it, saying that it is a good thing for the grower to learn the difficulties of selling wine in bottle.

Why is more wine not estate-bottled? It is mainly a question of finance. If one examines the difference between selling the 1976 in bulk and bottle, one finds that it incurred its first costs in November 1975, when the winter pruning took place. If one took as example a vineyard that needed replanting, there would be four additional years before the first crop could be sold.

The vineyard was tended and treated throughout the spring and summer of 1976, and the proprietor's family fed, so it is not surprising that many wines were sold immediately after the harvest, that is to say in October 1976. A few owners waited until the spring for a better price. So the seller in bulk financed his operations for between eleven and sixteen months, and the terms of payment which the buyer negotiated may have extended this by a further six months.

The man wishing to sell his wine in bottle must age it a further twelve to eighteen months in wood, continue to cultivate his vineyard and feed his family, finance the bottling expenses, and then let the wine rest a little in bottle. He will not start getting paid for November 1975's work until spring or autumn 1978.

It is not surprising that most proprietors start domaine-bottling in a small way. Also, it is undoubtedly a lot of trouble. '*Il faut aller moins souvent à la pêche si on fait de la bouteille*' ('there's less time for fishing if one goes in for bottling').

The good proprietor in less famous villages like Savigny, Saint-Romain or Givry must bottle to make a decent living, for his wine gets a relatively poor price from a merchant. Often growers sell any famous names they own in bulk, because of the high prices they command. They will bottle for themselves the cream of their lesser-known *cuvées*, the value-for-money wines.

Maurice Vollot, a Savigny wine-broker, sees two extreme types of grower on the Côte—the *Bourguignon de terre* and the *Bourguignon de table*. The first is in service to his vines, rising at dawn, in bed by early evening: a professional who spends vintage-time in the vat-house rather than supervising the pickers, and whose barrels are always topped up. The second, round and purple like a ripe grape, may own and cultivate vines, but he also goes *à la chasse*. Above all he eats well, and when he says of a wine: '*Ça irait bien avec une bécasse*,' ('that would go well with a woodcock') you know he speaks from experience. Of his stomach he will say, as he pats it fondly: '*Monsieur, ça, c'est du Pinot.*' When strangers are around he sees himself as a one-man repository of all Burgundy's

133

folklore, his favourite stories revolving round food and drink, for instance the one about the German who came to the Côte specially for the shooting season, and chose to accompany pheasant with a camomile infusion, and jugged hare with tea. They both hold the same opinion about one thing, however. Their own wine is the best.[1]

THE BROKERS

Wine-brokers are well placed to take an objective view of the Burgundian scene. Buying and selling wine can be a delicate, emotional business, for two or three transactions may decide a family's annual income and form a judgement on twelve months' work. The *courtier*, or broker, is the intermediary who smooths the way for the deal.

He neither buys nor sells any wine himself. Once a deal has been struck, he produces a written confirmation and, one hopes, keeps an eye on the wine, for he guarantees that the delivery, perhaps three or six months later, corresponds to the wine originally sampled. He is paid by commission, which he receives mainly from the buyer. It will be 2–3 per cent if a local shipper, rather more if a foreign buyer. He may also receive up to 3 per cent from the grower.

Dr Lavalle has recorded that in Burgundy until the sixteenth century it was almost always the *jurés-tonneliers*, the corporation of coopers, who were charged with tasting the wines offered for sale, to value them or establish if they had been spoiled or adulterated. Thereafter, gentlemen known as *gourmets* took over the responsibility for fixing prices, verifying if the wine indeed came from the vineyard indicated by the seller, whether it was pure Pinot or a mixture of Pinot and Gamay, and whether white wines had been mixed in, or various vintages. More often than not these *gourmets* were also brokers, their responsibility being to conduct the foreign merchant to the cellars, and not allow any wine to be sold if not of good quality. In those days it was a buyer's

---

[1] Maybe there are few wine-makers who do not think this. When the future Pope John XXIII visited the Hospices de Beaune as Papal Nuncio, he admitted to M. Louis-Noël Latour that he too was a wine-grower. He said that he knew there must be better wines than his in Italy, everyone said so and he agreed. But his own was the one for him.

market, the broker being rewarded only by the grower, at the rate of *dix sols par queue*. The *queue* represented 456 litres or two of today's *pièces*, there being twenty *sols* in the *livre tournois* or franc.

Although today some foreign merchants are successful in dealing directly with Burgundy growers, many employ a broker, perhaps one who is a qualified oenologist, and it is easy to see why. In an hour or two the importer can be given an idea of the availability of wine and the tendency of prices. His man-on-the-spot will know that one grower has sold most of his cellar to the Americans; that another had trouble with overheating during his vinifications; that a third has a stack of old vintages on offer.

Many growers have but a rudimentary grasp of the nuts and bolts of exporting, and the broker provides a follow-up service after the importer has flown home, ensuring that treatments are carried out, special labels affixed, collections co-ordinated, invoices established, and payments distributed on time.

It is less easy to appreciate the value of the broker's contribution to the local trade. I have always been surprised at the arm's-length treatment of the vineyard-owners by Burgundian merchants, many of whom, when I was living in Burgundy in the late 1960s, would not be seen within miles of the growers—not to taste, not to talk, certainly not to socialize. Their buying was done without contact with the vineyard-owners, after assembly of samples by their brokers. While the best brokers certainly fulfil a useful role, it seems to me that some are a block to communication between grower and shipper. It has been estimated that brokers are involved in 60 per cent of today's trade in Burgundy.

THE MERCHANTS AND CUSTOMERS

The role of the merchant is defined in Poupon and Forgeot's *Les Vins de Bourgogne* (eighth edition) as buying fine wines, usually young, at the property, assuring them the care, treatment and maturation necessary to develop their natural qualities, correcting any possible faults, and thus satisfying the tastes and requirements of the customers. By holding large stocks, the *négociant* can guarantee a regular supply of wine from year to year, and to some extent smooth out dramatic price fluctuations at the property. Many merchants specialize in export, and their efforts have undoubtedly brought wealth and prestige to the region.

But what are the requirements of the customers? The trouble is that everyone who has heard of wine has heard of Burgundy; all those people would like to drink it, and they would like to drink it now. The Burgundians have become too market-orientated—involved in finding out what people will buy, or can be persuaded to buy, and then making it and selling it at a profit—and it is the road to disaster. Burgundy is a tiny wine area, capable of producing bottles of wine which astound one by their harmony, their complex perfumes and flavours. The renown of its villages and vineyards has circled the earth, its ease of access attracts visitors in their hundreds of thousands. It has more customers than can possibly be supplied, yet Burgundians rush headlong into the trap of trying to supply them all. Increased yields produce more wine, it matures earlier—and the product is transformed out of recognition in the process. Here is Max Léglise, Director of the *Station Oenologique de Bourgogne*: 'Fruity wines and early-maturing *cuvées*, every wine-making region in the world can make them. But *vins de garde* are the prerogative of certain privileged zones.'[1]

And what are the tastes of the customers? There undoubtedly are connoisseurs who look for finesse, for delicacy, for balance in their Burgundies, but most people expect what they have in the past been given: something full-bodied, rich and smooth. Most of these wines were fortified from the south, so the only way shippers pursuing a policy of authenticity have felt able to gain a place for themselves is by offering powerful wines, the power emanating from the sugar-bags. As we saw, the same problem has had the same effect on many of the top estates.

To what extent is the customer responsible for this state of affairs? Here is another quotation from Max Léglise:[2] 'He to whom one offers blackbird, saying that it is thrush, and who has never tasted either, has obviously no means of protesting.' Perhaps the moment is overdue for more of us to discover the taste of thrush. Professor Dion has pointed out that the quality and character of the products of a vineyard are to a large extent decided by the demands of the markets to which it is most convenient to dispatch them. So, given that the customer is

---

[1] *Congrès des Sociétés Savantes*, Beaune, 1972.
[2] *Une Initiation à la Dégustation des Grands Vins*, DIVO, Lausanne, 1976.

always right, and that in the Common Market the consumer is king, should we not be a little more exacting? Until we are, we will have only ourselves to blame if the Burgundians continue to deliver what they think we want.

The merchant handling the biggest volume of wine in Burgundy in 1975 was G. Corbet of Morey Saint-Denis, and this company came second as regards turnover.[1] Not many people have heard of it outside Burgundy; within, it is well-known. It handles large quantities of *vin ordinaire*, but also many of the region's most famous *appellations*. If one were a *négociant-éleveur* needing some *vin de table*, or a grower with a parcel of wine on one's hands that one wished to dispose of rapidly, one might think of telephoning Corbet.

First as regards turnover that year was the Patriarche group (including Kriter and Noémie Vernaux), its sales being around F.200m (£22·2m @ F.9·00 = £1·00). Four companies had a turnover in excess of F.32m (£3·6m): Bichot, Bouchard Père, Moillard, Reine Pédauque. Then, at around F.25m (£2·8m), came: Chauvenet, Geisweiler, Mommessin, Piat, A. Rodet. The following had turnovers of about F.15m (£1·7m): Bouchard Aîné, Calvet, Chanson, Drouhin, Jaboulet-Vercherre, Jadot, Leroy. In general, a growing part of their business is made up of wines imported from other regions and sold (legally and quite properly) under brand names, such as the above-mentioned Kriter.

The largest vineyard-owners amongst the merchants are: Faiveley (112 ha.), then Geisweiler (90 ha.), Bouchard Père (81 ha.), Reine Pédauque (50 ha.), Louis Latour (46 ha.), Drouhin (45 ha.) and Chanson (40 ha.). Out of a total of 5,000 ha., 800 ha. of AC vineyard were owned by merchants by 1962, according to Françoise Grivot.[2] The total in 1976 was 6,594 ha., and I would estimate that the merchants' share had stayed about the same, around one-sixth.

'*Negociants* are a necessary evil. Without them the bad vintages would be very hard, even for good wine-makers.' 'The great wine companies ... dynasties indeed ... a veritable racial and traditional aristocracy, issuing—like all ancient and true noble

---

[1] Source: M. Louis-Régis Affre, *Délégué Général du Syndicat des Négociants en Vins Fins de Bourgogne.*
[2] *Le Commerce des Vins de Bourgogne*, SABRI, Paris, 1962.

strains—from modest, courageous, even heroic beginnings.' The first quotation is from a leading grower, the second from *La Bourgogne Tastevin en Main* (1949) by Georges Rozet. The truth lies somewhere between the two. To an extent the merchants have become divided into two camps, the one buying heavily after good vintages, the other after mediocre or bad ones. If members of the first group have their own estates they may sell the wines of the mediocre or bad vintages to members of the second, who then do the dirty work. Others however blend the wines of two or three vintages, as described in the vinification chapter.

Many merchants lay themselves open to criticism for their passive acceptance of the role of buying and rendering palatable a third-rate product. Very few expend much effort in insisting on, let alone helping in, the creation of a first-rate product.

One way they could do this (without investing in vineyards) would be to buy grapes, and vinify themselves. Drouhin, Faiveley, Jaboulet, Moillard, and a few others already do this in a small way. In Champagne and Alsace it is common for merchants to buy grapes and vinify themselves. The growers are persuaded to give up making the wine in exchange for cash payments, and here the merchants have the edge over co-operatives, which must wait for their members' wines to be made and then sold, before sharing out profits. The Alsatian merchants do not find that they get the wines significantly cheaper: the benefit comes from the greater quality obtained by a controlled vinification. One or two merchant-operated vinification centres exist in the Gironde, the best-known being perhaps the Cave Bel-Air of Sichel & Cie.

One cannot see the practice spreading in Burgundy, the biggest stumbling-block being that both grower and merchant see vinification as the grower's traditional responsibility. Also, it is common to pay the grower for his grapes approximately half what he would receive if he made the wine himself and kept it for sale the following spring.

The lack of co-operation between growers and merchants has worried leading members of each side for years. Attempts were made to get together before the First World War, and later in 1942 and 1957, but success was not finally achieved until 6 July 1966 when the *Comité Interprofessionel de la Côte d'Or et de L'Yonne pour les Vins d'Appellation Contrôlée de Bourgogne* was founded. The interests of the Côte Chalonnaise are looked after in Mâcon, by the *Comité Interprofessionel de Saône et Loire pour les Vins d'Appellation d'Origine Contrôlée de Bourgogne et de Mâcon.* (Since the creation of the *Office du Vin* the various Burgundian *Comités* have banded together in an Interprofessional Federation.) The main objects of the committees are to defend quality; to publicize Burgundy's wines at home and abroad, notably at fairs and receptions; to spread the renown of the lesser-known villages and generic appellations; and to bring about agreement between grower and merchant over wine prices. Their existence is a reason for optimism, for they are evidence that Burgundians are accepting that growers, brokers and merchants are all in the same boat, or should I say vat, together. Unless the merchants succeed in involving themselves rather more in the wine-making process, where their oenological know-how could be of great benefit to numbers of small *vignerons*, I see them continuing to lose ground to the domaine-bottling growers. But greater involvement in wine-making would necessitate a swallowing of pride by the merchants and a changing of attitudes.

10

Tasting

The best way of getting to know the wines of Burgundy is by tasting them on the spot. Of course, it is not the only way, but I think it is probably the quickest.

The area is a European crossroads and from England one passes through or near it whether bound for Italy, the Côte d'Azur or Switzerland. My favourite way of getting there is by car, on the overnight ferry from Southampton to Le Havre. One lands in Normandy at 7 a.m., fortifies onself with a *grand'crème* at the first café, stocks up with a bag of *croissants* or *petits pains au chocolat*, and is down the autoroute and tasting wines in Chablis or Saint-Bris by noon. Not the ideal prelude to a tasting, for one's ears are still ringing from the traffic, and one's nerves taut; so, in fact, a relaxing lunch is a better idea. The afternoon can be spent finding a hotel, and exploring the vineyards of the Auxerrois, whose *vignerons* will happily lay out their wines for you that evening.

It is best to start tasting in Burgundy's lesser-known villages, which here means Irancy, Coulanges or Saint-Bris. Further south I would aim for the region of Mercurey, the Hautes Côtes or the backwoods of the Côte de Beaune—villages like Givry or Montagny, Marey-les-Fussey, Saint-Aubin and Saint-Romain.

It might seem that Burgundy is a perfect hunting ground for the private wine enthusiast, for the great wines of any vintage are produced in such small quantities that little is available for importers. However, dealing direct with growers can be an expensive and risky game, as this story may show. Maurice Vollot is a broker who covers the villages of Savigny, Pernand-Vergelesses, Aloxe-Corton, Ladoix-Serrigny and Chorey-les-Beaune. If one of his wholesale clients in Beaune asks him for some Pommard and it cannot be found in his five villages (it is a normal thing for a proprietor to own vines in several communes), he knows better than to venture off his territory to Pommard itself. For immediate *vigneron* reaction will be that, if Vollot comes this far, he must *really* need the wine, so prices will be firm.

Imagine then how foreigners may fare. Imagine also the temptation which exists for a grower to dispose of his second-rate wines to inexperienced or unsuspecting travellers. Nevertheless, calling on growers for a case or two of wine on one's way through Burgundy is an experience not to be missed. You will be welcomed right through the year, but the first problem is to find your proprietor.

Rainy days in January and February are best, for it is a slack time of the year in the vines and there is a fifteen-month-old wine for tasting, soon to be bottled. The great horizontal presses are ranged silently against the walls of the vat-rooms, surrounded by geraniums in pots and tubs of orange trees (the oranges still on them), both brought in from the frosts.

The first thing to look for in a grower's cellar is whether his *cuvées* really taste different. Then, whether there is a variation in quality between vintages. One may note whether all his casks are fully topped up, for this is perhaps the most important part of *élevage*; one will welcome the sight of new oak casks, for these expensive items are rarely indulged in by half-hearted wine-makers. However, cleanness of cellar floor, pipette and glasses do not necessarily mean a thing.

How does one go about forming, or reforming, one's Burgundian palate? How does one taste wine? On pages 142–5 is a Burgundian introduction, with the original *patois* (many of the turns of phrase are still in use).

Personally I have never got used to tasting with a *tastevin*, preferring a glass; and it is now rare for one to come across a straight Gamay north of the Beaujolais-Mâconnais. But familiarity with the grape-types is essential, as is the necessity of finding something safe to say if one is a beginner yet thinks one has detected a major fault. Every grower always tells you that his wine has just been racked or fined, so should really be resting, or else needs to be racked or fined the day after your visit. When you have tasted, the grower looks at you, and you know you have to comment. Only one thing matters: to be honest. If it is the first

Viens là mon gas, viens, qu'y t'eppreune[1]
C'ment qui faut far pour deguster.
Te y es. Desciale![2]
Tout d'abord, ça e son importance
5   Te te passe au doigt la tasse d'argent
Dont la bague quasiment te fiance
Au métier que te feras ben brament[3]
Plonge le pipette dans le trou de la bonde.
Bien. Varse le jus um cho[4] en biais
10 E peu regarde le une seconde.
L'est-il clair, brumeux vou bien[5] épais?
Halte-la! Je voyo qu' t'allo boire[6]
T'es pressé c'ment un maquignon
Contemple le dans toute sa gloire
15 A-t-il une couleur p'lure d'oignon[7]
Avant d'y gouter, a faut qu'a te plaise
Que te le voye mobile, vivant
Moiré à l'oeil, te c'ment de la braise
E peu te sauré[8] le reste en buvant.

20 Attends! faut encore que te l'sente
Promène voir ton grand nez au dessus!
Comment c'est y qu'o s'presente[9]?
Sent-y la grappe ou ben le verjus[10]
Maintenant oui, prends en une gorgée
25 Sans l'avaler c'est évident!
Fais la tourner, ... fais la bouger
Comme qui dirait, rince-toi les dents!
La! maintenant avale une gorgée qu'on sache
c'qu'o va dire[11] quand y sera au fond!
30 Les Marchands qui passent y s'y crachent!

---

[1] *apprenne*   [2] *Descelle la bonde du tonneau*
[3] *convenablement*   [4] *un peu*
[5] *ou bien*   [6] *Je vois que tu allais boire*
[7] *pelure d'oignon*   [8] *tu sauras*
[9] *Comment se présente-t-il?*
[10] *vinaigre de vin* (in this context. Normally *verjus* means the unripe grapes which are left on the vine for the birds)
[11] *Ce qu'il va dire*

142

Come here, boy, come so I can teach you
What you need to do to taste wine.
Are you ready? Knock the bung out.
First of all, and this is important,
5   You put the silver *tastevin* on your finger
Whose ring as it were betroths you
To the *métier* you will stoutly undertake.
Plunge your pipette in the bung-hole.
Right. Pour out the juice a bit askew
10 And then look at it a moment.
Is it clear, hazey, or else thick?
Halt there! I saw you starting to drink
You're hurrying like a horse-dealer
Contemplate it in all its glory
15 Has it the colour of onion-skin?
Before tasting it, it should please you
You should see it moving about, lively
Watered silk to the eye, like embers
You'll know the rest when you drink it.

20 Wait! You've still got to smell it
Let that great nose of yours have a look at it!
How does it appear?
Does it smell of grapes or vinegar?
Now yes, take a mouthful
25 Without swallowing it of course
Make it turn, make it move around
As one might say: Rinse your teeth!
There! Now swallow a mouthful so as to know
What it'll have to say when it's down below.
30 The merchants who pass, spit it out

143

Aoi! bois y, c'est pas de la poison
Y o pas tout[12]. Pour qu'y ait aucun doute
Te laisse un moment s'ecouler
Te dis ran[13]! te réflechis! te l'écoute
35   Après te sauras en parler.

S'agit pas de dire, après cette pause:
O, l'est fameux, l'a du bouquet!
Comme te dirais ça ou aut-chose
Faut que tu soye tout plein de ton sujet!
40   Du premier coup, faut que te débrouille!
Pinot—Passe-tout-grain—Gamay?
Pour ça j'sais qu't'es pas une andouille
Que t'as le bec honnête et franc, mais . . .
S'il arrive qu'o soye un peu aigre?
45   Ou qu'il a besoin d'etre reposé
Ou qui soye jeune, ou qu'o soye maigre . . .
Faute de tannin, te dis: o l'o rusé!
S'il est bon te fais claquer ta langue
Et te dis: o l'o grand, loyal! . . .
50   Te v'la mon gars sorti de ta gangue
Et de premier jus, te passe caporal!

[12] *Ce n'est pas tout*   [13] *Tu ne dis rien*

You—drink it—it's not poison.
That's not all. So there's no possible doubt
You let a moment slip by
You say nothing. You reflect! You listen to it
35 Afterwards you'll know how to talk about it.

It's not a question of saying, after that pause
Oh, it's capital, what a bouquet!
For you to say that, or anything else
You really must be full of your subject.
40 At the start, you must have your wits about you
Pinot—Passe-tout-grains—Gamay?
Here I know you're no fool,
That you've an honest nose, and free,
But if it happens to be a bit sour?
45 Or if it needs resting
Or if it's young, or if it's thin . . .
Lack of tannin, you say: that's a crafty one!
If it's good you clap your tongue
And say: this is good, loyal! . . .
50 There you are boy, out of the mould
And from private soldier promoted Corporal!

time you have ever tasted in a grower's cellar, then say so. He will be delighted, and will take you from cask to cask; you will end up tasting his oddities, the Puligny *rouge* or the Charmes-Chambertin *'qui n'a pas d'appellation, mais c'est du vrai, je peux vous le promettre.'* Finally, maybe, you will hear that sentence which never fails to cut short my determined farewells: *'Tenez,'* he says, reaching for a bottle, unlabelled, from a small unmarked pile in a corner, *'je vais vous faire goûter quelque chose de bon.'* He picks up a corkscrew with vine-stock handle, screws it into the cork, puts the bottle between his knees, and pulls.

But how does one taste? Given normally functioning senses, does it really only require enthusiasm and a croissant- rather than a bread-line income? I maintain so, and after a few years of attentive tasting one becomes so familiar with certain basic colours, smells and tastes (as long as one is training oneself on authentic examples) that one tastes with confidence.

You will recognize the difference between the perfume of young Chardonnay aged in old oak casks and one in new—the latter having a distinct smell of vanilla, or clean fresh-cut wood. Such a smell is quite different from the fault of woodiness, which comes from an imperfect cask. You will notice volatile acidity or oxidation and pick up smells of yeast, or milkiness. Because the growers have had it so easy for so long, there is much careless wine-making and bottling. If the chaptalization sugar is not measured out accurately and fermentations not completed because far too much was added, the wine will be sweet when you taste it. If the malolactic fermentation takes place in bottle when it should have been completed in casks—here the wine may be cloudy, the bouquet diminished, and a prickle noticeable on the tongue. With white wines, a common fault is oxidation, a premature deepening of colour, a lack of crispness on the finish.

For the first two or three years I was in the wine trade, I was secretly beset with dread lest I had a defective palate. The difference between wines seemed so small. I come from a family which drinks wine only rarely, and it is regular tasting which allows one to build up one's knowledge. There is no substitute for experience—so if you lack confidence about your tasting, do not despair, just start working on it.

'It seems to me sometimes,' writes Pierre Poupon, 'when I taste with extra attention, that antennae are growing at the base of my

146

nose.'[1] Tasting requires concentration, and quiet and space and light. It is much easier to assess a wine if one is tasting it blind than if one has read the label or been told what it is. It is also easier if there is a range of six to ten wines, all anonymous. The object is not to attempt to identify them, but to arrive at an honest assessment without being influenced by what one *thinks* the wine should taste like. One makes notes about each wine's looks, aroma, taste, and comes to a conclusion. And then, having seen the key, goes back to re-examine whether one's assessment is wildly out of line with what a given wine *should* taste like. If one is prepared to taste wines blind, one can call oneself a wine-taster.

Do not expect a Burgundian grower or shipper to put his wines up blind to you, though he may do if you get to know him. After all, he is trying to sell them, and telling you that you are about to taste Vosne-Romanée Les Suchots will pre-dispose you to like it. Or will it?

You must decide what importance you attach to authenticity, for the wine trade is divided on the subject. Growers, brokers, *négociants*, importers and merchants all know that what keeps them in business is providing the customer with wines he will enjoy. Nowhere is the reconciliation of attractiveness with authenticity more difficult than in Burgundy.

How does one recognize a pure Burgundy from one diluted with 10 per cent, 20 per cent or more of fortifying wine from the south? It is very difficult. Familiarity with the unblended article is the first requirement, and one of this book's main objectives is to indicate how to find it. Authentic red Burgundy is essentially clean-tasting, and leaves the mouth fresh. With practice you will recognize the distinctive Pinot Noir flavour and know when it is partially masked by bone-setter Mediterranean red, or by over-chaptalization. Remember that it is a characteristic of the Pinot Noir grape, when grown in Burgundy, to produce wines which are light in colour and alcohol. Is the wine you are tasting heady and alcoholic?

Great Burgundy smells of shit. It is most surprising, but something the French recognized long ago, *Ça sent la merde* and *Ça sent le purin* being common expressions on the Côte. Not always,

---

[1] *Nouvelles Pensées d'un Dégustateur, Confrérie des Chevaliers du Tastevin*, Nuits Saint-Georges, 1975.

of course; but frequently there is a smell of decaying matter, vegetable or animal, about them. This is nothing new. The Greeks had a wine called Saprias, of which H. Warner Allen has written:[1] 'The word σαπρος, which literally means rotten, raises a curious gastronomic paradox.... In the world of wine and food, decay may sometimes be a virtue.... To my mind σαπρος suggest[s] the razor edge of perfection between going up and going down the hill of development.' The last sentence does not apply to Burgundies, for they taste rotten long before they reach the razor edge, if they are good.

How can one define the difference between a fine bottle and a great bottle of wine? Not by their classifications, nor their origins or ages. It is the effect on the drinker which matters. A fine wine will have a lovely colour, attractive bouquet, and the balance, flavour and smoothness to be expected of it. A great wine will have all these things, but in addition something to make the pulse race, to make one exclaim: 'How *can* it smell and taste like that? That is amazing!' A fine wine may remind one of flowers or spices or fruits, but there is something animal, often something erotic about great Burgundy. *Un verre de Nuits prépare la vôtre* goes the saying about Nuits Saint-Georges. Perhaps I should translate the play on words: 'A glass of "Night" paves the way for yours.'

In the late 1960s there was no shortage of shippers and merchants absolutely convinced that the public preferred Algerianized Burgundy (as it then was), and they offered nothing else. Things have improved since then and it is now widely understood that a wine's taste-characteristics should not be at odds with its *appellation*. But the problem of making drinkable red Burgundy remains; and old habits die hard.

Have confidence in your palate, however untrained it is. If at a shipper's or merchant's tasting you have great difficulty in finding any difference between, say, an Aloxe-Corton and a Gevrey-Chambertin, you should be suspicious. Maybe your host's palate is deformed by years of adding 15 per cent, or buying and selling such wines. This is, I believe, what M. Pierre Poupon was referring to when he wrote: 'In order for quality to triumph like the naked truth wines would have to be anonymous, as are the masterpieces of the Middle Ages. That way there would be no more doubts,

[1] *A History of Wine*, Faber and Faber, 1961.

deceptions or illusions. But how many *négociants* would have to relearn how to taste, how many *vignerons* have to relearn how to make wine?'[1]

The Burgundians themselves run a certain number of tasting commissions. The judges will include a cross-section of growers, brokers and merchants who will ensure, as so they should, that no bad wines and no blatant substitutions carry famous names. But many of the members of the three categories have a vested interest in maintaining the blending *status quo*. The grower able to sell his Chambertin 1977 as such, without declassing it, got a good price for it; the broker got his commission; the merchant who then made it saleable by blending was able to set up a reasonable profit margin (which is difficult in famous years when the growers' prices are high).

Concours Agricole de Paris and *Foire Nationale des Vins à Mâcon* certificates are usually a good guide to merit—though it has happened, I think, that the Aligoté prize be carried off by someone who submitted a sample which included some of the overproduction from his Corton-Charlemagne!

The *Confrérie des Chevaliers du Tastevin* has held blind tastings since 1950 at the Clos de Vougeot in order to identify estimable bottles, which thereafter carry *Tastevinage* labels. Complete authenticity has not, I believe, always been the first requirement of wines submitted to these tastings. Today, I think one can argue that it should be.

[1] *Nouvelles Pensées d'un Dégustateur, Confrérie des Chevaliers du Tastevin*, Nuits Saint-Georges, 1975.

PART TWO

Introduction

~~~~~~~~~~~~~~~

Part Two describes the wines, places and people of Burgundy, village by village from Chablis in the north down to the Beaujolais. Nearly 300 of the leading domaine-bottling growers are described and over fifty of those merchants most often associated with the great wine names of Burgundy.

The sizes of *Grand Cru* (Great Growth) and *Premier Cru* (First Growth) vineyards are given to the nearest tenth of a hectare, except in Chablis where only Great Growth sizes are given. After every grower's name is shown the total size of his vineyard in hectares, followed by a percentage figure. This is the approximate percentage of his total production which, in a good year, he bottles himself. When a grower owns more than one First Growth in the same village, the name of the village is not repeated. In most cases the sum of the First Growths and Great Growths is considerably less than a proprietor's total vineyard holding. The balance will be made up by commune wines, Bourgognes, Passe-Tout-Grains and Aligotés. The word Monopole appears whenever a grower is sole proprietor of the listed vineyard—there are over a hundred of these, summarized in Appendix A. Often a grower or merchant owns vineyards in several communes. Details of the grower's estate appear wherever the vat-house and cellars are located; in the case of merchants, where his business is based.

The figure in brackets after a merchant's name indicates the year his company was founded. No percentage figure is given after merchants' vineyard possessions for they practically always bottle all their wines themselves.

Metric measures have not been converted into their British or American equivalents, for these details will chiefly be of interest to the visitor to Burgundy. When discussing wine with a proprietor,

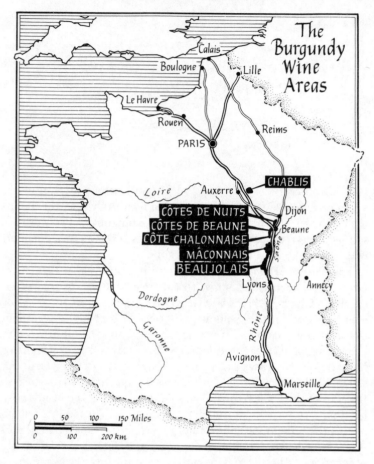

it is essential to feel at home with hectolitres and hectares. Here is
a simple conversion table:

1 hectare (ha.): approximately 2½ acres
1 hectolitre (hl): 100 litres: 22 gallons or 11 dozen bottles
1 barrel (*une pièce*): 223–8 litres: 25 dozen bottles
(In Chablis the standard barrel is the *feuillette*, holding 132 litres;
Mâconnais-Beaujolais barrels hold 212–16 litres.)

Be warned, however, that vineyard-owners will often confuse
matters by talking not of hectolitres and hectares, but of quarter-
casks and *ouvrées*, the game being played with the persistence of

154

shopkeepers counting out change in a mixture of old and new francs. The *ouvrée* is an old measure equivalent to 0·0428 ha. It is most often met with in the following conversation: 'In the old days yields were far smaller; my father used to make a quarter-barrel (*quartaut*) per *ouvrée*. If he made half a barrel it was miraculous. But these days people make a whole barrel, even two barrels.' Here are the modern equivalents:

quartaut à l'ouvrée: 13½ hl/ha.
½ *pièce à l'ouvrée*: 27 hl/ha.
1 *pièce à l'ouvrée*: 54 hl/ha.
2 *pièces à l'ouvrée*: 108 hl/ha.

There is scarcely an estate which does not bottle off the odd barrel of wine for family consumption; overnight it can begin to commercialize such wine as domaine-bottled. However, it takes practice to succeed in this, so I have tried to make a choice of those estates equipped and experienced in wine-making, tending and bottling, to whom I would go, or have gone, first when buying wine in bottle. Selection was made after consultation with merchants, brokers, and the growers themselves, particularly the last two. Once I had met with a first-class grower in a village he was usually happy to indicate other cellars he respected. Most are over five hectares in size and bottle over 30 per cent of their produce in a good year.

The accuracy of my figures cannot be guaranteed. A proprietor who in fact bottles all his wine in a fine year may only have admitted to bottling 60 per cent for fear merchants would black him the next bad year. Also there may be some duplication of vineyards. An aging proprietor who has leased out his vines on the half-fruit system may have declared himself the owner of all the land even though he only sells half of the wine; the lessee may have done the same.

The material has been collected over a ten-year period. I have tried to keep abreast of marriages and deaths, of changes within businesses, of land acquisitions and sales, but am aware that some errors will have crept in. I should be most grateful for any corrections from readers (however angry); mistakes will be rectified when the book is reprinted.

The reason I have listed, wherever possible, the exact size of a proprietor's holding in a vineyard is that where it is less than one-fifth of a hectare in size, there is some danger that the red grapes will not have been fermented separately. This can be done (for instance, in a small container whose sides slope inwards), but very often the grapes are mixed with others in a big vat. When the vat is drawn off the same wine will be given two or more names. However, the best proprietors ferment their different wines separately, even down to the produce of one-tenth of a hectare (thought this was virtually impossible in a year of small production like 1969). The problem is not so acute with small-holdings of white vines, for it is normal for white wines to ferment in a cask. All that is needed is the time and effort to make an individual pressing of a small quantity of grapes.

To spend half a page describing a merchant's own vineyards may be said to be missing the point if they represent a mere 5 per cent of his turnover. But often they are his prestige products, and ownership of vineyards is of increasing importance as more growers refuse to part with their wines to the trade. Many merchants only differ from their colleagues by their vine possessions.

The *appellation* laws stipulate different minimum levels of sugar in the grapes for each wine of Burgundy, but I have not listed them. They are totally ignored by growers, brokers, merchants and enforcement authorities whenever it suits them, and we might as well ignore them too.

11

Chablis and the Auxerrois

The vineyards of the Yonne *département* are divided between two valleys, the Yonne and its tributary, the Serein. The latter is the narrower, and consequently more subject to spring frosts. In twenty communes in the low hills and combes which border the Serein are to be found the vineyards of Chablis. We shall come to them in detail in a moment, but first let us look at the history of both areas.

Vines ran up to the walls of Auxerre as long ago as A.D. 680, so the account of Bishop Vigile tells us. And from the beginning, the small craft of the Yonne river, which runs past the town, were responsible for distributing the wines. Nearby Chablis and its territory belonged to the monks of Saint-Martin de Tours, thanks to a gift in A.D. 867 by Charles the Bald. Another monastery was to play a part in establishing the renown of Chablis, that of Pontigny, twenty kilometres away. This was a daughter of Cîteaux, founded in 1114. It is a magnificent white church, almost the size of Notre Dame, where three Archbishops of Canterbury, including Thomas à Becket, gained sanctuary in the Middle Ages. Although the monks had a small vineyard called *la Vieille Plante* nearby, they lost no time in seeking agreement with those of Saint Martin de Tours to exploit land at Chablis. A house was obtained in 1118, with enclosable land and thirty-six *arpents*[1] of vineyard.

At this time it was said of the Comte de Gatinois that his Auxerre vines gave 'delicious wine beyond all expression'. Two kings, François I and Henry IV looked favourably on the region, the one allowing its wines to be sold throughout the kingdom, the other removing taxation on them.

---

[1] An old French measure roughly equal to an acre.

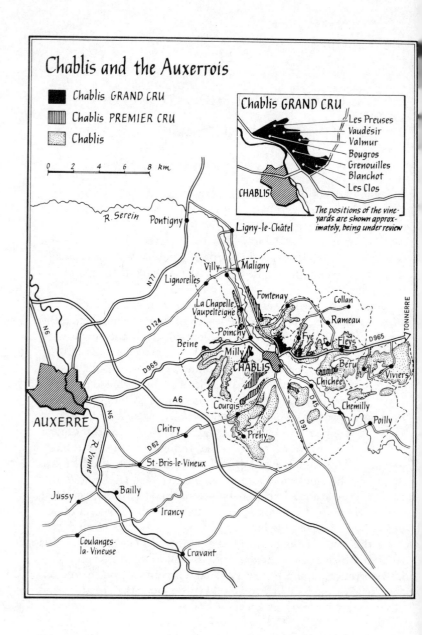

Chablis and the Auxerrois

- ■ Chablis GRAND CRU
- ▥ Chablis PREMIER CRU
- ▦ Chablis

0 2 4 6 8 km

Chablis GRAND CRU

Les Preuses
Vaudésir
Valmur
Bougros
Grenouilles
Blanchot
Les Clos

CHABLIS

The positions of the vineyards are shown approximately, being under review

R. Serein
Pontigny
Ligny-le-Châtel
Villy
Maligny
Lignorelles
Fontenay
Collan
La Chapelle Vaupelteigne
Rameau
Poinchy
Fye
Fleys
Beine
Béru
Milly
CHABLIS
Chichée
Viviers
Courgis
Chemilly
Poilly
Préhy
Chitry
St-Bris-le-Vineux
AUXERRE
R. Yonne
Jussy
Bailly
Irancy
Coulanges-la-Vineuse
Cravant
TONNERRE

N77 N6 D124 D965 A6 N6 D62 D965 D45 D91 D965

'Few wine reputations in France are so anciently attested as that of Auxerre,' writes Professor Dion. 'From the twelfth century, at a time when texts concerning the export trade of wines are still silent about Beaune and Bordeaux, clerks are using emphatic adjectives: *superlativum, pretiosissimum*, to describe Auxerre's wines. One sees King John being given a *tonneau*, in 1203, in gratitude for affixing the royal seal on an act confirming an agreement between the Earl of Leicester and the Bishop of Lincoln.'

Through the centuries, Paris was the outlet for the wine of the region, as for its wood, its charcoal, its cattle, and its building stone, which went down to the capital via the Yonne and its tributaries. Often the barrels did not stop in Paris, but went on to Rouen, Normandy, and overseas. The correspondence of the Chevalier d'Eon, who lived in London in the eighteenth century, shows that wine from nearby Tonnerre was much appreciated in England at that time.

By the seventeenth century, Professeur Dion describes how 150 itinerant merchants habitually brought Yonne wines for sale in Paris. It was fashionable for nobles, churchmen and bourgeois (described in 1607 as *ces gros-milours, ces ventres-gras*) to own their own vines in the region. But disaster was to overtake the Auxerrois.

Because of its proximity to Paris, the north, and the east of France, it became a most important table-wine production area in the eighteenth and nineteenth centuries, indeed the most important in Burgundy. In 1788 there were 32,000 hectares planted, in 1888 over 40,000 hectares. Three-quarters of the production was red wine, one-quarter white, but Pinot Noir and Chardonnay had given way before large-yielding varieties, particularly Gamay and Sacy. Only in the small enclave of Chablis and its nearest communes had the Chardonnay retained its hold.

The vineyards of the Auxerrois received three body-blows during the second half of the nineteenth century, from which they are only now coming round. Mildew ravaged them, the phylloxera devastated them, and then they lost their traditional market to wines from the Midi, which could reach Paris cheaply thanks to the newly-opened railways. A Chablis merchant today will pointedly remark that Midi wines were 'of good quality then'. Of the 40,000 hectares planted in the 1880s there remain today less than 3,000 over a third of which produces *vin ordinaire* for home consumption. The details of the quality wines are as shown in the table opposite.

THE AUXERROIS

As can be seen, the Auxerrois produces all manner of wines. They come from four principal communes, Saint-Bris-le-Vineux (the most important), Chitry, Irancy and Coulanges-la-Vineuse. The first two produce mainly white wines, the last two mainly reds. This century the area has lived in the shadow of Chablis; indeed at one time it hoped for an extension of that *appellation*. Is not Chitry part of the canton of Chablis, with its vineyards on similar Kimmeridgian subsoil? But it is in a different watershed, on the wrong side of the autoroute; an AC such as *Bourgogne des environs de Chablis* was not to be. Instead, the communes seek to offer a range of wines which are complementary to the famous neighbour. Perhaps their success will come from the new AC for *méthode champenoise* Sparkling Burgundy, Crémant de Bourgogne; perhaps from Sauvignon de Saint-Bris; or perhaps from the very diversity of wines which this mini-region can offer.

This century a large part of the wines of the Auxerrois has always been made into sparkling wine, for it is here that one comes across the Sacy grape. It gives fairly high yields of a wine which is strong in acidity, low to average in alcohol (10°–10·5°)—not unsurprisingly therefore a base for sparkling wine. In the bad old pre-AC days it went to Rheims and Epernay and was sold as Champagne, then for many years it was purchased by Henkell for making into Sekt. On the flotation of the Deutsche Mark in 1970 this market collapsed, and now the growers are doing the job themselves. In 1971 they founded a co-operative known as the *Société d'Intérêt Collectif Agricole du Vignoble Auxerrois* (SICAVA) and leased three hectares of underground cellars in a disused limestone quarry at Bailly, a hamlet of Saint-Bris. Its stone once went to build the Panthéon. Champagne methods are being used on *assemblages* of the local grapes in the following approximate proportions: 50 per cent Sacy, 35 per cent Aligoté, 10 per cent Pinot Noir, and a little Gamay.

It is surprising to come across the Sauvignon grape in Burgundy, but it has been found at Saint-Bris since the mid-

160

TABLE 3. AOC AND VDQS VINEYARDS AND WINES OF THE YONNE DÉPARTEMENT

	1975 VINTAGE	1981 VINTAGE	Vines
	Vines in production (ha.)		
LE CHABLISIEN (SEREIN VALLEY)			
Chablis *Grand Cru*	83	91	Chardonnay (known as Beaunois)
Chablis *Premier Cru*	306	474	
Chablis	544	924	
Petit Chablis	174	113	
	1,107	1,602	
L'AUXERROIS (YONNE VALLEY)			
Crémant de Bourgogne	101	191	Principally Sacy and Aligoté, a little Pinot Noir and Gamay
Bourgogne *blanc*	18	29	Chardonnay (known as Beaunois)
Bourgogne Aligoté	155	152	Aligoté
Bourgogne *Grand Ordinaire blanc*	116	56	Sacy
Sauvignon de Saint-Bris (VDQS)	65	63	Sauvignon
Bourgogne *rouge*	134	189	Pinot Noir
Bourgogne *Grand Ordinaire rouge*	26	19	Gamay
Bourgogne Passe-Tout-Grains	21	71	Gamay ($\frac{2}{3}$) Pinot Noir ($\frac{1}{3}$)
	636	770	
Total AOC	1,678	2,309	
Total VDQS	65	63	
GRAND TOTAL	1,743	2,372	

nineteenth century, at that time being mixed in with other wines. Now grown and vinified apart, its wine enjoys VDQS status, and serves to lure Parisians and foreign buyers in search of value for money away from Sancerre and Pouilly-sur-Loire. The wine from the Aligoté grape is not very pronounced, indeed there is nothing in its character to hook the private customer—that is the role of the Sauvignon, and within a year or two that customer will happily be buying both. Not to mention the red! For recently there has been some replanting of Pinot Noir, 1976 seeing the birth of a specific Bourgogne-Irancy AC for wines from that commune and neighbouring Cravant.

In additon to the Pinot, some César (otherwise known as Romain) is planted. This is a singular vine, with jagged leaves, big long bunches and an irregular production, whose introduction to the area is attributed to one of Caesar's legionaries. Recently a bas-relief dating from the second or third century was discovered at Escolives, between Coulanges and Auxerre. A small naked vintager is picking a bunch of grapes whose leaf, much indented, has been recognized by experts as the local César. Its wine is very deep in colour, full of tannin and backbone. Normally it is planted in amongst the Pinots, in the proportion of 5–10 per cent, to give body to the light wines and it has a reputation for being *ingueulable* (undrinkable) if ever vinified on its own. But the curious will find this far from the truth if they seek out M. Michel Esclavy in Saint-Bris, currently the only person vinifying César apart. The wine would be quite impossible to identify as a Bourgogne by deduction in a blind tasting, having nothing in common with Pinot or Gamay. It has the astringency of a claret or something from the hills of the Midi, but is certainly not *ingueulable*.

The legislation still permits Bourgogne *rouge* in the Yonne to be made from the Tressot grape, however this has virtually disappeared. It is a low-yielder and its wine without merit, according to Monsieur Esclavy. It is surprising that it should have lasted so long. In a letter from Charles VI of 1394 mention is made of a fifteen-year-old grape-picker at Saint-Bris who was struck down and killed by the owner of a vineyard because he '*mettait des treceaux et autres raisins avec des pynoz.*' This is one of the earliest mentions of the Pinot grape known to Professor Dion.

A date worth noting is the weekend preceding 11 November

each year, when the growers of the Auxerrois organize the *Fête des Vins de l'Yonne* at Saint-Bris. It apparently consists of a varied *folklorique* programme, a *bal populaire* and a permanent tasting of the wines of six communes: Saint-Bris, Chitry, Irancy, Coulanges, Auxerre and Vaux. I have never been; you might wish to arrange a trip to coincide with it, or alternatively to give it a wide berth.

CHABLIS

Chablis is to wine what Corot is to painting: three out of four are false—or so the saying used to go. Perhaps it is still true if one takes into account all the Californian, Australian and other wines whose makers are too lazy or just incapable of building a reputation in their own right; fortunately it is no longer the case with Chablis AC.

As we have seen, the grape is the Chardonnay, locally known as Beaunois. It is grown on clayey-limestone plateau and hillside soils, which are stonier and deeper than those of the Côte d'Or. The bedrock is twenty million years younger, being upper Jurassic.

Yonne vines must be grafted on to specially lime-resistant root-stocks, and for this reason *Riparia* × *berlandieri* crosses are favoured, particularly a root-stock developed at Oppenheim named SO4 which brings the grapes to an early maturity and is not too productive. The Côte d'Or's 3309C is not widely found, a *Vinifera* × *berlandieri* cross, the 41B, being the other most common stock. This is the same stock as is used in Jerez where its resistance to lime is also valued. As always, much care must go into selecting compatible vines for grafting, taking into account the health and analysis of the soil, and its drainage.

The Yonne is experimenting with clonal selection of Chardonnays in liaison with the Côte d'Or, having established fourteen families in 1974. Because of the greater richness of the soil the pruning is different to the rest of Burgundy being a double Guyot with two long fruit-bearing canes. They are often bent downhill, to diminish vegetation and encourage the production of fruit.

Frost has always been a far greater problem in Chablis than elsewhere in Burgundy. In the years 1945, 1951, 1953 and 1957 the crop was totally wiped out; from 1955 to 1961 parts of the

163

vineyard were touched every year except 1958. The *Grands Crus* were always the worst hit, for the narrow Serein valley tends to trap cold air masses, to the extent that growers gave up replanting. The great vineyards of Clos and Grenouilles were stubble-fields on which people skied and tobogganed in the winter only thirty years ago. The most dangerous period is 15–31 May, for if the young buds are caught then it is too late for them to shoot again.

Anti-frost systems are normally installed in the vineyards around 25 April, when the pruning and one ploughing have taken place. Various methods have been tried: paraffin candles (which tend to burn the nearby vines); various heaters using fuel-oil; and thermostatically-controlled gas burners, though these sometimes fail to raise the temperature sufficiently. The most imaginative installation is a network of underground pipes connected to fifteen pumps on a specially dug horseshoe-bend of the river Serein. Fifty hectares of Fourchaume and neighbouring vineyards are protected from frosts by overhead water-sprinklers, which come into operation when the temperature drops below freezing, covering the young shoots with a thin layer of ice; they are then as snug and safe as snowdrops under the snow. It needs a lot of water and the likelihood of frost on subsequent days is increased once you start to sprinkle, because of the increased humidity in the vineyard. But it is an economical system, if requiring delicate handling. Following its success, an artificial lake has recently been built on the road between Chablis and Auxerre so that vines in the communes of Beine, Poinchy and Milly can be similarly protected.

The area under vines in Chablis has tripled over the last twenty years. Monsieur J. P. Couillaut of the *Station Agronomique et Viticole de l'Yonne* in Auxerre explains the expansion in various ways. There is the possibility of protection against spring frosts, and the ease with which land can be chemically disinfected, thus eliminating the need for ten or fifteen years between grubbing up and replanting a vineyard. And progressively more estates have moved over to cultivating the vine exclusively, thereby requiring a larger area under cultivation.

As recently as 1945–55 a Chablis merchant hesitated before encouraging his son into the business. At that time there were a lot of old *vignerons*, for much labour had been lost to the towns. A *vigneron* would have cows and cornfields, and in order to make both ends meet the wives would keep rabbits, hens and a pig. The merchant was really someone in those days. When he went a few kilometres down the road, to La Chapelle perhaps, the word would go round: '*Il est dans le pays, il va peut-être passer.*' There was an additional link in the distribution chain, for he would use a *courtier de campagne* to aid the transaction. One such broker was a certain Simon of Fleys, a bachelor. The broker had title to a free lunch whenever a deal had been done and the wine taken away, and Monsieur Simon would artfully insist on his right even if he had arranged three deliveries in a morning, storing up free lunches for days ahead.

A *vigneron-raconteur* not to be missed by the visitor curious for old Chablis stories is Monsieur Robert Fèvre. He has a striking Mr Punch nose, and surveyed, perhaps, your arrival at the Hôtel de l'Étoile from the window of his house nearby. He recalls pressing in the old days, when the whole Chablis harvest went through twenty-six presses owned by twenty-two families. A pressing needed five men, and even then they only managed one day-time and one night-time *marc*. The small *vigneron* would bring his grapes to a bourgeois house; they would be pressed, and the must carried back to his cellar slung between the shoulders of two carriers walking in step. A crown of rye straw would be put in the container to prevent the must from slopping over. The owner of the press would obtain payment according to the number of *feuillettes* produced.

And those *cabanes*, shaped like igloos, still to be seen in the vines. When earth was brought by donkeys from hill-top or valley to replace the winter's erosions, the large stones would be set on one side. Communal effort would then build them into domed shelters, with a hole in the top, which let the smoke out, or the sun in, and could be blocked in times of rain. Since there was no cement, something had to be done to fill the crevices between the stones. So a trench would be dug round the outside of the *cabane* and earth piled against it, at least high enough to keep the draughts above the heads of those sitting inside, their backs against the stones.

It was a harder life in those days, and some of the old generation like Père Collet still remember the spring frosts of 1926, 1927 and 1928 when as a newly-married man he had no wine to sell for three consecutive years. There were no foreign holidays then. Now the

165

Crédit Agricole organizes wine-growers' trips to Tunisia, Sri Lanka and the United States.

In addition to Chablis itself, nineteen communes have the right to the *appellation*. Progressing down the Serein valley they are: Poilly, Chemilly, Préhy, Chichée, Béru, Viviers, Courgis, Fleys, Milly, Fyé, Rameau (a hamlet of Collan), Beine, Poinchy, Fontenay, La Chapelle, Lignorelles, Villy, Maligny and Ligny-le-Châtel. It is a pretty valley, the roadsides dotted with cowslips in April. If you go for a walk in the mixed evergreen and deciduous woods you may see traces of old rows of vines, for some of these woods were once vineyards, and may well be again. The twenty communes cover about 20,000 hectares, of which it is said that 5,000 hectares could be planted with vineyard. The table on page 161 showed that a mere 1,100 hectares were in production in 1975. How much more should be planted, and to which AC the new wines should be entitled, have provoked bitter disputes. Indeed the Serein valley is not serene at all.

The Chablis Controversy

Two rival growers' syndicates are in competition in the Chablis wine-field. On the one hand the *Syndicat de Défense de l'Appellation Chablis*, headed by M. William Fèvre, on the other a breakaway organization under M. Jean Durup, the *Fédération des Vignerons du Chablisien*. Monsieur Fèvre is the son of a Chablis grower, an ex-student of the prestigious Paris *École Nationale d'Administration* and owner of a large estate, the Domaine de la Maladière. He is also a civil servant, one of France's forty Contrôleurs d'État, responsible for the financial control of *Sociétés d'Autoroutes*. Monsieur Durup's father is a Maligny grower. The son took a Paris law degree, then spent ten years in the Ministère des Finances before setting up a company to give advice on tax problems, at the same time creating a large estate, the Domaine de l'Eglantière.

Chablis was recognized by the tribunals in 1923, and the INAO in 1938, as being grown on a subsoil of Kimmeridgian limestone (the name comes from the Dorset village of Kimmeridge). Petit Chablis could be grown anywhere else within the twenty communes—theoretically on as much as 17,000 hectares. It has been Monsieur Durup's contention that this was a major error—

for is not orientation of the vineyard frequently of greater importance? Has not some Chablis always been grown on Portlandian limestone?

He succeeded in persuading the INAO to appoint a highly-qualified commission of experts to re-open the investigation, and in November 1976 decrees were published which more or less vindicated his views, removing the reference to Kimmeridgian and taking into account all factors, such as aspect and microclimate, when arriving at the classification. Much of the land around Monsieur Durup's home village of Maligny has been upgraded from Petit Chablis to Chablis, to the fury of Monsieur Fèvre, whose battle-cry remains Kimmeridge.

Needless to say, the antagonists are of different political colours, Fèvre being left and Durup right of centre. There have been some memorable Clochemerle-type incidents indeed, once the struggle took to the air. A Durup man tells how suddenly one day the news got out that Monsieur Fèvre had organized a survey in Petit Chablis territory. His henchmen were mapping out the *appellation*, they must be followed, they must be stopped! The barricades went up, and local merchant Michel Laroche took off in his aeroplane, with walkie-talkie connection to the ground, to plot their progress. It was *la guerre*. Fortunately no blood was spilled, but *per capita* Chablis consumption rose spectacularly that day, the chase being hot.

And then there was the story of the Bois de Milly. A Parisian gentleman, Monsieur des Courtis, bought a plot of land in the wood above Milly to build a house. Suddenly the bulldozers had moved in, the trees were down and he was requesting permission to plant a vineyard and make Petit Chablis. Vines in the Bois de Milly, exclaimed Monsieur Fèvre's syndicate, certainly not! But Monsieur Durup thought otherwise (was this not hillside land of excellent aspect, just uphill from the First Growth Côte de Léchet?) and somehow pushed it through. And now the INAO's commission of experts has declared that the wine will be worthy of the AC Chablis, not mere Petit Chablis. What grindings of teeth must there not be in the Fèvre camp!

In fact they do more than grind their teeth. They have lodged an appeal against the 1976 decrees before the Council of State, the highest court in the land for disputes between individuals and the state. A result is unlikely before 1981 or 1982, for all the evidence must be submitted in writing, and such trials often last three to four years.

While the judgement is awaited, one side's views can be followed blow by blow in William Fèvre's latest publication, *Les Vrais Chablis et les Autres*. He describes how the *appellation* Chablis has now been extended, by the 1976 decrees, from the hillsides, its traditional home, on to the plateaux, of dubious viticultural value. One indeed is known as Champ de Raves, the turnip field. Wooded hillsides, including that known as Les Landes et Verjus (*verjus* meaning unripe grapes) have been classified as *Premiers Crus*, without anyone having the remotest idea of what the wine they are to yield will taste like. W. Fèvre states:

Chablis est un cru de Bourgogne like Montrachet, Meursault, Pouilly-Fuissé. No-one is either surprised or shocked by the fact that Chassagne-Montrachet produces 4,000 hl of white wine per year, Puligny-Montrachet 7,000 hl, Meursault 15,000 hl, Pouilly-Fuissé 25,000 hl. At present Chablis produces 50,000 hl yearly, and could produce 100,000 hl, without leaving Kimmeridgian hillsides, and with no loss to its distinctiveness.

If it were to produce 200,000 hl through expansion on to the plateaux opened to its development by the decrees and survey of 1976, it would cease to occupy a place 'in the first ranks of the wines of France', as Guyot described it in 1868. It would fall to a level alongside many foreign dry white wines which call themselves Chablis.

'May true Chablis wines, by their lively, stimulating effect on the mind's lucidity,' (Guyot again), 'hold back the producers and those tempting them from what would be a fatal slope.'

One suspects that W. Fèvre[1] is not entirely convinced that the INAO has been pointing in the right direction since the departure of H. Pestel as Director in the late 1960s, and the arrival of his successor M. de Marquet. He sees the INAO believing less and less in the influence of natural factors on the quality of wine, and more and more in the importance of man and his technical advances, as in Germany or California.

---

[1] The Council of State dismissed William Fèvre's appeal in 1982, so the vineyard extensions have been definitively recognized.

The Chablis debate will go on for years no doubt, continuing to spread the renown of the area. The wine was costing (in 1979) as much as a bottle of Champagne. But let us not begrudge the Chablis growers their splendid incomes—they need them to pay the legal fees.

And what about the wines? '*Légers, secs, brillants et digestifs,*' was how a nineteenth-century gourmet described the wines of Chablis, and ideally that is how they should be. But not many are light today. Demand has been for full-bodied white Burgundies; and well-chaptalized wines stand up best to foreign travel. Chablis is dependable, but it often lacks zip.

Main Merchants and Growers (89800 Chablis)

BACHEROY-JOSSELIN

A *négociant* business, founded in 1973 by Michel Laroche, who describes himself as a *véritable savant du vin*. He is certainly a lively trader, the last twenty-five years having seen the expansion of the Domaine Laroche in Maligny from one to over twenty hectares, and the creation of the Domaine La Jouchère.

Here are the details of the vineyards:

Domaine Laroche   22 ha.
Chablis Blanchot $4\frac{2}{3}$ ha., Les Clos 1 ha., Bougros $\frac{1}{3}$ ha., Fourchaume 7 ha., Vaillons 1 ha., Montmains $\frac{4}{5}$ha.

Domaine La Jouchère   potentially 55 ha.
Chablis Vaillons $4\frac{3}{4}$ ha., Beauroy $1\frac{1}{3}$ ha., Vaudevey (to be planted) $11\frac{1}{3}$ ha., Chablis, Petit Chablis.

J. BILLAUD-SIMON   7 ha. (100 per cent)
Chablis Les Clos $\frac{2}{3}$ ha., Vaudésir $\frac{2}{3}$ ha., Mont-de-Milieu, Montée de Tonnerre, Vaillons.

These wines have been bottled every year since 1955, mainly for the American market.

ADHÉMAR BOUDIN   9 ha. (25 per cent)
Fourchaume 2 ha.

M. Boudin is one of the most experienced of the estate-bottling growers in La Chapelle Vaupelteigne, a neighbouring commune to Chablis.

LA CHABLISIENNE
This co-operative was founded in 1935 and accounts for about a fifth of Chablis production. It sells 80 per cent in bulk to the Burgundy trade.

DOMAINE JEAN COLLET ET FILS   21 ha. (35 per cent)
Chablis Valmur ½ ha., Vaillons 3½ ha., Montmains 4½ ha., Epinotte 3 ha., Mont-de-Milieu ½ ha., Montée de Tonnerre ⅔ ha., Chablis 5 ha.

DOMAINE PIERRE DES COURTIS
Chablis 10 ha.
This is the vineyard which was bulldozed from the Bois de Milly and initially classified as Petit Chablis. Its first harvest was in 1977.

RENÉ DAUVISSAT   7 ha. (80 per cent)
Chablis Les Clos 1½ ha., Les Preuses 1 ha., Forêts 3½ ha., Séchet.
M. Dauvissat's enthusiasm for wine-making was described in some detail by Alexis Lichine in his *Wines of France*. He still ages his wines in wood for a year or more.

PAUL DROIN-BAUDOIN   6 ha. (70 per cent)
MARCEL DROIN-MARY
Chablis Vaudésir ⅓ ha., Grenouilles 1 ha., Valmur 1 ha., Les Clos 1 ha., Montée de Tonnerre, Montmain, Vaillons.

MARCEL DUPLESSIS ET FILS   4 ha. (30 per cent)
Chablis Les Clos ⅓ ha., Montée de Tonnerre, Montmain, Fourchaume, Châtain.

DOMAINE DE L'EGLANTIÈRE   50 ha. (100 per cent)
DOMAINE DE LA PAULIÈRE
Chablis Fourchaume 10 ha., Montée de Tonnerre 1 ha., Montmains ½ ha., Vaucoupin, Chablis, Petit Chablis.
M. Durup's estate, which started to sell in bottle in 1974. 70 per cent of the wine is exported. It is based in Maligny, north of Chablis.

MAURICE FÈVRE   4 ha. (100 per cent)
Chablis Les Clos 1¼ ha., Valmur 1¼ ha., Les Preuses ⅔ ha., Fourchaume.

Maurice Fèvre was for a long time one of the most respected wine-makers in Chablis. He supplied Pruniers in Paris for many years, and in London until it closed. Now his estate is being integrated into the Domaine de la Maladière.

ROBERT FORGEOT

M. Forgeot owns a vineyard at Bernouil, near Tonnerre, where pre-phylloxera vines may be seen growing healthily, producing Bourgogne *blanc*. They are Chardonnay *franc de pied*—ungrafted Chardonnays, in clay soil, planted originally in a crowd, as the saying went, but now pushed into rows. Nothing very remarkable about the wine, but cuttings from these old vines have gone to vine research stations at Montpellier and Mulhouse, and have been used on more than one fine Chablis estate.

RAOUL GAUTHERIN   8½ ha. (15 per cent)

Chablis Les Clos ⅕ ha., Grenouilles ⅕ ha., Séchet, Butteaux, Lys, Mellinot.

DOMAINE DE LA GRENOUILLE   10 ha. (100 per cent)

Chablis Grenouilles 10 ha.

This estate was bought by the Testut family in 1966. The *cuverie* is inside the Grenouilles vineyard.

LAMBLIN ET FILS   (1920) 7 ha.

Chablis Valmur ⅔ ha., Mont-de-Milieu, Beauroy, Fourchaume.

M. Lamblin's offices were for many years in Maligny in the Rue Chante-Pinot; now he has large new temperature-controlled installations north of the village.

DOMAINE A. LONG-DEPAQUIT   25 ha.

Chablis Les Clos, Vaudésir, Les Preuses, Vaillons, Lys, Beugnons.

A famous estate which is being reconstituted. The wines are distributed by Bichot of Beaune.

DOMAINE DE LA MOUTONNE   2·35 ha. (100 per cent)

For years the whereabouts of one of Chablis' best-known wines, Chablis Moutonne, has been obscured by disputes. There have been wrangles over alleged abuses of the name and squabbles between the heirs to the estate. Was it a brand or a vineyard? No two Chablisiens seemed to agree.

Thanks to an article by Pierre Bréjoux, published in 1978 in *La*

Revue du Vin de France, all has become clear. I am indebted to it for much of what follows.

'*Pissatif et léger, faict saulter le bûveur comme un petit mouton*'— so wrote the monks of the Abbey of Pontigny about their Chablis in the eighteenth century. They owned a vineyard of 1·11 ha. in the *climat* of Vaudésir, known as La Moutonne, which was sold to Simon Depaquit at the Revolution. His descendants, the Long-Depaquit family, extended the Moutonne name to cover wine from nearby plots in the *Grand Cru* Les Preuses, then further adjoining Vaudésir rows. Louis Long-Depaquit also owned vines in Les Clos, Valmur and *Premiers Crus*. Moutonne became for a time a commercial brand covering wines from several origins.

In 1950 an agreement was reached that the *appellation* should only be used on wines from a plot of 2·35 ha., situated in the *Grands Crus* Vaudésir and Les Preuses. After Louis Long-Depaquit's death in 1967, the seven heirs took some time dividing their valuable inheritance.

The vineyard now belongs to the Société Civile de la Moutonne, the wines being distributed by Bichot (82·5 per cent) and Drouhin (17·5 per cent) of Beaune.

Half of the vineyard is so steep that the cultivation is done by winch.

DOMAINE DE LA MALADIÈRE   25 ha. (100 per cent)
Chablis Les Clos 3½ ha., Bougros 5⅔ ha., Les Preuses 2⅓ ha., Vaudésir 1⅖ ha., Valmur 1⅔ ha., Grenouilles ½ ha., Vaulorent, Vaillons, Montée de Tonnerre, Lys, Forêts, etc.

The creation of this estate during the last twenty years by the determined William Fèvre undoubtedly stimulated others to expand and replant. He was one of the first to fight frosts in the 1950s. When I first met him in 1969, he believed that Chablis should be *le meilleur des vins de café, le moins cher des vins de restaurant* and was barely in favour of restricting yields, except for *Grands* and *Premiers Crus*. A decade later the story is very different, as we saw earlier in this chapter.

LOUIS MICHEL ET FILS   18 ha. (65 per cent)
Chablis Vaudésir 1¼ ha., Grenouilles ⅔ ha., Les Clos ½ ha., Montmain, Fourchaume, Vaillons, Butteaux, Montée de Tonnerre, Forêts.

Louis Michel recalls his father pulling up their Les Clos vines in

172

1959. After eighteen harvests they had produced wine precisely twice, so often had the frosts struck. But in the twenty years which followed, the estate has quadrupled in size.

The wines have regularly been imported into England by O. W. Loeb & Co.

J. MOREAU ET FILS (1814)

The firm has its own 70 ha. estate:

Chablis Les Clos 8 ha., Valmur 2 ha., Vaudésir 1 ha., Vaillons 9 ha., Chablis 50 ha.

It is sole proprietor of a trade mark: Clos des Hospices, which is a 2·4 ha. part of Les Clos. It handles white wines from other French regions as well as Chablis.

LOUIS PINSON 4 ha. (100 per cent)

Chablis Les Clos 1 ha., Mont de Milieu, Forêts, Montmain.

FRANÇOIS RAVENEAU 4 ha. (100 per cent)

Chablis Les Clos $\frac{1}{2}$ ha., Blanchot $\frac{1}{3}$ ha., Montée de Tonnerre 1 ha., Chapelot $\frac{3}{4}$ ha., Butteaux $\frac{1}{2}$ ha., Forêts $\frac{1}{6}$ ha.

M. Raveneau, who is a wine-broker as well as a proprietor, ages his wines six months in vat and eight months in wood. He bottles them after two finings, but no filter, and they are almost invariably sold within weeks of their being available. However, the local Hôtel de l'Étoile has stocks of many of his past vintages, and if you wish to discover that Chablis can have exceptional depth of flavour, I recommend one of his bottles.

A. REGNARD ET FILS (1870)

This company has passed from father to son-in-law since its foundation. It owns no vineyards but buys a lot of must for carefully-tended vinification. Fourchaume is its speciality.

Its Managing Director, Michel Rémon, looks after a third of a hectare of Vaudésir for Peter Reynier, the London wine shipper. The vines were bought by the latter's father in the 1930s, when much of Vaudésir was still abandoned to the weeds. The wine is French-bottled and shipped to England.

MARCEL SERVIN 12 ha. (75 per cent)

Chablis Les Preuses $\frac{4}{5}$ ha., Bougros $\frac{3}{4}$ ha., Les Clos $\frac{4}{5}$ ha., Blanchots $\frac{1}{2}$ ha., Montée de Tonnerre, Vaillons, Butteaux.

SIMMONET-FEBVRE (1840)

For many years, half of this company's turnover was in Sparkling Chablis, which has an interesting origin. After the Napoleonic wars a certain Tisserand began putting a bubble into his local wines (Chablis is in fact closer to the Champagne than the Côte d'Or wine-field). Bearing the noble name of Moët the wines sold successfully in England for several years until one day his customer omitted to pay for a large consignment. Since a court action could hardly be brought, Tisserand went out of business.

His equipment was bought by the first M. Febvre, who wisely began production under his own name. The company owns a couple of hectares in Chablis Les Preuses and Mont de Milieu and is broker for several Beaune merchants. It also handles a little red and rosé Irancy.

DOMAINE ROBERT VOCORET ET SES FILS 12 ha. (40 per cent)

Chablis Les Clos $1\frac{1}{3}$ ha., Valmur $\frac{1}{3}$ ha., Blanchot 3 ha., Montée de Tonnerre, Beugnon, Forêts, Séchet, Châtain.

Robert Vocoret was elected mayor of Chablis in 1966. He has been exporting to the USA since the mid-1950s.

There are thirteen other growers who bottle their wines in Chablis itself and sixty-three in the surrounding villages. In the four villages of the Auxerrois there are over seventy—details may be had from the *Fédération Interprofessionelle des Vins de Bourgogne*, rue Henri Dunant, 21200 Beaune.

The Côte de Nuits

DIJON, LARREY AND CHENÔVE

The most northerly village of the Côte de Dijon is Larrey, but it has virtually disappeared beneath the suburbs of Dijon. Already in 1892 Danguy et Aubertin described how country houses had been built halfway up the slopes, thus gaining a magnificent view. Vineyards were probably planted there contemporaneously with those at Chenôve; they certainly existed in A.D. 587, and in the seventh century Duke Amalgaire gave vines from this commune to the Abbey of Bèze—we will meet the Duke again later, in Gevrey-Chambertin.

Neither of the villages has right to a commune *appellation*, but both produce some good Bourgognes. Larrey's best-known vineyard is Les Marcs d'Or, whose wines did not lack finesse, according to the early nineteenth-century writer Dr Morelot. It used to belong to the cellist Maurice Maréchal, and faces north-east, which is rare on the Côte. I understand that his son has so far won the battle to prevent a school being built on the vineyard. The only Larrey wine I have come across is the Bourgogne Montre-Cul of M. Quillardet.

Chenôve may have got its name from the fact that *Chanvre*, or cannabis, was cultivated there. In the old days, the territory was divided between three owners—the chapter of Autun, the Benedictines of Saint-Bénigne and the Dukes of Burgundy, who owned the famous Clos du Roi with its vat-house and magnificent presses. The Clos du Roi now belongs to M. Michel Pont of Volnay (see page 275), the presses to Messrs Pascal of Dijon. They were constructed by Alix de Vergy in 1238.

It is recounted that in 1648 the wines of Chenôve sold at higher

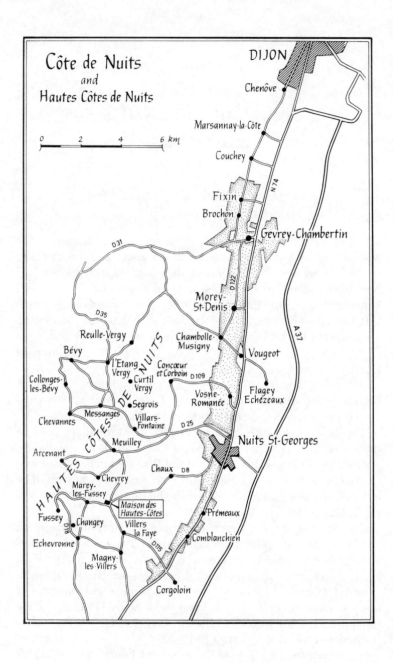

prices than those of Gevrey. Perhaps the presence of the Duke of Burgundy's Clos had an influence on consumer demand.

There are three or four attractive interior courtyards in Chenôve and on the main square a fifteenth-century façade which has been turned into four separate houses. Around the sanatorium grows the most northerly forest of cedars in Europe, so the locals claim.

There are half a dozen merchants in Dijon, but I do not know of any estate-bottling growers based in either Dijon, Larrey or Chenôve.

MARSANNAY-LA-CÔTE AND COUCHEY

'La Côte s'achève sur une gentille frivolité, sur un pas de gavotte dégustative.' G. Rozet, Tastevin en main.

The wines of Marsannay-la-Côte and Couchey have the right to the AC Bourgogne. The villages are best known for their rosé, which can be called Bourgogne Rosé or Bourgogne Clairet with the addition of either Marsannay or Marsannay-la-Côte. The wine is made by vinifying Pinot Noir grapes as if they were white. The last pressings give a rose-tinted must which should be enough to give the wine its grey-pink colour. If not, three bottles per hogshead of red Pinot from Marsannay have been known to do the trick. It is a full-bodied dry rosé with a clean Pinot flavour.

Marsannay has been producing wine since at least A.D. 658. It has had periods of great poverty, for instance after the Battle of Rocroy in 1643, when the population was reduced to thirty, of which two handled half the pruning, as the remainder were so miserable. But during the eighteenth century Dijon doubled in size, and the nearby villages were planted with Gamay to quench its thirst. Couchey and Marsannay-la-Côte made fortunes and they showed it by building enormous town-halls and churches which can still be seen (Marsannay pulling down a Romanesque church to do so). In 1855 Dr Lavalle wrote that there was not enough Pinot in the communes to make a single cuvée spéciale and in 1918 the situation had scarcely changed.

When the AC laws were formulated in the late 1930s there were only about forty hectares of Pinot plantations, which was not enough for the villages to be considered for Côte de Nuits Villages. However, since the war this plantation has tripled. The local

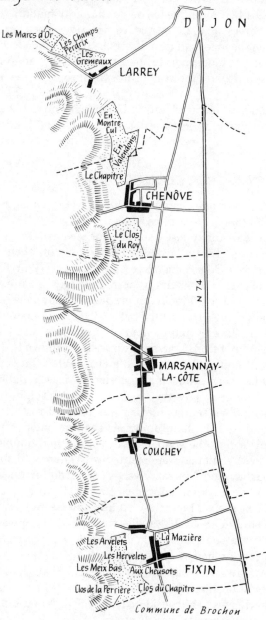

Dijon to Fixin

DIJON

Les Marcs d'Or
Les Champs
Perdrix
Les Gremeaux
LARREY

En
Montre-
Cul

En Valendons

Le Chapitre

CHENÔVE

Le Clos
du Roy

N 74

MARSANNAY-
LA-CÔTE

COUCHEY

Les Arvelets
La Mazière
Les Hervelets
Les Meix Bas
Aux Cheusots
FIXIN
Clos de la Perrière
Clos du Chapitre

Commune de Brochon

growers admit that the best vineyards on the slope are more suited to the making of red than rosé wine; it is to be hoped that Marsannay and Couchey may receive the AC Côte de Nuits Villages on condition that their wines pass a tasting panel first. As in Chenôve, there is a danger that spreading Dijon may further encroach on the vines. The superior AC would help to prevent this, as such vineyards are considered to be of 'public utility' and planning permission for building is harder to obtain.

Perhaps Marsannay's greatest claim to fame today is that the following great estate is based there:

DOMAINE CLAIR-DAÜ 35 ha. (100 per cent of its *Premiers* and *Grands Crus*)

Chambertin Clos de Bèze 2 ha., Chapelle-Chambertin $\frac{2}{5}$ ha., Gevrey-Chambertin Clos Saint-Jacques 2 ha., Etournelles Saint-Jacques $\frac{2}{5}$ ha., Lavaux Saint-Jacques $\frac{1}{4}$ ha., Cazetiers 1 ha., Combe aux Moines $\frac{1}{6}$ ha., Clos du Fonteny Monopole $\frac{9}{10}$ ha., Musigny $\frac{1}{3}$ ha., Bonnes Mares $2\frac{3}{4}$ ha., Chambolle-Musigny Les Amoureuses $\frac{1}{6}$ ha., Clos de Vougeot (middle and bottom) $\frac{1}{2}$ ha., Savigny Dominode $1\frac{3}{4}$ ha., Santenay 2 ha., Fixin, Marsannay.

This domaine invented Bourgogne Rosé de Marsannay on 22 September 1919. For many years it has been one of the foremost estates on the Côte with a reputation for long-lasting, tannic wines. One should approach it with care, however, for unrelenting demand is never a good thing for wine-makers. Its recent director M. Bernard Clair was one of the few to be experimenting extensively with different varieties of Pinot when I last met him. He had some Chardonnay rosé, and was trying to develop a rot-resistant Pinot, called Tête de Nègre because of the blackness of its grapes. He had several plantations of Hautes and mi-Hautes Vignes (he favoured two rather than three metres between the rows), and found that although maturity came a week later, they produced a deeper-coloured wine than that of ordinarily-pruned vines. The high vines are now mainly used for producing Marsannay rosé.

Bernard Clair's sister, Madame Vernet, took over as director of the estate in 1981, her wine-maker being a Montpellier-qualified oenologist, Gerard Ploy.

Part of the property is the old chapel of the bishop-dukes of Langres, and against it grow two climbing vines which are perhaps the oldest vines in France. They are thought to date back to the sixteenth century (a third is recorded as having died at a great age in 1840), and still produce magnificent bunches of grapes. They ripen in November, and are used as table grapes, or for making mustard.

Other Growers (21160 Marsannay-la-Côte)

JEAN FOURNIER 6 ha. (20 per cent)
Gevrey-Chambertin $\frac{2}{3}$ ha., Côte de Nuits Villages, Marsannay.

Jean Fournier has been running this estate single-handed since the age of seventeen.

ROGER HUGUENOT 9$\frac{1}{2}$ ha. (40 per cent)
JEAN-LOUIS HUGUENOT
Charmes-Chambertin $\frac{1}{5}$ ha., Gevrey-Chambertin *Premier Cru* 1$\frac{1}{3}$ ha., Fixin 4$\frac{1}{3}$ ha., Marsannay.

As in many Marsannay cellars, there is some excellent Bourgogne *rouge* here, made from the Pinots on the slope.

CHARLES QUILLARDET 17 ha. (90 per cent)
Bourgogne Montre-Cul 2 ha., Gevrey-Chambertin 2 ha., Marsannay *rouge* and rosé 11 ha., Côte de Nuits Villages 2 ha.

Charles Quillardet and his friends Derey in Couchey cultivate Dijon's last vineyard—Le Montre-Cul—so-named because the steepness of the slope affords unusual perspectives to those working below. They used a bulldozer to make the terraces and, because of their awkward width, adopted an unusual form of Lenz-Moser pruning. To reach this vineyard one has to pass beside the apartments and office blocks of the Dijon suburb of Chenôve which, with a population of 40,000, is the Côte d'Or's second largest town. The bronzed and earth-stained Quillardet says he feels 'some sort of fossil' in these surroundings, though once arrived in his vineyards the view over Dijon is superb.

He has tripled the size of his domaine in twenty years.

There are six other growers who offer wine in bottle from Marsannay-la-Côte.

Main Growers (21160 Couchey)

LOUIS BROCARD 4 ha. (60 per cent)
Fixin 1 ha.

All M. Brocard's sons-in-law work in the town, so the little domaine and local clientele he has built up are not destined to last for long.

CLÉMANCEY FRÈRES   5 ha. (10 per cent)
Fixin Les Hervelets 1⅘ ha.

From outside, the Clémanceys' house looks brand new. But inside is an ancient oak-beamed front room with a wide open hearth, and an alcove for the family bed beside it. The kitchen is situated in what used to be the bread-oven.

The Clémancey brothers say that they are strongly against over-sugaring their wines. They are farmers as well as *vignerons*.

DEREY FRÈRES   10 ha. (75 per cent)
Fixin Les Hervelets 1 ha., Gevrey-Chambertin 1 ha., Fixin, etc. Bourgogne Montre-Cul 1 ha.

The Derey brothers cultivate Montre-Cul, along with Quillardet of Marsannay.

The family bought its Hervelets from Noisot, the Napoleonic grenadier who set up the well-known monument to the Emperor above Fixin.

MARCEL SIRUGUE   2½ ha. (50 per cent)
Côte de Nuits Villages.

M. Sirugue has more cornfields than vineyards.

FIXIN

Fixin is the first village AC south of Dijon, and the beginning of the Côte de Nuits proper. Its annual harvest averages 1,300 hectolitres (or 14,300 dozen bottles), from an area under vines of 128 hectares. Its wines have neither the power of Gevrey nor the finesse of Vosne, but they are well-balanced when not over-chaptalized.

It was named Fiscinus in 830, Fiscentiae in 995. Its best-known vineyard has always been the Clos de La Perrière, and the Marquis Loppin de Montmort used to sell this at the same price as Chambertin. The vineyard is named after a once-famous quarry, and is attached to a manor house which belonged to the Abbey of Cîteaux. Next door is the Clos du Chapitre, giving in theory the second wine of the village. Also well-known is the Clos Napoléon, previously Aux Cheusots or Les Echézeaux, which borders Fixin's melancholy curiosity, the Parc Noisot. Claude-Charles Noisot was a *commandant aux grenadiers* in Napoleon's Guard who commissioned the Dijon sculptor Rude to erect a memorial to the Emperor. Bonaparte is cast in bronze, at the moment when he 'awakens to immortality' on a rock in Saint-Helena. Noisot's last wish was to be buried in the park, upright, with his sabre raised, mounting a deathly guard on his Emperor.

I think that Fixin is unlucky at the moment in its big land-owners. P. Joliet and P. Gelin's wines should be good, but I have rarely heard of anyone drinking a great bottle or come across one myself. The problem seems to be lack of technical expertise.

The following vineyards are classified as *Premier Crus*: Les Meix Bas (part), Clos du Chapitre (part), Aux Cheusots (part), La Perrière (part), Les Arvelets (part), Les Hervelets (part).

Main Growers (21710 Fixin)

GUY BERTHEAUT   7 ha. (30 per cent)
Fixin Les Arvelets $\frac{2}{3}$ ha., Crais 1$\frac{1}{2}$ ha., Gevrey-Chambertin 1 ha.

Savigny is not the only village of the Côte with wall-inscriptions. Over M. Bertheaut's garden gate is written '*Prend garde a toy maro* 1693' (*maro = maraudeur*). Elsewhere can be seen: '*Bien faire vax mieu que dire*' and '*Tout par amour et rien par forse*'.

ERNEST BOURGEOT   4 ha. (25 per cent)
Gevrey-Chambertin, Chambolle-Musigny, Fixin.

SOCIÉTÉ CIVILE DU CLOS SAINT-LOUIS   6 ha. (30 per cent)
Fixin Les Hervelets $\frac{1}{8}$ ha., Gevrey-Chambertin $\frac{1}{8}$ ha.

CAMILLE CRUSSEREY
Fixin Les Hervelets 1 ha., Clos du Meix Trouhans Monopole 2 ha.

M. Crusserey's son studied Beaux Arts, and has designed some unusual labels for him.

RENÉ DEFRANCE   4 ha. (25 per cent)
Fixin 4 ha.

DOMAINE PIERRE GELIN   16 ha. (80 per cent)
Chambertin Clos de Bèze $\frac{2}{3}$ ha., Mazis-Chambertin $\frac{1}{3}$ ha., Fixin Clos Napoléon Monopole 1$\frac{4}{5}$ ha., Fixin Clos du Chapitre Monopole 4$\frac{3}{4}$ ha., Fixin Les Hervelets $\frac{1}{2}$ ha.

This is the largest domaine in Fixin. M. Molin has a fine

182

ensemble, both *Monopoles* Clos having their own *cuveries* within their walls. The village church stands below them, the twelfth-century manor of La Perrière above, and in between his rolling hillside of vines.

When last I visited it, the youngest vines in the Clos du Chapitre dated from 1948.

DOMAINE DE LA PERRIÈRE   5 ha. (35 per cent)
Fixin Clos de la Perrière Monopole 5 ha.

This vineyard has one of the oldest reputations in Burgundy, but I remember being greatly depressed by my first tasting of Philippe Joliet's wine. It has been distributed by a variety of shippers: Moillard, Reine Pédauque, in 1978 Dufouleur Père et Fils.

Six other growers are listed as bottlers in Fixin.

BROCHON AND GEVREY-CHAMBERTIN

Danguy and Aubertin believe that it was probably a Roman colony which first reclaimed the Brochon hillsides from brambles to plant vines. Traces of their occupation in the form of coins, sculpted monuments and tombs have been found, as have remains of a Merovingian settlement in the form of large numbers of graves. The place was known as Bruciacus in the sixth century, Briscona villa in 878. Eleven of the southern *lieux-dits* of the commune of Brochon have right to the AC Gevrey-Chambertin, the remainder being Côte de Nuits Villages or Bourgogne.

Gevrey-Chambertin, situated 13 km south of Dijon, is the largest village *appellation* of the Côte de Nuits, covering nearly 500 hectares and producing on average 14,500 hectolitres (160,000 dozen bottles) of wine. Some of the longest-living village wines come from the hillside between Gevrey and Brochon, the reason being that *Grands Crus* and *Premier Crus* are so thick on the ground to the south of Gevrey that much of the commune wine comes from over the *Route Nationale* 74 down towards the railway.

The most important vineyard-owner in the history of Gevrey-Chambertin is the Abbey of Cluny. Its first acquisition was land which had been given to the Abbey of Sainte-Bénigne by Richard le Justicier, Duke of Burgundy, in 895; it purchased much more in

183

Brochon and Gevrey-Chambertin

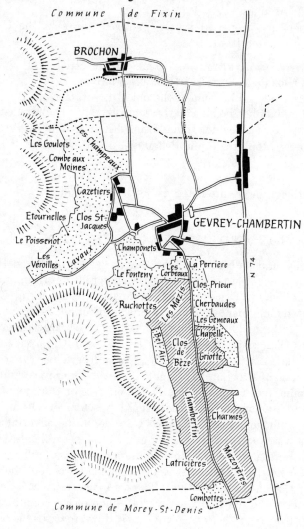

Commune de Fixin

BROCHON

Les Goulots
Combe aux Moines
Les Champeaux

Cazetiers

Etournelles
Clos St-Jacques
Le Poissenot
Les Véroilles
Lavaux

GEVREY-CHAMBERTIN

Champonets

Le Fonteny
Les Corbeaux
La Perrière

Clos-Prieur

Cherbaudes

Ruchottes
Les Mazis
Les Gemeaux

Chapelle

Bel-Air
Clos de Bèze
Griotte

Chambertin

Charmes

Mazoyères

Latricières

Combottes

N 74

Commune de Morey-St-Denis

1275 from another Burgundian Duke, Robert II. One of its abbots, Yves de Poissey, had begun the construction of the château on the rue Haute in 1257, and this, with its four strong towers, served as a refuge for the local population in times of invasion. Part of the château still stands and can be visited. There is still a family of *vignerons* in Brochon named Cluny—evidence, so the locals tell me, that the monks did more than bring protection and viticultural know-how to the village.

Gevrey-Chambertin is the birthplace of Gaston Roupnel, a professor at the Lycée de Dijon and historian of the French countryside. Between the two World Wars he wrote many purple passages on wine; here he is on Chambertin: 'It, on its own, is all that is possible in great Burgundy. Tough and powerful like the greatest of Cortons, it has the delicacy of Musigny, the velvet of Romanée, the perfume of a high Clos Vougeot. Its colour is that sombre scarlet which seems to emprison in its garnet reflections all the glory of a setting sun. Taste it: feel in the mouth that full and firm roundness, that substantial flame enveloped by the mat softness of velvet and the aroma of reseda! Chambertin, king of wines!'

No village in Burgundy has more *Grands Crus* than Gevrey, which added Chambertin to its name by *ordonnance* of Louis Philippe in 1847. Chambertin Clos de Bèze vineyards cover fifteen hectares and Chambertin thirteen hectares, making a total of twenty-eight hectares for the two top *Grands Crus*. Both wines are red, and the average harvest about 800 hl, or 9,000 dozen bottles. Chambertin Clos de Bèze may be called Chambertin on its own, but the opposite is not permitted. The Clos de Bèze was first planted after Duke Amalgaire had given a parcel of land to the Abbey of Bèze in A.D. 630. Tradition has it that a peasant named Bertin who owned the adjoining plot to the south decided to plant it with the same vines as the monks; its wine was perfect and soon the field (known in 1219 as Campus Bertini) became called the Champ de Bertin, then simply Chambertin.

The two vineyards (whose wines are said to taste the same) are divided between twenty-five owners. They have not always been as famous as they are today. Danguy and Aubertin record that their reputation was made in the eighteenth century, when the owner of the Clos supplied the Palatine court and Napoleon Bonaparte, the *queue* of Bèze-Chambertin being worth only 30 *livres* in 1651, but 700 or 800 *livres* by 1761.

The Dijon journalist Jean-François Bazin has shed light on Napoléon's liking for Chambertin, quoting from Frederic Masson (*Napoléon chez lui, La Journée de l'Empéreur aux Tuileries*). It would seem that the Emperor drank scarcely any wine except five- to six-year-old Chambertin, *much diluted with water* (*très trempé d'eau*). There was no cellar at the Tuileries nor any of the palaces. The wine cost six francs a bottle, and was supplied on a sale-or-return basis by the firm of Soupé et Pierrugues, 338 rue Saint-Honoré, in uniform bottles marked with a crowned N, manufactured at Sèvres. Either Soupé or Pierrugues accompanied the imperial headquarters on campaign, Bonaparte declaring that he had never been deprived of his wine 'even in the middle of the sands of Egypt'. J.-F. Bazin wonders whether it was really Chambertin, or rather wine coming from the village of Gevrey ... I would wonder further, for more than once have I added water to something masquerading as a *Grand Cru* of the Côte de Nuits to break it down from over 14° to a reasonable alcoholic strength. Perhaps Bonaparte had similar dislikes!

The other *Grands Crus* of the village are: Charmes-Chambertin (31·61 ha. Average harvest 870 hl, or 9,500 dozen bottles); Chapelle-Chambertin (5·39 ha. Average harvest 160 hl, or 1,760 dozen bottles); Griotte-Chambertin (5·48 ha. Average harvest 70 hl, or 770 dozen bottles); Latricières-Chambertin (6·94 ha. Average harvest 200 hl, or 2,200 dozen bottles); and Mazis-Chambertin (12·59 ha. Average harvest 280 hl, or 3,080 dozen bottles). Mazoyères-Chambertin is occasionally found, but the vineyard has been merged with the more easily-pronounceable Charmes-Chambertin.

The following are currently classed as *Premiers Crus*: Les Véroilles, Village Saint-Jacques known as 'Le Clos Saint-Jacques', Aux Combottes, Bel-Air, Cazetiers, Combe aux Moines, Etournelles, Lavaux, Poissenot, Les Champeaux, Les Goulots, Issarts, Les Corbeaux, Les Gemeaux, Cherbaudes, La Perrière, Clos-Prieur (top only), Clos du Fonteny, Champonets, Au Closeau, Craipillot, Champitonnois known as 'Petite-Chapelle', Ergots, Clos du Chapitre (part).

If one excludes the *Grands Crus*, the commune of Gevrey-Chambertin, including its First Growths, has about 430 ha. of vineyard, producing on average 12,000 hl or 132,000 dozen bottles of red wines.

Main Growers and Merchants (21220 Gevrey-Chambertin)

PIERRE BOURÉE FILS   (1864) 3 ha.
Charmes-Chambertin $\frac{3}{4}$ ha., Gevrey-Chambertin Clos de la Justice Monopole 2 ha.
   The Clos de la Justice is on the plain side of the Dijon–Chagny road.

CAMUS PÈRE ET FILS   17 ha. (100 per cent)
Chambertin $1\frac{3}{4}$ ha., Latricières-Chambertin $1\frac{1}{2}$ ha., Charmes-Chambertin 3 ha., Mazoyères-Chambertin 4 ha., Mazis-Chambertin $\frac{1}{3}$ ha.
   M. Camus says he is the only proprietor not to take advantage of the law which allows Mazoyères-Chambertin to be sold as Charmes-Chambertin. He is as well qualified as anybody to comment on the different characteristics of four of the Chambertin satellites and says that Mazoyères is the lightest, Mazis and Charmes the finest, and Latricières the closest to the real thing. He is the largest proprietor in Charmes.

DOMAINE PIERRE DAMOY   9 ha. (80 per cent)
Chambertin Clos de Bèze 5 ha., Chambertin $\frac{1}{2}$ ha., Chapelle-Chambertin $2\frac{1}{4}$ ha., Gevrey-Chambertin Clos Tamisot $1\frac{1}{2}$ ha.
   Damoy has the largest area of Clos de Bèze and Chambertin. At one time the same family also owned the Château du Moulin à Vent in the Beaujolais, and Château La Tour de By in the Médoc. A member of the Meurgey family has been *régisseur* of this estate from 1929 to 1982—which is the last vintage for which broker Henri Meurgey was responsible.

DOMAINE DROUHIN-LAROZE   15 ha. (100 per cent)
Chambertin Clos de Bèze $1\frac{1}{2}$ ha., Clos de Vougeot (top) $1\frac{1}{2}$ ha., Bonnes Mares 2 ha., Latricières-Chambertin $\frac{3}{4}$ ha., Chapelle-Chambertin $\frac{1}{2}$ ha., Mazis-Chambertin $\frac{1}{4}$ ha., Gevrey-Chambertin *Premier Cru* 2 ha., Chambolle-Musigny, Morey-Saint-Denis.
   This estate is one of those most committed to must-heating as a remedy for the colour problem of off-years. The plant for raising the temperature of the must to 90°C, maintaining it there for 2–3

minutes, and then refrigerating it down to 15°C, was installed and first used in 1964. It was used to heat the whole harvest in 1965, 1967 and 1968; it lay idle in 1966 and 1969. Bernard Drouhin informed me in 1978 that the plant is now used every year. It has enabled the estate to bottle its wines regularly, though in the early days many of the treated wines were declassed and sold as Bourgogne.

When asked whether the treated wines had a tendency to resemble each other, M. Drouhin said that, if true, this was to be preferred to their resembling nothing on earth.

Grands Crus here are always aged in new barrels.

DUROCHÉ   7 ha. (50 per cent)
Chambertin Clos de Bèze $\frac{1}{3}$ ha., Charmes-Chambertin $\frac{1}{3}$ ha., Gevrey-Chambertin Lavaux Saint-Jacques 1 ha.

M. Duroché usually makes two *cuvées* of Gevrey Villages, since some of his vines, situated on the *coteau* between Gevrey and Brochon, are superior to the rest, which are in the valley.

E. GEANTET-PANSIOT   4 ha. (100 per cent)
Charmes-Chambertin $\frac{2}{5}$ ha., Gevrey-Chambertin *Premier Cru* Poissenot $\frac{1}{2}$ ha.

This estate started bottling in the late 1950s, when M. Geantet-Pansiot found it too much to let his carefully-made wines disappear year after year into the merchants' cellars, 'never to be seen again'. He looks for wines with plenty of perfume.

GEOFFROY PÈRE ET FILS   5 ha. (70 per cent)
Mazis-Chambertin $\frac{1}{10}$ ha., Gevrey-Chambertin Clos-Prieur 1 ha.

The tendency here is towards short vatting times, giving wines which come round fairly quickly.

NAIGEON-CHAUVEAU ET FILS   (1890)
This company distributes the wines of the Domaine des Varoilles, $9\frac{4}{5}$ ha., consisting of four Gevrey-Chambertin Monopoles: Clos des Varoilles 6 ha., La Romanée 1 ha., Clos du Meix des Ouches 1 ha., Clos du Couvent $\frac{1}{2}$ ha., also Charmes-Chambertin $\frac{2}{3}$ ha., and Gevrey-Chambertin Champonets $\frac{2}{3}$ ha.

It tends the vines of two other estates:

Domaine Pierre Naigeon   1 ha.
Bonnes Mares $\frac{1}{2}$ ha., Gevrey-Chambertin Clos-Prieur $\frac{1}{3}$ ha.

Domaine P. Misset
Clos de Vougeot 1 ha.

This La Romanée (there is a third in Chassagne-Montrachet) produced white wine until 1965, when it was replanted with Pinot Noir. It is situated above Les Varoilles which has also been extensively reconstituted.

In the late 1960s the Clos du Meix des Ouches was still in old vines.

Three generations of the same family have run this company.

FERNAND PERNOT   7 ha. (50 per cent)
MME VEUVE JOSEPH BEAUDOT
Griotte-Chambertin $\frac{1}{4}$ ha., Gevrey-Chambertin Clos Saint-Jacques $\frac{7}{8}$ ha., Combe aux Moines $\frac{1}{2}$ ha., Les Champeaux $\frac{1}{4}$ ha.

Père Pernot resembles an amiable old bear. He describes himself as 'taken between the two fires'—of the English saying they want tannic wines, and the French quick-drinkers, and he tries to steer a middle course. When comparing the wines of Chambolle and Gevrey, he has a nice phrase: at the age of 15 the Gevrey will be at its best, when the Chambolle already has *le chapeau sur l'oreille*. He tips his cap over his ear to illustrate. It is a euphemism for the wine being past the point of no return to the vinegar barrel.

Today the wine is made by the next generation.

G. POULLEAU-MUET   1$\frac{1}{2}$ ha. (100 per cent)
Gevrey-Chambertin $\frac{1}{2}$ ha., Côte de Nuits Villages.

M. Poulleau lives in Brochon; he is one of the most colourful *vignerons* on the Côte, with his own theories on every aspect of wine-making. Spraying of vines against mildew is only necessary because the soil is overworked; sulphur should be eliminated from vinifications; fining should only be done with powdered marine algae. . . . He has a faithful private clientele.

DOMAINE JOSEPH ROTY
Charmes-Chambertin, Mazis-Chambertin, Griotte-Chambertin, Gevrey-Chambertin Clos-Prieur, Les Fontenys.

This estate is the new star in the Gevrey firmament, having scooped all manner of prizes for its 1976 and 1977 vintages at the Paris and Mâcon fairs. The wines have been making their way quietly to Belgium and Luxembourg for years; it will be interesting to see if the quality can be maintained now that other countries are beating on M. Roty's door.

DOMAINE ROUSSEAU   13 ha.   (100 per cent)

DOMAINE ARMAND ROUSSEAU PÈRE ET FILS

Chambertin Clos de Bèze $\frac{3}{4}$ ha., Chambertin 1 ha., Gevrey-Chambertin Clos Saint-Jacques $3\frac{1}{4}$ ha., Clos de la Roche (in Morey-Saint-Denis) $1\frac{1}{2}$ ha.,   Charmes-Chambertin $\frac{1}{2}$ ha., Mazoyères-Chambertin $\frac{4}{5}$ ha., Mazis-Chambertin $\frac{1}{2}$ ha., Gevrey-Chambertin Cazetiers $\frac{3}{4}$ ha., Lavaux Saint-Jacques $\frac{3}{4}$ ha.

These wines are listed in order of quality, *Premier Cru* Clos Saint-Jacques being rated higher by Charles Rousseau than the three *Grands Crus*.

Monsieur Rousseau finds that high-temperature fermentations obtain more character than low. He favours bottling after 23 months rather than 18 so that any carbon dioxide left dissolved in the wine will have bubbled off during the summer.

His father Armand made the fame of this domaine, which has been bottling since 1926. Three-quarters of its turnover is on the export market, and in a good year it has no difficulty in finding customers.

Since my last visit he has acquired a Monopole: Ruchottes-Chambertin Clos des Ruchottes 1 ha.—I do not know where he places it in the quality hierarchy.

THOMAS-BASSOT

A family business, founded in 1850, now run by Jean-Michel Thomas. It is one of the smallest firms to employ an oenologist, and discusses its affairs with an openness rare among merchants.

The estate in Gevrey-Chambertin consists of $10\frac{3}{4}$ ha: Ruchottes-Chambertin $\frac{3}{4}$ ha., Griotte-Chambertin $1\frac{3}{4}$ ha., Mazis-Chambertin $3\frac{1}{6}$ ha., Gevrey-Chambertin *Premier Cru* $2\frac{4}{5}$ ha.

Of the three *Grands Crus*, M. Thomas describes the Mazis (coming from the Mazis-*haut* position which is better than Mazis-*bas*) as being closest in character to Chambertin; Griotte, from old vines, has a savage, individual flavour; Ruchottes is more supple and elegant.

DOMAINE G. TORTOCHOT $10\frac{1}{2}$ ha.   (40 per cent)

Chambertin $\frac{2}{5}$ ha., Charmes-Chambertin $\frac{2}{3}$ ha., Mazis-Chambertin $\frac{2}{5}$ ha., Clos de Vougeot $\frac{1}{4}$ ha. (bottom), Gevrey-Chambertin Lavaux Saint-Jacques $\frac{1}{3}$ ha., Les Champeaux $\frac{4}{5}$ ha.

This is the place to come if you want the local news, Gabriel Tortochot being affectionately known as the Gevrey Gazette. He is a leading light in the Côte d'Or Growers' Union, presides over numerous Committees and is a director of the *Institut National des Appellations d'Origine* (INAO)

DOMAINE LOUIS TRAPET PÈRE ET FILS   16$\frac{1}{2}$ ha. (95 per cent)
Chambertin 3$\frac{3}{4}$ ha., Chapelle-Chambertin 1$\frac{1}{10}$ ha., Latricières-Chambertin 1$\frac{1}{2}$ ha., Gevrey-Chambertin Petite-Chapelle 1 ha., Clos-Prieur $\frac{4}{5}$ ha.

Père Trapet is one of Gevrey's characters, and his wine provokes arguments. One man will tell you that his Chambertin is without equal, another that half his vines are selected high-yielders. The estate has been in the family for six generations and is now run by Jean Trapet *fils* and Jacques Rossignol, a son-in-law.

A further twenty-seven estate-bottling growers are listed for Gevrey-Chambertin, with eleven in Brochon.

MOREY-SAINT-DENIS

The first mention of Morey is in 1120, when the place was known as Mirriacum Villa. The Abbey of Cîteaux was given a part of the village by Savaric de Vergy that year, and in 1171 another religious foundation, the Abbey of Bussières, received a donation of Morey land from the High Constable of Burgundy, Guillaume de Marigny. There have been many proprietors, including the Abbey of Saint-Germain-des-Près in Paris.

The name never used to be well known. To some extent this was because the wines were sold as Gevrey-Chambertin or Chambolle-Musigny until the AC laws were introduced; also the village is a small one, and there is no single outstanding vineyard like Chambertin or Corton to make its reputation. But a generation of wine merchants and writers saying that this was the best-value village of the Côte de Nuits has had its effect, and by the 1976 vintage, Morey-Saint-Denis was fetching the same price as Vosne-Romanée. Saint-Denis was tacked on to Morey as recently as 1927, but it is by no means agreed that this is the finest vineyard

191

Morey-Saint-Denis and Chambolle-Musigny

Commune de Gevrey-Chambertin

Monts-Luisants

Aux Charmes

Clos de la Roche

Clos des Ormes

Les Genevrières

Les Froichots

Les Charrières

Les Chaffots

Les Façonnières

Clos St Denis

Les Fremières

Les Millandes

Maison Brûlée

La Riotte
Les Gruenchers

Les Bouchots

Clos Baulet

Clos des Lambrays

Clos Sorbés

Les Sorbés

MOREY-ST-DENIS

Clos de Tart

Clos de la Bussière

Les Sentiers

Les Baudes

Bonnes Mares

Les Lavrottes

Les Groseilles

Les Noirots

Aux Beaux Bruns

Les Fuées

Derrière la Grange

Les Gruenchers

Les Cras

Aux Combottes

Les Châtelots

CHAMBOLLE-MUSIGNY

Les Fousselottes

Les Charmes

Les Plantes

Les Borniques

Les Hauts Doix

Les Amoureuses

Les Musigny

Les Petits Musigny

La Combe d'Orveau

Commune de Vougeot

N 74

Les Mochamps

Les Chaffots

Meix Rentiers

Les Ruchots

Les Chenevery

of the commune. Of the wines in general, Pierre Bréjoux says that they have 'a more tender firmness than those of Gevrey'.

There are five *Grands Crus* on the commune:

1. Bonnes Mares (1·84 ha.). The majority of this vineyard is in Chambolle-Musigny, so I will say no more here than that anyone wishing to taste the Bonnes Mares from one commune against the other cannot do better than visit the Georges Roumier estate, where two separate *cuvées* are often made.

2. Clos Saint-Denis (6·56 ha. Average harvest 180 hl, or 2,000 dozen bottles). These vines originally belonged to the Collégiale of Saint-Denis de Vergy, founded in 1203.

3. Clos de Tart (7·22 ha. Average harvest 170 hl, or 1,870 dozen bottles). A parcel of land known as 'Climat de la Forge' was sold to the nuns of Notre Dame de Tart near Genlis in 1141. The vendor was the Maison-Dieu in Brochon, the acquisition being confirmed by Pope Lucius III in a Bull of 1184. The property was sold at the time of the Revolution to a M. Charles Dumagner of Nuits for 68,200 *livres* (charges in addition). It is one of the rare places in Burgundy where press-house, *cuverie* and cellar are all to be found within the Clos.

4. Clos de la Roche (15·34 ha. Average harvest 390 hl, or 4,300 dozen bottles). This vineyard has expanded over the years, for in Dr Lavalle's time (1855) it was less than a third its present size. In a similar way we shall find the name of La Tâche being used for a much larger area than it used to be.

5. Clos des Lambrays (9 ha.). While the vineyard is being reconstituted, its annual yield will be decided by a Morey-Saint-Denis commission. This vineyard was upgraded from First to Great Growth status in 1981.

The following are currently classed as First Growths: Les Ruchots, Les Sorbés, Clos Sorbés, Les Millandes, Clos des Ormes (part), Meix Rentiers, Monts-Luisants, Les Bouchots, Clos de la Bussière, Aux Charmes, Les Charrières, Côte-Rôtie, Calouères, Maison Brûlée, Les Chabiots, Les Mochamps, Les Froichots, Les Fremières, Les Genevrières, Les Chaffots, Les Chénevery (part), La Riotte, Clos-Baulet, Les Gruenchers, Les Façonnières.

First Growth and commune Morey-Saint-Denis cover 93 hectares, producing on average 36 hl (400 dozen bottles) of white wine, 2,070 hl (23,000 dozen bottles) of red.

Main Growers and Merchants (21740 Morey-Saint-Denis)

HÉRITIERS COSSON   9¾ ha. (60 per cent)
Clos des Lambrays Monopole 9 ha., Morey-Saint-Denis Clos des Sorbés ¾ ha.

The Clos des Lambrays was up for sale for at least a decade before its disposal in 1979 to a group of three buyers. The price used to be 18 million francs, but by 1978 it was down to 12 million—about £60,000 per acre for the 22 acres, excluding vathouse and cellars.

I understand the vineyard needs some replanting, for during her lifetime, Madame Cosson claimed to have the only ungrafted vines remaining in Burgundy.[1] Many of her vines were still connected by an underground root system dating from the days of planting *en foule* by *provignage* or *marcottage* (a shoot from an old vine would be taken below the surface to form its own root system). They had been pushed into rows in order to facilitate cultivation.

DOMAINE DUJAC   11 ha. (100 per cent)
Clos Saint-Denis 1½ ha., Clos de la Roche 1⅕ ha., Bonnes Mares ⅓ ha., Echézeaux ⅔ ha., Charmes-Chambertin ⅔ ha., Gevrey-Chambertin Combottes 1 ha., Morey-Saint-Denis *Premier Cru* ⅓ ha., Chambolle-Musigny *Premier Cru* ⅓ ha.

Jacques Seysses came to Burgundy in his late twenties from banking and publicity, making his first harvest at this estate in 1968. A labour-saving *cuverie* was constructed and the house, parts of which date back to 1640, restored. Most of the vines (once the Domaine Graillet) were comparatively high-yielding Pinots, so replanting was done with Pinots from Gouges in Nuits Saint-Georges, which yield very little. The estate now supplies fourteen out of France's seventeen *Guide Michelin* three-star restaurants.

Jacques Seysses believes in the use of organic manure, in slow fermentations (stalks included), and neither fining nor filtration. He normally harvests later than the average.

---

[1] There are others near Tonnerre (see page 171).

His was the Morey-Saint-Denis served to President Giscard d'Estaing at the meal prepared by Paul Bocuse when the latter was decorated with the Légion d'Honneur.

DOMAINE ROBERT GROFFIER   7 ha. (100 per cent)
Chambertin Clos de Bèze ⅖ ha., Bonnes Mares 1 ha., Chambolle-Musigny Les Amoureuses 1 ha.

Robert Groffier was bottling very little when we first met, for he had recently bought some vines, and needed to sell his wine immediately after the harvest. He had a contract with Piat in Mâcon, and specified in it that he wished to sell wine and cask together—this enabled him to lodge all his *Grands Crus* in new oak every year which added considerably to their quality. Now he bottles virtually everything, and the estate is still well spoken of.

G. LIGNIER ET FILS   15 ha. (25 per cent)
Clos de la Roche 2 ha., Clos Saint-Denis 2 ha. (a *cuvée* each of old and young wines), Morey-Saint-Denis Clos des Ormes 4½ ha.

M. Lignier says that he makes his wine with the French preference for early-maturers in mind.

HENRI MAUFFRÉ   6 ha. (10 per cent)
Clos de la Roche ½ ha., Charmes-Chambertin ½ ha., Morey-Saint-Denis Clos des Sorbés 1½ ha.

DOMAINE PONSOT   8 ha. (60 per cent)
Clos de la Roche 3½ ha., Latricières-Chambertin ⅓ ha., Morey-Saint-Denis Monts-Luisants *blanc* 1½ ha., Gevrey-Chambertin, Chambolle-Musigny.

Jean-Marie Ponsot calls himself a *viticulteur-éleveur*, which is an encouraging start. The tradition of careful wine-tending was begun by his father who was more interested in this aspect than in viticulture.

This is one of the few places to offer a white Morey; it is a heavy wine, made from the Pinot Blanc, for which a bouquet of eglantine is claimed. But the speciality is Clos de la Roche.

MAISON HENRY RÉMY
Maison Henry Rémy used to control the Domaine Louis Rémy (6 ha.).
Chambertin 1 ha., Latricières-Chambertin 1½ ha., Clos de la Roche 1½ ha., Chambolle-Musigny Les Fremières ¾ ha., Derrière la Grange ¾ ha.

The estate was down to three hectares in size in 1978 and not forthcoming over which vineyards have been disposed of, and which kept.

Thirteen more growers are listed as offering wine in bottle from Morey-Saint-Denis.

CHAMBOLLE-MUSIGNY

Known as Cambolla in 1110, also Campus Ebulliens (*Champ Bouillant* or boiling field), Chambolle seems to have taken its name from the turbulent flood-waters of the Grone stream which used to cause severe damage. Musigny was added around 1880.

'In the opinion of many persons,' writes Dr Lavalle, 'this commune produces the most delicate wines of the Côte de Nuits.' This is echoed by many writers, but no longer seems valid to me. Are there any delicate wines on the Côte de Nuits? Chaptalization has killed delicacy, at least for the time being, and Chambolle, which lacks the backbone of Nuits or the vinosity of Gevrey, suffers more than most villages from flabby, cotton-wool bottles of wine.

Dr Morelot attributed the finesse and lightness of the village's wines to plantations of Pinot Blanc amongst the Pinot Noir: 'When this variety does not exceed a twelfth or a tenth one can suggest with certainty that, pressed and fermented with the red *noirien*, the wine which is drawn off will always be sufficiently coloured, and much superior in finesse and good taste to that which is made only with black grapes. Several proprietors who are aiming more at quantity than quality are destroying the white grape as it yields less in the vat; but it is mistaken speculation, they lose more by it than they gain.'

There are two *Grand Crus* in the village:

1. Musigny (10·65 ha. Average harvest 10 hl or 110 dozen bottles of white wine, 280 hl or 3,080 dozen bottles of red). The Musigny vineyard is situated to the south of the village, near the Clos de Vougeot. The earliest record of it dates from 1110, when the Canon of Saint-Denis de Vergy, Pierre Cros, gave his field of Musigné to the monks of Cîteaux.

2. Bonnes Mares (13·70 ha. Average harvest, including the wine

produced in the commune of Morey-Saint-Denis, 430 hl or 4,730 dozen bottles of red wine). Bonnes Mares would seem to take its name from the verb *marer*, to work the vines, thus meaning well-tended vines.

The following are classified *Premiers Crus*: part of Bonnes Mares, Les Amoureuses, Les Charmes, Les Cras (part), Les Borniques, Les Baudes, Les Plantes, Les Hauts Doix, Les Châtelots, Les Gruenchers, Les Groseilles, Les Fuées, Les Lavrottes, Derrière la Grange, Les Noirots, Les Sentiers, Les Fousselottes, Aux Beaux-Bruns, Les Combottes, Aux Combottes.

First Growth and commune Chambolle-Musigny cover 173 hectares, producing an average harvest of 4,800 hl (52,800 dozen bottles) of red wine only.

Main Growers and Merchants (21770 Chambolle-Musigny)

VEUVE A. CLERGET   6 ha. (50 per cent)
MICHEL CLERGET
GEORGES CLERGET
Echézeaux $\frac{1}{4}$ ha., Chambolle-Musigny Les Charmes $\frac{2}{3}$ ha., Vosne-Romanée, Morey-Saint-Denis, Vougeot.

This estate believes in aging at least a few wines in new oak each year.

DOMAINE GRIVELET   5 ha. (100 per cent)
Chambolle-Musigny Les Amoureuses $\frac{1}{10}$ ha., Les Charmes $\frac{2}{3}$ ha., Aux Beaux-Bruns $\frac{1}{3}$ ha., Les Hauts Doix $\frac{1}{10}$ ha.

PAUL HUDELOT ET SES FILS   12 ha. (10 per cent)
Bonnes Mares $\frac{1}{8}$ ha., Chambolle-Musigny Les Charmes $2\frac{1}{4}$ ha.

ALAIN HUDELOT-NOËLLAT   10 ha. (60 per cent)
Richebourg $\frac{1}{4}$ ha., Romanée Saint-Vivant $\frac{1}{2}$ ha., Clos de Vougeot (top) $\frac{2}{5}$ ha., Vosne-Romanée Les Malconsorts $\frac{1}{4}$ ha., Les Suchots $\frac{2}{5}$ ha., Nuits Saint-Georges Les Murgers $\frac{3}{4}$ ha., Chambolle-Musigny.

For long Noël Hudelot's Clos de Vougeot (half of the vines in the plot dating from 1920) was reckoned to produce one of the best Clos de Vougeots of the year. The estate has more than doubled in size in a decade, acquiring Richebourg and Romanée Saint-Vivant as it grew, and Noël Hudelot has now handed over to his son.

DOMAINE GEORGES ROUMIER ET SES FILS   16 ha. (80 per cent)
Musigny $\frac{1}{10}$ ha., Bonnes Mares $2\frac{1}{4}$ ha., Clos de Vougeot 1 ha. (top
and bottom), Chambolle-Musigny Les Amoureuses 1 ha., Morey-
Saint-Denis Clos de la Bussière Monopole $2\frac{1}{2}$ ha.

There are two Roumier brothers: Alan who is *régisseur* of the
Domaine de Vogüé, and Jean-Marie who looks after the family
domaine. Their *Monopole* used to belong to the Abbey whose name
it bears in the Ouche valley behind the Côte. Like many of the
estates on the Côte de Nuits, they advocate heating a part of the
harvest, say a third, in a poor year to get back some of the colour
which the rot has destroyed.

DOMAINE COMTE GEORGES DE VOGÜÉ $12\frac{1}{4}$ ha. (75 per cent)
Musigny (*rouge*) $6\frac{3}{4}$ ha., Bonnes Mares $2\frac{2}{3}$ ha., Chambolle-
Musigny Les Amoureuses $\frac{1}{2}$ ha., Musigny *blanc* $\frac{1}{2}$ ha.

When I visited the estate, three hectares of Musigny were
planted in vines which were forty or more years old, producing a
'*Cuvée Vieilles Vignes*'. Another $\frac{1}{2}$ ha. produces Musigny *blanc*.
This is the only white wine of Chambolle-Musigny, and is always
bottled at the domaine.

The *régisseur*, Alain Roumier, is not impressed by most of the
older generation's efforts at wine-making. 'Do you see these must-
coolers?' he quotes them, 'I leave them turned on right through
the vinification. Just to make sure.' Which would certainly not be
a very scientific way to proceed. But excessive chaptalization, of
which this estate is sometimes guilty, is also to be abhorred.

A further fourteen estate-bottling growers in Chambolle-Musigny
are listed.

VOUGEOT

This village used to be known for the quality of the wines produced
in the *Grand Cru* Clos de Vougeot; now, however, its principal
renown is due to the *Confrérie des Chevaliers du Tastevin* which
holds banquets and tastings (the latter were referred to on page
149) in the Château du Clos de Vougeot.

The *Confrérie* has been spectacularly successful in publicizing
the wines of Burgundy. It was founded in 1934, when cellars were
full and buyers scarce, and one of the proprietors of Richebourg

Vougeot and Vosne-Romanée

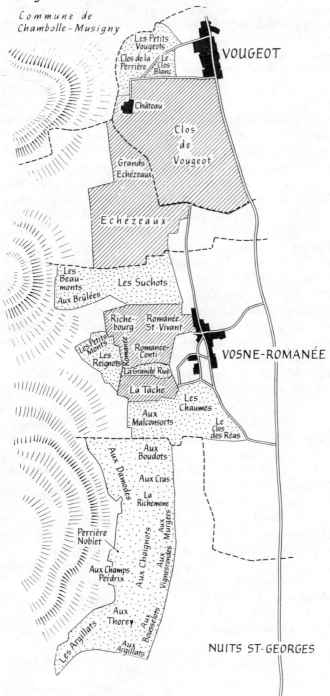

Commune de Chambolle-Musigny

Les Petits Vougeots

VOUGEOT

Clos de la Perrière

Le Clos Blanc

Château

Clos de Vougeot

Grands Echézeaux

Echézeaux

Les Beaumonts

Les Suchots

Aux Brûlées

Richebourg

Romanée St-Vivant

Les Petits Monts

Romanée

Romanée-Conti

VOSNE-ROMANÉE

Les Reignots

La Grande Rue

La Tâche

Les Chaumes

Aux Malconsorts

Le Clos des Réas

Aux Boudots

Aux Damodes

Aux Cras

La Richemone

Aux Chaignots

Aux Murgers

Perrière Noblet

Aux Champs Perdrix

Aux Vignesrondes

Aux Thorey

Aux Bousselots

Les Argillats

Aux Argillats

NUITS ST-GEORGES

was sending his wine to a Lyons café for sale by the carafe. Since no-one wants our wines, let us invite our friends and drink together, ran the idea, and soon it became apparent that people would pay a great deal to have dinner at the Clos de Vougeot. In 1978 a meal cost F.250 per head, and if you wanted to be enrolled as a member of the vinous brotherhood you could rapidly be relieved of a further sum. For this you would receive a colourful Certificate and a tasting-cup. Groups organize themselves eighteen months in advance to hire a Boeing and fly from Bermuda or Australia with the sole object of attending a banquet for 500 people, being enrolled, having a sing-song, and then flying back. Perhaps it is seen as a short-cut to being considered a wine expert. Certainly the idea is widely held that membership of the order is some sort of qualification. Here is the blurb to the magnificent book *Mastering the Art of French Cooking*, by Simone Beck, Louisette Bertholle and Julia Child (Penguin Books, reprinted 1972): 'In 1951 the authors, who have each studied under a number of distinguished French chefs, started a cooking school in Paris, *L'École des Trois Gourmands*, which has since become famous. All three are *Chevaliers de la Confrérie du Tastevin*.' It appears to be the final accolade. I am not wishing to stop people enjoying a dinner at the Clos de Vougeot, having enjoyed one there myself. But I wonder if some wine-lovers have not allowed themselves to become dazzled by Burgundian brilliance in the field of public relations.

Let us return to the wine. The *Grand Cru* Clos de Vougeot occupies 50·15 ha—over four-fifths of the land under vines in the commune (average harvest 1,500 hl or 16,500 dozen bottles). This is the part of the Côte nearest to the monastery of Cîteaux, which is ten kilometres into the plain. From 1110 onwards the monks started to receive gifts of land, so Dr Lavalle tells us, their poverty, saintliness and the austerity of their rule contrasting keenly with the opulence of other abbeys. The vineyard was too far from the monastery to be cultivated by the monks themselves, so a *maître du cellier* was appointed. The young wine spent its first year next to the vat-house in the vines, then being moved to greater safety at a château in the village of Vougeot. By the fifteenth century the monks' vineyard had been enclosed within the great wall which can still be seen.

The Clos de Vougeot was confiscated for the nation in 1789, but was not split up for another hundred years. In 1860 the English tried to acquire it, offering two-and-a-half million francs, but their offer was disdainfully thrust aside, so Camille Rodier[1] tells us. It was sold in 1889 for 600,000 francs to six Burgundians, five of them wine-shippers, and two years later the six had become fifteen. By 1977 the Clos had been divided into 107 plots, shared between seventy-five owners, of whom details may be found below.

The Clos de Vougeot has the most varied subsoil of any *Grand Cru* in Burgundy. There are six types according to R. Gadille: Bathonian and Bajocian limestone, Bajocian, Aquitanian and Pliocene marls, and alluvial deposits. In 1832 A. Jullien[2] wrote: 'The vines placed in the upper section give a very fine and delicate wine; the low sections, above all those which border the main road, give something much inferior.' Today, more than one Burgundian has been heard to say that the low land, being somewhat imperfectly drained, would be more aptly used for beetroot cultivation. It is to be hoped that the map of the Clos to be found on pages 202–3 which shows the position of the various owners' plots listed below, will be of interest. If we exclude the Ministry of Roads and Bridges (which presumably acquired its corner for road widening), it will be noticed that twenty-three owners have plots which are less than a quarter of a hectare in size, liable to yield about three barrels of wine per year. Such a small quantity is difficult to vinify successfully. Some proprietors do so, and some families certainly vinify together, but more than one owner solves the problem by throwing the Clos de Vougeot grapes into a vat of something else. When the wine is drawn off it is given two names of origin.

A few blind-tastings of lower, middle and upper Clos de Vougeot against *Grands Crus* and *Premiers Crus* of Vosne and Chambolle would seem to be well overdue. It would certainly be welcome alternative publicity to the news of yet another dinner of the *Confrérie des Chevaliers du Tastevin*, concerning which, let us give Pierre-Marie Doutrelant[3] the last word: 'One laughs for an hour, smiles for the next, sweats for the last three. It's too much.'

The following are classified *Premiers Crus*: Le Clos Blanc, Les Petits Vougeots, Les Gras (part), Clos de la Perrière.

[1] *Le Clos de Vougeot*, L. Venot, Dijon, 1949.
[2] *Topographie de tous les vignobles connus*, de Lacroix et Baudry, Paris.
[3] *Les Bons Vins et les Autres*, Éditions du Seuil, Paris, 1976.

The Clos de Vougeot

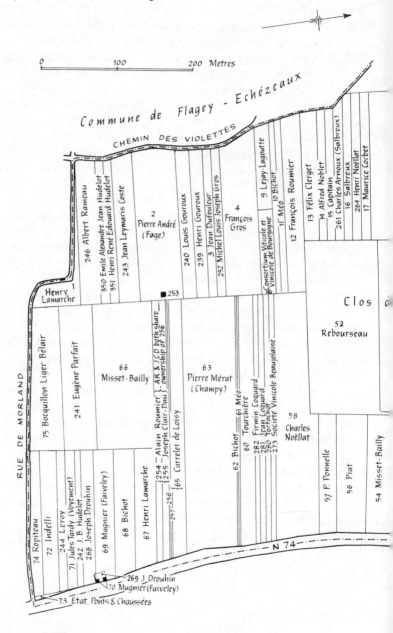

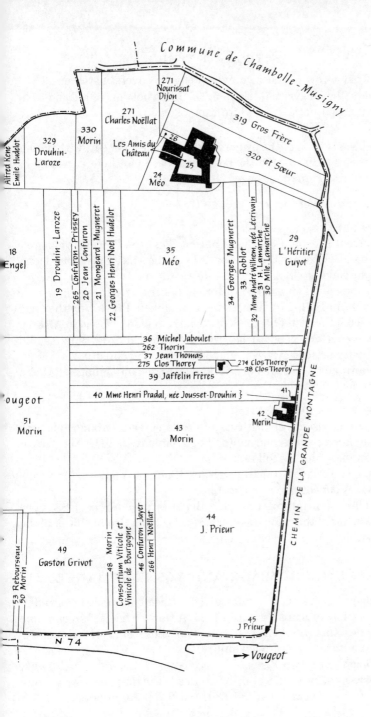

First Growth and commune Vougeot covers just over 12 ha., producing on average 450 hl (5,000 dozen bottles) of red and 55 hl (600 dozen bottles) of white wine per vintage.

Table 4 is a list of the owners in the Clos de Vougeot, with details of their holdings. (For the position of each plot, reference may be made to the map on pages 202–3.)

Main Growers in the village (21640)

ÉTS BERTAGNA   12 ha.
Vougeot *Premier Cru* 3 ha., Vougeot Clos de la Perrière Monopole $2\frac{2}{5}$ ha., Echézeaux $1\frac{1}{2}$ ha., Clos de la Roche $\frac{1}{2}$ ha., Clos Saint-Denis $\frac{1}{2}$ ha., Gevrey-Chambertin La Justice $1\frac{1}{2}$ ha.

Along with an estate in Morgon and Fleurie these vines were bought in 1961–2 by repatriated Frenchmen. Previously they had owned a thousand hectares or so in the region of Bone in Algeria. (It seems too good to be true that the Côte de Bone should actually exist in Algeria—but I have not invented it.)

Bertagna wines are not well known to me, but Julian Jeffs has a soft spot for them.

L'HÉRITIER GUYOT (1845)
A Dijon-based firm with its interests spread through liqueurs, fruit juices, wines and vines. The Domaine de l'Héritier Guyot comprises 5 ha. as follows:
Clos de Vougeot (top) 1 ha., Clos Blanc de Vougeot Monopole 3 ha., Vougeot *Premier Cru* 1 ha.

Three-quarters of the Clos Blanc is sold in the USA. The character of this wine was once described by a Grand Officer of the *Chevaliers du Tastevin* as being '*d'une rondeur carrée*'.

FLAGEY-ECHÉZEAUX AND VOSNE-ROMANÉE

Flagey-Echézeaux is a small village in the plain which belonged to the Abbey of Saint Vivant in 1188. A thin wedge of the commune divides the wines of Vougeot from those of Vosne-Romanée, whose *appellation* Flagey enjoys.

There are two *Grands Crus*: Grands Echézeaux (9·14 ha. Average harvest 270 hl or 3,000 dozen bottles); and Echézeaux (30·08 ha. Average harvest 880 hl or 9,700 dozen bottles).

TABLE 4. OWNERS IN THE CLOS DE VOUGEOT (April 1977)

Companies, etc.	Plot Number	Hectare (H)	Are (a)	Centiare (ca)
*The State (Ponts et Chaussées)	73		1	70
Consortium Viticole et Vinicole de Bourgogne, S.A., 13 rue de Tribourg, 21 Nuits Saint-Georges	8		18	80
	47		64	
		Total:	82	80
*Éts. Leroy 21 Auxey-Duresses	244		20	83
Éts. L'Héritier Guyot, S.A., 1 rue des Trois Ponts, 21 Dijon	29	1	05	20
Jaffelin Frères, Société en nom collectif 2, Bd. Clémenceau, 21 Beaune	39		62	70
Maison Albert Bichot, S.A., 6 bis Bd. Jacques Copeau, 21 Beaune	6			50
	10		17	70
	62		6	40
	68		38	42
		Total:	63	02
*Maison Lejay-Lagoutte, S.A., 19 rue Ledru-Rollin, 21 Dijon	9		18	80
Les Petits-Fils de Pierre Ponnelle, SARL, 2 rue Sylvestre-Chauvelot, 21 Beaune	57		34	28
S.C. Domaine Jacques Prieur 1 rue des Santenots, 21 Meursault	44	3	27	78
(Construction)	45			10
S.C. Domaine Joseph Drouhin 1 rue d'Enfer, 21 Beaune	268		28	89
	269			13
		Total:	29	02

205

TABLE 4—*cont.*

Companies, etc.	Plot Number	Hectare (H)	Are (a)	Centiare (ca)
S.C. Domaine Thorin				
Les Jacques,				
71 Romanèche-Thorins	262		31	00
*S.C. Domaine Ropiteau-Mignon				
13 rue du 11 novembre,				
21 Meursault	74		22	08
S.C.I. du Clos de Thorey				
Place Villeneuve,	274		7	56
21 Nuits Saint-Georges	275		21	15
		Total:	28	71
S.C.I. du Clos de Thorey				
Place Villeneuve,				
21 Nuits Saint-Georges				
(Construction)	38		8	00
S.C.I. Charles Noëllat	58	1	59	07
21 Vougeot	271	1	04	18
		Total: 2	63	25
S.C. Les Amis du Château du Clos de Vougeot				
au Château,	26		3	25
21 Vougeot (Construction)	25		58	90
S.C. Mongeard-Mugneret et Fils				
21 Vosne-Romanée	21		28	49
S.C. pour l'exploitation du				
Domaine Henri Rebourseau	52	2	10	00
21 Gevrey-Chambertin	53		10	96
		Total: 2	20	96
Société Piat et Cie, SARL				
21 rue de la République	56		61	30
71 Macon (Construction)	55			10
*Société Vinicole Beaujolaise, SARL				
Bd. Émile Guyot,				
69 Saint-Georges de Reneins	273		20	09
S.C. d'exploitation Drouhin-Laroze				
21 Gevrey-Chambertin	329		56	96

Individual Proprietors	Plot Number	Hectare (H)	Are (a)	Centiare (ca)
Pierre André (m. Fage)				
25 rue de l'Égalité,				
75019 Paris	2	1	09	72
(Construction)	253		0	08
Felix Bocquillon Liger Belair				
24 rue Crébillon,				
21 Nuits Saint-Georges	75		72	45
(Construction)	76		0	15
*Charles Arnoux (m. Salbreux)				
21 Vosne-Romanée	261		22	40
*Roger Capitain				
21 Serrigny	15		17	12
Mme Adonis Carrelet de Loisy				
(née Labouré)				
21 rue de Beaune,	65		59	82
21 Nuits Saint-Georges	257		4	88
		Total:	64	70
(Construction)	64			10
Joseph Clair-Daü				
21 Marsannay-la-Côte	255		29	68
	256		2	44
		Total:	32	12
Philibert Felix Clerget				
5, Pl. Marey,				
21 Beaune	13		34	24
*Christian Eugène Marie Confuron				
21 Prissey	265		17	12
Joseph Confuron (m. Jayer)				
21 Vosne-Romanée	46		25	39
Jules Paul known as Jean				
Confuron (succession)	20		34	24
*Firmin Coquard				
21 Morey-Saint-Denis	282		21	47
*Louis Coquard known as Jean				
21 Morey-Saint-Denis	281		21	40
*Maurice Corbet (m. Jayer)				
21 Morey-Saint-Denis	17		21	40
M. Alexandre Drouhin (m. Laroze)				
(succession)				
21 Gevrey-Chambertin	19		68	48

207

TABLE 4—*cont.*

Individual Proprietors	Plot Number	Hectare (H)	Are (a)	Centiare (ca)
*Jean Dufouleur				
Route de Dijon,				
21 Nuits Saint-Georges	3		20	85
René Engel				
21 Vosne-Romanée	18	1	36	96
Héritiers Henri Gouroux				
21 Flagey-Echézeaux	239		34	10
Louis Gouroux				
21 Flagey-Echézeaux	240		34	10
Gaston Grivot (m. Grivot)				
(succession)	49	1	86	75
Mlle Colette Marie-Thérèse Gros				
21 Vosne-Romanée	320		77	85
François Fernand Marie Gros				
21 Vosne-Romanée	4		93	00
(Construction)	5		0	20
Gustave René Gros				
21 Vosne-Romanée	319		77	85
*Michel Louis Joseph Gros				
21 Vosne-Romanée	252		20	85
Georges Henri Noël Hudelot				
(m. Mongeard)	22		42	80
*Jean-Baptiste Hudelot				
(succession)	242		14	22
Alfred René Émile Hudelot	23		35	16
*Émile Alexandre Jean Hudelot	350		20	15
*Henri René Edouard Hudelot	351		20	15
Paul Indelli				
99 rue de Courcelles,				
75 Paris	72		42	51
Michel Ulysse Henri Marie Jaboulet				
Château de la Commaraine,				
21 Pommard	36		31	00
Henri Emmanuel Constant Lamarche,				
21 Vosne-Romanée	1		22	75
	31		17	53
	67		42	25
		Total:	82	53

Individual Proprietors	Plot Number	Hectare (H)	Are (a)	Centiare (ca)
*Mlle Geneviève Henriette Marie Lamarche,				
21 Vosne-Romanée	30		19	12
Jean Leymaris Coste	243		52	60
Jean Alfred Émile Edouard Méo				
9 Villa Saïd,				
75016 Paris	7		0	70
	11		18	95
	24		24	25
	35	2	53	99
	61		5	54
	Total:	3	03	43
Pierre Mérat (Champy)				
21 rue Eugène Spüller,				
21 Beaune	63	2	25	66
Paul Missey-Bailly				
23 rue Vannerie,				
21 Dijon	54		60	40
	66	1	45	86
	Total:	2	06	26
Héritiers Jean-François Antonin Morin				
21 Nuits Saint-Georges	43	2	55	47
Mesdames J. Labet et N. Déchelette	48		12	00
	50		10	11
	51	2	10	85
	330		51	11
	Total:	5	39	54
(Construction)	42		8	50
Georges Mugneret				
21 Vosne-Romanée	34		34	24
Veuve Etienne Mugnier et Jacques Mugnier				
6 rue du Colonel de Grancey,	69		43	89
21 Dijon (managed by Faiveley)				
(Construction)	70		1	34
*Alfred Noblet				
21 Vosne-Romanée	14		17	12
Henri Noëllat (m. Jayer)	264		21	40
21 Vosne-Romanée	266		25	39
	Total:		46	79

TABLE 4—*cont.*

	Plot Number	Hectare (H)	Are (a)	Centiare (ca)
*Jean Nourrissat, Notaire 25 rue Buffon, 21 Dijon	272		16	09
Eugène Parfait 21 Chambolle-Musigny	241		83	53
Mme Henri Pradal (née Jousset- Drouhin) and co-proprietors 28 rue Chardon-Lagache, 75016 Paris	40		62	00
(Construction)	41			10
Albert Rameau 21 Morey-Saint-Denis	246		49	75
Raymond Roblot 21 Vosne-Romanée	33		34	24
Alain Roumier 21 Chambolle-Musigny	254		29	67
	256		2	44
	Total:		32	11
François Roumier 21 Chambolle-Musigny	12		53	31
*Mlle Marie Josephine Salbreux 2 rue de l'Hôpital, 21 Dijon	16		22	40
*Jules Tardy (m. Voyement) 21 Fontaine-Française	71		23	30
Jean Thomas 1 Pl. d'Argentine 21 Nuits Saint-Georges	37		31	29
*Veuve Adonis Tortochot 21 Gevrey-Chambertin	280		21	33
Mme Robert Tourchière 25 rue Eugène-Spüller, 21 Beaune	60		64	20
*Mme André Wilhem (née Suzanne Lécrivain)	32		17	54
Area within the Clos, as listed above:		50	92	61
Less plots with buildings:			77	57
Area available for vines:		50	15	04

Who dares criticize the wines of Vosne? The Abbé Courtépée, in the late eighteenth century, declared that there were no common wines in the village. Since then, apparently, no writer has contradicted him. But now it is a ridiculous statement. Fine wines are not made automatically, or by right or accident. And today there is more than one grower in Vosne-Romanée known to have planted curious Pinots, and several who have a heavy hand with the sugar-bags.

There are five *Grands Crus* in the village, some of the most famous and expensive wines in the world. In alphabetical order they are: La Tâche (6·01 ha. Average harvest 179 hl or 1,970 dozen bottles); Richebourg (7·99 ha. Average harvest 238 hl or 2,600 dozen bottles); Romanée (0·83 ha. Average harvest 30 hl or 330 dozen bottles); Romanée-Conti (1·80 ha. Average harvest 58 hl or 640 dozen bottles); and Romanée Saint-Vivant (9·14 ha. Average harvest 230 hl or 2,530 dozen bottles).

For centuries Romanée-Conti has been judged the finest. At the Revolution a document declared that its wine was the most excellent of all the vineyards of the Côte d'Or, indeed of all the vineyards of the French Republic, and could give life back to the dying. Today one has the impression that those who taste it regularly, and compare it with its peers, are not so starry-eyed.

Comparative blind-tastings of these *Grands Crus* of Vosne-Romanée and Flagey-Echézeaux, from different growers and merchants, are too rarely organized. The Burgundians lean happily on the descriptions and classifications of past centuries; customers are diverted by the expense of the bottles, and the difficulty of assembling them.

The following are classified as *Premiers Crus*: Aux Malconsorts, Les Beaumonts, Les Suchots, La Grande Rue, Les Gaudichots, Aux Brûlées, Les Chaumes, Les Reignots, Le Clos des Réas, Les Petits Monts.

First Growth and commune Vosne-Romanée covers 240 ha., producing an average harvest of 5,400 hl (60,000 dozen bottles) of red wine.

Notes to Table 4
1. There is a total of 107 plots, of which 11 have buildings on them.
2. 75 owners are listed, 23 of which (marked *) have plots of less than a quarter of a hectare. The produce of such plots is not always vinified separately (see page 156).

Main Merchants and Growers (21670 Vosne-Romanée)

J. CONFURON-JAYER   3 ha. (100 per cent)

Clos de Vougeot $\frac{1}{4}$ ha. (bottom), Vosne-Romanée Les Suchots $1\frac{1}{2}$ ha.

DOMAINE RENÉ ENGEL   7 ha. (65 per cent)

Clos de Vougeot $1\frac{1}{3}$ ha., Grands Echézeaux $\frac{1}{2}$ ha., Echézeaux $\frac{1}{2}$ ha., Vosne-Romanée Les Brûlées $2\frac{1}{2}$ ha.

M. René Engel was for fifteen years Professor of Oenology at the Dijon Faculté des Sciences. He is one of the most distinguished and gallant of the Clos de Vougeot after-dinner speakers.

The vines were managed by his son, Pierre, who divided his time between them and many other activities, among them flying, until his untimely death. Pierre's widow and son now look after the estate.

JEAN GRIVOT   12 ha. (60 per cent)

VEUVE GASTON GRIVOT

LOUIS JAYER PASQUIER

Clos de Vougeot (bottom) $1\frac{4}{5}$ ha., Echézeaux $\frac{1}{2}$ ha., Vosne-Romanée Les Beaumonts $\frac{5}{6}$ ha., Les Suchots $\frac{1}{5}$ ha., *Premier Cru* $\frac{1}{3}$ ha., Nuits Saint-Georges aux Boudots $\frac{4}{5}$ ha., Chambolle-Musigny.

It is often said that roadside Clos de Vougeot is of *Premier Cru* rather than *Grand Cru* quality.[1] With his Echézeaux, Beaumonts, Suchots and Boudots vines, M. Grivot is well-placed to comment, and he states that his Clos de Vougeot turns out superior every time, though it may require considerable bottle-age. He is one of Vosne's worthiest *vignerons*, so it really need not be thought that his large holdings in the Clos de Vougeot might bias him in its favour. He ages his wines the first winter in glass-lined tanks, finding that this speeds malolactic fermentation. Then, of course, in wood.

DOMAINE GROS FRÈRE ET SOEUR   7 ha. (25 per cent)

Richebourg 1 ha., Clos de Vougeot $1\frac{1}{2}$ ha. (what used to be called Les Musigny du Clos de Vougeot), Vosne-Romanée.

The section of Clos de Vougeot belonging to M. Gustave Gros is

---

[1] The people who classify roadside Clos de Vougeot as fit only for growing turnips (*terrain de betteraves*) are usually those without vines within its walls.

as close to Musigny as one can get. He is a black-bearded, modest bachelor with a philosophic air. It is as if Cîteaux had sent back a lay brother to till its finest plot.

GROS PÈRE ET FILS

A company set up in 1963 with the idea of buying grapes and vinifying them properly, as well as replanting in the Hautes Côtes at Chevrey near Arcenant.

Under the same roof are the domaines:

JEAN GROS AND FRANÇOIS GROS   12 ha. (50 per cent)

This is half of what used to be the Domaine Gros-Renaudot, the other half being Gros Frère et Soeur.

Richebourg 1 ha., Clos de Vougeot 1 ha. (top), Vosne-Romanée Clos des Réas Monopole 2 ha., Chambolle-Musigny, Vosne-Romanée.

The Renaudots were *vignerons* as far back as 1500, though perhaps the most celebrated member of the family is Théophraste, known as the Father of French Journalism for his founding of the *Gazette de France* in 1631. The literary prize awarded each year at the same time as the Goncourt is named after him.

Jean Gros is a voluble advocate of his own methods of wine-making. He believes that the answer lies in putting three people into the vats each evening, naked, to achieve a total submerging of the 'hat' of grapes and an intimate mixing of must and skins. At the beginning the 'hat' is so solid it can be danced on. Later the progress of fermentation can be checked by the ease with which the dancers sink into it.

The aim is to produce wines of sufficient delicacy to enable one to drink a whole bottle and wake up the following morning with a *'bouche d'enfant'*.

DOMAINE HENRY LAMARCHE   13 ha. (75 per cent)

Grands Echézeaux $\frac{1}{2}$ ha., Echézeaux $\frac{1}{2}$ ha., Clos de Vougeot 1 ha. (bottom, middle and top), Vosne-Romanée La Grande Rue Monopole 1$\frac{1}{2}$ ha., Aux Malconsorts 1 ha., Les Suchots $\frac{3}{4}$ ha., Pommard Les Epenots 1$\frac{1}{2}$ ha., Pommard 3 ha.

M. Lamarche's *Premier Cru Monopole* is surrounded by the following *Grands Crus*: La Tâche, La Romanée, Romanée-Conti, and Romanée Saint-Vivant. From this *climat* he recently pulled up vines which dated back to 1896.

ABBÉ LIGER-BELAIR   1½ ha. (100 per cent)
CHATEAU DE VOSNE-ROMANÉE

La Romanée Monopole ⅘ ha., Vosne-Romanée Les Reignots ⅔ ha.

La Romanée has been in the Abbé Liger-Belair's family for three and a half centuries. His wines are distributed by Bouchard Père et Fils.

A story is often told in Beaune of a *curé* who refused to celebrate Mass with anything less than a Meursault Perrières, saying: 'At communion, I do not care to make grimaces at my God.' I felt that the Abbé might provide a modern sequel, and am delighted to record that, on very special occasions (such as when asked by the *Confrérie des Chevaliers du Tastevin* to preach in Vosne-Romanée on the thirtieth anniversary of the Saint Vincent Tournante) he celebrates Mass with la Romanée.

JEAN MÉO   11 ha. (10 per cent)
Clos de Vougeot 3 ha. (top), Richebourg ⅓ ha., Vosne-Romanée Les Chaumes 2 ha., Nuits Saint-Georges Aux Boudots 1½ ha., Aux Murgers ⅔ ha.

M. Méo was President Director General of Elf petrol, and a technical adviser to General de Gaulle. Indeed, it is said that the General consoled himself with a bottle of Méo's Clos de Vougeot the day after his last referendum.

The vines are worked by one Louis Faurois, his two sons and a nephew. M. Faurois knows the Clos de Vougeot like the back of his hand, having lived in the Château (where his sons were born) for twenty-seven years. Half the vines in Méo's plot were planted by Faurois in 1920. There is an unusual 'accord' between owner and *vigneron*, for rather than dividing the grapes, they vinify together before splitting the harvest.

MONGEARD-MUGNERET   15 ha. (100 per cent)
Clos de Vougeot ⅔ ha., Grands Echézeaux 1 ha., Echézeaux 3 ha., Vosne-Romanée Les Suchots ½ ha., Nuits Saint-Georges Aux Boudots ½ ha., Vougeot Premier Cru 1 ha.

There is a proverb in French: Marry off your daughter, you're doing well; don't marry her off, you're doing better. Jean Mongeard adapts: De-stalk your grapes, you're doing well; leave the stalks in, you're doing better. He favours long vatting-times of eighteen to twenty days, at least two years in wood, and uses new casks for the *Grands Crus* when he can. Which all results in long-lasting and famous wines.

He is also experimenting with sowing grass between the rows—henceforth vineyards may have to be judged not by how well the garden is dug, but how skilfully the lawn is mown.

RENÉ MUGNERET $4\frac{1}{2}$ ha. (75 per cent)

Echézeaux $\frac{2}{3}$ ha., Vosne-Romanée Les Suchots $\frac{1}{3}$ ha., Nuits Saint-Georges Aux Boudots $\frac{1}{2}$ ha.

'Sometimes I taste my wines and I find them bitter, not good. And then other times I find them stunning. It depends on one's mouth—the palate changes.' René Mugneret refuses to filter his wines. His bottles are often capped with sealing wax.

A. MUGNERET-GIBOURG $6\frac{1}{3}$ ha. (100 per cent)

DR GEORGES MUGNERET

Clos de Vougeot $\frac{1}{3}$ ha. (top), Echézeaux $1\frac{1}{3}$ ha., Nuits Saint-Georges, Vosne-Romanée.

M. André Mugneret has now retired and handed over his vines to his son on half-fruit. His Clos de Vougeot touches the Château, whose floodlights stand between the rows. His Echézeaux in its turn touches the Clos de Vougeot wall. His vines have aged with him, and included some from 1923 when I visited him last.

CHARLES NOËLLAT   18 ha. (100 per cent)

Romanée Saint-Vivant nearly 2 ha., Richebourg 1 ha., Clos de Vougeot $2\frac{2}{3}$ ha. (top, middle and bottom unified), Vosne-Romanée Les Beaumonts $2\frac{1}{3}$ ha., Aux Malconsorts $\frac{1}{10}$ ha., Les Suchots $\frac{1}{2}$ ha., Nuits Saint-Georges Aux Boudots $1\frac{1}{2}$ ha., Aux Murgers $\frac{2}{3}$ ha.

This estate is a private company, with strong views on merchants. Its main-road advertisement announces '*Propriétaire non Négociant*', and its price-list adds: '*Mes vins sont garantis d'Origine absolue. Ni coupage, ni addition.*' Enormous sums have been spent here, on the advice of M. Léglise of the Beaune Station Oenologique, on modern equipment for heating and cooling the grapes. Local and brokers' comments on the results are not favourable, but the owner replies: 'One would no longer be French if one gave up criticizing.'

At one time he made a single *cuvée* of his top Clos de Vougeot, which is right above the Château, but he says his clients found that it lacked character.

HENRI NOËLLAT   10 ha. (25 per cent)

MICHEL NOËLLAT

Clos de Vougeot $\frac{1}{2}$ ha., Vosne-Romanée Les Suchots 1$\frac{1}{3}$ ha., Les Beaumonts 2 ha., Nuits Saint-Georges Aux Boudots $\frac{1}{2}$ ha., Chambolle-Musigny 2 ha.

In a good year Henri Noëllat makes two *cuvées* of his Clos de Vougeot, over half of which is in the top part and planted with vines dating back to 1925.

He is a charming man with a sparkling eye; his wines have a good reputation. He has now handed over the management of his domaine to his son Michel, who will be bottling more.

He says that quite often his Beaumonts or Suchots prove better than his Clos de Vougeot.

ALBERT NOIROT ET SES FILS   5 ha. (80 per cent)

MANIÈRE-NOIROT

Echézeaux $\frac{1}{4}$ ha., Vosne-Romanée Les Suchots 1$\frac{1}{2}$ ha., Nuits Saint-Georges Aux Boudots 1 ha.

Having run this domaine for twenty-five years, Madame Noirot has now handed over to her son-in-law, Marc Manière.

She recalls some original methods of treating wine: a fine cloth bag would be filled with vine-shoot cinders and lowered into a barrel to draw out impurities; or a piece of charcoal would be dropped in to improve the colour. The last time this happened was in 1944. You used cinders to clean saucepans and to whiten clothes (even if it did take three days' beating), so why not for wine too?

DOMAINE DE LA ROMANÉE-CONTI   25 ha. (100 per cent)

DOMAINE MAREY-MONGE

Romanée-Conti Monopole 1$\frac{4}{5}$ ha., La Tâche Monopole 6 ha., Richebourg 3$\frac{1}{2}$ ha., Romanée Saint-Vivant 5$\frac{1}{4}$ ha., Grands Echézeaux 3$\frac{1}{2}$ ha., Echézeaux 4$\frac{3}{5}$ ha.,. Montrachet $\frac{1}{2}$ ha.

The owner of the most famous *Grands Crus* on the Côte, a maker of deep-coloured, perfumed, long-lasting wines, one of the first and most consistent advocates of estate-bottling—for many people the Domaine de la Romanée-Conti is *the* domaine in Burgundy. In addition to its two famous *Monopoles* Romanée-Conti and La Tâche, it owns approximately half of Richebourg, over a third of Grands Echézeaux, and one-seventh of Echézeaux. The Domaine

Marey-Monge's Romanée Saint-Vivant, whose vines and wines it now tends, constitutes over half that *appellation*.

It is sometimes claimed that La Romanée and Romanée-Conti were once a single vineyard; however, research by the owners of the latter indicates the contrary.

The origins of the present Romanée-Conti are the five *journaux* of vines called in 1512 Le Cros (or Clos) des Cloux. They are not referred to as Romanée until 1651, Conti being tacked on after 1760 when the Prince de Conti bought them from the Croonemburgs. At this time a map was drawn which shows that the vineyard covered the identical area to that covered today, even to the dog-tooth edges at its south-west corner.

Uphill from this vineyard a certain plot belonging to the Oratoire de Dijon became known towards the end of the eighteenth century as '*au dessus de la Romanée*'. This, combined with adjoining plots, has become today's La Romanée.

Until the beginning of this century, La Tâche was a vineyard of merely $1\frac{3}{5}$ ha., and so it appears on the old maps. Today it includes most of Les Gaudichots, for in the early 1930s the Domaine de la Romanée-Conti was able to show that it had sold its Gaudichots as La Tâche for a long enough time to satisfy the makers of the AC laws that a 'local, loyal and constant' precedent had been set.

The Domaine is now jointly owned by the De Villaine and Leroy families, the latter being shippers in Auxey-Duresses. Cultivation of the vineyards is labour-intensive, along traditional lines. The bunches of grapes are sometimes thinned out if the harvest promises to be a large one. The wines are vatted a very long time on the skins, and in the cellar a filter is scarcely ever used. The domaine states: 'Nothing has changed in our methods of viticulture, wine-making or tending for very many years. It is team work, carried out every day for the best, taking into account the different conditions of each vintage.'

'The most celebrated and expensive red wine in the world, though seldom the best' is how Hugh Johnson has described Romanée-Conti.[1] If not, why not? It seems to me that the wines have sometimes been made with a heavy hand. Dr Lavalle wrote in 1855 on the Burgundian grape harvest as follows:

---

[1] Hugh Johnson, *Pocket Book of Wine*, Mitchell Beazley, 1977.

For the wines of Burgundy to be perfect, that is to say rich at the same time in colour, fire and bouquet, it is necessary that alcohol should only be present in a given proportion and that tartaric acid should exist in great quantity. For this to come about . . . it is important that the natural sugars should not be allowed to develop to excess by picking the grapes when they are exaggeratedly mature. . . . Did our ancestors not embody this idea in the old proverb '*Vin vert, riche Bourgogne*'?

Tartaric acid in great quantity is certainly not to be recommended in the Côte d'Or today, but Burgundies are cool-climate wines, and in the Domaine de la Romanée-Conti style I sometimes miss a refreshing finish on the palate. One really could not fault wonderful wines like La Tâche 1961 or La Tâche 1962—two of the greatest Burgundies I have ever drunk—or the outstanding Montrachets. But I have found many of the wines of the 1960s over-alcoholic, due either to late picking or to over-chaptalization.

From 1974 two new directors have been jointly responsible, with Chef de Caves André Noblet, for the wine-making: Madame Bize-Leroy and Aubert de Villaine. They ran into criticism (not exactly welcome) for releasing all their 1975s, when it was argued that the wines were likely to bring little credit to the famous names they bore. But it is difficult to assess their wines, particularly the lesser vintages, when young. The unfashionable years often prove agreeable surprises (though at a price, of course) when mature.

For decades this estate set the highest standards and has been Burgundy's flag-bearer. There is good reason to hope that the vintages of the late 1970s will mature into complex, finely balanced bottles, and that the estate will maintain its envied position as Burgundy's greatest domaine.

There are fourteen other estate-bottling growers listed for Vosne-Romanée.

Main Growers (Flagey-Echézeaux)

LOUIS GOUROUX $3\frac{1}{2}$ ha. (30 per cent)
Clos de Vougeot (top) $\frac{1}{3}$ ha., Grands Echézeaux $\frac{1}{2}$ ha., Echézeaux $1\frac{4}{5}$ ha.

COQUARD-LOISON 5 ha. (20 per cent)
Grands Echézeaux ⅕ ha., Clos de Vougeot ⅖ ha., Echézeaux 1 ha.,
Clos de la Roche ¼ ha., Gevrey-Chambertin, Vosne-Romanée.

NUITS SAINT-GEORGES

This is an important commercial centre for the area, grouping
shippers, brokers, liqueur-makers, fruit-juice factories, label-
printers, and sparkling-wine manufacturers. It used to have
strategic importance as a frontier-town on the French border with
Franche-Comté, but today there are few traces of its medieval
battlements, indeed few attractions for the tourist. If he is an
Englishman who stops to taste, on its home ground, a glass of the
wine whose name was until recently to be found on every wine-list
throughout the United Kingdom, he may be not a little confused.
For authentic Nuits Saint-Georges, if he finds it, is a far cry from
the easy-drinking velvety blend which used to be so widely
available; it is rough wine when young: austere, with a savage
individual perfume when coming from the best vineyards. He may
not like it.

Nuits stands on a stream, the Meuzin, which flows down from
two villages on the Hautes Côtes, Arcenant and L'Etang-Vergy.
In 1747 its flood-waters caused the death of five adults and seven
children. Over the years it has carried down alluvial deposits to
the detriment of the commune's low-lying vineyards, and those
along its banks.

Look for the rock, if you want to find texture in the wine. Some
of the best vineyards are in the adjoining commune of Prémeaux
(whose wines have right to the Nuits Saint-Georges *appellation*) in
a narrow strip between hill-top and valley.

The following are classified as *Premiers Crus*: from the com-
mune of Nuits: Les Saint-Georges, Les Vaucrains, Les Cailles, Les
Porets, Les Pruliers, Les Hauts-Pruliers (part), Aux Murgers, La
Richemone, Les Chaboeufs, La Perrière, La Roncière, Les Procès,
Rue de Chaux, Aux Boudots, Aux Cras, Aux Chaignots, Aux
Thorey (part), Aux Vignes-Rondes, Aux Bousselots, Les Poul-
ettes, Aux Crots (part), Les Vallerots (part), Aux Champs-
Perdrix (part), Perrière-Noblet (part), Aux Damodes (part), Les
Argillats (part), Chaines Carteaux (part), Aux Argillats (part).
From the commune of Prémeaux: Clos de la Maréchale, Clos

Nuits Saint-Georges and Prémeaux

NUITS ST-GEORGES

Rue de Chaux
Les Procès
Aux Crots
Les Pruliers
Les Hauts-Pruliers
La Roncière
Les Poulettes
La Perrière
Les Porets
Les Cailles
Les Chaboeufs
Les Vaucrains
Les Saint-Georges
Les Vallerots
Chaines Carteaux
Les Didiers
Le Clos des Forêts
Aux Perdrix
Clos des Corvées
Clos des Grandes Vignes
Les Corvées-Paget
PRÉMEAUX
Clos des Argillières
Le Clos Saint-Marc
Clos Arlots
Clos de la Maréchale

Commune de Prissey

Arlots, Clos des Argillières, Clos des Grandes Vignes, Clos des Corvées, Clos des Forêts, Les Didiers, Aux Perdrix, Les Corvées-Paget, Le Clos Saint-Marc.

The vineyard area covers a total of 375 ha., producing on average 8,900 hl (nearly 100,000 dozen bottles) of red wine, 30 hl (330 dozen bottles) of white.

Main Merchants and Growers (21700 Nuits Saint-Georges)

JEAN-CLAUDE BOISSET (1961)

This firm distributes the ten-hectare Gevrey-Chambertin estate of its founder, Jean-Claude Boisset. Its largest export market is the United Kingdom.

L. J. BRUCK (1807)

This firm was for a long time run by Mr Lionel Bruck, whose grandfather arrived in Burgundy in 1870, from the Liverpool cotton trade.

He owned the largest section (3½ ha.) of Corton Clos du Roi as well as some Nuits Saint-Georges Les Saint-Georges (¼ ha.).

Mr Bruck died recently and the company was taken over by Cruse et Fils Frères of Bordeaux.

F. CHAUVENET (1853)

A specialist merchant, one of the largest in Nuits, who does not attempt to combine care of vines with care of wine. Founded in 1853, Chauvenet exports two-thirds of its turnover. It is perhaps best known for White, Pink and Red Cap Sparkling Burgundy, which it does not make itself, but buys from different *mousseux* merchants in the area.

Colette once wrote a pleasant piece about the company, which is now owned by Margnat.

JEAN CHAUVENET 7 ha. (10 per cent)
CLAUDIUS CHAUVENET
Nuits Saint-Georges Les Vaucrains ½ ha., *Premier Cru* 1½ ha., Vosne-Romanée.

MAURICE CHEVILLON 13 ha. (20 per cent)
ROBERT CHEVILLON
Nuits Saint-Georges Aux Chaignots 3 ha., Les Cailles 2 ha., Les Saint-Georges ¾ ha., La Roncière 2 ha., Les Pruliers 1½ ha.

AUGUSTE CHICOTOT 3½ ha (75 per cent)
Nuits Saint-Georges Les Saints-Georges 1 ha., Les Vaucrains
¼ ha., Les Procès, Les Pruliers.

LUCIEN CHICOTOT 3½ ha. (35 per cent)
Nuits Saint-Georges Les Saint-Georges 1 ha., Les Vaucrains ¼ ha.

D. CHOPIN-GESSEAUME 5 ha. (100 per cent)
J. GESSEAUME
Nuits Saint-Georges Les Pruliers ½ ha., Les Cailles ¼ ha., Les
Chaignots ⅕ ha.

JH. FAIVELEY (1825) 112 ha.
This is one of the largest domaines in Burgundy, consisting of
42 ha. in the Côte d'Or and about 70 ha. in Mercurey. Chambertin
Clos de Bèze 1¼ ha., Latricières-Chambertin 1½ ha., Mazis-
Chambertin 1½ ha., Gevrey-Chambertin Combe aux Moines 1 ha.,
Premier Cru 3 ha., Musigny 1½ ha., Bonnes Mares ½ ha.,
Chambolle-Musigny Les Amoureuses ½ ha., *Premier Cru* 1½ ha.,
Echézeaux 1 ha., Clos de Vougeot 1½ ha. (⅔ bottom, ⅓ middle-top),
Nuits Saint-Georges Clos de la Maréchale Monopole 9½ ha., Les
Saint-Georges ½ ha., Les Porets 2 ha., *Premier Cru* 1½ ha., Corton
Clos-des-Cortons Faiveley Monopole 3 ha., Mercurey Clos des
Myglands Monopole 9 ha., Clos-du-Roi 3½ ha., Clos Rond Mon-
opole 5 ha., Les Mauvarennes Monopole 15 ha., Clos Rochette
blanc Monopole 2 ha., Clos Dardelin Monopole 2½ ha., La Fram-
boisière Monopole 6 ha.

With a domaine like this, it is not surprising that M. Guy
Faiveley has the air of a benign pixie, with a face which seems
specially built for smiling. His company exports to eighty
countries.

GEISWEILER ET FILS (1804)
After the First World War, this company looked around at the
Champagne, Cognac and Port trades and noted how much easier
it was to sell wine under the merchant's name than under a
multiplicity of vineyard names. For fifty years their main efforts
were directed towards building up brands called Geisweiler Grand
Vin and Réserve. They shipped their share of full-bodied, velvety
wines to England.

During the 1970s, they altered course and purchased twenty

hectares of land in the commune of Nuits Saint-Georges and seventy hectares in the Hautes Côtes de Nuits at Bévy. The latter is a brave experiment—it will be interesting to see how the wines taste alongside other Hautes Côtes de Nuits when the vineyards start bearing.

DOMAINE HENRI GOUGES   10 ha. (75 per cent)

Nuits Saint-Georges Les Saint-Georges 1 ha., Les Vaucrains 1 ha., Clos des Porets Saint-Georges Monopole 3½ ha., Les Pruliers 2½ ha., La Perrière ½ ha., Les Chaignots ⅓ ha.

With the Marquis d'Angerville from Volnay, Henri Gouges was at the forefront of the battles against fraud in Burgundy in the 1920s. He died in 1967. His two sons carry on the traditions of the estate (which has been bottling for fifty years) with reserve and modesty. Their vines are low-yielding Pinots.

Around 1934 Henri Gouges discovered a Pinot Noir bearing both red and white grapes. He thought it would be amusing to propagate it, so took cuttings of the white shoot. The offspring of this shoot now constitute ⅓ ha. of La Perrière: initial fears that they might become red again have not been justified. This white Nuits Saint-Georges is very full-bodied.

HOSPICES DE NUITS

This charitable foundation dates from 1692, and over the years has received several gifts of vineyards from well-wishers. Since 1961, the wines have been sold by auction, usually on the Sunday before Palm Sunday. They carry the names of benefactors, and come from the following nine hectares of First Growth Nuits Saint-Georges land:

Murgers ⅕ ha. = Cuvée Guyard de Changey
Porets ⅕ ha. = Cuvée Antide Midan
Boudots ⅕ ha. = Cuvée Mesny de Boisseaux
Didiers Monopole 1 ha. = Cuvée Fagon
Rues de Chaux ⅓ ha. = Cuvée Camille Rodier
Corvées Paget ⅓ ha. = Cuvée Saint-Laurent
Didiers Saint-Georges Monopole 2⅕ ha. = Cuvée Cabet and
= Cuvée Jacques Duret
Saint-Georges ⅗ ha. = Cuvée des Sires de Vergy
Five other cuvées (Claude Poyen, Guillaume Labye, Soeurs Hospitalières, Grangier and Mignotte) are made from lesser-known First Growths.

DOMAINE GEORGES JEANNIARD   7½ ha. (5 per cent)
Nuits Saint-Georges Les Pruliers 2⅕ ha., Les Perrières 1 ha., Les Argillats ⅔ ha.

JOUAN-MARCILLET   5 ha. (30 per cent)
Nuits Saint-Georges Clos des Perrières Monopole 1 ha., Aux Crots ⅔ ha.

LABOURÉ-ROI   (1832)
At the time of the phylloxera the founder of this company decided that Burgundy was *fichu*, so sold out to a M. Jeanniard whose grandson is now in charge. The company is of small to medium size, and owns 2½ ha. of vines in Nuits Saint-Georges Bellecroix and Tribourg. It distributes the 6 ha. René Manuel estate:
Meursault Bouches Chères 1½ ha., Les Poruzots 1⅓ ha., Clos de la Baronne Monopole (red) 2½ ha.

M. Manuel's Bouches Chères label is the attractive enlargement of a design of 1830 in white, gold and light blue. Bouches Chères derives from *bouchon*, meaning wood from which game is flushed. It quickly passed through *bouchères* (butchers' wives) to its present form.

LIGER-BELAIR ET FILS   (1720) 3½ ha.
Richebourg ½ ha., Clos de Vougeot (middle) ¾ ha., Nuits Saint-Georges Les Saint-Georges 2¼ ha.

This company also owns the Domaine du Vivier in the Beaujolais, with vineyards at Fleurie, Moulin à Vent and Romanèche-Thorins.

LUPÉ-CHOLET ET CIE   (1903)
This firm owns the *Monopoles* Nuits Saint-Georges Château Gris, 4 ha., situated in the First Growth vineyard of Aux Crots, and Bourgogne *rouge* Clos de Lupé, 2 ha.

The Italianate Château Gris with two terraces stands in a magnificent position above Nuits and is lived in by the *vigneron* who works the Clos. Its name comes from the unusual grey slate roof. It was built between 1796 and 1802 in order to give work to the local inhabitants. Those on the job received two bowls of soup and four sous a day.

From the death of Jacques de Lupé in 1952 and until 1969, the company was run by his two sisters, Countesses Liane and Inès de Mayol de Lupé. For a time the management of their cellars and all administrative work were handled for them by F. Chauvenet, then Moillard. Recently some members of the Bichot family have become involved in the firm.

DOMAINE MACHARD DE GRAMONT   30 ha. (75 per cent)
The estate has 9 ha. of *Grand* and *Premier Cru* in a wide variety of communes: Clos de Vougeot, Nuits Saint-Georges (6 ha.), Vosne-Romanée, Chambolle-Musigny, Aloxe-Corton, Pommard (8 ha.), Savigny-les-Beaune, Volnay, Beaune, Côte de Beaune Monopole, Clos des Topes Bizot (4¼ ha.).

This estate has recently been split, part becoming the Domaine Chantal Lescure.

DOMAINE TIM MARSHALL   ⅖ ha. (100 per cent)
Nuits Saint-Georges Les Perrières ¼ ha., Les Argillats ⅕ ha.

Tim Marshall is a Yorkshireman turned Burgundian export wine-broker. He has a famous palate and has pointed more than one confused Anglo-Saxon buyer in the direction of authentic, high-quality Burgundy. The wine from his own vineyards is mainly sold in France. He believes in slow fermentations, the removal of about 20 per cent of the stalks before a vatting of ten to fifteen days and aging in new oak.

He acts for ECVF Sélection Jean Germain in Meursault (see page 285).

DOMAINE HÉRITIERS ÉMILE MICHELOT   6 ha. (50 per cent)
Nuits Saint-Georges Les Vaucrains ⅔ ha., Les Porrets ½ ha., Les Saint-Georges ⅙ ha., Richemone ½ ha., *Premier Cru* 1⅓ ha.

This estate has plans to bottle more in the future.

P. MISSEREY ET FRÈRE (1904) 6 ha.
Nuits Saint-Georges Les Vaucrains 2 ha., Les Cailles 1 ha., Les Saint-Georges 1 ha., Aux Vignes Rondes 1 ha., Aux Murgers 1 ha.

The Misserey family has owned vines for four generations and been merchants for two. They believe in frequent rackings, and bottle *Grands Crus* straight from the barrel.

MOILLARD-GRIVOT (1850)
The origins of this company go back as far as 1848, to the marriage of Marguerite Grivot and her vineyards with Symphorien Moillard and his.

Although today still owning 19 ha. of vines, the company is

225

essentially a specialist merchant, and is the largest on the Côte de Nuits. The estate is mainly worked on the half-fruit system. It consists of small-holdings in Chambertin Clos de Bèze and Romanée Saint-Vivant, a slice of middle Clos de Vougeot, two important First Growth sections, Vosne-Romanée Aux Malconsorts 2½ ha., and Nuits Saint-Georges Clos de Thorey Monopole 3½ ha., and holdings in Vosne-Romanée Les Beaumonts, Nuits Saint-Georges La Richemone, Les Grandes Vignes Monopole 2 ha.,[1] Corton-Charlemagne, Corton Clos du Roi and Beaune Grèves. The company also distributes two *Monopoles* exclusively: Corton Clos de Vergennes 2 ha., and Volnay Clos de la Barre 1 ha.

The Thomas family which owns Moillard also controls Pampryl, the Nuits Saint-Georges fruit-juice company with a 40 per cent share of the French market.

Moillard has three functions, according to its Managing Director, Yves Thomas. It owns the well-situated vineyards listed above. It is one of the three or four companies in Burgundy to buy grapes from the growers and assume responsibility for the vinifications. Thirdly, it fills the traditional *négociant* role of buying, tending and bottling. There is a fourth: it acts as a stockholder and, to some extent, a banker for the Burgundy trade, as many firms draw wines from it, then put their own labels on.

It has experimented with must-heating and new methods of vinification with the object of producing wines which are 'more supple and complete'. It exports extensively and believes that pasteurization can solve some of a wine's stability problems.

UCGV MORIN PÈRE ET FILS (1822)
The estate consists of 4½ ha. Nuits Saint-Georges Les Cailles 2⅓ ha., Les Pruliers 1 ha., Les Vaucrains ¼ ha.

It used to be the largest proprietor of Clos de Vougeot, and unique in having an operational vat-house within the Clos, called the Château de la Tour. Parts of the building date from 1890, but most from 1947. One wine was made from holdings in the top, middle and lower sections of Clos de Vougeot. Following the death of M. Jean Morin, ownership of the Château de la Tour has passed to his daughters, Mesdames J. Labet and N. Déchelette.

---

[1] The Clos des Grandes Vignes in Prémeaux is one of the only First Growths to be found on the plain side of the Dijon–Chagny road.

HENRI REMORIQUET   4 ha. (30 per cent)
Nuits Saint-Georges Les Saint-Georges $\frac{1}{5}$ ha., Aux Damodes $\frac{1}{5}$ ha.,
Premier Cru $\frac{2}{5}$ ha.

Main Merchants and Growers in Prémeaux (21700 Nuits Saint-Georges)

MAISON JULES BELIN   (1817) 13 ha.
Nuits Saint-Georges Clos des Forêts Saint-Georges Monopole
7 ha., Clos de l'Arlot *rouge* and *blanc* Monopole 4 ha., Côte de
Nuits Villages Clos du Chapeau Monopole $1\frac{3}{5}$ ha.

The Clos de l'Arlot comes into view on the left as the main road
north to Dijon dips down into the village of Prémeaux, one of the
prettiest vineyards on the Côte. The steepest part is nicknamed
Montre-Cul, and is planted in Chardonnay; at the top right-hand
corner the fine old retaining wall supports La Terrasse de l'Anglais
where an Englishman is said to be buried beneath the vines.
Within the Clos but unseen from the road is a 100-ft-deep park
inside a disused quarry. The Arlot is a stream whose source is in
the vineyard—it passes under the road at the bottom of the Clos
where there used to be a small fish-rearing farm.

The firm of Belin make a speciality of their Marc à la Cloche—at
the end of the last century they were one of the first to age and
commercialize what used to be merely a *vigneron*'s drink.

DOMAINE JEAN CONFURON ET SES FILS   10 ha. (90 per cent)
Clos de Vougeot (top) $\frac{1}{2}$ ha., Bonnes Mares $\frac{1}{4}$ ha., Nuits Saint-
Georges Les Chaboeufs $\frac{1}{2}$ ha., Les Vaucrains $\frac{1}{4}$ ha.

This domaine has been going since the eighteenth century. Fifty
years ago it began bottling on a small scale, supplying at that time
the Belgian Court. It now delivers to NATO and the UN in
Geneva, and to the British Embassy in Germany.

ROBERT DUBOIS ET FILS   9 ha. (20 per cent)
Nuits Saint-Georges Les Porrets $\frac{1}{4}$ ha., Nuits Saint-Georges, Côte
de Nuits Villages.

This estate has doubled in size since 1966.

DOMAINE DU GÉNÉRAL GOUACHON   6 ha. (80 per cent)
GÉRARD ELMERICH—SUCCESSEUR
Nuits Saint-Georges Clos des Corvées Monopole 5 ha., Clos des
Argillières $\frac{4}{5}$ ha.

Gouachon was a local *vigneron* who made good in the army and returned to buy vines. This estate changed hands in the late 1960s.

Michel Thomas (of the family which owns Moillard-Grivot) is involved in its management and I am informed that the old vines in the estate are being replaced only very slowly, and that the pruning is particularly severe. It is to be hoped that its past great quality will be maintained.

BERNARD MUGNERET-GOUACHON   13 ha. (50 per cent)
Nuits Saint-Georges Aux Perdrix 3⅓ ha., Echézeaux 2 ha., Vosne-Romanée, Nuits Saint-Georges.

A few rows of Aligoté and some acacia trees are all that come between Bernard Mugneret and the Perdrix Monopole; he is the only proprietor producing wine under the name.

Like Louis Gouroux in Flagey he believes that the *Pinot droit* in careful hands produces worthwhile results.

CHARLES VIÉNOT
Richebourg 1 ha., Corton 3 ha., Nuits Saint-Georges Clos Saint-Marc Monopole 1⅖ ha., Clos des Corvées-Pagets 1½ ha., Vosne-Romanée, Aloxe-Corton.

This firm has been established in Prémeaux since before the French Revolution. The only other proprietor in the Clos des Corvées-Pagets is the Hospices de Nuits, so M. Viénot can assure himself its exclusive distribution by buying the Cuvée Saint-Laurent, as he did in 1970.

The company owns a fine collection of wine glasses, mostly from the eighteenth and nineteenth centuries. It is interesting to note that wine-professionals at that time were not insisting on a tulip-shape.

There are four more bottling growers in Prémeaux, and nine in Nuits Saint-Georges, which also has a further nine merchants.

PRISSEY, COMBLANCHIEN AND CORGOLOIN

Between Prémeaux and Ladoix, the first village of the Côte de Beaune, the scenery changes abruptly, for the Côte is dominated by large tips, the refuse of marble quarrying. Quarrying on a large scale dates from the Second Empire, when mechanical saws made it possible to obtain thin slabs, two to four centimetres thick, and the new railway carried the marble to the capital. The first quarry is above the Porets vineyard of Nuits Saint-Georges. It produces Rose de Prémeaux, not a wine but a compact light-pink limestone, in which can be seen the fossilized holes of tiny organisms which burrowed in the ooze before it solidified. It takes an excellent polish. Comblanchien marble proper is the stratum above the Prémeaux. It is a clear beige colour, and was used to build the Paris Opéra and Orly Airport. It is also widely seen in the Côte d'Or, as flooring in the houses of the more successful growers and shippers.

Leaving Prémeaux on the road towards Beaune one crosses three communes, Prissey, Comblanchien and Corgoloin whose wines may be sold under the *appellation* Côte de Nuits Villages. Fixin and Brochon at the northern extremity of the Côte de Nuits also have that right, and on average 5,100 hl (56,000 dozen bottles) of red wine are made each vintage, along with 10 hl (110 dozen bottles) of white. The five communes have the following areas delimited for vines: Fixin (128·04 ha.), Brochon (46·76 ha.), Prissey (11·80 ha.), Comblanchien (54·03 ha.), and Corgoloin (80·22 ha.), making a total of 320·87 ha.

Main Growers (21830 Comblanchien)

HENRI GILLES   6¾ ha. (90 per cent)
Nuits Saint-Georges Les Brûlées 1½ ha., Corton Renardes ¼ ha., Côte de Nuits Villages.

M. Gilles is now close to retirement.

TRAPET-LALLE   9 ha. (50 per cent)
Nuits Saint-Georges 1½ ha., Aloxe-Corton ½ ha., Côte de Nuits Villages 4 ha.

In this Comblanchien cellar one may taste a Côte de Nuits Villages made from Pinots *droits* against another made from classic Pinots. M. Trapet finds that the former is *plus flatteur* initially, but that it ages poorly. He invariably chooses to bottle the classic Pinot wine.

Main Growers (21730 Corgoloin)

DOMAINE DE LA POULETTE, L. AUDIDIER   15 ha. (100 per cent)
Corton Renardes ¼ ha., Vosne-Romanée Les Suchots ½ ha., Nuits

229

Saint-Georges Les Saint-Georges 1 ha., Les Vaucrains 2 ha., Les Poulettes 1 ha., Côte de Nuits Villages Les Langres 2 ha.

M. Audidier is a member of the *Académie d'Agriculture de France* and an *ingénieur agronome*.

Eight other growers and one merchant bottle wine in Comblanchien, besides three other growers and one merchant in Corgoloin.

13

The Côte de Beaune

HAUTES CÔTES DE NUITS AND HAUTES CÔTES DE BEAUNE

Leave the valley of the Saône behind you, break up through the Côte, and you find yourself in a constantly changing countryside of small hills, plateaux and streams. It is an area which is slowly coming to life again producing fine wine. There are about 400 wine-growers, in thirty-four communes, cultivating 750 hectares of vineyard. Many combine wine-making with the growing of *petits-fruits*—raspberries and blackcurrants—and some still keep a cow or a pig, a horse or a flock of sheep.

A century ago there was six times the area of vineyards, then a number of factors contributed to their abandonment. Post-phylloxera replanting was done with the Gamay grape, but also with Franco-American hybrids; both produced wines which were little better than ordinary. Hillside cultivation was costly, and mechanization difficult, and the wines were undercut in price by the higher-strength *ordinaires* of the Midi and Algeria. Many families had been ruined by the costs of reconstituting the vineyards, and had scarcely the means to fight mildew and Oidium. Then one man in ten never returned from the Great War; those that did found many hillsides lying fallow. In 1913 there had been 3,300 hectares planted in the Hautes Côtes, and by the mid 1950s 900 hectares were left, of which only 520 were planted with noble grapes. In one commune of the Hautes Côtes de Nuits, Arcenant, the area under vines evolved like this:[1] in 1880 there

---

[1] *Le Vignoble des Hautes Côtes de Nuits et de Beaune*, Jean-François Bazin, Les Cahiers de Vergy, 1973.

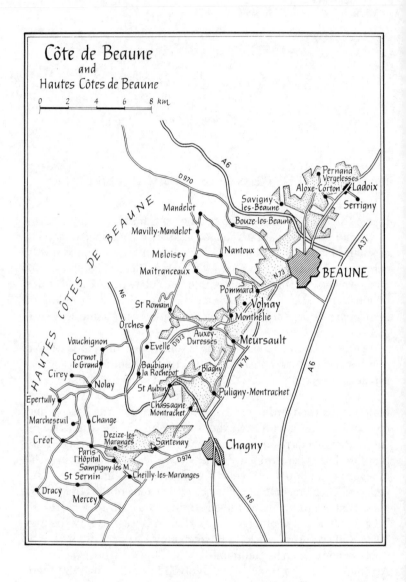

Côte de Beaune
and
Hautes Côtes de Beaune

0   2   4   6   8 km

were 360 hectares, by 1913 this had reduced to 230 hectares and in 1957 it was down to 40 hectares.

Vines have been recorded in the Hautes Côtes since A.D. 761, when a vineyard in Meuilley was given to the Church, according to Dr Lavalle. The Ducal Accounts of 1381 record that Philip the Bold had cellars in Beaune, Pommard, Volnay, Monthélie—and Meloisey, in the Hautes Côtes. Meloisey's wine had been served at the coronation of Philip-Augustus in 1180.

The renaissance of the Hautes Côtes vineyards over the last quarter of a century has come about thanks to replanting with Pinot Noir, and to a lesser extent with Chardonnay and Aligoté. The cost of bringing a hectare of vineyard from fallow land to its first harvest the fourth year after plantation was officially calculated in 1976 to be F.51,693 for high-trained, wider-spaced vines, F.80,492 for traditional low-trained vines. More than half of the new plantations, according to the leading grower Lucien Jacob, have adopted the former method.

In August 1961 the Hautes Côtes were granted the right to the ACs Bourgogne Hautes Côtes de Beaune and Bourgogne Hautes Côtes de Nuits in respect of wine produced from the Pinot Noir grape, within the delimited area, on condition that they passed a tasting examination. Thus the principle of obligatory tasting was introduced to the Côte d'Or. But the battle was not yet won, for the local *négociants* found the new names of little interest to them. Perhaps there was also room for improvement in their vinification methods. A co-operative had been founded at Orches in 1957, and this was expanded to embrace all the Hautes Côtes, opening new premises on the road out of Beaune towards Pommard, in 1968.[1] Hautes Côtes growers tried to establish a *rapprochement* with those of the Côte, for were their wines not complementary? Less prestigious certainly, but of approachable price and there was scope for the existing area under vines to be doubled as demand grew.

It was not the Burgundians but the Swiss who took up the

---

[1] In 1978 grapes from 250 hectares of vineyard were vinified at the Co-operative for the following *appellations*: Bourgogne Hautes Côtes de Nuits, Bourgogne Hautes Côtes de Beaune, Nuits Saint-Georges, Pommard, Savigny-les-Beaune, Côtes de Nuits Villages, Côtes de Beaune Villages, Bourgogne Passe-Tout-Grains, Rosé d'Orches, Bourgogne Aligoté. About 50 per cent is bottled at the property after a good vintage.

challenge of the new *appellation contrôlée*. The Savigny merchant Henri de Villamont, owned by Schenk of Switzerland, signed an eighteen-year distribution contract in 1970 for the Co-operative's Bourgogne Hautes Côtes de Beaune and Bourgogne Hautes Côtes de Nuits, which appears to give satisfaction to both sides.

Parallel with the success of the Co-operative is that of the new generation of growers, specializing in domaine-bottling and direct selling. The making of fine wine in this region, where the grapes ripen later than those of the Côte because of its altitude, is often a risky and difficult proposition. Currently there are thirty-two growers in the Hautes Côtes de Beaune and eighteen in the Hautes Côtes de Nuits engaged in offering their wines in bottle. Their *appellations* sometimes include wines from the Côte (as with the Louis Jacob estate), but more often are limited to Hautes Côtes de Beaune or Nuits, Bourgogne *blanc*, Bourgogne Passe-Tout-Grains, Bourgogne Aligoté.

The following communes must be mentioned in the Hautes Côtes de Beaune:

ECHEVRONNE (21420 Savigny-les-Beaune)
The leading grower is Domaine Louis Jacob, with 16 ha. in production, of which 60 per cent is bottled at the estate. It is run by Lucien Jacob, on whose land are planted the experimental clones of Pinot Noir which were described on pages 94–8. He is a much respected man, one of the INAOs representatives in Burgundy, a dynamic and determined fighter for progress. His vineyards are distributed as follows: Savigny Vergelesses 2 ha., Savigny 6 ha., Beaune *Premier Cru* $\frac{2}{3}$ ha., Aloxe-Corton, Pernand-Vergelesses, Hautes Côtes de Beaune 6 ha.

LA ROCHEPOT (21340 Nolay)
Charles Labry and Maurice Pouleau.

MELOISEY (21950)
Guillemard-Dupont et Fils and Pierre Mazilly.

NANTOUX (21114)
Joliot et Fils, where five or six hectares are said to produce good wine from vines trained in the traditional manner.

In the Hautes Côtes de Nuits:

MAGNY-LES-VILLERS (21700 Nuits Saint-Georges)
Henri Naudin Fils has about twelve hectares and bottles much of
the wine himself; Claude Cornu is another leading grower.

MAREY-LES-FUSSEY (21700 Nuits Saint-Georges)
Simon Fils and Maurice Thevenot-le-Brun et Fils are both
growers who have replanted extensively over the last ten years.
Thevenot-le-Brun has fifteen hectares planted and a number of
export customers. He has some unusual wines to offer: Bourgogne Aligoté with an intentional bubble, offered as Aligoté
perlant, and Gold-Medal-winning Pinot Gris.

VILLARS-FONTAINE (21700 Nuits Saint-Georges)
Henry Hudelot's is a large estate, specializing in high-vine
cultivation and his own bottling.

Of course, some of the largest estates in the Hautes Côtes are
owned by growers and merchants from the Côte. Bouchard Père of
Beaune own the Château de Mandelot with its vines; Geisweiler of
Nuits Saint-Georges have replanted extensively at Bévy; Jean
Gros, a Vosne-Romanée grower with holdings in Richebourg, has
vineyards at Chevrey near Arcenant; and Dominique Guyon of
Savigny has twenty hectares in a single block on the south-facing
Myon hillside in Meuilley. I understand that this took some
assembling, for there were 350 individual plots and seventy
owners, who had to be seen one by one.

ALOXE-CORTON, LADOIX-SERRIGNY AND PERNAND-VERGELESSES

On the territory of Aloxe begins the Côte de Beaune, according to
Dr Lavalle. The eastern slope of the hill of Corton constitutes one
of the largest and most beautiful vineyards of the Côte.

It has been planted with vines since at least A.D. 858, when the
Bishop of Autun, Modoin, donated his Aloxe vines to the
cathedral. The Dukes of Burgundy owned vineyards here, as did
the Knights Templar and the Kings of France; in 1534 Charlotte
Dumay, wife of Gauldry, *garde de la Monnaie* in Dijon, gave
a hundred *ouvrées* of vineyard to the Hôtel-Dieu in Beaune,
which still has them. Perhaps Charlemagne drank wine from
this hillside, before giving his vines to the Collégiale of Saulieu, in
A.D. 775.

Aloxe-Corton, Ladoix and Pernand

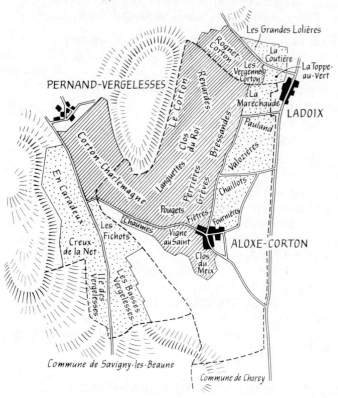

There are two *Grands Crus*, both of which extend on to the adjoining communes of Ladoix and Pernand:

1. Corton (to which the name of individual vineyards—Clos du Roi, Bressandes, Renardes, Pougets, Perrières, Languettes etc.—is often added). Average harvest: 2,600 hl (28,600 dozen bottles) of red wine, 35 hl (385 dozen bottles) of white. This is the largest *Grand Cru* in Burgundy. Much of the land is owned by shippers making wine which matures rapidly. In Dr Lavalle's day, these wines contained a lot of tannin, and were the firmest and most frank of the Côte de Beaune, needing seven or eight years'

maturity and able, when of good vintage, to last thirty or forty. Who would bother to mature them for ten years today?

The first and last word in Cortons, for many, is Louis Latour's Ch. Corton-Grancey. An expensive branded wine, conveniently available, which is often bought and sold without being tasted, no questions asked. What does it look like in a tasting alongside Cortons from Drouhin, Tollot-Beaut, Senard, Jadot, Mallard-Gaullin, Mérode, Lequin, Laleure-Piot? Or Cortons from Thénard, Dubreuil-Fontaine, Chevalier-Dubois, Bouchard Père, Thévenot, Voarick or Chandon de Briailles?

2. Corton-Charlemagne (Average harvest: 1,040 hl or 11,500 dozen bottles). This can be astonishingly rich and full of flavours for a dry white wine. Says P. Bréjoux: 'One can distinguish Cortons-Charlemagnes from Meursaults although they are close. Some are tender and fine, others vigorous. The less successful are a bit flabby and heavy.'

The following are classified as First Growths of Aloxe-Corton:

COMMUNE OF LADOIX-SERRIGNY
La Maréchaude, La Toppe-au-Vert, La Coutière, Les Grandes Lolières, Les Petites Lolières, Les Basses Mourettes.

COMMUNE OF ALOXE-CORTON
Valozières (part), Chaillots (part), Clos du Meix (part), Fournières, La Maréchaude (part), Pauland (part), Les Vercots, Les Guérets.

There is an average production of First Growth and commune Aloxe-Corton amounting to 4,100 hl (45,000 dozen bottles) of red wine, 40 hl (440 dozen bottles) of white.

The growers of Ladoix maintain that their commune provides the best First Growth Aloxe-Cortons. Most of their red wine (1,500 hl or 16,500 dozen bottles) is sold as Côte de Beaune Villages. There is a little white Ladoix (80 hl or 880 dozen bottles). Altogether the area delimited for First Growth and commune wines is 135.49 hectares.

On the further side of the Corton hillock, facing south-west, are the Corton-Charlemagne vineyards of Pernand-Vergelesses, first mentioned in 1375. Across a narrow valley from them are red wines, the best from the vineyard of Ile des Vergelesses. Pernand has a local reputation for its Aligoté.

The following are currently classified as First Growth vineyards of Pernand-Vergelesses:

ILE DES VERGELESSES

Les Basses Vergelesses, Creux de la Net (part), Les Fichots, En Caradeux (part).

The average production is 1,900 hl (20,900 dozen bottles) of red wine, some of which is sold as Côte de Beaune Villages, and 320 hl (3,500 dozen bottles) of white. Altogether 143.30 hectares are delimited for viticulture.

Main Merchants and Growers (21550 Ladoix-Serrigny)

CAPITAIN-GAGNEROT   (1802) 8 ha.
Corton Renardes and La Maréchaude $\frac{3}{4}$ ha., Aloxe-Corton Les Moutottes 1 ha., Les Lolières $1\frac{1}{2}$ ha., Corton-Charlemagne $\frac{1}{10}$ ha., Clos de Vougeot (top) $\frac{1}{6}$ ha., Ladoix Côte de Beaune $3\frac{1}{4}$ ha.

Les Moutottes is virtually the *Monopole* of M. Capitain. It was planted in fifty- and seventy-year-old vines when I was there, its quality then usually surpassing that of his Cortons.

CHEVALIER-DUBOIS   8 ha. (80 per cent)
Corton-Charlemagne $\frac{1}{6}$ ha., Corton 1 ha., Aloxe-Corton, Ladoix Côte de Beaune.

M. Chevalier has been bottling extensively for many years. He is well placed, just off the Dijon–Lyon road and, as well as his fine wines, he has on offer a fund of amiable Burgundian wisdom.

MICHEL MALLARD   9 ha. (90 per cent)
Corton $\frac{1}{2}$ ha., Aloxe-Corton, Côte de Beaune, Côte de Nuits.

DOMAINE DE SERRIGNY

PRINCE FLORENT DE MÉRODE $10\frac{2}{5}$ ha. (90 per cent)
Corton $3\frac{4}{5}$ ha., Aloxe-Corton $\frac{2}{3}$ ha., Pommard Clos de la Platière $3\frac{2}{3}$ ha.

The Prince de Mérode is of Belgian origin. He has lived in Burgundy for thirty years in a moated castle in the plain opposite his Corton vineyards. His estate is managed by Bitouzet of Savigny (q.v.).

ANDRÉ NUDANT   5 ha. (60 per cent)
M. Nudant is a master-grafter of vine-stocks who nearly went off to the Cameroons as a Jesuit father. Instead he is well situated on

the main Dijon–Lyon road for attracting private customers. His $\frac{1}{3}$ ha. in Corton-Charlemagne he reclaimed himself from the pine trees. He also has vines in Aloxe-Corton La Coutière, La Toppe-au-Vert, and Ladoix Côte de Beaune.

Main Growers in Pernand-Vergelesses (21420 Savigny-les-Beaune)

DOMAINE BONNEAU DE MARTRAY   11 ha. (100 per cent)
Corton-Charlemagne $8\frac{2}{3}$ ha., Corton $2\frac{1}{2}$ ha.

This property has two links with Burgundy's history. Its owner (until his death in 1969) was René Bonneau du Martray, a direct descendant of Nicolas Rolin who caused the Hôtel-Dieu to be built in Beaune in 1443. And it would seem that the Bonneau du Martray estate, lying on the borders of Pernand-Vergelesses and Aloxe-Corton, corresponds exactly to the site of the vineyards owned by the Emperor Charlemagne before he presented them to the collegiate church of Saulieu in 775.

Today the estate is managed by Mme du Martray's nephew, Jean le Bault de la Morinière.

P. DUBREUIL-FONTAINE PÈRE ET FILS   17 ha. (80 per cent)
Corton Clos du Roi 1 ha., Bressandes $1\frac{1}{2}$ ha., Perrières $\frac{3}{5}$ ha., Pernand-Vergelesses, Ile des Vergelesses $\frac{2}{3}$ ha., Savigny Les Vergelesses $2\frac{1}{2}$ ha., Corton-Charlemagne $1\frac{1}{3}$ ha., Pommard Les Epenots $\frac{1}{6}$ ha.

Pierre Dubreuil was for long mayor of Pernand. He has recently acquired the village's only *Monopole*, Pernand-Vergelesses Clos Berthet (2 ha.) which he replanted with red and white vines. His son Bernard now runs the property.

LALEURE-PIOT   7 ha. (50 per cent)
Pernand-Vergelesses, Ile des Vergelesses $\frac{1}{2}$ ha., Corton Bressandes $\frac{1}{3}$ ha., Beaune Les Blanches Fleurs $\frac{1}{3}$ ha., Savigny Vergelesses $\frac{1}{3}$ ha., Corton-Charlemagne $\frac{3}{4}$ ha.

Following the death of conscientious wine-maker Gabriel Laleure (who was incidentally a hail expert, called upon to assess vineyard damage from Champagne to the Rhône), the estate is now run by his son Jean-Marie. He is a qualified oenologist with an understanding probably second to none of the workings of the Burgundian wine trade.

239

ROBERT RAPET ET FILS   12 ha. (75 per cent)
Corton and Corton Perrières 1 ha., Corton-Champagne 1½ ha.,
Beaune *Premier Cru* ½ ha., Pernand-Vergelesses Les Vergelesses
2½ ha., Savigny Fourneaux 1 ha., Aligoté 3 ha.

The late Robert Rapet was the archetype of my idea of the
typical *vigneron* before I went to Burgundy: baggy corduroys,
several days' stubble, mistrust of intruders, a wide-screen
television in a grubby room. But after a few minutes his
prickliness disappeared. The massive family *tastevin* came out
(inscribed L. Rapet D. Pernand 1792), the old boy clapping it
between his hands, saying it was built to withstand the pressures
of heated conversation. By the end he was as difficult to escape
from as any other Burgundian when launched on the subject of his
own wine. It is now his son Roland who ensures that replanting is
carried out, and who is expanding the estate when he can.

ANDRÉ THIÉLY   8 ha. (100 per cent)
Corton-Champagne ¼ ha., Corton ⅓ ha., Pernand-Vergelesses Les
Fichots 1¼ ha., Aloxe-Corton, Savigny.

M. Thiély bottles his wines every year.

Main Merchants and Growers (21920 Aloxe-Corton)

P. A. ANDRÉ

LA REINE PÉDAUQUE
These are the creations of Pierre André who founded his first wine-
firm in Burgundy in 1923.

In 1937 he bought the Rôtisserie de la Reine Pédauque in Paris
(drawing publicity by placing a magnum each of red, white and
rosé wine before every guest), and in 1939 Victor Clicquot
champagne in Rheims.

In 1950 Reine Pédauque wines were first launched and in the
same year the best site in Beaune was secured and developed for
the tempting of tourists to make a cellar-descent. The company
now runs several estates:

Domaine de la Juvinière   23⅘ ha.
Clos de Vougeot (top) 1 ha., Corton Clos du Roi, Pougets,
Combes, Côte de Nuits Villages, Clos des Langres Monopole
7 ha., Savigny, Pommard, Aloxe-Corton.

Domaine Les Terres Vineuses 24⅘ ha.
Corton Clos du Roi, Corton Renardes, Aloxe-Corton *Premier Cru*,
Ladoix Clos les Chagnots Monopole 7 ha., Corton-Charlemagne.

Domaine du Clos des Guettes
Savigny Clos des Guettes 2½ ha.

Domaine Viticole des Carmes
Mâcon 18 ha.

The firm specializes in Savigny wines, claiming at one time to
commercialize 40 per cent of the production of the village.

CHAPUIS 11 ha. (30 per cent)
Corton 5 ha. (Perrières, Languettes, Chaumes, Voiroses, a little
Bressandes), Corton-Charlemagne ⅔ ha.

'Cultivation is more efficient now,' says M. Chapuis. 'When you
had to lean on a plough you got tired quickly and the furrow went
less deep.'

His wines have been described as elegant.

DANIEL SENARD

DOMAINE DES MEIX 7½ ha. (65 per cent)
Corton Clos du Roi ½ ha., Bressandes ½ ha., Aloxe-Corton Val-
ozières ¾ ha., Corton Clos des Meix Monopole 1⅘ ha., Corton ⅘ ha.,
Aloxe-Corton 2¾ ha., Beaune, Côte de Beaune Villages.

In the old days, 5 per cent of Corton was planted with Pinot
Gris, locally called Beurot, which softened the roughish wines.
(This is the same grape as the Tokay d'Alsace and the Ruländer of
Germany.) Comte Senard still has a little in his vineyard (as did
Chapuis and Quenot when I visited them), which he makes as a
straight white wine.

The Senard estate is more successful than most in off-vintages,
its formula being as follows:
(1) Remove rotten grapes from the harvest; (2) Fill each vat in a
single day; (3) Vat for a long time in order to obtain colour; (4)
Add enough sugar to obtain a 12°–12.5° wine—no more or the wine
will be unbalanced; (5) Rather than pumping the must over the
'hat' of grape-skins, it is preferable to push them down under the
surface (having first taken care to wash the feet, so that Anglo-
Saxon customers may not be shocked).

HENRI POISOT 5½ ha. (10 per cent)

HERITIERS PIERRE POISOT
Corton-Charlemagne 1 ha., Bressandes 1 ha., Languettes 1 ha.

When I visited it, the estate was making two *cuvées* of Corton-Charlemagne, one of them, although coming from a vine merely eight years old, quite exceptional.

This estate is managed by Michel Voarick (see below).

MAX QUENOT FILS ET MEUNEVEAUX $6\frac{1}{2}$ ha. (40 per cent)
Corton Bressandes 1 ha., Perrières $\frac{2}{3}$ ha., Chaumes $\frac{1}{3}$ ha.

MICHEL VOARICK ET FILS   14 ha. (100 per cent)
Corton Renardes $\frac{1}{2}$ ha., Languettes 1 ha., Clos du Roi $\frac{1}{2}$ ha., Corton-Charlemagne $1\frac{1}{3}$ ha.

Michel Voarick is a difficult man to catch—he had just come back from killing a wild boar north of Dijon when I eventually met him.

He began bottling in 1961 when ten barrels were left on his hands, and by 1969 was bottling 30 per cent of his crop in a good year—now it is 100 per cent. He also cultivates the Hospices de Beaune Cuvée Dr Peste vines. When talking of the changes which have taken place, he mentions the greater care given to vinifications. His father would spend all day in the vines picking, then be up half the night making the wine. The son spends all his time in the *cuverie* during the harvest.

During 1969, this estate took on the running of the Henri Poisot domaine, in exchange for two-thirds of its grapes at each vintage.

There are a further eight bottling growers in Ladoix, fifteen in Pernand and one in Aloxe.

SAVIGNY-LES-BEAUNE AND CHOREY-LES-BEAUNE

Savigny-les-Beaune comes third, after Beaune and Pommard, as regards quantity of red wine produced on the Côte de Beaune. It is situated at the mouth of the valley of the Rhoin, its vines being found on two hillsides, differently orientated. The wines from the Vergelesses Côte are fine and perfumed; those from the Marconnets slope on the Beaune side are more full-bodied.

Savigny lays claim to having seen the invention in 1863 of the first *tracteur-enjambeur*, for cultivating vines by straddling the rows. It was horse-drawn and had wooden wheels and can apparently be seen at the Ferme de Chenôve.

There are fifteen or more wall-inscriptions in Savigny, ranging from the unfashionable '*Travailler est un devoir indispensable à l'homme, riche ou pauvre, puissant ou faible, tout citoyen oisif est un fripon*' through the expedient '*Il ne faut pas donner son appât au goujon quand on peut espérer prendre une carpe*' to the calm '*Malgré les imposteurs, traîtres et jaloux, l'homme patient viendra à bout de tout*'. They were inscribed between the seventeenth and nineteenth centuries, no one knows why or by whom.

Currently the following vineyards are classified as First Growths: Les Vergelesses, Les Vergelesses known as Bataillière, Les Marconnets, La Dominode, Les Jarrons, Basses-Vergelesses, Les Lavières, Aux Gravains, Les Peuillets (part), Aux Guettes (part), Les Talmettes, Les Charnières, Aux Fourneaux (part),

Savigny-les-Beaune

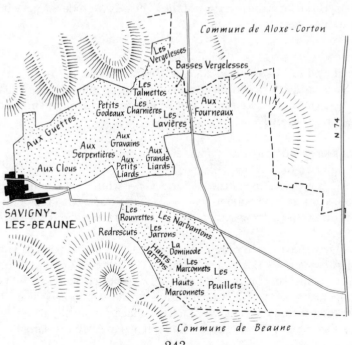

Aux Clous (part), Aux Serpentières (part), Les Narbantons, Hauts Marconnets, Hauts Jarrons, Redrescuts (part), Les Rouvrettes (part), Aux Grands Liards (part), Aux Petits Liards (part), Petits Godeaux (part).

The total area delimited for vineyards is 378.47 hectares, producing on average 340 hl (3,740 dozen bottles) of white wine, 8,400 hl (92,400 dozen bottles) of red.

The vineyards of Chorey-les-Beaune lie in the plain to the east of Savigny. Most of the wine is red, and sold as Côte de Beaune Villages. I confess I have rarely drunk it. The area under vines is 121·57 hectares, producing 2,660 hl (29,260 dozen bottles) of wine.

Main merchants and growers (21420 Savigny-les-Beaune)

P. BITOUZET   2 ha. (100 per cent)
Savigny Les Lavières ½ ha., Aloxe-Corton Valozières ⅓ ha.

M. Bitouzet is the *régisseur* of the Prince de Mérode estate, with some vineyards of his own.

SIMON BIZE ET FILS   10 ha. (100 per cent)
Savigny Les Vergelesses 2 ha., Les Marconnets ⅔ ha.

'A lack of education has brought about people wanting their wines to burn their stomachs. But wine should be light and natural and fine,' says Bize.

VALENTIN BOUCHOTTE   5 ha. (85 per cent)
Savigny Haut Jarrons 2 ha.

M. Bouchotte owns the historic vines which Dr Guyot first trained horizontally and in lines—they are a kilometre long—thus inventing the pruning system now universal throughout the Côte d'Or.

This is how he describes his wine-making methods: 'Do you know how to make an ice-cream sorbet? That's how I vinify. I've a large copper cauldron, into which I pack ice and salt at a temperature of $-6°C.$, which stands in the vat to keep it cool. Carbonic fermentation gives the fruit, maceration the substance. It's like making good cheese, the system's exactly the same.'

DOMAINE CHANDON DE BRIAILLES   18 ha. (50 per cent)
MM. DE NICHOLAY PROPRIÉTAIRES
Savigny Les Lavières 3 ha., Pernand Ile des Vergelesses 4 ha.,
Corton Les Bressandes 3 ha., Clos du Roi 1 ha., Les Maréchaudes
$\frac{1}{2}$ ha., Corton *blanc* $\frac{1}{3}$ ha. (planted in the Bressandes vineyard, half
in Pinot *blanc*, half in Chardonnay).

This domaine, whose proprietors are cousins of the Chandons of
Moët fame, has an important Paris clientele, including Lasserre,
Prunier and the Tour d'Argent. They are the largest proprietors in
Pernand Ile des Vergelesses, which has been described as a lady's
Corton.

A fair proportion of replanting took place here in the 1960s.

DOUDET-NAUDIN   (1849) 5 ha.
Beaune Clos du Roi $\frac{1}{2}$ ha., Savigny Aux Guettes 1 ha., Redrescuts
$\frac{4}{5}$ ha., Corton Les Maréchaudes 1 ha., Aloxe-Corton Les Bout-
tières 1 ha., Pernand-Vergelesses Les Fichots $\frac{3}{5}$ ha.

M. Doudet is not an easy man to draw out, perhaps because of
his strong views on wine-writers: 'You always take your facts from
existing books. Have you read Camille Rodier, Poupon and
Forgeot? It's all been said before, you know.'

He claims to make his wines by the ancient methods, and I dare
say they have given pleasure to thousands. But if this is how the
ancients did it, I am all for progress.

PAUL DUBREUIL-BIZE   6 ha. (75 per cent)
Savigny Les Vergelesses 2 ha., Les Lavières 1 ha.

Paul Dubreuil created this entire estate himself—his father had
no vines at all. He is happier making wine than tending vines, to
the extent that in 1959 he nearly asphyxiated himself by spending
three almost uninterrupted weeks in the *cuverie* tending his vats
and breathing in carbon dioxide.

LOUIS ECARD-GUYOT   12 ha. (30 per cent)
Savigny Aux Serpentières 3 ha., Les Jarrons 1 ha., Les Narbantons $1\frac{1}{2}$ ha.

The name of Aux Serpentières is thought to have come not from
finding serpents in this particular vineyard, but from the snakings
of the boundaries between the many holdings.

245

LES FILS D'ANTONIN GUYON   13½ ha. (100 per cent)
DOMAINE DES HERITIERS D'HYPPOLITE THÉVENOT
DOMAINE DE LA GUYONNIÈRE
DOMAINE DU VILLAGE DE CHAMBOLLE
Corton-Charlemagne ½ ha., Corton Clos du Roi ¾ ha., Les Bressandes 1 ha., Le Corton ¼ ha., Volnay Clos des Chênes 1 ha., Meursault Les Charmes ½ ha., Gevrey-Chambertin 2 ha., Aloxe-Corton 2 ha., Pernand-Vergelesses 2 ha., Beaune 2 ha.

The Domaine Thévenot was acquired in the 1960s by a Dijon wine-merchant, M. Guyon, and the wines are offered under a variety of domaine names. One of the Guyon brothers, Dominique, has large holdings in the Hautes Côtes de Nuits (see page 235).

LAURENT GAUTHIER   (1898)
This is a small company, which sells mainly to private customers in France. It used to own a few rows of vines in Beaune and Aloxe-Corton so that the title *négociant-propriétaire* could be used. Now these have been sold, though the odd barrel of Savigny Les Lavières is still made.

PIERRE GUILLEMOT   5 ha. (25 per cent)
Savigny Aux Serpentières 1⅓ ha.
A good estate—though, sadly, its old Serpentières vines have finally been pulled up and the vineyard replanted.

ALBERT LACROIX   2½ ha. (30 per cent)
Savigny Aux Serpentières ½ ha., Les Rouvrettes ½ ha.
Many proprietors introduce their wines with the words: '*Moi, je cherche à faire de la qualité.*' But not Albert Lacroix. He talks quietly of the importance of storing fine wine in new casks; of the dangers of vines becoming over-cultivated, too cossetted. A combination of lucky factors, he says—healthy grapes and a hot, dry day to pick them on—accounts for the character of his Aux Serpentières 1966. '*C'est un beau métier. Quand on fait quelque chose de bien on peut en garder le souvenir, en le mettant en bouteilles.*'

246

PAVELOT-GLANTENAY   8 ha. (10 per cent)
Savigny La Dominode 1⅓ ha., Les Peuillets 1 ha., Aux Guettes
¾ ha.

This estate is included primarily for its old vines of La
Dominode. When I lived in Burgundy it nearly always outshone
all else in the village when the new wines were tasted, and at the
time was sold under contract to Joseph Drouhin.

PIERRE PETITJEAN   15 ha. (100 per cent)
Savigny Aux Serpentières 1 ha., Les Lavières 1 ha., Les Char-
nières 1 ha., Aux Gravains 1 ha., Hauts Jarrons ½ ha., Beaune
Avaux ⅓ ha., Les Bressandes ⅓ ha., Champimonts ⅓ ha., Corton
Renardes ½ ha.

M. Petitjean's estate has grown from 4 ha. in fifteen years, and
is efficiently run. He is a quiet, active man, and was one of the
founders of the Cousinerie de Bourgogne with Maurice Vollot. A
major outlet for his wines is his hotel-restaurant in Savigny, called
L'Ouvrée. This has prospered, in spite of having had the
misfortune to open on 13 May 1968—the first day of the
événements.

SEGUIN-MANNUEL
The origins of this small company date back to 1824. Pierre Seguin
owns 3 ha. of Savigny vines, of which 1 ha. is Les Lavières. His
cuverie bears a famous inscription, which I have here translated as:
'If my memory serves me right there are five reasons for drinking:
the arrival of a guest, present and future thirst, the quality of the
wines and any other reason you like (1772).'

HENRI DE VILLAMONT   6½ ha.
Grands Echézeaux ½ ha., Savigny Clos des Guettes 2 ha.,
Chambolle-Musigny.

This company is of Swiss origin and has been established in
Savigny since the mid-1960s. It belongs to the Schenk group, the
largest European wine company.

The Clos des Guettes has been replanted with vines where
lettuces and potatoes had been growing. This was one of the first
merchants to carry a range of estate-bottled wines, and has been in

the vanguard of those offering the wines of the Hautes Côtes de Beaune and de Nuits.

There are a further four merchants and seventeen bottling growers in Savigny.

Main Growers in Chorey-les-Beaune (21200 Beaune)

ARNOUX PÈRE ET FILS   15 ha. (10 per cent)
Beaune *Premier Cru* 2 ha., Aloxe-Corton, Savigny, Chorey.

DUBOIS-GOUJON   6 ha. (10 per cent)
Beaune Les Bressandes ¾ ha., Cent Vignes ¼ ha., Savigny, Aloxe, Chorey.

M. Dubois has been mayor of Chorey. His Bressandes vines were sixty years old in the early 1970s.

DOMAINE GERMAIN, CHÂTEAU DE CHOREY   12½ ha. (100 per cent)

DOMAINE DE SAUX
Beaune Teurons 2 ha., Cras 1½ ha., Vignes Franches 1 ha., Boucherottes 1 ha., Cent Vignes ½ ha., Chorey-les-Beaune, Château de Chorey (Monopole) 1 ha., Pernand-Vergelesses, Bourgogne Château Germain.

François Germain runs this estate and also a small merchant's business. His fine Beaunes sell well.

DOMAINE GOUD DE BEAUPUIS   12 ha. (60 per cent)
Pommard Les Epenots ¼ ha., La Chanière ½ ha., Beaune Clos des Vignes Franches 1⅔ ha., Grèves 1½ ha., Toussaints ¼ ha., Savigny Les Vergelesses ⅓ ha., Aloxe-Corton Valozières ¼ ha., Ladoix, Chorey, Bourgogne Château des Montots.

Although holding a merchant's licence M. Goud de Beaupuis considers himself more as a proprietor. One of his claims to fame lies in being a pioneer of amateur radio; his house can be recognized by a bristling of antennae on its roof.

DANIEL MAILLARD-DIARD   10 ha. (30 per cent)
Aloxe-Corton Les Lolières 1 ha., Beaune, Savigny, Chorey.

MALDANT-PAUVELOT ET FILS   11 ha. (30 per cent)
Savigny 4 ha., Aloxe 4 ha., Chorey 3 ha.

DOMAINE MAURICE MARTIN ET FILS   13 ha. (25 per cent)
Beaune Teurons ¼ ha., Aloxe-Corton, Savigny, Chorey.

The Teurons vines were over forty years old when I visited the domaine.

DOMAINE TOLLOT BEAUT ET FILS   20 ha. (90 per cent)
Corton Les Bressandes 1 ha., Le Corton ⅗ ha., Beaune Clos du Roi 1 ha., Les Grèves ¾ ha., Savigny Les Lavières 1⅓ ha., Champ Chorey Monopole 1½ ha., Aloxe-Corton, Chorey-les-Beaune.

In the late 1960s the Clos du Roi was in very old vines, most of them dating from 1922. This is a reputable estate.

C. TOLLOT ET R. VOARICK   22 ha. (90 per cent)
Beaune Clos du Roi ½ ha., Pernand-Vergelesses Ile des Hautes Vergelesses ¾ ha., Aloxe-Corton, Savigny, Chorey, Pernand, Ladoix, Côtes de Nuits Villages.

In 1965 the firm opened a restaurant, Le Bareuzai, on the Dijon–Beaune road as an outlet for its wines, which were then cheaper drunk at the table than if bought to take away. Half of its production goes to this one restaurant.

BEAUNE

'At the heart of the vineyards of the province, famed for its cellars and the wines of its Côte, a centre for viticulture and oenological teaching, its wine-trade radiating across the globe, animated by fairs and fêtes, adorned with remarkable monuments, Beaune is the wine capital of Burgundy.' So runs a sign in its Wine Museum (the translation is mine) and nobody disputes it. Every visitor to Burgundy goes to Beaune and its Hospices, and quite right too.

This was where the Dukes of Burgundy resided until their move to Dijon in the fourteenth century, and their palace can still be seen. So can many fine houses in its old streets like the Renaissance no. 18 rue de Lorraine, dedicated to the Muses, in an attic of which this book began.

It is a town of greedy eaters (though you may eat better in a Beaunois home than in the restaurants), the Saturday-morning market yielding Cîteaux cheeses, corn-coloured Bresse chickens, perhaps a haunch of young wild boar (the blood supplied separately, no extra charge, in a jam jar). The inhabitants will tell you how to choose your butcher, this one for pork, that one for

Beaune

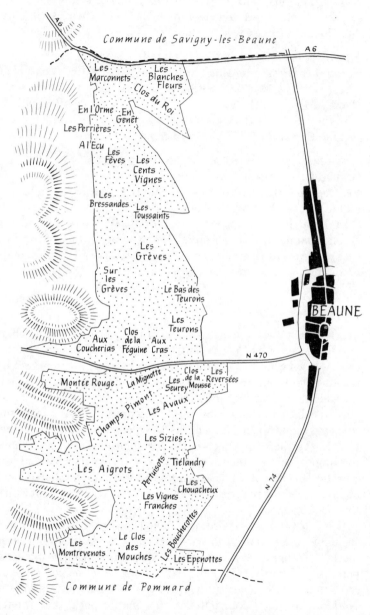

Commune de Savigny-les-Beaune

A 6

Les Marconnets
Les Blanches Fleurs
Clos du Roi
En l'Orme
En Genêt
Les Perrières
A l'Ecu
Les Fèves
Les Cents Vignes
Les Bressandes
Les Toussaints
Les Grèves
Sur les Grèves
Le Bas des Teurons
Les Teurons
Aux Coucherias
Clos de la Féguine
Aux Cras

N 470

Montée Rouge
La Mignotte
Clos de la Mousse
Les Seurey
Les Reversées
Champs Pimont
Les Avaux
Les Sizies
Les Aigrots
Pertuisots
Tiélandry
Les Chouacheux
Les Vignes Franches
Les Boucherottes
Les Montrevenots
Le Clos des Mouches
Les Epenottes

BEAUNE

N 74

Commune de Pommard

veal, another for *volaille*. In Beaune, the weather is predicted by feeling the bread: '*Le pain est mou; il va pleuvoir.*' One should never leave the place without allowing Madame Bazeron of the rue Carnot to sell one some *gâteaux* (made of nothing but butter) in her inimitable fluty voice. Her husband is a master *pâtissier* and his *mille-feuilles*, his shiny dark-brown chocolate fish, his ice-creams, his *pâté bourguignon en croûte* (the last must be ordered in advance) are part of Beaune's treasures. Go quickly, for Madame Bazeron deserved a peaceful retirement years ago.

And of course there is the wine. Here are the names of Beaune's First Growths: Les Marconnets, Les Fèves, Les Bressandes, Les Grèves, Les Teurons, Le Clos des Mouches, Champs Pimont, Clos du Roi (part), Aux Coucherias (part), En l'Orme, En Genêt, Les Perrières, A l'Ecu, Les Cent Vignes, Les Toussaints, Sur les Grèves, Aux Cras, Clos de la Mousse, Les Chouacheux, Les Boucherottes, Les Vignes Franches, Les Aigrots, Pertuisots, Tiélandry or Clos-Landry, Les Sizies, Les Avaux, Les Reversées, Le Bas des Teurons, Les Seurey, La Mignotte, Montée Rouge (part), Les Montrevenots (part), Les Blanches Fleurs (part), Les Epenottes (part).

There are 538 hectares of vineyard delimited, producing on average 440 hl (4,840 dozen bottles) of white wine, 10,500 hl (115,500 dozen bottles) of red.

Main Merchants and Growers

ALBERT BICHOT & CIE (1831)

For many years this company has grouped local merchants, now numbering over fifty, under its wing. It distributes the wines of the Domaine du Clos Frantin, 10 ha., which once belonged to Général Legrand, Maréchale de Camp of the Emperor Napoleon:

Chambertin $\frac{1}{3}$ ha., Richebourg $\frac{1}{14}$ ha., Clos de Vougeot $\frac{3}{5}$ ha. ($\frac{1}{3}$ top, Grand Maupertuis, $\frac{2}{3}$ bottom), Vosne-Romanée Aux Malconsorts $1\frac{3}{4}$ ha., Grandes Echézeaux $\frac{1}{4}$ ha., Echézeaux 1 ha., Corton Languettes, Gevrey-Chambertin, Vosne-Romanée, Nuits Saint-Georges. The Clos Frantin itself (in Vosne-Romanée) is too small to be worth marketing, and one imagines they must have difficulty vinifying the Richebourg.

Three Bichots assure the continued expansion of this firm, which originally sprang from Monthélie and is now the largest exporter of Burgundy *appellations*. A cousin of their grandfather, incidentally, founded Paul Masson in California.

DOMAINE GASTON BOISSEAUX $7\frac{1}{2}$ ha. (100 per cent)
Beaune Montée Rouge $4\frac{1}{2}$ ha., Savigny Les Peuillets $\frac{1}{4}$ ha., Chorey-les-Beaune $2\frac{1}{2}$ ha.

BOISSEAUX-ESTIVANT (1878)
This merchant works extensively with restaurants and hotels in the four local *départements* of Côte d'Or, Saône et Loire, Jura and Doubs. It is small but expanding. André Boisseaux, the man who took Patriarche to fame, came from this company.

BOUCHARD AÎNÉ ET FILS (1750)
This company stems from the same family as Bouchard Père et Fils; their ways parted back in 1750. It has a 22 ha. estate on the Côte Chalonnaise:

Mercurey Clos La Marche Monopole 3 ha., Clos du Chapitre 4 ha., Mercurey *blanc* $1\frac{1}{2}$ ha.

In addition it regularly buys the grapes and makes the wine of the Domaine Dr Henri Marion (6 ha.):

Chambertin Clos de Bèze $1\frac{4}{5}$ ha., Fixin La Mazière $1\frac{1}{4}$ ha., Côte de Nuits Villages 3 ha.

Its energetic director Paul Bouchard serves as a magnet to countless English-speaking visitors to Beaune, for he was born and educated in Britain. His father was running the firm's London office when the Second World War broke out, and the family lived in Sussex with the late André Simon while it lasted.

BOUCHARD PÈRE ET FILS (1731)
With over $81\frac{1}{2}$ ha. of wines, this company owns by far the largest estate on the Côte de Beaune:

Corton Le Corton $3\frac{2}{3}$ ha., Corton-Charlemagne 3 ha., Savigny Les Lavières 4 ha., Beaune Les Teurons $3\frac{1}{3}$ ha., Les Marconnets $2\frac{1}{3}$ ha., Clos de la Mousse Monopole $3\frac{1}{3}$ ha., Les Grèves Vigne de l'Enfant Jésus Monopole 4 ha., Clos-Landry Monopole $1\frac{3}{4}$ ha., Beaune du Château $28\frac{2}{3}$ ha. (a non-vintage wine made from the following First Growths: Les Aigrots $6\frac{2}{5}$ ha., Les Sizies 1 ha., Pertuisots $\frac{1}{3}$ ha., Les Avaux $4\frac{1}{3}$ ha., Les Seurey $\frac{2}{5}$ ha., Clos du Roi $\frac{3}{4}$ ha., Les Cent Vignes $2\frac{1}{5}$ ha., En Genêt $1\frac{1}{4}$ ha., Les Bressandes

$\frac{1}{6}$ ha., Les Toussaints $\frac{2}{3}$ ha., Les Grèves 1$\frac{1}{5}$ ha., Sur les Grèves 1$\frac{1}{6}$ ha., Champs Pimonts $\frac{3}{4}$ ha., Tuvillains 4 ha., Bellissandes 1$\frac{2}{3}$ ha., Le Bas de Teurons 1$\frac{1}{2}$ ha., Les Boucherottes $\frac{1}{4}$ ha.); Pommard Les Rugiens $\frac{2}{5}$ ha., Les Combes $\frac{3}{4}$ ha., Volnay Caillerets (Ancienne Cuvée Carnot) 3$\frac{3}{4}$ ha., En Chevret $\frac{1}{4}$ ha., Taille-Pieds 1 ha., Chanlin $\frac{2}{5}$ ha., Fremiet Clos de la Rougeotte Monopole 1$\frac{1}{2}$ ha., Chambertin $\frac{1}{6}$ ha., Montrachet 1$\frac{1}{10}$ ha., Chevalier-Montrachet 1$\frac{2}{5}$ ha., Meursault Les Genevrières 1$\frac{2}{5}$ ha., Beaune du Château *blanc* 4 ha. (principally grown in Les Aigrots and Les Sizies).

The Clos de la Mousse is one of the earliest developing Beaunes. Of the Vigne de l'Enfant Jésus it has been said that it received its name because of the smoothness of the wine, 'which goes down the throat like little Jesus in velvet pants'. However, M. Claude Bouchard states that the vineyard was named by its one-time owner, the Carmelite Monastery, in honour of their miraculous 'Enfant Jésus' who had something to do with Anne of Austria eventually conceiving Louis XIV. Another house speciality is Volnay Caillerets Ancienne Cuvée Carnot, these vines having once belonged to the French President. The company distributes the wines of the Château de Vosne-Romanée (see page 214) and the Château de Mandelot in the Hautes Côtes de Beaune, details of which are as follows:

DOMAINE DU CHÂTEAU DE MANDELOT   6 ha.
Bourgogne Hautes Côtes de Beaune 2$\frac{1}{3}$ ha., Bourgogne Passe-Tout-Grains 1$\frac{1}{5}$ ha., Bourgogne Aligoté 1$\frac{3}{4}$ ha.

These wines are vinified at the château under the control of Bouchard Père et Fils. A further 3 ha. of Hautes Côtes de Beaune are still to be planted.

E. BROCARD ET FILS
Founded in 1890 in Paris. It moved to Beaune in 1950, though the capital remains a large outlet for its sales.

CALVET S.A.   (1818)
The first Calvet to sell wine was Jean-Marie, at Tain l'Hermitage in the northern Rhône in 1818; five years later he moved to Bordeaux. His son Octave, who expanded the business, initially drew his Burgundies from the house of Pierre Ponnelle, but by the

end of the century his own vast installations had been built on Beaune's boulevards. The company has always been directed by a Burgundian, for a Bordelais would have to relearn his trade in this area where wine is scarce and properties tiny. It was recently bought by Whitbreads of London, so perhaps we shall see an Englishman move in.

CHAMPY PÈRE ET FILS (1720)

This is one of the oldest wine merchants in Burgundy. At its head for most of this century has been M. Mérat, an autograph-collector, international polo player and cavalry colonel. He has ensured that an old-world leisured air survives in the Victorian-style offices and cellars. Still in use, for instance, is an unusual turn-of-the-century spitoon, called a vomitorium. The firm possesses the original 1720 price-lists, which feature many First Growth Nuits. These wines would have been loaded on to the back of a cart for sale in Belgian market-places. Louis Pasteur wrote to the company when experimenting with must-heating. His letters are preserved and it is not surprising that Champy's vinification methods should owe something to his experiments. The system of heating the must in double-walled copper cauldrons has been described elsewhere.

The estate consists of $7\frac{1}{2}$ ha.:
Clos de Vougeot (bottom and middle) $2\frac{1}{4}$ ha., Savigny La Dominode $1\frac{3}{4}$ ha., Beaune Le Clos des Mouches $1\frac{3}{4}$ ha., Les Avaux $1\frac{3}{4}$ ha.

PAUL CHANSON

Paul was the last remaining Chanson, but the only time he had much to do with the running of the firm was in 1923. He was a bachelor who loved his independence. He had crossed the Sahara and travelled from Queensland to Tahiti, so was a natural for the title of *Ambassadeur de Vins de France* when a group of French Academicians and Duff Cooper launched the idea after the Second World War.

In his shooting-lodge-*garçonnière* behind the Côte were zebra skins and grass skirts and Romanesque carvings; on the walls a dog's-head gargoyle with grinning teeth, a mermaid angel, a pagan cross he rescued from the path of the Paris–Nice autoroute. There (although he had houses in Beaune and Paris), his *penates* were set up, in the form of a small Celtic god, found at a spring nearby.

254

He planted Pinot Blanc (not Chardonnay) above the First Growths of Beaune, in Bourgogne Clos de Pierres Blanches, as in the white part of his Corton Vergennes vineyard.

He also owned vines in Pommard Trois-Follots (three fools), Beaune Avaux and Grèves. Most he bottled himself and if sometimes this happened before the alcoholic or malolactic fermentations were quite completed, his friends usually forgave him the unwanted bubbles in their wines. His prices were high, but his yields small and his vattings long.

On the subject of Burgundian merchants, he was stimulating, on wines quotable: 'Our Aligotés are better than our Chardonnays. For Chardonnays you have to wait, two years in wood, two years in bottle. But Aligoté, it's a girl in a mini-skirt, hop, off she goes to earn her keep straight away.'

Paul Chanson died in a car accident during the winter of 1974/5. His Corton-Vergennes he left to the Hospices de Beaune, where the *cuvée* bears his name. His mottos were *Marche ou crève* and 'It's in ourselves that we are thus and thus.'

CHANSON PÈRE ET FILS   (1750) 40 ha.
This firm lists the greatest number of Beaune wines:
Clos des Fèves $3\frac{3}{4}$ ha., Les Bressandes $1\frac{1}{3}$ ha., Les Grèves $2\frac{1}{5}$ ha., Le Clos des Mouches $4\frac{1}{3}$ ha., Les Marconnets $3\frac{3}{4}$ ha., Clos du Roi $2\frac{2}{3}$ ha., Champs Pimont 3 ha., Les Teurons $3\frac{4}{5}$ ha., Les Blanches Fleurs $1\frac{1}{4}$ ha., Savigny La Dominode $1\frac{3}{4}$ ha., Les Marconnets $2\frac{1}{5}$ ha., Pernand-Vergelesses Les Vergelesses $5\frac{1}{2}$ ha.

Chanson aims to produce wines where finesse counts for more than body. I have found them sound, but they have never yet got me excited. Two brothers, Philippe and François Marion (their father married a Chanson) run the firm, which stores most of its wine in the largest of Beaune's bastions, behind walls eight metres thick. Voltaire was once a customer.

CO-OPÉRATIVE DES HAUTES CÔTES DE BEAUNE ET NUITS
This £80,000 investment is situated on the main road south of Beaune, opposite the village of Pommard. It vinifies and commercializes the produce of about 250 ha. of vines—for further details, see page 233.

255

CORON PÈRE ET FILS   (1879) 3 ha.
Beaune Les Cent Vignes $\frac{4}{5}$ ha., Clos du Roi $\frac{4}{5}$ ha., Champs Pimont 1 ha., Les Grèves $\frac{1}{2}$ ha., Le Clos des Mouches $\frac{1}{5}$ ha.

HENRI JEAN DARVIOT   16 ha. (75 per cent)
DOMAINE DARVIOT
Beaune Les Grèves $\frac{3}{4}$ ha., Le Clos des Mouches 1 ha., Les Aigrots $\frac{3}{4}$ ha., Montagne Saint-Désiré 2 ha., Meursault La Goutte d'Or $\frac{1}{2}$ ha., Clos de la Velle Monopole 1 ha., Monthélie Clos Gauthey Monopole 1 ha., Les Duresses $\frac{3}{4}$ ha., Savigny.

M. Darviot is a friend of the cartoonist Peynet, who has drawn his famous French lovers for the front of this domaine's price-list.

JOSEPH DROUHIN
It was in 1880 that Joseph Drouhin bought out an old Beaune merchant, founded in 1756, in order to sell wine under his own name. Soon afterwards he acquired the cellars of the Dukes of Burgundy, the Kings of France and the Collégiale of Beaune. Under his son Maurice Drouhin the company expanded after the First World War. It concentrated on quality and bought vineyards on the Côte de Beaune.

The latter's nephew and adopted son, Robert Jousset-Drouhin, took control in 1957 at the age of twenty-three. He foresaw that demand for Burgundies would rise while supply remained stable, and adopted a policy of extension of his estate on the Côte de Nuits—now, thanks to tractors, close enough for cultivation. He also took steps to guarantee the authenticity of his wines by allowing none foreign to Burgundy and Beaujolais into his cellars. This means no Châteauneuf du Pape, no Côtes du Rhône, and no *ordinaire* wines at all.

The 45 ha. estate consists of:
Chambertin Clos de Bèze $\frac{1}{8}$ ha., Griotte-Chambertin $\frac{1}{2}$ ha., Bonnes Mares $\frac{1}{4}$ ha., Musigny $\frac{2}{3}$ ha., Chambolle-Musigny Les Amoureuses $\frac{1}{2}$ ha., *Premier Cru* $1\frac{1}{5}$ ha., Clos de Vougeot (middle and bottom) $\frac{7}{8}$ ha., Grands Echézeaux $\frac{1}{2}$ ha., Echézeaux $\frac{2}{5}$ ha., Corton $\frac{1}{2}$ ha., Beaune Clos des Mouches red and white 13 ha., *Premier Cru* $2\frac{1}{2}$ ha., Volnay Clos des Chênes $\frac{1}{4}$ ha., Chablis *Grand Cru* 2 ha., *Premier Cru* 7 ha., Chablis $11\frac{1}{2}$ ha.

After a poor harvest all but the best of these wines will be on sale to the local commerce in bulk. No VSR or non-vintage wine is ever sold.

The company makes and distributes the famous Montrachet Marquis de la Guiche (see page 299), as well as Puligny-Montrachet Clos du Cailleret (see page 293).

In 1927 it was among the first to experiment with *vinification ferré* or must-heating. The process was found unsatisfactory then and again in 1957. Robert Drouhin finds that this treatment gives different wines a uniform character. His concern for authenticity and apparent conviction that the Burgundy wine-trade is about exceptional bottles have always attracted me. I have often chosen his wines—and sometimes been disappointed. This goes to show, perhaps, how difficult it is to produce fine Burgundy regularly, and does not stop me continuing to try his bottles.

DOMAINE DUCHET   5 ha. (60 per cent)
Corton-Charlemagne $\frac{1}{4}$ ha., Savigny Les Peuillets $\frac{2}{5}$ ha., Beaune Les Bressandes 1 ha., Les Cent Vignes 1 ha., Les Grèves $\frac{1}{3}$ ha., Pertuisots, Les Teurons, Blanchisserie, a little Pomard.

Mme Duchet's husband used to be mayor of Beaune; she began running the estate in 1961. It took her six years to learn to vinify, she says.

Her Bressandes vines, which are on ground so steep that pulleys are needed to cultivate them, were a ripe age in the early 1970s.

HOSPICES DE BEAUNE
The 55 ha. of vines belonging to the Hospices de Beaune are situated on almost every hillside of Beaune's Côte. But rather than being sold under their village and vineyard names like other Burgundies, the wines from one village which complement each other are blended to form different *cuvées*. This system is designed to produce well-balanced wines. It also simplifies labelling and commercialization and ensures continuity, for if one part of a *cuvée* gets hailed on or needs replanting, the remaining vineyards keep the joint flag flying.

The wines are sold by auction on the third Sunday of November each year. It is one of the so-called glorious events of Burgundy's *Trois Glorieuses* that weekend, the other two being a Clos de Vougeot dinner and the Paulée lunch in Meursault (see pages 200 and 286). Each wine always used to carry the name of the *vigneron* who made it until in 1899 it was decided to use instead the names of the Hospices's major benefactors. Nicolas Rolin and Guigone de Salins had founded it; the Dames Hospitalières care for its sick. Others now posthumously famous on wine-bottle labels donated its 600 ha. of woodland or 800 ha. of farmland. Some, of course, gave vines. The first to do this, with a vineyard in the climat of 'En le Faye' was a Beaune baker's family in 1459. One of the most recent was Thomas Collignon, an inhabitant of Gevrey-Chambertin with no heirs, who gave a large plot of Mazis-Chambertin, the Hospices's only vineyard on the Côte de Nuits. The *cuvée* was named after his mother, and auctioned for the first time in 1977. The latest acquisitions are two *cuvées Cyrot Chaudron*, a Beaune and a Pommard.

At present, the red wine *cuvées* are composed as follows:

Charlotte Dumay: Corton Renardes 2 ha., Les Bressandes 1 ha., Clos du Roi $\frac{1}{2}$ ha.

Docteur Peste: Corton Bressandes 1 ha., Chaumes et Voirosses 1 ha., Clos du Roi $\frac{1}{2}$ ha., Fiètre $\frac{2}{5}$ ha., Les Grèves $\frac{1}{10}$ ha.

Rameau-Lamarosse: Pernand-Vergelesses Les Basses Vergelesses $\frac{3}{5}$ ha.

Forneret: Savigny Les Vergelesses 1 ha., Aux Gravains $\frac{2}{3}$ ha.

Fouquerand: Savigny Basses Vergelesses 1 ha., Les Talmettes $\frac{2}{3}$ ha., Aux Gravains $\frac{1}{3}$ ha., Aux Serpentières $\frac{1}{7}$ ha.

Arthur Girard: Savigny Les Peuillets 1 ha., Les Marconnets $\frac{4}{5}$ ha.

Nicolas Rolin:[1] Beaune Les Cents Vignes $1\frac{1}{2}$ ha., Les Grèves $\frac{4}{5}$ ha., En Genêt $\frac{2}{5}$ ha.

Guigone de Salins: Beaune Les Bressandes 1 ha., En Senrey $\frac{4}{5}$ ha., Champs Pimont $\frac{3}{5}$ ha.

Clos des Avaux: Beaune Les Avaux 2 ha.

Brunet: Beaune Les Teurons $\frac{7}{8}$ ha., Les Bressandes $\frac{2}{3}$ ha., La Mignotte $\frac{1}{2}$ ha., Les Cents Vignes $\frac{1}{3}$ ha.

---

[1] I have always been somewhat surprised by Nicolas Rolin's pre-eminence, considering that several *cuvées* have origins just as noble and vines as old. One theory would have it that Les Cent Vignes (whence much of it comes) is one of the most favoured spots on the Côte de Beaune, whose grapes are nearly always the first to swell, turn colour and ripen.

Maurice Drouhin: Beaune Les Avaux $\frac{4}{5}$ ha., Les Boucherottes $\frac{2}{3}$ ha., Champs Pimont $\frac{3}{5}$ ha., Les Grèves $\frac{2}{5}$ ha.

Hugues et Louis Bétault: Beaune Les Grèves $\frac{7}{8}$ ha., La Mignotte $\frac{1}{2}$ ha., Les Aigrots $\frac{2}{5}$ ha., Les Sizies $\frac{1}{3}$ ha., Les Vignes Franches $\frac{1}{5}$ ha.

Rousseau-Deslandes: Beaune Les Cent Vignes 1 ha., Les Montre-venots $\frac{2}{3}$ ha., La Mignotte $\frac{2}{5}$ ha., Les Avaux $\frac{1}{3}$ ha.

Dames Hospitalières: Beaune Les Bressandes 1 ha., La Mignotte $\frac{2}{3}$ ha., Les Teurons $\frac{1}{2}$ ha., Les Grèves $\frac{1}{3}$ ha.

Dames de la Charité: Pommard Les Epenots $\frac{2}{5}$ ha., Les Rugiens $\frac{1}{3}$ ha., Les Noizons $\frac{1}{3}$ ha., La Refène $\frac{1}{3}$ ha., Les Combes Dessus $\frac{1}{5}$ ha.

Billardet: Pommard Petits-Epenots $\frac{2}{3}$ ha., Les Noizons $\frac{1}{2}$ ha., Les Arvelets $\frac{2}{5}$ ha., Les Rugiens $\frac{1}{3}$ ha.

Blondeau: Volnay Champans $\frac{3}{5}$ ha., Taille Pieds $\frac{3}{5}$ ha., Ronceret $\frac{1}{3}$ ha., En l'Ormeau $\frac{1}{5}$ ha.

General Muteau: Volnay le Village $\frac{4}{5}$ ha., Carelle sous la Chapelle $\frac{1}{3}$ ha., Cailleret Dessus $\frac{1}{5}$ ha., Fremiet $\frac{1}{5}$ ha., Taille Pieds $\frac{1}{5}$ ha.

Jehan de Massol: Volnay-Santenots Les Santenots $1\frac{1}{2}$ ha.

Gauvain: Volnay-Santenots Les Santenots $1\frac{1}{2}$ ha., Les Pitures $\frac{1}{3}$ ha.

Lebelin: Monthélie Les Duresses $\frac{7}{8}$ ha.

Boillot: Auxey-Duresses Les Duresses $\frac{3}{4}$ ha.

Madeleine Collignon: Mazis-Chambertin $1\frac{1}{2}$ ha.

Cyrot Chaudron: Beaune 2 ha.; also Pommard 2 ha.

White wines

Françoise de Salins: Corton-Charlemagne $\frac{1}{4}$ ha.

Baudot: Meursault-Genevrières Les Genevrières Dessus $\frac{2}{3}$ ha., Les Genevrières Dessous $\frac{3}{4}$ ha.

Philippe le Bon: Meursault-Genevrières Les Genevrières Dessus $\frac{1}{5}$ ha., Les Genevrières Dessous $\frac{2}{5}$ ha.

de Bahèzre de Lanlay: Meursault-Charmes Les Charmes Dessus $\frac{1}{2}$ ha., Les Charmes Dessous $\frac{2}{5}$ ha.

Albert-Grivault: Meursault-Charmes Les Charmes Dessus $\frac{1}{2}$ ha.

Jehan Humblot: Meursault Le Poruzot $\frac{2}{3}$ ha., Grands Charrons $\frac{1}{10}$ ha.

Loppin: Meursault Les Criots $\frac{2}{3}$ ha.

Goureau: Meursault Le Poruzot $\frac{1}{3}$ ha., Les Pitures $\frac{1}{3}$ ha., Les Cras $\frac{1}{5}$ ha.

Paul Chanson: Corton-Vergennes $\frac{1}{4}$ ha.

The exact make-up of the *cuvées* changes from time to time. Until 1968, for instance, there were two Beaune wines called Virely and Estienne. Now part of Estienne has gone into the Dames Hospitalières, and the remainder, along with Virely, has been rented to the Lycée Viticole et Agricole de Beaune. A Monthélie Henri Gélicot, and a Savigny Du-Bay-Peste-Cyrot have also fallen by the wayside over the years.

It is traditional for the vines making up each *cuvée* to be tended by the same family down the generations, and there is much rivalry at the time of the auction, for a bonus is paid according to the prices attained. At present, five *cuvées* are tended by ladies (Dames de la Charité, Arthur Girard, Jehan de Massol, Lebelin, and Boillot), the last three by the same person, Mme Monthélie-Leblanc.

A lot of replanting was done after the war, but the Hospices vineyards now show a good balance between young and old vines. In 1968 and 1977, André Masson, the estate manager, produced a table to illustrate this:

	Percentage *1968*	*1977*
Fallow land	3	2
Young vines (less than 4 years old)	7	5
Youngish vines (4–15 years old)	28	27
Vines of adult age (16–30 years old)	45	35
Old vines (30 years or more)	17	31

As may be seen, he had slightly increased the average age of the vines.

What was less admirable, however, was what happened after the grapes had been picked. Yields had gone up in the Hospices vineyards, as elsewhere in Burgundy, but without a corresponding increase in vat-space to handle the larger quantities of grapes. If the harvest was not to be stopped, some vats had to be drawn off after only a few days' maceration, to make room for the newly-arriving grapes. The resulting wines lacked substance and length. Nor was the after-care always impeccable, the most notorious 'accident' being the loss of over 100 hogsheads of the 1976 harvest.

A new estate manager, André Porcheret (an ex-*tonnelier* and *chef-caviste*), has recently taken over; the vat-house has been extended and new cellars acquired. No longer will the young wines have to be stored at ground level (said to be one of the causes of the 'accident' with the 1976s, another being that the wine was drawn off into vinegary barrels). Every year the young wine is now lodged in new oak, and the barrels are sold with the wine. Of the enormous 1982 harvest 25 per cent was excluded from the auction, the wine withdrawn being the produce of young vines and those which had overcropped.[1]

This is all greatly to be welcomed, but in addition, a bit of post-auction quality control is overdue. Since 1969, the Hospices have been issuing their own labels, giving an air of authenticity to the wines, indeed the impression that they go out around the world with the Hospices' blessing. Yet some of the contents are unrecognizable. Recently one of the finest tasters I know bought a bottle of Hospices wine from a Beaune wine shop. He was so disgusted with it, he poured it down the drain. That seems a waste—for while his fondness for accurate description perhaps prevented him from using it in a *boeuf bourguignon*, it would surely have made a richly-flavoured *coq au vin*.

In 1896, when Durand and Guicherd were describing the year's work in the vineyard, they included this comment in their passage for November: 'First tastings of the bright wines at the Hospices de Beaune sale; first appraisals, often too hasty, of the quality of the new wines.' It is no different today. To judge the Hospices wines in November each year is to judge them at what is often the most attractive moment in their lives—just recognizably wine, their meagre structures masked by sweet grapiness.

Fellow wine-buyer, why do you bid at the Hospices auction? Do you have to stop off in Beaune when your reason for coming to

---

[1] The *appellation* certificates and the valuable wine they accompany are of course not to be wasted, but are finding their way into the local *commerce*, there no doubt to improve with *élevage*. Did the Hospices consider declassifying some or all of these 250 *pièces*, which are arguably unworthy of the famous AC names they bear?

Burgundy is to secure good new Beaujolais? Would your customers really desert you if your wine-list was bare of Hospices bottles? If the Hospices de Beaune is the most deserving charity you know, then why not send a donation?

There has sometimes been pressure on the Hospices from overseas importers (as well as from the tens of thousands of tourists who annually visit the Hôtel-Dieu) for estate-bottlings to take place. But while the auction is so successful, there is unlikely to be any change. Selling in bulk to the local trade simplifies the wine-maker's life, and the local *négociants* are keen to stay in the circuit. They find fulfilment in their traditional role.

In fact, not all the wine is sold in bulk. A few barrels are kept back and bottled at the Hospices so that the sick and old, who are its *raison d'être*, may always have fine old wine to drink on feast-days.

JABOULET-VERCHERRE (1834) 9 ha.
Pommard Clos du Château de la Commaraine Monopole 1½ ha., Clos Blanc 2 ha., Volnay Caillerets ¼ ha., Beaune Clos de l'Écu Monopole 2⅘ ha., Corton Les Bressandes ½ ha., Clos de Vougeot (middle) ⅓ ha., Chambertin ¼ ha.

This company was founded in Tain l'Hermitage. It is one of the largest grape-buyers on the Côte, and has used the *vinification ferré* must-heating process for many years. The end product is very supple and does not need excessive aging. It claims that the system was invented by monks.

LOUIS JADOT (1859)
On the death of the third Louis Jadot the present director M. André Gagey was asked to run the company while awaiting the maturity of Louis-Alain Jadot. But the latter was killed in a car accident in 1968 at the age of twenty-three.

The company's fine domaine of 25 ha. dates from the nineteenth century:
Les Corton Pougets 2¼ ha., Corton-Charlemagne 1½ ha., Pernand-Vergelesses en Caradeux Clos de la Croix de Pierre Monopole 2 ha., Beaune Clos du Roi ½ ha., Les Teurons 1 ha., Les Bressandes 1½ ha., Les Vignes Franches ½ ha., Les Vignes Franches Clos des Ursules Monopole 2½ ha., Les Boucherottes 3 ha., Chevalier-Montrachet les Demoiselles ½ ha.

The last vineyard is shared with Louis Latour,[1] the two companies being very friendly.

Jadot own (and used to work in) one of the most extraordinary buildings in Beaune *not* open to the tourists: the 1470 Couvent des Jacobins, which was built thirty years after the famous Hospices, in the same style. It has a magnificent vaulted roof which is carved with gargoyles and monsters' heads like the Salle des Povres, but in this case left unpainted. The Jadot stocks of cardboard cartons were until recently piled up to the beams, while down below bottles were labelled beneath Gothic arches, in side-chapels of the convent.

Today the bottling and cartonning takes place outside Beaune's walls and the convent is used for receptions and tastings. André Gagey is a vaguely familiar figure to many English people, for he once appeared on BBC Television describing the life of a Burgundian wine-merchant during the Hospices de Beaune auction weekend in November. His voice is rich and deep, his wine advice impeccable, his good humour irresistible.

JAFFELIN (1816) 4 ha.
Clos de Vougeot (middle) $\frac{2}{3}$ ha., Beaune Les Bressandes $2\frac{1}{2}$ ha., Les Avaux $\frac{1}{2}$ ha.

This firm owns the Caves du Chapitre, situated within the Gallo-Roman Castrum which was Beaune's first settlement. It is associated with Joseph Drouhin, sharing a small computer and a bottling line; but the stocks of wine are different, as are the sales networks.

MAISON LOUIS LATOUR (1797)
Most of the Louis Latour domaine dates from the phylloxera crisis, when the Comte de Grancey, who lived in Paris, lost confidence in the future of wine-making and sold his estate at Aloxe-Corton. Since then it has been extended north to Chambertin and south to Chevalier-Montrachet (but see footnote below). The estate consists of about 46 ha. and accounts for a quarter of the firm's turnover.

[1] The vineyard in question is part of the Les Demoiselles section of the Caillerets *climat* of Puligny-Montrachet. In the past its AC was Puligny-Montrachet Les Demoiselles; it has now been upgraded.

Chambertin 1 ha., Romanée Saint-Vivant Quatre Journaux 1 ha., Corton 16 ha. (sold at Château Corton-Grancey), Corton Clos de la Vigne au Saint Monopole $2\frac{2}{3}$ ha., Corton-Charlemagne 7 ha., Aloxe-Corton Les Chaillots $4\frac{1}{2}$ ha., Pernand-Vergelesses Ile des Vergelesses $\frac{3}{4}$ ha., Beaune Les Vignes Franches $2\frac{2}{3}$ ha., Les Perrières 1 ha., Clos du Roi $\frac{1}{2}$ ha., Les Grèves $\frac{1}{5}$ ha., Pommard Les Epenots $\frac{1}{2}$ ha., Volnay Les Mitans 1 ha., Chevalier-Montrachet Les Demoiselles $\frac{1}{2}$ ha.

Until his death in 1982, Louis Latour senior was the *doyen* of négociants and a well-known figure in Beaune. He used to see no merit in the tendency to return to vinifying with the stalks included, for the latter hindered pressing, and sufficient tannin could be had from the skins and pips. He would recount how during his forty years as director of the Hospices de Beaune Museum (containing the famous Roger van der Weyden's 'Last Judgement') a succession of experts had informed him that great paintings should be exposed to, or shielded from, the light. As fashions changed in caring for pictures, so they did in wine-making.

As I have written in the chapter on vinification, Louis Latour's red wines are pasteurized (being heated to 70°C, and kept at that temperature for one minute). In style they are early-maturing, high in alcohol, very round—not my idea of fine Burgundy. The white wines on the other hand are often splendid, and exactly what one hopes for.

LYCÉE VITICOLE   23 ha.
Beaune Champs Pimont, Montée Rouge, Les Bressandes, Les Aigrots, Les Perrières, Côte de Beaune, Chorey-les-Beaune, Puligny-Montrachet, Bourgogne Passe Tout Grains.

MAIRE ET FILS   (1780) 7 ha.
This company is owned by M. Pierre Labet of Émile Labet & Cie, a specialist in *marc*, *cassis*, *framboise*, and *prunelle*. A *marc* made from Pinot Noir, he says, is very strongly flavoured, and needs greater aging than a Gamay *marc*. The descriptions 'Three Star' and 'VSOP' have no legal definition when applied to *marc*. M. Labet has discovered that the first M. Maire used to trade in olive oil as well as wine. He toured the Russian and Central European courts with a horse and cart. The firm now distributes the Beaune

Premier Cru of the Domaine P. Labet, and also the Clos de Vougeot of the Domaine du Château de la Tour.

MALLARD-GAULLIN   (1875) 22 ha.

Corton Renardes 1½ ha., Corton-Charlemagne 1½ ha., Aloxe-Corton *Premier Cru*.

In off-years this company will sell its wines to the local commerce in bulk, in good years to a French private and restaurant clientele in bottle. Many are *tastevinés*.

P. DE MARCILLY FRÈRES   (1849) 15 ha.

Chassagne-Montrachet Clos Saint-Jean, Morgeot, La Conière, Beaune Les Grèves and *Premier Cru*, Bâtard-Montrachet, Les Criots-Bâtard-Montrachet, a little Chambertin.

Since 1924, this company has followed a policy of declassifying these wines to sell them, blended with others they may have bought, as branded Bourgognes named Marcilly Réserve or Marcilly Première. So such a wine as Bâtard-Montrachet de Marcilly rarely, if ever, exists. The firm only moved to Beaune in 1912, having been founded in Chassagne-Montrachet. They still have a *cuverie* there, including a fine pair of nineteenth-century presses.

DOMAINE MATHOUILLET-BESANCENOT   6 ha. (35 per cent)

Beaune Les Grèves 1 ha., Clos de Roi 1 ha., Les Cent Vignes 3 ha., Corton-Charlemagne ¾ ha.

Bernard Besancenot's late father used also to run the Domaine Chandon de Briailles in Savigny. He was an energetic committee-man, being president of various associations and a leading light in the Comité Interprofessionel. He exported most of his estate-bottled wine, and had a listing in the Swedish State Monopoly.

ÉTS ANDRÉ MOREY   (1868)

Jean-Paul Belmondo is an associate and shareholder in this company. It owns 12½ ha. in Villié-Morgon in the Beaujolais.

ALBERT MOROT   (1820) 7 ha.

Beaune Les Bressandes 1⅓ ha., Les Marconnets ⅘ ha., Les Cent Vignes 1⅓ ha., Les Teurons 1 ha., Les Toussaints ¾ ha.

This company works in the 1890 Château de la Creusotte. Three-quarters of its turnover is in the wines from its own vineyards.

PATRIARCHE PÈRE ET FILS (1780)

Until its purchase by M. André Boisseaux after the Second World War, this company was one of the quieter traditional shippers. Since then, by dynamic marketing, it has become the largest merchant in Burgundy after Corbet. The cellars are visited by coachload after coachload. At the time of the Hospices de Beaune wine sale, a tasting is organized of vintages covering half a century. M. Boisseaux's other interests include branded wines and the sparkling Kriter.

The Patriarche estate consists of a dozen or so hectares of Beaune:

Les Fèves, Les Grèves, Les Bressandes, Les Avaux, Clos du Roi, Les Blanches Fleurs, Les Cent Vignes, Les Toussaints.

It also recently acquired the Château de Meursault estate (see page 288).

PIERRE PONNELLE

This house was founded in 1875 by the man who was subsequently asked to direct Calvet's first operations in Burgundy. It has a domaine of $4\frac{3}{4}$ ha. in the following vineyards:

Beaune Clos du Roi, Beaune Les Grèves, Corton Clos du Roi, Vougeot Domaine du Prieuré, Clos de Vougeot (bottom), Chambolle-Musigny, Charmes-Chambertin, Bonnes Mares, and Musigny.

POULET PÈRE ET FILS

This house was founded in 1747. It possesses all its accounts since that date, and all its correspondence since 1810. One interesting fact to be had from their study is that at the end of the eighteenth century Volnay was the most popular wine, followed by Beaune and Nuits Saint-Georges. Pommard was not to gain its ascendancy until the English-speaking countries became Burgundy buyers.

REMOISSENET PÈRE ET FILS (1879)

This company has a small estate of $2\frac{1}{2}$ ha. in the Marconnets, Grèves, Toussaints and Bressandes vineyards of Beaune. It believes that a larger domaine would be a disadvantage, for one is tempted to find one's own wines good and call them by famous names when they should be declassed. M. Roland Remoissenet's speciality is combining the roles of *courtier* and merchant. His company has a file devoted to vineyards planted in old vines, and makes its own oak casks. He mentions the desirability of using wood from trees growing at the edge of the forest (these being tougher after greater exposure to the elements).

LÉON VIOLLAND (1844) 10 ha.
Beaune Montée Rouge 4½ ha., Savigny Les Marconnets 2 ha., Pommard 4 ha., and small sections of Corton, Corton-Charlemagne and Beaune Clos du Roi.

This company deals mostly with French private customers and restaurants.

DOMAINE VOIRET 15 ha. (35 per cent)
Beaune Aux Cras ⅔ ha., Pertuisots 1⅔ ha., Les Grèves ⅖ ha., Les Avaux ½ ha., Les Aigrots ⅖ ha., Les Teurons ⅓ ha., *Premier Cru* 3 ha., Côte de Beaune Grande Châtelaine 1 ha.

This domaine is the only one I know to offer that rare red and white *appellation* Côte de Beaune (not to be confused with Côte de Beaune Villages). Their Grande Châtelaine is planted with Chardonnay. They are experimenting with must-heating, and do not find that it makes the different *crus* resemble one another.

There are a dozen more merchants in Beaune, and nine estate-bottling growers, with a further twelve growers in Bligny-les-Beaune, and four in Bouze-les-Beaune.

POMMARD

The wines of Pommard have an old reputation for aging and travelling well. They are described as solid, well-constructed wines of deep colour, comparable to good Cortons or Gevrey-Chambertins in their need to be laid away to soften up.

The sound of the name Pommard corresponds to most people's idea of what Burgundy should be. It is not just easy to pronounce—it has a full-bodied, generous ring to it. Faced with a wine-list, if you lack confidence, say Pommard. Your spirits will rise. Or rather, they should. Personally I avoid Pommards like the plague, for life has been relatively so easy for the growers (because of international demand) that interesting bottles are very hard to find. The wines are usually the worst value for money in Burgundy.

267

Pommard and Volnay

Commune de Beaune

Les Boucherottes

Les Saucilles

Les Pézerolles

Les Argillières

Les Épenots

N 73

N 74

La Platière

La Chanière

Les Charmots

Les Arvelets

Clos de Verger

La Refène

Clos Blanc

Clos de la Commaraine

POMMARD

Derrière St-Jean

Les Rugiens Bas

Les Chaponnières

Les Croix Noires

Les Poutures

Clos Micot

Les Rugiens Hauts

Les Jarollières

Les Fremiets

Les Bertins

Les Combes Dessus

Les Chanlins Bas

Chanlin

Pointes d'Angles

Pitures Dessus

Fremiet

Les Brouillards

Clos des Ducs

Les Angles

Les Mitans

VOLNAY

La Barre

Bousse d'Or

En l'Ormeau

En Verseuil

Carelle sous la Chapelle

Carelle Dessous

Taille-Pieds

Champans

Ronceret

En Cailleret

Les Aussy

Clos des Chênes

Cailleret Dessus

En Chevret

Les Lurets

Robardelle

Les Santenots

Commune de Meursault

The following vineyards are currently classed as First Growths: Les Rugiens Bas, Les Rugiens Hauts (part), Les Epenots, Les Petits Epenots (part), Clos de la Commaraine, Clos Blanc, Les Arvelets, Les Charmots, Les Argillières, Les Pézerolles, Les Boucherottes, Les Saucilles, Les Croix Noires, Les Chaponières, Les Fremiers, Les Bertins, Les Jarollières, Les Poutures, Clos Micot, La Refène, Clos de Verger, Derrière Saint-Jean, La Platière (part), Les Chanlins Bas (part), Les Combes Dessus (part), La Chanière (part).

First Growth and commune Pommard covers 340 hectares, the average production being 10,400 hl (114,400 dozen bottles) of red wine.

Main Merchants and Growers

COMTE ARMAND, PROPRIÉTAIRE $5\frac{1}{4}$ ha. (80 per cent)

DOMAINE DU CLOS DES EPENEAUX
Pommard Clos des Epeneaux Monopole $5\frac{1}{2}$ ha.

The *cuverie* and cellars here form part of a fine old *vigneron*'s house with a stony balcony. The *régisseur* is Philibert Rossignol of Volnay.

BIDOT-BOURGOGNE   5 ha. (35 per cent)
Pommard Les Epenots $\frac{1}{4}$ ha., Volnay, Beaune.

According to local custom, M. Bidot added his wife's name to his own on marriage, thus assuring himself of the *appellation* Bourgogne for a lifetime.

DOMAINE BILLARD-GONNET   12 ha. (20 per cent)
Pommard *Premier Cru* $5\frac{1}{2}$ ha. (Les Rugiens, Clos de Verger, Les Jarollieres, Les Pézerolles, Les Charmots, Les Chaponières, Les Poutures, Les Bertins).

GEORGES CAILLET
BERNARD CAILLET $6\frac{1}{2}$ ha. (100 per cent)
Pommard Les Charmots $\frac{1}{2}$ ha., Beaune *Premier Cru*.

Bernard Caillet was thirty-five when I met him in the late 1960s, and taking over the running of this estate from his father. His methods were modern—in 1968 he got reasonable results from heating half of his must.

FÉLIX CLERGET   18 ha. (30 per cent)

Pommard Les Rugiens $\frac{3}{4}$ ha., *Premier Cru* 5 ha. (Les Arvelets, Les Charmots, Les Saucilles, Les Charmières, Clos Blanc, Les Chanlins Bas), Volnay En Cailleret $\frac{1}{3}$ ha., Les Mitans 1 ha., Puligny-Montrachet Champ Gain $\frac{1}{3}$ ha., Beaune Les Grèves $\frac{2}{3}$ ha., Les Aigrots 2$\frac{1}{2}$ ha., Saint-Désiré 3 ha., Corton Renardes $\frac{2}{5}$ ha., Corton Vergennes $\frac{3}{4}$ ha., Clos de Vougeot $\frac{1}{3}$ ha. (top).

The origins of this estate date back to 1270. A member of the Clerget family has been mayor or assistant mayor of his village some twenty-seven times. Monsieur Félix Clerget has strong feelings about the tendency to over-chaptalize: 'It is to turn a dancer into a wood-cutter. And a wood-cutter without any conversation at all.' To bring a wine of 10.5° up to 11.5° is one thing, but up to 13.5° quite another. '*Laboria vincit*, they say. It's false. In wine, laziness, or rather, discretion, conquers all. You need to put the brake on production.'

His Saint-Désiré wine from Beaune (uphill from the Clos des Mouches) is one of his favourites, being 'simple, slender, un-clogged. Beaune wine is sad, in a minor key, recalling autumn mists, wood-smoke, the *retour de chasse*. And never vulgar. Wine must be a courtesan. It must try to please, yet must keep a certain severity, must even have something which shocks. In any cellar you should always be able to find a friend.'

ROGER CLERGET   14 ha. (100 per cent)

Pommard Les Rugiens $\frac{1}{2}$ ha., Les Epenots $\frac{1}{2}$ ha., Les Pézerolles 1$\frac{1}{2}$ ha., Clos Blanc $\frac{1}{2}$ ha., Savigny Les Vergelesses 1$\frac{1}{2}$ ha., Aloxe-Corton 1 ha.

From 1947 until his death in 1974 Roger Clerget bottled all his wine, good year and bad. This was made possible by heating the grapes up to 85°C for ten to thirty minutes, and then bringing them down to 25°C, for pressing and fermentation without their skins. His first experiments with this system were made with an old pig-potato cauldron. His face used to register a continuous grin as he described his methods and their success. His wines had a concentrated flavour which perhaps came from his needing 400 kg rather than the normal 300 kg to make one barrel of wine, due to evaporation. Initially a smell could be detected similar to that of raspberry jam in the making, but this was said to disappear before bottling. The vines are now tended by Georges Pinte of Savigny.

DOMAINE DU CLOS SAINT-JEAN 7½ ha.

LAHAYE PÈRE ET FILS
Pommard 4½ ha., Meursault ⅔ ha.

M. Lahaye is a broker as well as a proprietor who bottles occasionally.

DOMAINE DE MME BERNARD DE COURCEL 13 ha. (90 per cent)
Pommard Les Epenots 8 ha., Les Rugiens 1 ha.

This domaine has a very large sale to the USA in famous years.

DOMAINE MICHEL GAUNOUX 12 ha. (100 per cent)
Pommard Les Grands Epenots 3 ha., Les Rugiens Bas 1 ha., Les Arvelets ½ ha., Les Charmots ⅓ ha., Beaune *Premier Cru* ¾ ha., Corton-Renardes 1½ ha.

Vigneron's wisdom from Père Gaunoux: 'We are very irregular in character, and the sun much more so than us. Pay more attention to the vintage than the *cru*.' Wearing an old *caviste*'s apron, he was sitting next to a marble slab with glue spread over it, sticking the 1937 neck-slip on to some Pommard Les Rugiens. 'You must not believe that one is better just because one is old. It depends on the wind of the epoch whether bottles sell well. Off-years are always thoroughbreds, even if they're a bit lame.' This domaine has a stock of 150,000 bottles, and can supply vintages back to 1929. In the cellars one or more casks may carry the discreet visiting-card *'Réserve des Caves de la Tour d'Argent'*.

DOMAINE JULES GUILLEMARD 8 ha. (35 per cent)
GUILLEMARD-FAIVRE
Pommard Les Rugiens ½ ha., Les Epenots ½ ha., La Platière 1 ha., Beaune Le Clos des Mouches ½ ha., Les Epenottes ½ ha.

DOMAINE LEJEUNE 8 ha. (30 per cent)
Pommard Les Rugiens 1 ha., Les Argillières 1½ ha., Les Poutures 1 ha., Cras 1½ ha., Les Chaponières ½ ha.

The *régisseur* of this domaine, M. Jacquelin-Vaudoisey, himself owns 2 ha. of Pommard, with ⅓ ha. in Les Epenots. The domaine possesses a seventeenth-century vat, claimed to be the oldest in Burgundy, which is still held together by osier and birch stems.

HÉRITIERS RAOUL LENEUF 4 ha. (50 per cent)
Pommard and Beaune.

M. Leneuf's tasting-room is simple and attractive. Built of old stone, it is triangular with a large open fireplace in one of the walls.

DOMAINE PARENT 11½ ha. (100 per cent)

Pommard Les Chaponières ¾ ha., Les Epenots 2½ ha., Les Chanlins Bas ⅓ ha., Beaune Les Epenottes 2 ha., Les Boucherottes ½ ha.

Jacques Parent is a conscientious tender of vines and wine. He has little patience with the dabblers who, for instance, rack their wine when rain prevents their being in the vineyard, rather than when the wine needs it. He and his wife form a powerful team. A bottle of First Growth Pommard is one of the great luxuries of life, like an outfit from Dior: equivalent care and ideals should go into its making, they would have you know.

CHÂTEAU DE POMMARD 20 ha. (100 per cent)

JEAN-LOUIS LAPLANCHE

Clos de Château de Pommard Monopole.

This is the largest Clos under single ownership in Burgundy, and is surrounded by two kilometres of walls. As every inhabitant of Pommard will tell you, the vines are situated between the village and the road, almost in the plain.

Dr Jean-Louis Laplanche is a well-known psycho-analyst and Sorbonne professor who spends four days a week in Paris and three in Pommard. There are two châteaux within the Clos. The older was built in 1726 and sold by the Marey family in 1789 'because people were burning châteaux everywhere'. Five years later they regretted it, and being unable to buy it back, built another close by. The two are now united for the first time.

DOMAINE V. POTHIER-RIEUSSET 8 ha. (35 per cent)

Pommard Les Rugiens ¾ ha., Les Epenots ⅙ ha., Clos de Verger 1 ha., Beaune Les Boucherottes ½ ha.

M. Virgil Pothier is a *courtier* as well as being a proprietor. He sells his domaine-bottlings to local merchants, and holds certain stocks of old vintages, including, when I went there, some remarkable Les Rugiens off-years such as 1946 and 1938.

A further twenty-two estate-bottling growers are listed in Pommard, and two merchants.

VOLNAY

The village of Volnay sits high up on its hillside, as befits a place whose wines have long been reputed the finest of the Côte de Beaune. Today it has some outstanding estates, setting standards for the whole of Burgundy, and at least one providing inspiration to other wine-makers.

The names of many of the individual vineyards have been unchanged for 700 years. In the thirteenth century, the Order of Malta owned six *ouvrées* of En Cailleret, and the Priory of Saint-Étienne in Beaune had vines in En Verseux, Les Angles and Carelle. The Dukes owned part of Taille-Pieds and Chevrey, and in 1250 constructed a château, for the view was so varied, the air so good, and the wines and water so excellent. In 1509 the King owned parts of En Cailleret, Champans, En l'Ormeau and Taille-Pieds. On the collapse of Valois Burgundy with Charles the Bold's death, one of Louis XI's first actions was to have the 1477 Volnay harvest brought to his château at Plessis-les-Tours. There is only one Volnay in France, goes the old saying.

The classified First Growths are: En Cailleret, Cailleret Dessus, Champans, En Chevret, Fremiet, Bousse d'Or, La Barre or Clos de la Barre, Clos des Chênes (part), Les Angles, Pointes d'Angles, Les Mitans, En l'Ormeau, Taille-Pieds, En Verseuil, Carelle sous la Chapelle, Ronceret, Carelle Dessous (part), Robardelle (part), Les Lurets (part), Les Aussy (part), Les Brouillards (part), Clos des Ducs, Pitures Dessus, Chanlin (part), Les Santenots (red), Les Petures (red), Village-de-Volnay (part).

The average production of the village is 7,900 hl (87,000 dozen bottles) of red wine, from a delimited area of 214.64 hectares.

Main Merchants and Growers

MARQUIS D'ANGERVILLE 14 ha. (90 per cent)
Volnay Clos des Ducs Monopole 2 ha., Caillerets ½ ha., Fremiet 1½ ha., Champans 4 ha., Taille-Pieds 1 ha., Meursault Les Santenots 1 ha.

In the early days of the *appellation contrôlée* laws the present Marquis's father waged unceasing war against dishonest practices. Consequently the local commerce closed against him, and he was forced to bottle his own wine and sell direct.

His son recalls that at this time, when Beaune station was probably the largest producer of Burgundy, the wines arrived from the south to be rebaptized and despatched without leaving their trains. As well as combating fraud, the late Marquis undertook the most rigorous selection of quality-producing vines, which became known as Pinots d'Angerville, and are still to be found on this famous estate.

DOMAINE HENRI BOILLOT 22 ha. (100 per cent)
Puligny-Montrachet Clos de la Mouchère Monopole 4 ha., Pucelles $\frac{1}{2}$ ha., Meursault Les Genevrières 1 ha., Volnay En Chevret 2 ha., Caillerets $\frac{3}{4}$ ha., Les Angles 1$\frac{1}{2}$ ha., Pommard Les Jarollières 1$\frac{1}{4}$ ha., Les Rugiens $\frac{1}{2}$ ha., Beaune Les Epenottes $\frac{1}{2}$ ha.
This is one of the largest estates to sell direct.

MME BUFFET 6 ha. (30 per cent)
Volnay Champans $\frac{1}{2}$ ha., Clos des Chênes 1 ha., Pommard Les Rugiens $\frac{1}{10}$ ha.

DOMAINE CLERGET 5 ha. (75 per cent)
Volnay Caillerets $\frac{1}{3}$ ha., Clos du Verseuil Monopole $\frac{2}{3}$ ha., Les Santenots $\frac{3}{4}$ ha., Carelle sous la Chapelle $\frac{2}{3}$ ha., Pommard Les Rugiens $\frac{2}{3}$ ha.
There have been Clergets in Volnay since 1270.

BERNARD DELAGRANGE ET FILS 20 ha. (100 per cent)
Volnay Caillerets $\frac{1}{3}$ ha., Champans $\frac{1}{3}$ ha., Pommard Les Chanlins Bas $\frac{1}{3}$ ha., Beaune Les Boucherottes $\frac{1}{3}$ ha.
M. Delagrange is oriented towards attracting the passing tourist, and has a tasting-room full of varnished barrels, brochures and vine-root lamp-standards. When I visited him, the animal-skins on the walls seemed to have been improperly cured, giving his tasting-room an unusual smell—but no doubt that problem has been put right.

GEORGES GLANTENAY 6 ha. (30 per cent)
Pommard Les Rugiens $\frac{1}{4}$ ha., Volnay Les Santenots $\frac{1}{3}$ ha., Les Brouillards 1 ha.

LOUIS GLANTENAY 8 ha. (50 per cent)
Volnay Clos des Chênes $\frac{1}{2}$ ha., Caillerets $\frac{1}{4}$ ha., Les Santenots $\frac{2}{3}$ ha., Pommard Les Rugiens $\frac{1}{4}$ ha.
Louis Glantenay has been Mayor of Volnay.

MICHEL LAFARGE 8 ha. (65 per cent)
Volnay Clos des Chênes 1 ha., Beaune Les Grèves $\frac{1}{2}$ ha., Meursault $\frac{1}{2}$ ha.

HENRI MONNOT 6 ha. (100 per cent)
Volnay Caillerets $\frac{1}{5}$ ha., *Premier Cru* 3 ha., Pommard Les Fremiets $\frac{1}{3}$ ha., Les Chanlins Bas $\frac{1}{4}$ ha.
Monsieur Monnot's major clientele is French restaurants.

MME FRANÇOIS DE MONTILLE 6 ha. (100 per cent)
Pommard Les Rugiens 1 ha., Les Epenots $\frac{1}{4}$ ha., Les Pézerolles 1 ha., Volnay Taille-Pieds $\frac{4}{5}$ ha., Champans $\frac{2}{3}$ ha., *Premier cru* 1 ha., Les Mitans $\frac{3}{4}$ ha.
Maître Hubert de Montille is a Dijon lawyer. A *vigneron* cultivates his mother's vines (it is her name which appears on the label), but he supervises the vinification himself. During the 1959 vintage, he made a mistake in calculating the amount of sugar to be used for chaptalizing, with the result that a wine of only 11.5° of alcohol was produced. To his great surprise this developed better in bottle than any of his other 1959s. As a result, very little chaptalization now takes place on this estate. In addition, its vines are mostly of mature age and their yield is kept low.

This estate has been producing fine and fascinating bottles, whatever the weather, for twenty years now; and Hubert de Montille has become a wine-maker's guru, at whose feet more than one inexperienced Côte d'Or grower has been delighted to sit.

MICHEL PONT—LE CELLIER VOLNAYSIEN 40 ha. (60 per cent)
Auxey-Duresses Le Val 2 ha., Les Duresses 1 ha., Monthélie Les Champs Fulliot $1\frac{1}{2}$ ha., Sous Roches 1 ha., Meursault Les Chevalières $\frac{1}{2}$ ha., Volnay Caillerets $\frac{1}{2}$ ha., Clos des Chênes 1 ha., Pommard Les Chanlins Bas 1 ha., Beaune, Savigny-lès-Beaune, Marsannay-la-Côte, Bourgogne Clos du Chapitre Monopole $1\frac{1}{2}$ ha., Le Clos du Roy 1 ha., Le Chapitre $1\frac{1}{2}$ ha.
The last-mentioned Burgundy vineyards are in Chenôve, the Dijon suburb. Camille Rodier praised the quality of these wines, which now have the lowliest of *appellations*, attributing their decline to the spread of both the Gamay grape and Dijon's outskirts. But the Gamay has been beaten back and the builders temporarily halted. M. Pont much extended his estate in 1979

with the purchase of the Château de Savigny, which now also houses a motor-bike museum.

DOMAINE DE LA POUSSE D'OR   13 ha. (100 per cent)
Volnay Bousse d'Or Monopole 2⅓ ha., Cailleret Dessous 2⅖ ha., Cailleret Dessus Clos des 60 Ouvrées Monopole 2⅔ ha., Clos d'Audignac Monopole ⅘ ha., Pommard Les Jarollières 1⅓ ha., Santenay Le Clos de Tavannes 2 ha., Les Gravières 2 ha.

At the time of the French Revolution, this estate was joined to the Domaine de la Romanée-Conti, when a People's Commissary in Dijon chopped off the heads of the owners of the finest vineyards in order to take over their lands. It is the largest proprietor of Volnay Caillerets, owning one-third of this vineyard. Its Clos d'Audignac was in young vines in the late 1960s. Within five years of coming to Volnay from farming in the Aisne, its director, Gérard Potel had earned the respect of some of the most critical wine-makers on the Côte. His special method of vinifying in poor years (described on page 109) enables him to bottle all his wines every year. The different vintages sell at greatly varying prices. He is a man who goes out of his way to taste and discuss other growers' wines. The estate is owned by a syndicate put together by the late Jean Ferté, a French gastronome who belonged to the Académie des Vins de France, the Académie des Gastronomes and the Club des Cent.[1] It supplies some of France's finest restaurants.

F. ROSSIGNOL-BOILLOT   4½ ha. (80 per cent)
Beaune, Pommard, Volnay, Monthélie *blanc*.

RÉGIS ROSSIGNOL-CHANGARNIER   7 ha. (80 per cent)
Volnay, Pommard, Beaune, Meursault.

No *Premiers Crus* here, but an enthusiastic owner, who has invented and built his own must-cooler.

PHILIBERT ROSSIGNOL-SIMON ET FILS   8 ha. (50 per cent)
Volnay 6 ha., Pommard 1½ ha., Meursault ½ ha.

Monsieur Rossignol (who is *régisseur* of the Comte Armand

---

[1] Members meet regularly for a *gueuleton* (to use the Burgundian word). Contrary to popular belief, membership is not restricted to those weighing over 100 kg—the Club simply consists of one hundred persons.

domaine in Pommard) has strong feelings about not over-chaptalizing. His wines can be drunk at Maxim's.

I met him in June, when the vines were flowering, and one of his bottled wines showed a prickle of gas on the tongue. I asked him whether this could really be due to the flowering, as the stories always tell, or whether it was that the warming up of the cellar provoked a slight refermentation. He rejected this: 'A man who gets pneumonia one winter may well start coughing and sneezing at the same period for several years afterwards. I give you an idiotic comparison. But a wine lives, and it follows the vines' cycle.'

Five other growers in Volnay are listed as bottling their wines.

MONTHÉLIE

In 1855 Dr Lavalle recorded that the wines of Monthélie were worth three-quarters those of Volnay; if Volnay was offered at 400 francs *la queue* (456 litres), Monthélie would be offered at 300 francs. The relationship was almost identical in respect of the 1976 vintage over a hundred years later. According to Henri Meurgey & Cie, *Courtiers en vins*, the prices registered when the last *cuvées* of 1976 were disposed of were F.4,200 per hogshead (228 litres) for Volnay, F.3,000 per hogshead for Monthélie.

Vines were recorded at Monthélie as early as the ninth century, when Counte Adalhard gave a *finage* to the church of Saint-Nazaire d'Autun. No stream crosses the commune, and there is no arable land; it is dedicated to wine-producing.

Here are the First Growths: Sur Lavelle, Les Vignes Rondes, Le Meix-Bataille, Les Riottes, La Taupine, Le Clos Gauthey, Le Château-Gaillard, Les Champs Fulliot, Le Cas Rougeot, Les Duresses (part).

The average production is 2,100 hl (23,100 dozen bottles) of red wine, 45 hl (500 dozen bottles) of white, from 93.35 hectares of vineyard.

P. Bréjoux remarks that the Champs Fulliot vineyard is contiguous with Volnay-Caillerets, the two wines being comparable; and he feels that Monthélie is unfortunate in producing relatively little wine, not enough to spread the name.

Monthélie, Auxey and Meursault

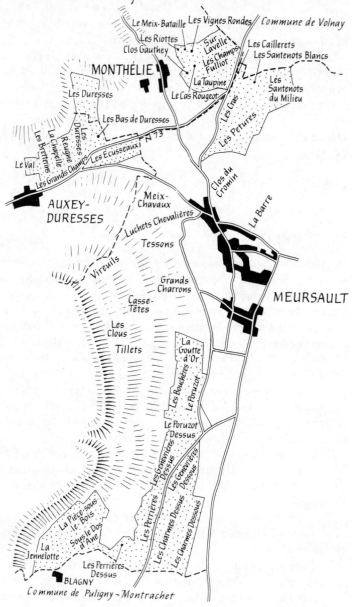

Le Meix-Bataille · Les Vignes Rondes · Commune de Volnay
Les Riottes
Clos Gauthey
Sur Lavelle
MONTHÉLIE
Les Champs Fulliot
Les Caillerets
Les Santenots Blancs
Les Duresses
La Taupine
Le Cas Rougeot
Les Santenots du Milieu
Les Bas de Duresses
Les Crôs
Les Duresses
La Reugne
Les Petures
La Chapelle
Les Brettérins
N 73
Les Écusseaux
Le Val
Les Grands Champs
Clos du Cromin
AUXEY-DURESSES
Meix-Chavaux
La Barre
Luchets Chevalières
Tessons
MEURSAULT
Vireuils
Grands Charrons
Casse-Têtes
Les Clous
Tillets
La Goutte d'Or
Les Bouchères
Le Poruzot
Le Poruzot Dessus
Les Genevrières Dessus
Les Genevrières Dessus
La Pièce sous le Bois
Sous le Dos d'Ane
Les Perrières
Les Charmes Dessus
Les Charmes Dessous
La Jennelotte
Les Perrières Dessous
BLAGNY
Commune de Puligny ~ Montrachet

Main Growers

CHARLES BOUSSEY   10 ha. (75 per cent)
Volnay Taille-Pieds ¼ ha., Monthélie Les Champs Fulliot 1 ha.,
Pommard ¾ ha., Meursault.

This domaine has been bottling for over thirty years. The wine
is sold under a simple but attractive label showing a medieval
wine-press embossed in gold.

DOMAINE MONTHÉLIE-DOUHAIRET   9 ha. (90 per cent)
Volnay Champans 1 ha., Clos des Chênes ⅔ ha., Fremiet ½ ha.,
Pommard *Premier Cru* ⅕ ha., Meursault Les Santenots ⅔ ha.,
Monthélie.

The origins of this domaine go back 200 years to the building of
Mlle Douhairet's house and *cuverie*. The latter was constructed
round a massive wooden press, worked by a 'squirrel wheel' which
can still be seen.

HENRI POTINET-AMPEAU   11 ha. (90 per cent)
JOSEPH POTINET
Volnay Clos des Chênes ¾ ha., Les Santenots 2 ha., Pommard
Premier Cru ½ ha., Meursault Les Perrières ⅓ ha., Les Charmes
½ ha., Monthélie.

R. DE SUREMAIN   8 ha. (75 per cent)
Château de Monthélie *rouge*, Rully *Premier Cru blanc*.

Monsieur de Suremain has combined the functions of mayor,
president of the local *syndicat*, and *châtelain* of the village. Parts of
his house date back to the fourteenth century. He says that his
Chardonnay in Rully have a slight taste of muscatelle—they are
closer to a Pouilly Fuissé than a Côte de Beaune white.

Ten other growers and the Co-operative (which may be visited
from Easter to November) also bottle wines in Monthélie.

SAINT-ROMAIN

Saint-Romain is a steep little village, surrounded by precipices,
really part of the Hautes Côtes, yet attached to the Côte de
Beaune. It has a barrel-maker, François Frères, who supplies the
Domaine de la Romanée-Conti, the Domaine Leflaive and some of

the top Napa Valley estates such as Robert Mondavi and Spring Mountain.

There are no classified First Growths on the 140 hectares delimited for vineyard; the average production is 950 hl (10,450 dozen bottles) of white wine, 550 hl (6,050 dozen bottles) of red.

Main Growers

FERNAND BAZENET $4\frac{1}{2}$ ha. (75 per cent)
ARMAND BAZENET
Saint-Romain *rouge* and *blanc*.

In the hands of careful wine-makers like Fernand Bazenet Saint-Romain *blanc* can equal wines from the Côte de Meursault.

HENRI BUISSON   5 ha. (100 per cent)
Saint-Romain *rouge* and *blanc*.

M. Buisson remarks that the reputation of Saint-Romain has been rising ever since replanting with Pinot, instead of Gamay, began around 1935.

BERNARD FÈVRE   5 ha. (35 per cent)
Saint-Romain 4 ha., Auxey-Duresses 1 ha.

ÉMILE GRIVELET   8 ha. (60 per cent)
NAUDIN-GRIVELET
Saint-Romain *rouge* and *blanc*, Auxey-Duresses *rouge* and *blanc*.

DOMAINE RENÉ THÉVENIN   10 ha. (30 per cent)
Volnay, Beaune, Meursault, Monthélie, Saint-Romain.

ROLAND THÉVENIN ET FILS   (1856)
This company has exclusive distribution of the following estates:

Domaine du Château de Puligny-Montrachet   11 ha.
Montrachet $\frac{1}{5}$ ha., Puligny-Montrachet Les Folatières 3 ha., La Garenne $\frac{4}{5}$ ha., Champs Gain $\frac{4}{5}$ ha., Clos de Chaniot $\frac{1}{2}$ ha., Nosroyes 1 ha., Meursault Casse-Têtes $\frac{1}{2}$ ha.

Domaine du Moulin aux Moines $6\frac{1}{2}$ ha.
Auxey-Duresses Clos du Moulin aux Moines Monopole $2\frac{4}{5}$ ha., Les Ecusseaux $2\frac{1}{4}$ ha.

Domaine de la Corgette 7 ha.

Saint-Romain Clos des Ducs Monopole 1 ha., Clos de la Branière 1½ ha., Beaune Les Teurons ⅖ ha., Les Perrières ¾ ha., Pommard.

I gather that in 1980 M. Thévenin was disposing of some of these vineyards. Montrachet has been acquired by the Domaine de la Romanée-Conti, Puligny Clos de la Garenne by the Duc de Magenta.

GERMAIN THÉVIOT   5 ha. (20 per cent)

MAURICE BOURGEOIS
Monthélie 2 ha., Saint-Romain 3 ha.

There are nine other growers who estate-bottle in Saint-Romain.

AUXEY-DURESSES

The best vineyards of this village are south or south-east facing, situated in the small valley which runs back from the Côte towards La Rochepot. The wines were sold as Volnay or Pommard before the arrival of AC legislation.

The following are classified as *Premiers Crus*: Les Duresses, Les Bas de Duresses, Reugne, Reugne known as La Chapelle, Les Grands Champs, Climat du Val known as Clos du Val (part), Les Ecusseaux (part), Les Bretterins known as La Chapelle, Les Bretterins.

From a delimited area of 149.98 hectares, there is an average production of 920 hl (10,120 dozen bottles) of white wine, 2,300 hl (25,300 dozen bottles) of red.

Main Growers and Merchants

GÉRARD CREUSEFOND   8 ha. (25 per cent)
Auxey-Duresses Le Val 2 ha., Meursault Le Poruzot ½ ha., Volnay.

F. LAFOUGE-CLERC ET FILS   8 ha. (40 per cent)

PIERRE LAFOUGE

JEAN LAFOUGE
Auxey-Duresses La Chapelle 1 ha., Les Duresses ¼ ha., Meursault.

The La Chapelle vineyard used to belong to the Counts of La

Rochepot, its income maintaining their chapel at Auxey. It is a suave wine, considered by some superior to Les Duresses. (The village would hardly have elected to add the name of what is virtually a family Monopole on to its own.)

M. François Lafouge remembers a time when Pinots were first trained on metal wires, and horses introduced between the rows. It was feared that they would kick over the vines and break the wires. Decades later, the introduction of tractors produced the same response.

HENRI LATOUR   6 ha. (25 per cent)

Auxey-Duresses La Chapelle ½ ha., Les Grands Champs ½ ha.

This expanding estate works closely with Domaine René Roy in replanting the Hautes Vignes (see page 283).

ÉTABLISSEMENTS LEROY   (1868)

This is a family business, where the boss is the buyer. Several million bottles of Burgundy's oldest and finest vintages lie aging in its old stone cellars. There is an estate of 6 ha., stituated as follows:

Chambertin ⅔ ha., Clos de Vougeot (bottom) ⅓ ha., Musigny ⅖ ha., Pommard ¾ ha., Meursault 2⅕ ha., Auxey-Duresses 1½ ha.

Except in the United States of America and the United Kingdom, the firm distributes exclusively the Domaine Marey-Monge and the Domaine de la Romanée-Conti of Vosne-Romanée, the Leroy family being co-proprietor of the latter. The firm has been able to concentrate on the top end of the wine market and now has a fine reputation, particularly amongst France's top restaurateurs. It is run by Mme Bize-Leroy, who entered her father's firm in 1955. She is frequently the subject of articles about dynamic women in business and said to be an indefatigable taster.

Judging from the relatively small number of Leroy bottles I have drunk, her taste seems to be for well-constituted, powerful wines. They certainly last, which is a great point in their favour. They are very expensive, for the company seems to follow Dr Lavalle's advice of 1855: '*Soyez très-sévère sur la qualité, soyez tres-facile sur le prix.*'

JEAN PRUNIER ET FILS   19 ha. (35 per cent)

Auxey-Duresses Clos du Val Monopole 1 ha., Volnay Caillerets
⅓ ha., Meursault, Pommard, Monthélie.

It is when one meets a grand old *vigneron* like Jean Prunier (or
Père Pernot, or Rapet, or Roulot) that thoughts come to mind of
loose floorboards and all that privately-owned yellow stuff that
the French are meant to hoard. Outward signs of wealth are non-
existent, except for one give-away—the old stones of their houses
have always been repointed.[1] Here there is a home-made *méthode
champenoise* sparkling wine named Cristal Michel after one of the
sons—who have now divided the estate since the father's death in
1978.

DOMAINE RENÉ ROY   10 ha. (50 per cent)

Volnay Les Santenots ¼ ha., Auxey-Duresses Les Duresses ¾ ha.,
Le Val 5 ha.

M. Roy is one of the foremost exponents of the Hautes Vignes
system of pruning. The vines are planted at intervals of 1.20 m
and 3.30 m (three times the normal span between rows) and
allowed to grow to shoulder-height. One-third as many vines
produce three times as many grapes per vine, so the overall yield
remains stable, but both frost damage and rot are reduced by the
greater distance between foliage and soil. The biggest advantage is
the cutting of labour costs in working the vineyard. The initial
outlay on material is heavy, and experiments to find the most
suitable grafts are unfinished, so outstanding results cannot yet be
shown. But M. Roy continues to convert all his vines to the new
system.

The larger space between the rows enables him to use a harvest
transporter of his own invention. This de-stalks and crushes, or
presses (depending on the grape-colour), immediately after
picking. It is the closest anyone has come to the oenologist's ideal
of pressing white grapes immediately, to ensure maximum
freshness. The must is stored under CO_2 pressure until it reaches
the vats. Manpower is saved here also, since the transporter only
needs emptying at midday and in the evening. He is also
experimenting with the growing of rye-grass between the rows, to
prevent erosion. He has one vineyard he has not ploughed for three

---

[1] Eventually the floorboards are replaced by something heavier to lift, like
Comblanchien marble.

years, with the same object in mind. (See Domaine Clair Daü, page 179, for further Hautes Vignes details.)

Five other growers bottle their wines in Auxey-Duresses.

MEURSAULT AND BLAGNY

More white wines are grown in this commune than in any other of the Côte d'Or, and they have made its reputation. They are less vigorous and racy than Montrachet or Chevalier-Montrachet, according to P. Bréjoux. He points out (and it is worth reading between his lines) that the tint of Meursault is a beautiful green-gold, and that the wines keep their bouquet, freshness and flavour perfectly when their development in hogshead allows a fairly early bottling.

The first mention of vineyards is in 1102 when Duke Eudes II of Burgundy gave vines to Cîteaux. The vineyard of Santenot is mentioned in 1218, that of Charmes in 1366. Les Santenots today is of course a red wine vineyard. It stands on the boundary with Volnay, and is sold under its neighbour's name.

The hamlet of Blagny is uphill from Meursault's finest vineyard, Les Perrières. The Blagny vines straddle the commune boundary with Puligny, well sheltered and perfectly orientated. P. Bréjoux finds Meursault-Blagny *'un grand vin très franc de goût. C'est lui qui se rapproche le plus du Montrachet et du Chevalier-Montrachet'*.

The following are classified First Growths of Meursault: Les Perrières, Les Perrières Dessus, Les Perrières Dessous, Les Charmes Dessus, Les Charmes Dessous (part), Les Genevrières Dessus (part), Les Genevrières Dessous (part), Le Poruzot Dessus, Le Poruzot (part), Les Bouchères, Les Santenots Blancs, Les Santenots du Milieu, Les Caillerets, Les Petures, Les Cras, La Goutte d'Or.

In the commune of Blagny: La Jennelotte, La Pièce-sous-le-Bois, Sous le Dos d'Ane (part).

The average production of the village is 10,500 hl (165,500 dozen bottles) of white wine, 550 hl (6,050 dozen bottles) of red, from 416.79 hectares.

Meursault has more growers offering their wines in bottle than any other village in Burgundy.

284

Main Growers and Merchants

CHARLES ALEXANT 5 ha. (100 per cent)
Puligny-Montrachet Les Folatières 1 ha., Volnay-le-Village $\frac{1}{2}$ ha., Beaune Les Bressandes $\frac{2}{3}$ ha., Corton $\frac{1}{3}$ ha., Meursault Clos des Bouches Chères $\frac{3}{4}$ ha., Meursault Côte de Beaune Clos de la Baronne 1 ha.

ROBERT ET MICHEL AMPEAU 10 ha. (100 per cent)
Puligny-Montrachet Les Combettes $\frac{2}{3}$ ha., Meursault Les Perrières 1 ha., Les Charmes $\frac{1}{2}$ ha., Blagny La Pièce-sous-le-Bois $\frac{3}{4}$ ha. Red: Auxey-Duresses Les Ecusseaux 1 ha., Volnay Les Santenots $1\frac{1}{2}$ ha., Pommard 1 ha., Beaune Clos du Roi $\frac{1}{2}$ ha., Savigny Les Lavières $\frac{2}{3}$ ha.

In the 1960s Robert Ampeau was undoubtedly one of Meursault's best white wine-makers. Whether or not success spoiled him in the 1970s is a moot point.

BALLOT-MILLOT 7 ha. (75 per cent)
Meursault Les Genevrières $\frac{1}{2}$ ha., Les Charmes $\frac{1}{2}$ ha., Beaune Les Epenottes 1 ha., Volnay Les Santenots $\frac{1}{2}$ ha., Puligny-Montrachet *Premier Cru* $\frac{1}{3}$ ha.

ANDRÉ BRUNET $7\frac{1}{2}$ ha. (50 per cent)
Meursault Les Charmes $1\frac{1}{2}$ ha., Les Genevrières $\frac{1}{8}$ ha., Volnay Les Santenots $\frac{1}{3}$ ha., Meursault *Premier Cru rouge* $\frac{2}{3}$ ha.

HÉRITIERS DARNAT 1 ha. (30 per cent)
Meursault Les Cras Clos Richemont Monopole $\frac{2}{3}$ ha.

FRANÇOIS GAUNOUX $8\frac{1}{2}$ ha. (100 per cent)
Meursault La Goutte d'Or 1 ha., Les Genevrières $\frac{1}{3}$ ha., Puligny-Montrachet Les Folatières $\frac{1}{3}$ ha., Bâtard Montrachet $\frac{2}{3}$ ha., Pommard *Premier Cru* 1 ha., Beaune Le Clos des Mouches 1 ha., Les Epenottes 1 ha.

The name Gaunoux on a bottle, whether it be from the Pommard domaine, or this one (created in the 1960s by a brother), is a good beginning.

SÉLECTION JEAN GERMAIN ECVF (1972)
Jean Germain was for long Bernard Michelot's right-hand man. He is an enthusiastic must-beater during the fermentation, thus

ensuring that yeasts do not take up winter quarters at the bottom of the cask.

The wines from his own vineyards (Puligny-Montrachet Grands Champs $\frac{2}{5}$ ha., Meursault $\frac{1}{3}$ ha.) are sold through the merchant's business he runs in association with the Nuits broker, Tim Marshall. The firm specializes in fine white wines and takes great care over their tending and bottling.

DOMAINE CHARLES GIRAUD   9 ha. (30 per cent)
PIERRE LATOUR-GIRAUD
Pommard La Refène $\frac{1}{4}$ ha., Volnay Clos des Chênes $\frac{1}{4}$ ha., Meursault Les Genevrières $1\frac{1}{2}$ ha., Les Charmes $\frac{1}{4}$ ha., Les Perrières $\frac{1}{5}$ ha., Côte de Beaune Villages.

Pierre Latour, the manager of this estate, is also one of Burgundy's most helpful brokers.

DOMAINE ALBERT GRIVAULT $3\frac{1}{2}$ ha.
Meursault Clos des Perrières Monopole 1 ha., Les Perrières $1\frac{1}{2}$ ha., Pommard Clos Blanc 1 ha.

This domaine bottles on demand, mainly for exportation. The Clos des Perrières should be the *crème de la crème* of Meursault; but the wine was not getting the care it deserved when last I visited the estate.

RAYMOND JAVILLIER   5 ha. (50 per cent)
Meursault Clos du Cromin, Tillets.

M. Javillier is a *courtier-éleveur* as well as a proprietor, dealing mainly with the export market.

DOMAINE DES COMTES LAFON   12 ha. (75 per cent)
Montrachet $\frac{1}{3}$ ha., Meursault Les Charmes $1\frac{1}{2}$ ha., Les Perrières $\frac{3}{4}$ ha., Les Genevrières $\frac{3}{4}$ ha., La Goutte d'Or $\frac{1}{2}$ ha., Clos de la Barre Monopole 2 ha., Volnay Les Santenots $2\frac{1}{2}$ ha., Clos des Chênes $\frac{1}{2}$ ha., Champans 1 ha.

The Lafons received their title from the Pope in 1905, following their refusal to be a party to the State's expropriating the goods of the Church during the *Période des Inventaires*.

In the mid-1920s the count resurrected the tradition of the Paulée, or post-vintage feast for the vineyard workers, in Meursault. A literary prize has been awarded since 1932, on the Monday after the Hospices de Beaune wine sale.

The Lafon cellar is one of the deepest and coolest in Meursault.

'*C'est un vrai frigo,*' they say. No filter is ever used there. The Montrachet is always put into new casks, and bottles of previous vintages are uncorked for topping-up purposes, so I gather.

DOMAINE PIERRE-YVES MASSON   11 ha. (100 per cent)
CHÂTEAU MASSON
Vosne-Romanée Aux Malconsorts ¾ ha., Au-dessus des Malconsorts ½ ha., Nuits Saint-Georges *Premier Cru* 2¼ ha., Les Pruliers 1½ ha., Corton-Bressandes 2⅔ ha., Beaune Les Grèves 2¾ ha.

This estate was taken over by M. Masson in 1965, and is now based at the Château de Bligny-les-Beaune.

PIERRE MATROT
DOMAINE JOSEPH MATROT   15 ha. (65 per cent—all his fine wine)
Meursault Les Charmes 1 ha., Les Perrières ½ ha., Blagny 2 ha., Puligny-Montrachet Les Chalumeaux ¾ ha. Red: Blagny La Pièce sous le Bois 2 ha., Volnay Les Santenots 1½ ha.

This domaine is an old hand at bottling, which it likes to do early—white 1959s bottled in February 1960 showed much greater fruit than those bottled eight months later.

When the Volnay Santenots vineyard was acquired, it was planted with Chardonnays, but so strange was the character of the white wine produced that Monsieur Matrot soon replanted with Pinots Noirs. (The Santenots vineyard may of course legally yield Volnay or Meursault, according to the colour of the grapes planted.)

MICHELOT   20 ha. (80 per cent)
Meursault Les Genevrières 1½ ha., Les Charmes 1 ha., Les Perrières ¼ ha., Clos Saint-Félix ½ ha.

Probably more enthusiasts pass through Bernard Michelot's cellar than any other in the village. He is small and round and tanned, and he grins a lot. He has often fermented his wines entirely in new wood, the clean oaky character later somewhat overpowering the Chardonnay's fruit. But he is by no means the only Côte de Meursault grower to use too much new oak.

JEAN MONNIER ET SON FILS   15 ha. (75 per cent)
Meursault Les Genevrières ⅓ ha., Les Charmes ⅔ ha., Pommard Clos de Cîteaux Monopole 3 ha., Les Epenots 3 ha., Les Argillières ⅔ ha., Les Fremiers ⅓ ha., Beaune Les Montrevenots ⅔ ha., Puligny-Montrachet.

The Clos de Cîteaux was planted in 1207 by Duke Eudes III and given to the monastery whose name it now bears, who owned it for the next four centuries. M. Monnier acquired it in 1950 from M. Chevillot of the Hôtel de la Poste in Beaune. Amongst his village Meursaults, the Clos du Cromin (1½ ha.) is one of the rare vineyards whose plantation dates from the last century and the reconstitution of the vines after the phylloxera. Its yield is now, of course, low, but it is more reliable than a younger vine.

DOMAINE RENÉ MONNIER   22 ha. (80 per cent)
Meursault Les Charmes 2 ha., Les Chevalières 2½ ha., Beaune Les Toussaints ¾ ha., Les Cent Vignes 1½ ha., Volnay Clos des Chênes ¾ ha., Puligny-Montrachet Les Folatières ¾ ha., Pommard ¾ ha.

This estate used to be run by the late René Monnier's son-in-law, Hubert Monnot, who was President of the Meursault *syndicat*. It possesses one of the finest rounded vaults in the village, but suffers from lack of cellar space, which could mean that the bottle stocks got an uncalled-for warming when the cellar was heated to receive the new wine in cask.

Hubert Monnot's widow is now *gérante* of the estate, which is jointly controlled, so she informs me, by Kenneth Ingleton of Maldon, Essex, who is responsible for the entire production and marketing for the Domaine. In ten years it has expanded from 14 to 22 hectares—so no doubt by now the problem of cellar-space has been solved.

BERTHE MOREY   10 ha. (30 per cent)
Meursault Les Perrières ½ ha., Les Charmes ¼ ha., Clos de Grands Charrons Monopole Volnay Les Santenots ¼ ha., Corton Renardes ¼ ha., Pommard 1 ha., Meursault 6 ha.

COMTE DE MOUCHERON, CHÂTEAU DE MEURSAULT   10 ha.
Volnay Clos des Chênes 3½ ha., Meursault Les Perrières 1 ha., Les Charmes 4½ ha.

In the wall of the Comte's Volnay Clos des Chênes can be seen four large holes. They were caused by de Lattre de Tassigny's advancing tanks as they swept straight across the vineyards, liberating France.

The Comte is the last of his line. From time to time he puts some of his vines up for sale, indeed to the best of my knowledge they have all now been acquired by Patriarche Père et Fils of Beaune, along with the Château de Meursault.

DOMAINE JACQUES PRIEUR   14 ha. (100 per cent)
Chambertin 1 ha., Musigny 1 ha., Clos de Vougeot $1\frac{1}{4}$ ha. (bottom), Beaune Aux Cras Clos de la Féguine Monopole 2 ha., Volnay Champans $\frac{1}{3}$ ha., Clos des Santenots Monopole 1 ha., Les Santenots $\frac{3}{4}$ ha., Meursault Clos de Mazeray red and white Monopole 3 ha., Les Perrières $\frac{1}{3}$ ha., Puligny-Montrachet Les Combettes $1\frac{1}{2}$ ha., Montrachet $\frac{2}{3}$ ha., Chevalier-Montrachet $\frac{1}{5}$ ha.

This estate was leased by J. Calvet & Cie of Beaune from 1930 to 1975. The author Pierre Poupon is one of its shareholders and the estate now includes his Meursault Les Perrières vines which were previously part of the Domaine Poupon.

ROPITEAU FRÈRES   (1848)
This company was taken over by Chantovent in June 1974, and is building larger warehousing and bottling facilities. It continues to distribute the wines of the two family-owned Ropiteau estates, which have fine old reputations and total 35 hectares:

Domaine A. Ropiteau-Mignon
Meursault Les Genevrières 1 ha., Les Charmes $\frac{2}{5}$ ha., La Goutte d'Or $\frac{1}{5}$ ha., Le Poruzot $\frac{2}{3}$ ha., Les Chevalières $\frac{1}{3}$ ha., Clous $3\frac{1}{2}$ ha., Volnay Clos des Chênes 1 ha., Pommard Les Chanlins $1\frac{1}{3}$ ha., Monthélie Les Champs Fulliot 1 ha., Les Duresses $1\frac{1}{3}$ ha., Beaune Les Grèves 1 ha., Clos de Vougeot (bottom) $\frac{1}{3}$ ha.

Domaine Maurice Ropiteau
Meursault Les Perrières $1\frac{1}{4}$ ha., Les Grands Charrons $1\frac{1}{4}$ ha.

H. ROUGEOT   10 ha. (100 per cent)
Meursault Les Charmes 1 ha., Volnay Les Santenots 1 ha., Ladoix Côte de Beaune, Meursault.

M. Rougeot was the Comte de Moucheron's *régisseur* and one of the few people in Burgundy to be experimenting with the development of different types of Pinot and root-stock. In addition, he runs a road-building enterprise.

GUY ROULOT ET FILS   15 ha. (90 per cent)
'I've got five children, but I can't be sure that they're all mine, not really sure, do you get me? But my wine—it was I who made it, I know. There are no direct vines (ungrafted vines) in my

vineyards, no Noahs, no Otellos or 5455s as they were all planted after the war. Put this down as you're taking notes: you must never drink wines at room temperature—let a red wine warm in the glass by all means, but serve it fresh. You ask how methods have changed over the years—well, we're cleaner than we used to be.' That was the late Paul Roulot talking, Guy Roulot's father, a self-styled '*brande-vinier*' (patois for distiller). As well as being a member of the Brotherhood of the Knights of the Tasting-Cup, he was a Commander of the Bresse Chicken and the Blue Ribbon, a Knight of the Fir-Cone and the Fish-Stew. His walls were hung with the arms of this record number of outlandish gastronomic brotherhoods.

His vines were mostly in straight Meursault, a little in Les Perrières and Les Charmes. Distilling was his hobby: for instance, a light plum brandy to fill that awkward gap after the fish course when he felt a pause was indicated and digestion should be helped. Also ratafia made from *fine*, not *marc* and *pernod* (or was it real absinthe?)—limpid green and pungent from the steeping of fennel and wormwood leaf, liquorice root and artemisia. In his *cuverie* I saw the pressed skins and pips waiting for distillation. They looked like sultanas and smelt damply of fresh fruit.

Guy Roulot was a first-rate white wine maker but tragically died in the prime of life. The estate is now run by his widow and daughter.

DOMAINE DE BLAGNY 9½ ha. (15 per cent)
COMTESSE P. DE MONTLIVAULT
Meursault Blagny La Genelotte Monopole *blanc* and *rouge* 3 ha., La Pièce-sous-le-Bois 2 ha., Sous le Dos d'Ane 2 ha., Puligny-Montrachet Les Chalumeaux ⅖ ha., Hameau de Blagny 2 ha.

From this hamlet up the slope between Meursault and Puligny it is said that all the clocks of the Côte can be heard to strike. The monks of Maizières were the first to plant vines here. They built a farm and the fifteenth-century chapel.

A further three merchants and fifty-four growers offer their Meursault wines in bottle.

PULIGNY-MONTRACHET

Puligny added Montrachet to its name in 1879. The village is of Gallo-Roman origin, first recorded as Puliniacus in a *diplôme* of Pope Urbain II in 1095. There are four *Grands Crus* on the territory:

1. Montrachet (7.49 ha. Average harvest: 230 hl. or 2,530 dozen bottles). Montrachet is something of a *parvenu* amongst *Grands Crus*, Courtépée stating that it was not *en réputation* at the beginning of the seventeenth century, when twenty-four *ouvrées* were acquired for a mere 750 *livres*. It was first mentioned in 1482, already much divided according to Dr Lavalle. But nobody disputes its place today as potentially the greatest white wine of Burgundy. As might be feared, it is not always up to scratch. I recall tasting Amiot's tiny production one year, and a sorry tale of

Puligny-Montrachet, Blagny, Gamay and Saint-Aubin

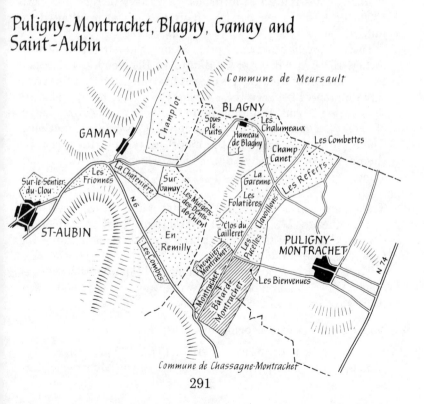

291

careless wine-making it told: a Paul Fleurot, oxidized; an indifferent Baron Thénard; a heavyweight Roland Thévenin. Dr Lavalle declares that a distinction should be drawn between the Puligny section of Montrachet, which faces south-east, and that of Chassagne, turned more to the south; the first producing wine of exquisite finesse, divine perfection. P. Bréjoux makes the same point, adding: '*C'est le vin le plus merveilleux à servir sur une belle truite, surtout si c'est vous-même qui l'avez pêchée, et c'est la grâce que je vous souhaite.*'

2. Chevalier-Montrachet (7.14 ha. Average harvest: 150 hl or 1,650 dozen bottles). This *Grand Cru* is situated uphill from Montrachet, its produce rated only just behind it.

3. Bâtard-Montrachet (11.83 ha. Average harvest: 350 hl or 3,850 dozen bottles). Bâtard-Montrachet straddles the Puligny/ Chassagne border.

4. Bienvenues-Bâtard-Montrachet (2.30 ha. Average harvest: 100 hl or 1,100 dozen bottles). This *Grand Cru* is situated in Puligny.

Tasters note a downward progression of quality from Mont-rachet, through Chevalier to Bâtard to Bienvenues. I daresay three centuries of wine-tasters cannot be wrong, and that there are tiny differences between these *Grand Cru* wines, attributable to their varied origins. But much more significant is the broad range of quality, caused by differing human skills and inclinations. There are bottles to make the mouth water and the heart go thump, and others, heavy and lifeless, which sell by the names alone.

The *Premiers Crus* of Puligny-Montrachet are: Clos du Cailleret, Les Combettes, Les Pucelles, Les Folatières (part), Clavoillons, Champ Canet, Les Chalumeaux, Les Referts, Sous le Puits, La Garenne, Hameau de Blagny.

The average production of commune and First Growth wines is 5,300 hl (58,300 dozen bottles) of white wine, 260 hl (2,860 dozen bottles) of red, from 233.91 hectares.

Main Growers and Merchants

DOMAINE CARILLON PÈRE ET FILS   10 ha. (30 per cent)
Mercurey En Champs Martin ½ ha., Chassagne-Montrachet Les

Macherelles *rouge* ½ ha., Les Chenerottes ½ ha., Puligny-Montrachet Les Combettes ½ ha., Champ Canet ½ ha., Les Referts 1 ha., Puligny-Montrachet *rouge* ½ ha., Saint-Aubin.

There have been Carillons at Puligny since 1632. Their *cuverie* is situated in a most unusual house, which was built with the stones of the old château. They claim that Saracen influence may show in the pointed arches of the vat-room, and perhaps in the entry down a corridor. The *curé* of Puligny hid himself here during the Revolution; his makeshift confessional and escape-route at the back of the house can still be seen.

DUPARD AINE   9½ ha.

Chevalier-Montrachet 1 ha., Puligny-Montrachet Clos du Cailleret Monopole 3½ ha., Les Pucelles 1¼ ha., Les Folatières ⅔ ha.

This company is run by the mayor of Puligny, M. Jean Chartron, whose grandfather founded it in 1860. The estate includes the Clos de Cailleret, which is adjacent to Montrachet, the wine being vinified and commercialized by Joseph Drouhin in Beaune. There are other proprietors in the Clos du Cailleret, but they sell their wine under the alternative name of Puligny-Montrachet Les Demoiselles.

DOMAINE RENÉ GUÉRIN   9 ha. (50 per cent)
DOMAINE GÉRARD GUÉRIN

Puligny Hameau de Blagny ½ ha., Blagny ¾ ha., Les Chalumeaux ½ ha., Champ Gain 1½ ha.

DOMAINE LEFLAIVE   18 ha. (65 per cent)

Chevalier-Montrachet   1 ha.,   Bâtard-Montrachet   2 ha., Bienvenues-Bâtard-Montrachet   1 ha.;   Puligny-Montrachet Clavoillons 5 ha., Les Combettes ⅔ ha., Les Pucelles 3 ha.; Blagny *rouge* 1½ ha.

This domaine borders a peaceful grassy square with triple rows of chestnut trees, stone benches and a boules-pitch. The *régisseur* is M. Jean Virot, an ex-broker. If his prominent nose did not suggest him as a wine man, one might mistake him for a melancholy country curate. He is one of the few people I met who said in 1969 that he was decreasing his domaine-bottling in favour of bulk sales—the cost of exploitation and labour having risen faster than the price of wine. But demand has made him change his tune. The domaine makes richly elegant wines.

VEUVE HENRI MORONI

'*Une brave dame*' who has been running her business since the 1940s. She owns 4½ ha.:

Bâtard-Montrachet ⅓ ha., Puligny-Montrachet Les Combettes ⅓ ha., Les Pucelles ⅕ ha., Puligny *rouge*.

DOMAINE ÉTIENNE SAUZET   12 ha. (80 per cent)

Bâtard-Montrachet, Bienvenues-Bâtard-Montrachet, Puligny-Montrachet Les Combettes, Champ Canet, Les Referts, *Premier Cru*, Clos de Meix Monopole.

Étienne Sauzet used to declare that he never racked his wines, and fined them while still on their original lees. He recommended this to all who would lend him an ear, and since he was President of five different associations connected with wines or wine-making an audience was often to be had. He described himself as the son of a *petit vigneron*, and brought this estate to prominence from virtually nothing. He died in 1975.

There are eight other growers offering wines in bottle from Puligny, two of whom hold merchant's licences.

SAINT-AUBIN AND GAMAY

These villages stand in a fold of the hills behind the Côte, their vineyards facing a variety of directions, south-east to south-west. Gamay probably gave its name to the vine which produces Beaujolais; it is now a hamlet of Saint-Aubin.

Certain Saint-Aubin vineyards, which cover 119.70 hectares are classified as First Growths: La Chatenière, Les Murgers-des-Dents-de-Chien, En Remilly, Les Frionnes, Sur-le-Sentier-du-Clou, Sur Gamay, Les Combes, Champlot.

The average production of the village is 1,400 hl (15,400 dozen bottles) of red wine, 700 hl (7,700 dozen bottles) of white. A lot of the red wine is sold as Côte de Beaune Villages.

Main Growers

BLONDEAU-DANNE   12 ha. (100 per cent)

Volnay, Meursault, Puligny-Montrachet, Chassagne-Montrachet, Saint-Aubin, a little Criots-Bâtard-Montrachet.

Where most proprietors are keen to talk about their vines and methods, information here was hard to come by. The estate, which operates with a '*Mis en bouteille au Château de Saint-Aubin*' label, has bottled everything since the war, and has grown from four hectares. I was not invited to taste the wine, and the dog bit me.

JEAN LAMY ET SES FILS   22 ha. (100 per cent)
Chassagne-Montrachet, Puligny-Montrachet, Santenay, Bâtard-Montrachet, Saint-Aubin, Côte de Beaune Villages, Aligoté.

Several of M. Lamy's *cuvées* have had Concours Agricole de Paris or Tastevinage honours, some have even gone on an international polar expedition to Antarctica. He produced famous Aligotés from old vines until his retirement. Now the vineyards are split between his two sons, Hubert in Saint-Aubin and René in Chassagne-Montrachet, the latter making Bâtard-Montrachet, Chassagne Clos Saint-Jean and Morgeot, Santenay and Saint-Aubin; the former Puligny-Montrachet, Chassagne-Montrachet and Saint-Aubin. 'The sons follow the methods of the father, quality and reasonable prices,' states the old boy.

ROUX PÈRE ET FILS   10 ha. (90 per cent)
Chassagne-Montrachet Clos Saint-Jean $\frac{1}{6}$ ha., *Premier Cru* $\frac{1}{4}$ ha., Santenay *Premier Cru* $1\frac{1}{3}$ ha., Puligny-Montrachet $\frac{1}{3}$ ha., Saint-Aubin *rouge* and *blanc* 3 ha.

As one might expect from relations of the Lamys, the Rouxs are careful wine-makers and bottlers.

There is one other grower and a merchant offering wine in bottle from Saint-Aubin.

CHASSAGNE-MONTRACHET

In this village and in Santenay re-appear the strata of oolitic Bathonian limestone which are partly responsible for the characteristics of the great red wines of the Côte de Nuits. Good reds of Chassagne and Santenay can easily be mistaken for wines of that Côte.

The place has long been occupied, for a text of A.D. 1007 mentions a villa in the *climat* La Romanée—presumably a Roman farm. There is some quarrying of pink, beige and veined limestone, which polishes well. In the hillside may be seen small abandoned quarries, whence the villagers no doubt extracted stone for their

Chassagne-Montrachet

homes and the altars and altar-steps of nearby fourteenth- and fifteenth-century churches. This is one of the villages where *Cordon-de-Royat* pruning and training of the vines is still to be seen. Its success requires particular skills when the vine is young. It was described on page 84.

Chassagne-Montrachet is of course world-famous for its white wines. Just under half of both Montrachet and Bâtard-Montrachet are in this commune, as is the whole of the tiny *Grand Cru*: Criots-Bâtard-Montrachet (1.6 ha. Average harvest: 35 hl or 385 dozen bottles).

The following are classified as *Premiers Crus*:

RED WINES

Clos Saint-Jean (part), Morgeot (part), Morgeot known as Abbaye de Morgeot (part), La Boudriotte (part), La Maltroie (part), Les Chenevottes, Les Champs Gains (part), Grandes Ruchottes, La Romanée, Les Brussonnes (part), Les Vergers, Les Macherelles, En Cailleret (part).

WHITE WINES

Morgeot (part), Morgeot known as Abbaye de Morgeot (part), La Boudriotte, La Maltroie, Clos Saint-Jean, Les Chenevottes, Les Champs Gains, Grandes Ruchottes, La Romanée, Les Brussonnes, Les Vergers, Les Macherelles, Chassagne ou Cailleret.

The average production of commune and First Growth wines is 4,800 hl (52,800 dozen bottles) of red and 3,100 hl (34,100 dozen bottles) of white from 356.38 hectares of delimited vineyard.

Main Growers and Merchants

PIERRE ET GUY AMIOT PÈRE ET FILS 8 ha. (50 per cent)

Montrachet $\frac{1}{10}$ ha., Chassagne-Montrachet En Cailleret $\frac{2}{3}$ ha., Puligny-Montrachet Les Demoiselles $\frac{1}{3}$ ha., Chassagne-Montrachet Clos Saint-Jean *rouge* $\frac{1}{3}$ ha.

At first Monsieur Amiot *père* seems somewhat dour, but he speaks with quiet authority, and his wines are usually respected.

BACHELET-RAMONET PÈRE ET FILS 9$\frac{1}{2}$ ha. (75 per cent of the First Growths)

JEAN-CLAUDE BACHELET

Bâtard-Montrachet $\frac{1}{2}$ ha., Chassagne-Montrachet *Premier Cru* 2 ha. (En Cailleret, La Romanée, Grandes Ruchottes, Grande Montagne, Morgeot). Red: Chassagne-Montrachet Clos de la Boudriotte 1 ha., Clos Saint-Jean 1 ha., Morgeot *rouge* 2$\frac{1}{2}$ ha.

Here is the third part of the Ramonet family *Monopole*, the Clos de la Boudriotte. M. Bachelet exports a lot, and tends wines for certain estates who are not equipped to do so. His Clos Saint-Jean is in old vines.

BAUDRAND ET FILS

DOMAINE DES VIEILLES VIGNES

Chassagne-Montrachet Clos Saint-Marc Monopole, Clos Saint-

Jean, Mercurey Clos Marcilly Monopole, Puligny-Montrachet, Santenay, Savigny-les-Beaune.

FRANÇOIS COLIN ET FILS   6 ha. (50 per cent)
Chassagne-Montrachet *rouge* and *blanc*.

DELAGRANGE-BACHELET   10 ha. (50 per cent)
Bâtard-Montrachet $\frac{1}{2}$ ha., Criots-Bâtard-Montrachet $\frac{1}{2}$ ha., Chassagne-Montrachet En Cailleret 1 ha., La Maltroie $\frac{1}{2}$ ha., Morgeot red and white 2 ha., Volnay Champans $\frac{2}{5}$ ha., Clos des Chênes $\frac{2}{5}$ ha., Pommard Les Rugiens $\frac{1}{5}$ ha.

While his white wines are fermenting, M. Edmond Delagrange favours regular stirrings-up of lees with wine. He has no sons, so sells a lot of his wine in barrel. He reduced the size of his estate from the above-listed ten hectares to four in 1979—but is not forthcoming with the details.

Until his death at the age of ninety-seven, this household harboured Père Bachelet, a charming old *vigneron* who was born in 1873. I asked him whether post-phylloxera wines equalled the pre-louse products and he was sure they did. 'When you graft a pear tree on to a quince root you don't harvest quinces. In any case, one didn't make only good wine in the old days.'

GEORGES DELÉGER   4$\frac{1}{2}$ ha. (30 per cent)
Chevalier-Montrachet $\frac{1}{6}$ ha., Chassagne-Montrachet Les Chenevottes $\frac{1}{4}$ ha.

JOSEPH DELÉGER   6 ha. (50 per cent)
Criots-Bâtard-Montrachet $\frac{1}{4}$ ha., Chassagne-Montrachet En Cailleret $\frac{1}{4}$ ha., Santenay La Comme $\frac{2}{3}$ ha., Puligny-Montrachet, Saint-Aubin.

JEAN-NOËL GAGNARD   7 ha. (80 per cent)
Bâtard-Montrachet $\frac{1}{3}$ ha., Chassagne-Montrachet En Cailleret $\frac{1}{3}$ ha. Red: Chassagne-Montrachet Clos de la Maltroie $\frac{1}{3}$ ha., Morgeot 1 ha., Santenay Le Clos de Tavannes $\frac{1}{3}$ ha.

Most wives help their husbands in the vines (though the latter tend to do all the pruning), but here is a remarkable team, and one prepared to give a straight answer to any questions. As in Meursault, I heard how a thunder-clap can turn the grapes violet. This sudden excess of maturity gives fantastic wines, but the grapes must be harvested immediately, or they will fall. For some reason, this phenomenon is often met with in Bâtard-Montrachet.

Of the two Gagnard brothers Jean-Noël is perhaps the red-wine man, Jacques the white (see the following estate).

GAGNARD-DELAGRANGE $4\frac{1}{2}$ ha. (50 per cent)
Montrachet $\frac{1}{10}$ ha., Bâtard-Montrachet $\frac{1}{4}$ ha., Chassagne-Montrachet La Boudriotte $1\frac{1}{5}$ ha., Morgeot *rouge* and *blanc* 1 ha., Clos Saint-Jean $\frac{1}{3}$ ha.

Jacques Gagnard states that good white wine is made or lost in the twenty-four hours which follow picking. He believes that the lees are very important, so does not *débourbe* (the practice of leaving the must for twenty-four to forty-eight hours in a tank to drop its largest impurities before fermentation in wood). 'In the end he'll eat his lees, it'll disappear,' he says of one of his wines.

He has a story of how a distiller used to clear a cloudy brandy. He would drop a fig in it and leave it quiet; three years later the brandy would be clear, and the fig completely solid. He has owned his rows of Montrachet since 1978—just enough to make a barrel a year.

MARQUIS DE LAGUICHE ET SES FILS $4\frac{3}{4}$ ha. (100 per cent)
Montrachet 2 ha., Chassagne-Montrachet Morgeot *blanc* $1\frac{3}{4}$ ha., *rouge* 1 ha.

This estate, which owns the largest slice of Montrachet, sells its must under contract to Joseph Drouhin, who vinifies, tends and bottles the wines in Beaune. The *régisseur* in Chassagne is l'Abbé Colin. With his beret, cigarette-holder, and round tortoiseshell glasses, his food-stained cassock and electric foot-warmer he might have stepped out of a twentieth-century Balzac novel; until 1971 he was mayor of the village, and is most generous with advice and information. His research into vintage date-records in Chassagne seems to indicate that the harvest has got later since grafted vines came in. The average date around 1820 was 4 September; in 1883 they even began on 24 August. Although the 1950 vintage began on 5 September, the 25th of that month is the most usual date for this century.

DOMAINE DU DUC DE MAGENTA $12\frac{1}{3}$ ha. (100 per cent)
Chassagne-Montrachet Abbaye de Morgeot Clos de la Chapelle Monopole $4\frac{1}{2}$ ha. ($\frac{2}{3}$ red, $\frac{1}{3}$ white), Puligny-Montrachet Clos de La

Garenne Monopole $1\frac{4}{5}$ ha., Meursault $\frac{3}{4}$ ha., Auxey-Duresses Les Bretterins 1 ha.

This estate doubled in size in the late 1960s, its owner, the Duc de Magenta, taking a keen interest in it. He seems more successful with his white wines than his reds.

CHÂTEAU DE LA MALTROIE 13 ha. (100 per cent)
Bâtard-Montrachet $\frac{1}{3}$ ha., Chassagne-Montrachet Clos du Château de la Maltroie Monopole *blanc* and *rouge* $2\frac{1}{2}$ ha., Grandes Ruchottes $\frac{1}{2}$ ha., Vigne Blanche $1\frac{1}{2}$ ha., Clos Saint-Jean $\frac{1}{3}$ ha., Santenay La Comme 2 ha.

This estate was taken over from the Picard family by André Cournut in the 1970s.

MARCEL MOREAU ET FILS $6\frac{1}{2}$ ha. (35 per cent)
Chassagne-Montrachet Grandes Ruchottes *blanc* $\frac{1}{3}$ ha., Morgeot *rouge* La Cardeuse Monopole $\frac{3}{4}$ ha., Les Chenevottes *blanc* $\frac{1}{2}$ ha.

ALBERT MOREY ET FILS 16 ha. (100 per cent)
Bâtard-Montrachet $\frac{1}{6}$ ha., Chassagne-Montrachet En Cailleret $\frac{3}{4}$ ha., Les Embrazées 1 ha., Morgeot red and white $\frac{1}{2}$ ha., Beaune Les Grèves $1\frac{1}{3}$ ha., Sautenay Clos Rousseau $\frac{4}{5}$ ha.

Albert Morey can often compare his own bottlings done twelve and eighteen months after the harvest, and invariably finds the former superior—a white wine's fruit will last much longer if it can be imprisoned early.

Discussing today's overproduction, he recalls stories of the even greater yields in 1902 and 1903 when over 100 hectolitres per hectare were produced. At that time the wine was worth less than the barrel which held it, so the 1902 was poured into the gutter to make room for the 1903. An interesting solution to this problem was proposed in 1905 by Trébar in *Le Réveil de la Bourgogne*. He suggested that the excess wines should be distilled and the result used for heating, lighting and running the new cars. 'The national alcoholic product would thus replace the stinking, repellent and very dangerous foreign-product petrol.'

DOMAINE MARC MOREY ET FILS 8 ha. (90 per cent)
Bâtard-Montrachet $\frac{1}{6}$ ha., Chassagne-Montrachet En Cailleret red $\frac{2}{3}$ ha., Les Chenevottes 2 ha., Morgeot red $\frac{1}{4}$ ha., Virondot $\frac{3}{4}$ ha., Puligny-Montrachet Les Pucelles $\frac{1}{2}$ ha., Beaune $\frac{1}{2}$ ha.

Marc Morey reclaimed and planted Virondot from scrubland.

His daughter is a qualified oenologist; they have recently installed refrigeration facilities to eliminate the danger of tartrate crystals forming after bottling.

MICHEL NIÉLLON
Chevalier-Montrachet, Bâtard-Montrachet, Chassagne-Montrachet Clos Saint-Jean, Les Vergers.

DOMAINE ALPHONSE PILLOT 6½ ha. (50 per cent)
Chassagne-Montrachet Morgeot *rouge* and *blanc* 1 ha., Les Chenevottes.

PAUL PILLOT 10 ha. (50 per cent)
Chassagne-Montrachet La Romanée ½ ha., Grandes Ruchottes ⅙ ha., Clos Saint-Jean 2 ha.

RAMONET-PRUDHON 14 ha. (100 per cent)
ANDRÉ RAMONET
Bâtard-Montrachet ⅓ ha., Bienvenues-Bâtard-Montrachet ⅓ ha., Chassagne-Montrachet Grandes Ruchottes 1 ha., En Cailleret ½ ha., Morgeot 5½ ha., Clos de la Boudriotte ¾ ha., Clos Saint-Jean ⅔ ha.

If the village of Chassagne ran a competition to choose from its inhabitants the one who most resembled a nineteenth-century Paris road-sweeper, there is not much doubt that Pierre Ramonet-Prudhon would beat all-comers. His wines have been served at the White House and the Court of the Belgians. Name a Michelin three-star restaurant and he supplies it. Because his is a one-man-show, his wines have occasionally been bottled a bit late, indeed it was fashionable in the late 1970s to say that he had lost his touch. But he does not lack practice, having first exported to the USA in 1934. To the above fine estate he recently added Montrachet, ⅕ ha.

CLAUDE RAMONET 6 ha. (100 per cent)
Bâtard-Montrachet ⅓ ha., Bienvenues-Bâtard-Montrachet ¼ ha., Chassagne-Montrachet Morgeot 1¼ ha., Grandes Ruchottes ¼ ha. Red: Clos Saint-Jean ⅖ ha., Clos de la Boudriotte ⅔ ha.

Claude Ramonet is a bachelor. He is as famous in the USA, to which three-quarters of his wine is sold, as his brother Pierre.

A further four estate-bottling growers, and one merchant, are listed in Chassagne-Montrachet.

SANTENAY

Santenay is the most southerly village of the Côte d'Or devoted to wine-making. It stands on a small river, the Dheune, and possesses, as H. Delonguy and Claude Sauvageot wrote in *Notice sur Santenay* in 1884, everything that can be expected of the countryside: woods, meadows and springs. The waters of Santenay are extremely salty, and prescribed for gout and rheumatism; its wines can be deep-coloured and stoutly-constructed, longer-lived than some Côte de Beaunes.

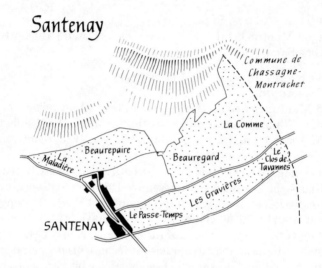

The following are classified as *Premiers Crus*: Les Gravières (part), Le Clos-de-Tavannes (part), La Comme (part), Beauregard (part), Le Passe-Temps, Beaurepaire, La Maladière.

The average production is 8,200 hl (90,200 dozen bottles) of red wine, 110 hl (1,210 dozen bottles) of white, 380·50 hectares being delimited.

Main Growers and Merchants

DOMAINE DE L'ABBAYE DE SANTENAY   12 ha. (40 per cent)

LOUIS CLAIR

Santenay Les Clos de Tavannes 2 ha., Les Gravières 2 ha., La Comme 1 ha., Chassagne-Montrachet Morgeot *rouge* ½ ha.

The eleventh-century abbey of which M. Clair is owner makes a very fine *cuverie* and cellar.

DOMAINE JOSEPH BELLAND   13 ha. (30 per cent)
Santenay Les Gravières 1½ ha., La Comme 1 ha., Beauregard 3 ha., Chassagne-Montrachet Clos Pitois Monopole red and white 3 ha.

BRENOT PÈRE ET FILS   (1876)
This company owns Bâtard-Montrachet (⅓ ha.), Santenay Les Gravières (½ ha.), and also small-holdings of Montrachet, Puligny-Montrachet, Santenay *blanc* and Chassagne-Montrachet.

M. Max Brenot fears for the future of small family merchants such as his, and believes in ensuring that his sons 'have the necessary baggage' to do other things.

SOCIÉTÉ CIVILE D'EXPLOITATION DU CHÂTEAU DE SANTENAY
Mercurey 76 ha.

The Château de Santenay stands above the village—it was one of Philippe le Hardi's fortresses. In its grounds are two magnificent plane trees, claimed to be the oldest in France. The property used to be directed by Pierre-Yves Masson, but is now managed by Joël Pidault of Chagny.

CLAIR-CAUTAIN   7½ ha. (20 per cent)
Santenay Le Clos de Tavannes ½ ha., La Comme 1 ha., Santenay *blanc* ¼ ha.

François Clair makes well-respected reds.

DOMAINE DU CLOS DE MALTE   7 ha. (10 per cent)
JOLY PÈRE ET FILS
Santenay Clos de Malte Monopole 7 ha.

This Clos takes its name from its association with the Knights of Malta, some of whom are buried in the Romanesque church beside it. The wine is lighter than most Santenays.

DOMAINE FLEUROT-LAROSE   17 ha.
Montrachet ⅓ ha., Bâtard-Montrachet ⅙ ha., Chassagne-Montrachet Abbaye de Morgeot *rouge* and *blanc* 7 ha., Santenay Clos du Passe-Temps 3 ha., Clos Rousseau 2 ha.

This domaine is run by Rene Fleurot; his brother Paul's name also used to appear on the labels. Until 1965 they were merchants, but now they only sell the wines from the domaines; the percentage of bottling varies.

DOMAINE DES HAUTES CORNIÈRES   12 ha. (100 per cent)

PHILIPPE CHAPELLE ET FILS
Corton $\frac{1}{2}$ ha., Santenay Les Gravières 2 ha., La Comme 1 ha., Chassagne-Montrachet Morgeot 2 ha., Aloxe-Corton 3 ha.

One of the Chapelle brothers has started a small merchant's business, demand for his own wines having exceeded the supply. He has been bottling 100 per cent of his harvest for fifteen years. After experimenting with short vatting-times of four to five days he has gone back to double this, but still produces relatively fast-developing wines. His brother runs an oenological laboratory behind the Église Notre-Dame in Beaune.

JESSIAUME PÈRE ET FILS   (1880) 10 ha.
Santenay Les Gravières 5 ha., Beaune Les Cent Vignes $1\frac{1}{3}$ ha.

DOMAINE LEQUIN-ROUSSOT
RENÉ ET LOUIS LEQUIN FRÈRES   15 ha. (50 per cent)
Bâtard-Montrachet $\frac{1}{4}$ ha., Corton $\frac{2}{5}$ ha., Chassagne-Montrachet Morgeot $1\frac{1}{4}$ ha., Santenay La Comme 2 ha., Le Passe-Temps $1\frac{1}{4}$ ha., Petit Clos Rousseau $\frac{1}{4}$ ha.

Jean Lequin (father of René and Louis) compares the modern *vigneron* to a country doctor, knowing a little about a lot, relying on experience and observation and only needing to call in a specialist (the oenologist) when affairs get out of control. He is really describing himself—most aptly too. One of his proudest possessions is a hand-written notebook inscribed '*J'appartien à Antoine Lequin, vigneron à Santenay 1783*'. The estate is best known for its red wines.

PROSPER MAUFOUX   (1860)
The majority (85 per cent) of this company's turnover is on the export market. Its director, Pierre Maufoux, has been known to advance the idea that Burgundy's problem of supply might be attacked by expanding the vineyard area across the road, which is an odd one. The firm distributes the wines of the Domaine Saint-Michel in Santenay and the Château de Viré (Mâcon-Viré AC).

JEAN MOREAU 4½ ha. (50 per cent)

Santenay Clos des Mouches 1 ha.

'*Pour faire un bon vigneron,*' M. Moreau says, '*il faut un bon palais. Il faut tout goûter.*'

G. PRIEUR 13 ha.

DOMAINE PRIEUR-BRUNET

Bâtard-Montrachet $\frac{1}{10}$ ha., Santenay La Comme $\frac{1}{2}$ ha., La Maladière 4⅘ ha., Meursault Les Charmes 1 ha., Chassagne-Montrachet Morgeot *rouge* ¾ ha., Volnay Les Santenots $\frac{1}{3}$ ha., Pommard La Platière $\frac{1}{5}$ ha.

This firm, founded in 1804, markets its domaine wines mainly in France, though it exports a little. It makes a speciality of La Maladière, which develops earlier than would La Comme or Les Gravières.

Four other growers and a merchant offer wine in bottle from Santenay.

DEZIZE-LES-MARANGES, CHEILLY-LES-MARANGES AND SAMPIGNY-LES-MARANGES

The red wine from these three villages is normally sold as Côte de Beaune Villages, and a good thing too, for three obscurer wine names would be hard to find. (They are over the border between the Côte d'Or and the Saône et Loire, about 230 hectares having plantation rights.)

The *appellation* Côte de Beaune Villages applies to red wines only, produced in any one of the following sixteen villages: Auxey-Duresses, Blagny, Chassagne-Montrachet, Cheilly-les-Maranges, Chorey-les-Beaune, Dezize-les-Maranges, Ladoix, Meursault, Monthélie, Pernand-Vergelesses, Puligny-Montrachet, Saint-Aubin, Saint-Romain, Sampigny-les-Maranges, Santenay, Savigny.

In the five years between 1972 and 1976, on average 9,600 hl of wine were declared under the name Côte de Beaune Villages.

Main Growers and Merchants

DOMAINE DU CHÂTEAU DE MERCEY (Cheilly)

305

JACQUES BERGER SA   40 ha. (60 per cent)
Mercurey 15 ha., Bourgogne Hautes Côtes de Beaune 25 ha.
  Most of this wine is sold in France, but a third of the production
goes to Switzerland.

L. LAURENCE, COURTIER ET VITICULTEUR (DEZIZE)   12 ha.
(60 per cent)
Santenay Les Gravières 1 ha., Puligny-Montrachet, Côte de
Beaune Villages.

ANDRÉ MONNOT (DEZIZE)   10 ha. (15 per cent)
VEUVE PAUL MONNOT
Santenay, Côte de Beaune Villages.

14

The Côte Chalonnaise

RULLY

Rully is the first village *appellation* of the Côte Chalonnaise, or Région de Mercurey. The village is said to take its name from a wealthy Gallo-Roman owner, Rubilium. A legacy of vines to the Abbey of Saint-Marcel was made in the eleventh century; in the seventeenth a gift of '*22 feuilletes de vin clairet très exquis*' was made by the inhabitants of Châlons to Louis XIII.

P. Bréjoux recounts that the inhabitants of Rully and Givry were unfortunate to fail in their application in 1923 for certain of their wines to be sold as Mercurey. The name of Rully was chiefly associated with the manufacture of sparkling wine, some by the Champagne method, some from outside the Burgundy area; the village's own still wines were hardly known. A hundred years ago there were 600 hectares of vines in the village, by the late 1940s a mere forty hectares producing AC wine. During the years 1953–7 the average production was only 430 hl of white, and 115 hl of red Rully. Replanting since has brought it up to 1,600 hl (17,600 dozen bottles) white and 1,000 hl (11,000 dozen bottles) red. There is still a sparkling wine industry, producing Bourgogne *mousseux*.

P. Bréjoux records an '*excellent climat*' in the commune of Chagny, called Saint-Jacques; I have never come across its wine, presumably a Bourgogne AC. Between Rully and Chagny is a small village, Bouzeron, known for its Aligoté, but also producing good red and white Bourgogne AC.

The following vineyards of Rully are *Premiers Crus*: Margoté, Grésigny, Vauvry, Mont-Palais, Meix-Caillet, Les Pierres, La Bressande, Champ-Clou, La Renarde, Pillot, Cloux, Raclot,

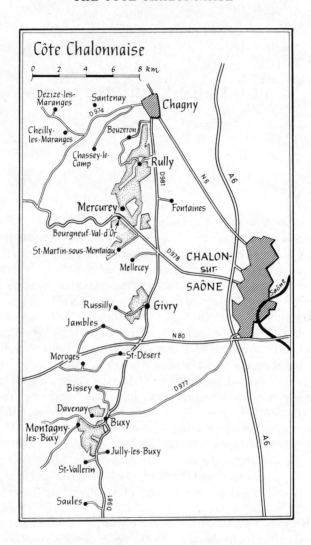

Côte Chalonnaise

Rabourcé, Ecloseaux, Marissou, La Fosse, Chapitre, Préau, Moulesne.

Main Growers and Merchants

COMTE J. D'AVIAU DE TERNAY   3 ha. (100 per cent)
Château de Rully *rouge* 2 ha., *blanc* 1 ha.

The Comte de Ternay owns an unusual sixteenth-century wine glass, large enough to hold three litres or four bottles of wine. Tradition has it that an ancestor, Charles de Saint-Ligier, used to drain it in one, though this seems impossible, for the rim is so wide that the wine pours past the sides of one's mouth.

He believes in long fermentations and refuses to filter.

RENÉ BRELIÈRE   15 ha. (100 per cent)
Rully *blanc* Margoté 3 ha., Champ-Clou 1 ha., Rully *rouge* Le Pria 3 ha., La Barre 8 ha.

Like many proprietors in Rully, M. Brelière 'Champagnizes' the products of his off-years and his young vines.

ÉMILE CHANDESAIS   (1933)
The founder of this firm in Fontaines (71150 Chagny) still directs it. The company does 65 per cent of its trade in France, mainly with wholesalers. It distributes the wines of the Domaine de la Folie[1] in Rully and the Beaujolais Villages Château de Néty.

There are five other estate-bottling growers in Rully, three in Bouzeron, two in Chassey-le-Camp and one in Chagny (which also has two merchants).

LES CAVES DELORME-MEULIEN   (1942)
Jean-François Delorme is one of the most forward-looking, least hidebound of Burgundy's merchants. He is fortunate in having the freedom to develop his family business in the way he sees fit, which has meant the creation over the last twenty years of the *Domaine de la Renarde* (40 ha.), of which a quarter is still to be planted. As well as Mercurey, Givry and Rully it includes the *Monopole* Rully Les Varots *rouge* and *blanc* (18 ha.). He is a promoter of the new sparkling wine Crémant de Bourgogne, but feels that the future of Rully lies in its still white and red wines. The whites are not far removed from the Meursault style, the reds finer, and readier earlier, than Mercurey.

[1] I learn in 1982 that M. Noel-Bouton's Domaine de la Folie now bottles 90 per cent of its production at the property. The 19 ha. estate consists of a 7 ha. red wine Monopole, Rully Clos de Bellecroix, the balance being white Rully from the Clos St Jacques. The latter is an unusually fine, lemony wine.

I have had a limited experience of his red Rully Les Varots, which has lacked concentration for my taste.

HENRI ET PAUL JACQUESON   5 ha. (75 per cent)
Rully *rouge* 2 ha., *blanc* 1½ ha., Mercurey 1½ ha.

M. Jacqueson used to 'Champagnize' some of his production, though stressing that Chardonnay wines from Rully are rather heavy for this. Now his main efforts go into his red wines; the 1973 and 1974 both won Gold Medals in Paris.

CELLIER MEIX-GUILLAUME   10 ha. (100 per cent)

RENÉ NINOT RIGAUD
Rully *blanc* La Bergerie, Rabourcé, La Gaudine 6½ ha., Rully *rouge* Le Meix Guillaume Monopole 1 ha., La Bergerie 1 ha., Mercurey 1⅔ ha.

These wines are quite often served at Clos de Vougeot dinners.

ARMAND MONASSIER
Rully *blanc*, *rouge*.

These wines can be drunk in Paris at the Restaurant Chez les Anges, owned by M. Monassier, accompanying *Oeufs en meurette* or other Burgundian dishes.

A. ET P. DE VILLAINE   12 ha. (100 per cent)
Bourgogne *rouge* Le Digoine, La Fortune, Bourgogne *blanc*, Aligoté.

This estate in Bouzeron (71150 Chagny) belongs to one of the co-directors of the Domaine de la Romanée-Conti, Aubert de Villaine and his American wife Pamela. Fine and perfumed wines are made and even in 1975 a respectable bottle of Bourgogne *rouge* was produced, showing what could be done.

In 1977, the Aligoté grapes failed to ripen—so much of the wine was sold in bulk to a local shipper.

Since March 1979, Aligotés grown in this commune have their own *appellation*: Bourgogne Aligoté de Bouzeron.

MERCUREY

The reputation of Mercurey's wines goes back to charters of A.D. 557 and 885, the name recalling a Roman temple to Mercury, later replaced by a windmill. The wines are harvested in

310

three communes, Mercurey, Saint-Martin-sous-Montaigu and Bourgneuf-Val-d'Or. This is the most important *appellation* of the Côte Chalonnaise. After the last war the average annual production was scarcely 5,000 hl, now it is 16,000 hl (176,000 dozen bottles) of red Mercurey, 800 hl (8,800 dozen bottles) of white. There are several large merchants in the area to assure the commercialization, and the Côte d'Or shippers J. Faiveley and Bouchard Aîné both have large vineyard holdings (see pages 222 and 252), the former a record number of *Monopoles* (see Appendix A).

Five vineyards are classified *Premiers Crus*: Clos-du-Roi, Clos-Voyen or Les Voyens, Clos-Marcilly, Clos-des-Fourneaux, Clos-des-Montaigus.

Main Growers and Merchants

DOMAINE BORDEAUX-MONTRIEUX   8 ha. (15 per cent)
Mercurey Clos Fortoul Monopole 4½ ha., Clos l'Évêque ⅛ ha.

ROLAND BRINTET   8 ha. (100 per cent)
Mercurey La Charmée, La Levrière, Les Ormeaux, Le Champillot, Les Vasées, La Corvée.

This domaine has been bottling since 1946, a time when there was little enough sugar for personal needs and none for chaptalization.

DOMAINE JEANNIN-NALTET   10 ha. (40 per cent)
Mercurey Clos-Voyen Monopole 4 ha., Clos l'Évêque 2 ha., Les Chezeaux, Les Naugues.

The Jeannin-Naltet family live most of the year round in Dijon. Their property in Mercurey is unusual in having all its vines gathered closely round it. Hail is therefore much feared and rockets used whenever storm-clouds threaten. They are reported effective so long as several owners fire off at once, when the clouds can be dispersed and the hail persuaded to fall as rain.

MICHEL JUILLOT   10 ha. (100 per cent)
LOUIS JUILLOT
Mercurey Clos des Barreaux 1 ha.

This domaine bottles its Mercureys whatever the weather.

YVES DE LAUNAY   7 ha. (60 per cent)
Mercurey Clos du Château de Montaigu Monopole 2 ha.

An unusual vein of light soil crops up here, which has given the name of Meix-Foulot or 'Mad Clos' to the house. Half a hectare of white grapes are grown on it.

PAUL MARCEAU   9 ha. (50 per cent)
Mercurey.

JEAN MARÉCHALE   6 ha. (100 per cent)
AUGUSTE MARÉCHALE
Mercurey.

FRANÇOIS PROTHEAU ET FILS   25 ha.
Mercurey Clos des Corvées 4 ha., Clos l'Évêque 7 ha., La Fauconnière 5 ha., Les Ormeaux 1½ ha. (*blanc*).

Half of this company's trade is done in France. They have been '*vignerons depuis 1720*'.

AUGUSTE RAQUILLET   8 ha. (40 per cent)
JEAN RAQUILLET
MICHEL RAQUILLET
Mercurey.

ANTONIN RODET   (1815) 20 ha.
DOMAINE DU MARQUIS DE JOUENNES D'HERVILLE
CHÂTEAU DE CHAMIREY
Mercurey Clos-de-Roi 3 ha., Clos l'Évêque 3 ha., Mercurey *blanc* La Mission Monopole 2 ha.

This firm exports to seventy countries.

DOMAINE DE SUREMAIN   12 ha. (35 per cent)
HUGUES DE SUREMAIN
Mercurey Clos l'Évêque 1 ha., Petit Sazenay 1 ha.

M. de Suremain attributes the fact that Mercurey has always sold well to there being a number of merchants based in the village.

ÉMILE VOARICK   50 ha. (50 per cent)
Aloxe-Corton *Premier Cru* Clos des Fiètres ¾ ha., Beaune Montée

rouge 1 ha., Mercurey Clos-du-Roi Monopole 1 ha., Château Beau 3 ha., Givry 8 ha.

Despite the size of his estate, M. Voarick, who started from nothing after the war, attaches great importance to keeping his many *cuvées* separate. The estate is in Saint-Martin-sous-Montaigu.

There are two more merchants and four more Mercurey growers offering wine in bottle.

GIVRY

The growers of Givry would have it that in the Middle Ages their wines were on an equal footing with those of Beaune. Certainly they paid the same taxes, for an *ordonnance* of 1349 states: '*Tonnel de vin de Beaune . . . et de Givry paiera six sous d'entrée à Paris.*' In 1390 Philippe le Hardi's wife Marguerite de Flandre stocked her cellars at the Château de Germolles with ten *queues* of Beaune and forty-five *queues* of '*Givry et environs*' according to P. Bréjoux.

There are no classified *Premiers Crus*, but the following vineyards can be noted: La Barande, Bois-Chevaux, Cellier aux Moines, Clos Saint-Paul, Clos Saint-Pierre, Clos Saloman. Champ Poureau is a white wine *climat*, according to P. Bréjoux.

Like the other villages of this region, Givry has seen replanting in recent years. The production is now 2,500 hl (27,500 dozen bottles) of red wine, 800 hl (8,800 dozen bottles) of white.

Main Growers and Merchants

PROPRIÉTÉ DESVIGNES   9 ha. (50 per cent)
Givry *rouge* and *blanc*, Clos du Vernois $\frac{2}{3}$ ha.

DU GARDIN   7 ha. (100 per cent)
Givry Clos Saloman Monopole 6 ha.

This Clos takes its name from the Saloman family which held land in Givry in the thirteenth century. It is recorded that in 1375 Hugues Saloman sold wine to the Pope.

It has been in the hands of its present owners for over three centuries and was for many years most carefully tended by M. Emmanuel du Gardin. He bottled every vintage but only after it had spent three years in wood, for he believed in neither fining nor filtering. Since the deaths of J. du Gardin in 1977 and Emmanuel du Gardin in 1978, the estate has been managed by their widow and daughter, with the help of two employees.

DOMAINE JOBLOT   6 ha. (100 per cent)
Givry *rouge* Clos du Cellier aux Moines 2 ha., Givry *blanc* Clos de la Servoisine 2 ha.

This estate has been bottling all its production every year since 1959.

MORIN FRÈRES   7 ha. (30 per cent)
Givry *rouge* and *blanc*.

CHARLES ET GÉRARD MOUTON   4 ha. (10 per cent)
Givry.

ROBERT NOLET   3 ha. (50 per cent)
Givry *rouge* and *blanc*.

RAGOT, JEAN-PIERRE ET JEAN-PAUL   7 ha. (50 per cent)
Givry *rouge* and *blanc* 2 ha.

Givry white is something of a rarity, made from the Chardonnay grape.

SOCIÉTÉ CIVILE DU DOMAINE THÉNARD   24 ha. (40 per cent)
Montrachet 1⅕ ha., Corton Clos du Roi 1 ha., Pernand-Vergelesses *rouge* 1 ha., Chassagne-Montrachet Clos Saint-Jean ⅕ ha., Mercurey ¾ ha. Givry Clos Saint-Pierre Monopole 2 ha., Cellier aux Moines 5 ha., Bois-Chevaux 11 ha.

Over two-thirds of this domaine was in young vines in the early 1970s, for it was neglected at one time. The climb back up the slope is inevitably a slow one, and the vinifications are not yet perhaps what they might be.

MONTAGNY

Montagny is a name which applies only to white wines, from the Chardonnay grape, grown in the communes of Buxy, Montagny, Jully-les-Buxy and Saint-Vallerin. There is an average annual production of 2,600 hl (28,600 dozen bottles) from a delimited area of 305·35 hectares. The local reds are Bourgogne and Passe-Tout-Grains.

The name is a recent one, for previously the wines, both red and white, were sold as Côte de Buxy. Here may be found the wall-inscription: '*Ne laeseris vinum*' (Do no harm to wine).

The words *Premier Cru* may appear on a label of Montagny if the wine had a minimum alcoholic content of 11·5° before the grapes were picked. That, at any rate, is the theory.

There is an important co-operative and one notable private estate in Montagny:

CAVES DES VIGNERONS DE BUXY-SAINT-GENGOUX LE NATIONAL (71390 Buxy)
This Co-operative dates from 1929. It handles most of the grapes harvested in Buxy, Montagny, Saint-Vallerin, Jully-les-Buxy, Saules, Saint-Boil, and Culles Les Roches—in all, the produce of 490 ha.

The Co-operative specializes in direct sales to French private customers and foreign importers. As well as Montagny *Premier Cru* and Montagny, it makes Passe-Tout-Grains, Aligoté and straight Bourgogne.

DOMAINE MARTIAL DE LABOULAYE, Château de Buxy 7 ha. Montagny *blanc* Le Vieux Château 3½ ha., Bourgogne *rouge* and Passe-Tout-Grains 3½ ha.

M. de Laboulaye was a Paris lawyer and a most charming old gentleman who had been bottling 20 per cent of his harvest every good year since 1937. He died in the mid-1970s; the estate is now run by his son-in-law, M. Courtet. There is a fine old machine for dissolving the chaptalization sugar, and thermostatically controlled cellars. Montagny should be drunk youngish, M. de Laboulaye used to say, though fine vintages can last ten years. The estate has a collection of old implements which includes a decanting cradle, an eighteenth-century wood-fuelled copper brandy-still, and an anti-phylloxera implement looking like a pneumatic drill. Beneath the twelfth-century tower, the highest point in Buxy, is a sundial with the inscription: '*Je ne marque l'heure que des beaux jours.*'

There is one merchant in Chalon-sur-Sâone, and twelve growers offering wine in bottle from the villages around Buxy: Bissey-sous-Cruchaud (which has a co-operative), Davenay, Moroges, Saint-Désert, Saint-Vallerin and Saules.

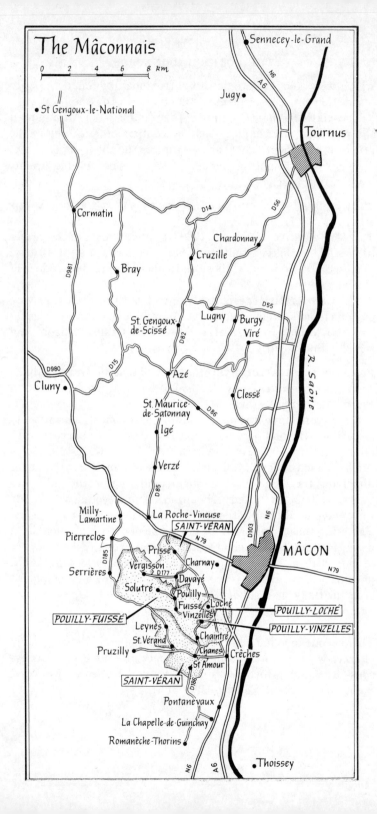

15

The Mâconnais

The reputation of the wines of the Mâconnais dates back to a mention by the Latin poet Ausonius, but it was not until the eleventh and twelfth century that vineyards were widely cultivated. The monks of the Abbey of Cluny, founded on the western edge of the vineyard area, were responsible for the extension, according to P. Bréjoux.

In the seventeenth century, southern Mâconnais wines went to Paris. The French market was partitioned by customs barriers under the Ancien Régime, Dijon and Châlons obstructing the sale of Mâcon wines in Franche Comté and Alsace, the Lyon market being virtually closed to all wines not harvested in the *gouvernement du Lyonnais*. Although heavy transport charges were incurred in reaching Paris these were incidental if the wine was of high quality. During the Revolution and under the Empire the wines were exported to Belgium, the Low Countries and Germany, at the expense of Bordeaux, whose deliveries were disrupted by the British blockade of coastal shipping. Getting the wines to Paris was never easy. As Pierre Goujon[1] describes, in summer the Saône or the Canal du Centre were often too low for navigation, while in winter ice might halt all movement. It became usual to make two despatches to Paris, one in October after the harvest, and one in the spring. There were numerous trans-shipments, from the Saône to the Canal du Centre, from the latter to the Loire or another canal. The boats on the Loire were one-third smaller than those on the Canal. Navigating the sandbanks of the Loire was tricky, and those living on the banks were used to digging out passing boats. Losses were important, and two

---

[1] *Le Vignoble de Saône et Loire au XIX Siècle*, Université Lyon II, Lyon, 1973.

tonneaux of wine had to be allowed for the personal consumption of the boatmen. Sometimes the autumn convoys became blocked, not reaching Paris till the spring. Pierre Goujon quotes from family papers assembled by A. Bernard:[1] 'Here I am at last arrived on the banks of the Loire; I had much trouble with my wines. We have already lost ten hogsheads from breakages, yawning staves, worm-holes in the wood; generally there has been much seepage. From our three boats we are loading on to eight.'

In 1854 the arrival of the railway changed everything. Nine years later Guigue de Champvans wrote in *Le Vignoble Mâconnais*: 'Not long ago the wine merchant, whose deliveries took place regularly twice a year, made his purchases twice, in spring and autumn. The railway has thrown the trade in completely new directions. Today he buys constantly, at any season, depending on what he sells and requires. The ease and speed of transport removes the need to store unless for speculative or blending purposes. His central warehouse is the vineyard itself.'

The Mâconnais is a region of chains of small hills, mostly running north–south, parallel to the river Saône; it is about 35 km long by 10–15 km wide, limited to the east by the plain of the Saône, to the west by the foothills of the Morvan and Charollais.

The bedrock is a continuation of the Jurassic strata we have met in the Côte d'Or. A lifting of the south of the Mâconnais has resulted in the erosion of the limestone and the emergence of the Hercynian bedrock—which is where the Beaujolais begins. Particularly resistant Jurassic strata have survived, forming the startling rock crests of Solutré and Vergisson which characterize the Pouilly-Fuissé countryside.

The Mâconnais is less dominated by its vineyards than the Beaujolais. It is a countryside of undulating wood-capped hills with rounded summits, 400–500 metres high, but it is less densely-populated and poorer than the Beaujolais. Vineyards alternate with meadows, divided by spinneys of sweet chestnut and acacia. Cherry trees and walnuts stand in the fields, and parallel to the rows of vines one may see rows of potatoes, both in flower together. As one drives down the roads light-brown kids, their horn-stumps just visible, disappear into the grass verge like baby

[1] A letter of 2 June 1830 (SAAST (T.XXXIII, 1933–4)).

roe-deer. There seems plenty of room for extension of the vineyard area if the current popularity of white Mâcon wines lasts.

The climate in the Mâconnais is a temperate but uncertain one, with extremes of cold in February, and heat in July and August. Frost is feared until the Foire de Mâcon is past—which usually corresponds to the Ice Saints in the calendar. The average annual rainfall is about 800 mm. The instability of the climate accounts for the importance of soil, orientation and altitude of the vineyards; and is responsible for many farms cultivating more than one crop or also raising animals. According to R. Boidron,[1] 60 per cent of the estates have a herd of cows (though this is diminishing), and a quarter own goats and make their own cheese.

The role of the wife is very important, indeed R. Boidron shows that only 7 per cent of vineyard concerns are run by bachelors. Tending vineyards is time-consuming (500 hours per hectare per year for Chardonnay, according to a 1974 survey by the CETA), and the wife's contribution is vital at certain times: for the bending and tying of the shoots, the trimming of excess leaves, the attaching, the chopping back of vegetation, the harvest. The careful arching and firm attachment of the two fruit-bearing Chardonnay shoots in the Mâconnais is a delicate task, demanding dexterity and skills often acquired as a child in her parents' vines. It should be done on humid days, never when there is a dry wind from the north or east. In certain vineyards it is perfectly executed and a beautiful symmetrical sight they make.

The Mâconnais has about 6,000 hectares of AC vineyard; a hundred years ago there was over three times that area under vines, for Mâcon wines were known as the Grands Ordinaires de France, the most widely planted vine being the Gamay. Today the Chardonnay has taken over, and it covers nearly 60 per cent of the vineyard area, the Gamay accounting for one-third, the Pinot Noir one-tenth. Co-operative cellars handle 85 per cent of white Mâcons, and 65 per cent of the red; altogether there are sixteen of them.

The co-operative movement in the Mâconnais dates from the 1920s when the storage capacity of the growers was stretched to its limit, prices were on the floor, yet still the wines failed to sell.

---

[1] *Le Mâconnais Viticole*, CETA Viticole du Mâconnais, Chambre d'Agriculture de Saône et Loire.

Many wines, it must be admitted, were made from hybrid vines, and frequently the growers did not possess proper vinification equipment. Contact was made with co-operatives in the Midi to obtain advice, and the first *Cave* built in the Mâconnais, at Saint-Gengoux de Scissé, in 1926. It was followed by Lugny a year later, then seventeen others before 1934.

As we have seen, co-operatives now occupy an important place in the Mâconnais. Let us therefore look at one in greater detail: Lugny, which has had considerable success exporting its wines directly since the collapse of the wine market in 1974. The Co-operative has 484 members, cultivating 825 hectares of vineyard in eleven communes. Five of these are devoted exclusively to the vine: Lugny (mainly white wines), Saint-Gengoux de Scissé (mainly red), Bissy-la-Mâconnaise, Cruzille and Péronne. The *Cave* makes a total of 50,000 hl of wine, 70 per cent being Mâcon Villages from the Chardonnay grape, 15 per cent Mâcon Supérieur *rouge* and *rosé* from the Gamay, and 15 per cent Bourgogne *rouge* from the Pinot Noir. Some Bourgogne Passe-Tout-Grains and Crémant de Bourgogne are also produced. Lugny merged with its neighbour Saint-Gengoux de Scissé in 1965 when, as in the 1920s, few buyers could be found for the wines in spite of low prices. The two cellars transformed themselves into a *Groupement de Producteurs*, which gives access to larger funds and is a significant psychological sales aid. For customers, be they foreign importers or passing Frenchmen, prefer the idea of dealing with a group of producers rather than a co-operative. In five years they have progressed from selling 10 per cent to selling 40 per cent of their production directly to consumers or foreign buyers. Now they have requested the extension of the *appellation contrôlée* Mâcon-Lugny to cover white wines from four communes in addition to Lugny itself. Perhaps they will succeed, for the wine produced in this northerly section of the Mâconnais seems to have its own originality: less steely, more flowery than, say, a Mâcon-Prissé. To some extent this is due to the presence of Chardonnay *musqué* vines in the vineyards; small proportions in a blend add relief to the wines.

In general the quality of red Mâcons has improved over the last decade, due to the wider adoption of the Beaujolais method of uncrushed grape vinification. In 1967 P. Bréjoux was advocating in *Les Vins de Bourgogne* that Mâcon's Gamay grapes should be vinified as rosés, or the best vineyards replanted with Pinot. But co-operative cellars such as Igé and Saint-Gengoux have pursued a different course, seemingly with success, for some 1978 red Mâcons fetched higher prices than Beaujolais.

More and more growers are using selective weed-killers, and reducing the number of ploughings and hoeings. The advantages have been summarized as follows:[1] It is not expensive (F.1,000 per hectare in 1975), requires little manpower, keeps the soil clean all year, reduces erosion, renders movement through the vineyard easier in wet weather, seems dangerous for neither vine nor man and is particularly appreciated on steep slopes. The experiments of the Lycée Agricole de Davayé over the seven years prior to 1975 show that generally the natural alcoholic degree is slightly increased, as is the yield.

Plantations of vines in wide rows, trained high, have been less successful however. The advantages of the system are that it requires fewer vines per hectare, that cultivation does not call for an expensive *tracteur-enjambeur*, and that fewer man-hours are required. But ten years of experiments in the Saône et Loire[2] reveal that yields are regularly lower with high vines, allied, in the case of the Chardonnay, to lower natural sugar production. Acidities are always greater, for high vines do not benefit from heat reflected off the ground. Comparative tastings favour the traditionally-trained vine in the case of the Aligoté and the Chardonnay. They were inconclusive for the Pinot Noir, and the high vines in this case proved the more resistant to grey rot. Comparable quality can only be obtained from high vines if a quarter to a third of the normally-expected yield is sacrificed— which more or less eliminates the benefits gained from lower-cost plantation and cultivation.

As might be expected, a fair proportion of Burgundy's regional *appellations* are produced in the Saône et Loire *département*, which is the countryside between the Côte d'Or and the Beaujolais (and includes the Côte Chalonnaise, the Mâconnais, Saint-Amour and parts of Chénas and Moulin à Vent). Here are to be found a quarter of the Bourgogne *rouge*, half the Bourgogne *blanc* and the

[1] *Beaujolais Mâconnais: Ecologie, Archéologie et Oenologie*, Derognat, Donnot, Defer and Lagoutte, Lyon, 1975.

[2] R. Boidron, *Vignes Hautes et Larges*, L'Exploitant Agricole, Saône et Loire, Mars, 1978.

base wine for Crémant de Bourgogne, and just under half the Bourgogne Aligoté, the Bourgogne Passe-Tout-Grains and Bourgogne Grand Ordinaire. The *appellations* which are specific to the Mâconnais, with their average production over the five years 1972–6 are:

	Average of the total harvest 1972–1976 (hectolitres)	
Mâcon *blanc*	2,346	
Mâcon Supérieur *blanc*	30,792	
Mâcon with village name, *blanc*	73,367	
Total Mâcon *blanc*		106,505
Mâcon *rouge* and *rosé*	3,070	
Mâcon Supérieur *rouge*	56,272	
Mâcon with village name, *rouge*	2,355	
Total Mâcon *rouge*		61,697
Pouilly-Fuissé	32,560	
Pouilly-Fuissé with vineyard name	2,109	
Pouilly-Loché	1,122	
Pouilly-Vinzelles	2,045	
Total Pouilly		37,836
Saint-Véran	11,783	11,783
		217,821 hl

POUILLY-FUISSÉ, -LOCHÉ, -VINZELLES AND SAINT-VÉRAN

These are the best white wines of the Mâconnais. They differ considerably in price, Pouilly-Fuissé being the greatest in demand, but are extremely similar in style and quality, a good Saint-Véran from Davayé, for instance, being to my mind at least the equal, at half the price, of many Pouilly-Fuissé from Chaintré. The names have been allotted haphazardly, I suppose on the Beaujolais principle (which we will come to in a moment) that if you call a wine by four names rather than one you have a chance of selling four times as much. The name to go for, therefore, is the one

322

which currently is the cheapest, because the most recently invented: Saint-Véran. It is harvested in the communes of Chânes, Chasselas, Davayé, Leynes, Prissé, Saint-Amour, Saint-Véran and Solutré.

In the Mâconnais and the Beaujolais I have not visited and described the most important merchants and estate-bottling growers (as was attempted in Chablis, the Côte d'Or and the Côte Chalonnaise), for the nature of the wines does not warrant it.

There are about seventy Mâconnais growers currently bottling, and twenty merchants, whose addresses may be had from the *Comité Interprofessionel de Saône et Loire pour les vins d'Appellation Contrôlée de Bourgogne et de Mâcon*, in Mâcon.

16

The Beaujolais

The Beaujolais region is part of the Lyonnais. It came into being in the eleventh century, founded by Béraud, first Lord of Beaujeu, its capital, which sits strategically on the shortest passage between the Saône and Loire valleys. It is named as Bellijocum in 1031.

Villefranche has been the commercial and administrative capital of the region since the sixteenth century. It owes its importance to its position as a market-town, surrounded by the agricultural lands of Bresse and Beaujolais, on the main north–south trade route. It was granted its charter of freedoms in 1260 by Guichard IV, Sire of Beaujeu.

Only in the last two hundred years has the Beaujolais become dominated by viticulture. Before the Revolution it was one of the most miserable and least populated regions in France, according to Cochard and d'Aiguperse.[1] The sandy soil gave a harvest of rye or barley every three or four years and a few sheep cropped amongst the briars. The transformation took place as a result of the division of the large estates after the Revolution and thanks to the opening up of new markets in the north of France after the road had been improved from the Saône to the Loire. The suppression of internal customs barriers encouraged the growers to bring more land into cultivation. The population is said to have tripled in sixty years.

In *Jadis en Beaujolais*, Justin Dutraive describes how the completion of the Canal de Briare in 1642 had enabled the Beaujolais growers to take their wines economically to Paris. The

---

[1] Quoted in Justin Dutraive, *Jadis en Beaujolais*, M. Lescuyer et Fils, Lyon, 1976.

first communes entitled to do so were Saint-Lager, Fleurie and Chénas. The land route through Burgundy had been expensive—twenty-nine *pièces* loaded on to three carts and a four-wheeled wagon requiring eighteen horses to pull them. River transport by the Loire and the new canal was longer and slower, but cheaper. There were three routes to the Loire but the most used was from Port de Belleville to Port de Pouilly. Horses were used for the first stage, and Charollais oxen, strong as oil-presses, on the uplands, then horse-drawn carts downhill to the Loire. It was thirsty work and there were as many public houses on the road as there were kilometre-posts. There was no river navigation at night, everything stopped in fog, and there were sixteen tolls, to the profit of local *seigneurs*. When Briare was reached, a tasting took place—anything *piqué* went on down the Loire to the vinegar establishments of Orléans. A month's navigation was required before Port-au-Vin, Paris, was reached.

The secret of success in the Beaujolais today is that six thousand estates and two hundred shippers are all selling one wine. It has been given different names to keep people guessing, tasting, comparing, drinking—but the wines are variations on one simple theme. Good Beaujolais is light purply-red, fruity on the nose, and slips easily down the throat. More accurately, each year they sell three wines rather than one. The first, probably from the southern part of the area, is light purply-red, fruity on the nose and slips easily down the throat from mid-November, straight after the harvest. The second is . . . yes, that is right, and you drink it the following March, April and May—it is probably called Beaujolais Villages. The third, well, you know what it tastes like, and it is called Brouilly or Fleurie or some such name. You drink it through the summer and autumn up to mid-November when the new wine arrives. After poor summers, like 1980, many wines of the southern Beaujolais bear no resemblance to anything purply-red and fruity; one must go to the more prestigious hillsides, from Saint-Amour to Brouilly, to find it. And in hot years like 1978, those hillsides give deep-coloured rich wines, again far removed from the ideal. They are bought by optimists who mistakenly believe that aging will bring them charm, perfume and elegance. Aging never transforms the product of the Gamay grape into something of comparable quality and interest to an aged Syrah, Pinot Noir, or claret. So after rich vintages, one should go straight

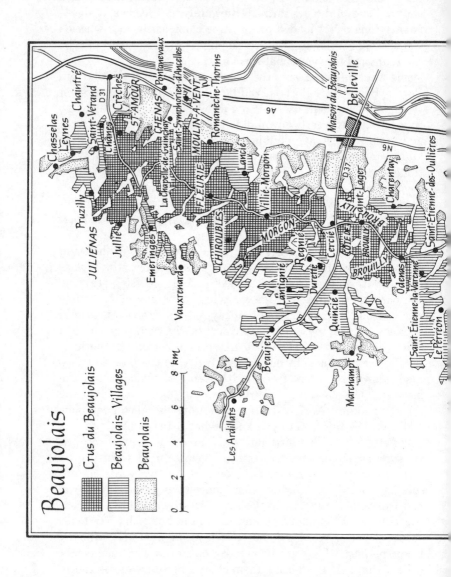

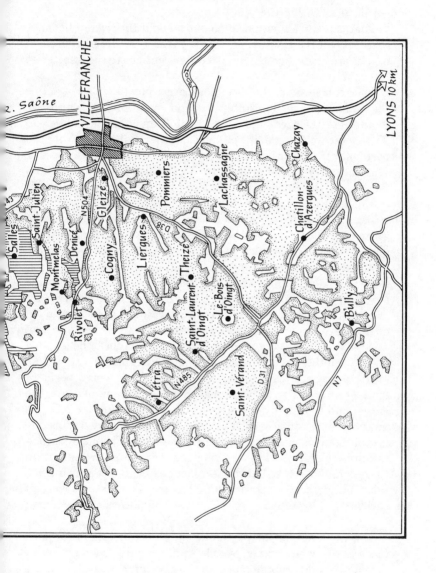

to the basic *appellations*, Beaujolais and Beaujolais Villages—and drink them within the year.

That is really all one needs to know about the region. I cannot quite leave it there, however, for each year over a hundred million bottles are made, and there are a few exceptions to the rule. So let us begin again.

The great secret of the Beaujolais, according to Dr J. Guyot,[1] is the Gamay grape. It established and maintains its legitimate reputation. Well, yes and no. For the Gamay grape, unless you know how to handle it, produces rather dull wine, with no particular fruitiness or character. What transforms it is a special vinification. I am indebted to M. Pelletier of the Sicarex-Beaujolais, the Government-backed vine and wine research unit in Villefranche, for his description of the process.

The first objective is to pick the bunches carefully and bring the grapes whole and unsquashed to the vat-house, and for this small plastic tubs holding no more than sixty kilograms of grapes are required. No *fouloir-égrappoir* is used, the machine which in most red-wine-making areas squashes the grapes, at the same time removing all or some of the stalks. Ideally, vinification takes place in a vat no larger than sixty hectolitres (though most vats in co-operative cellars are over twice that size). About six hectolitres of juice will be produced by the natural pressure of the bunches piled one on another; the proportion in a 150-hectolitre vat will be greater, which is their disadvantage. The juice may begin to ferment; in any case, the wine-maker will pump some of it over the grapes and heat it to get it going. Sugar is added to increase the final alcoholic degree of the wine, and about five grams per hectolitre of the anti-oxidant sulphur dioxide. The ideal fermentation temperature for extracting the maximum perfumes from the grape is 25°–28°C, but this is difficult to control. Fermentation takes place *within* each uncrushed grape, in an atmosphere of carbon dioxide produced by the fermenting juice at the bottom of the vat.

This method is an adaptation of the classic system of carbonic maceration wine-making, which would require no addition of sulphur dioxide, no pumping over of juice, but a saturation of the vat with bottled carbon dioxide immediately it was filled,

---

[1] *Étude des Vignobles de France*, Paris, 1868.

followed by ten to twelve days' maceration. In the Beaujolais the process takes five to six days, at the end of which the vat contains about thirty hectolitres of liquid; the grapes are pressed to extract the rest.

It is this method of wine-making, not the Gamay grape alone, which gives Beaujolais wines their characteristic fruitiness and soft finish. The Gamay grape itself has no great individuality—as can be seen by tasting Gamays from Savoie, or Saint-Pourçain on the upper Loire, squashed and fermented traditionally. It should be added that the Beaujolais climate suits the grape ideally. To obtain wine of mouth-watering freshness, the grapes are picked just before ripeness. A natural alcoholic degree of 10° or 11° allied to six grams of acidity is a good balance; the hot year of 1976 produced natural degrees of 11·5° and acidities of five grams or less, so some growers acidified the wines with tartaric acid to redress the balance.

The visitor to the Beaujolais discovers a countryside which is very different from northern Burgundy. Water is found in many places, so farms and manor-houses are spread regularly over the countryside, vineyards and people being cheek by jowl. Each village has clusters of hamlets around it. There are islands of woodland in the vines, meadows in the valleys, lollipop trees and red-roofed houses in a story-book landscape; a mixed agricultural economy, with a high population density. It is one immense village submerged in a vast vineyard, cut by countless twisting up-and-down roads, the hand of man evident wherever you look.

Up in the hills above Chiroubles, or in the vast amphitheatre of vines around Vauxrenard, horses still hoe between the rows on the steep slopes. Wild purple lupins grow from rock outcrops and the roadside verges in June. One rounds a corner and comes upon a green woodpecker standing with its beak in the air, or a hoopoe feeding in the long grass. One reaches a hilltop to find oneself fifty feet from a helicopter spraying at eye-level, or a circling black-and-white flecked buzzard.

'*La Bourgogne méridionale est un véritable puzzle de plaines, de bassins, de collines et de coteaux dissymétriques*', wrote Dr J. Guyot in 1868. The vineyards of the Beaujolais are to be found on a wide variety of bedrocks, dating from the primary to the tertiary eras. It can be divided into three parts, the Haut-Beaujolais, the Bas-Beaujolais and the valley of the Saône.

The Haut-Beaujolais is a chain of hills with steep slopes, cut by east–west valleys, running from Saint-Amour in the north to the level of Villefranche in the south. The soil is acid, sandy and made up of permeable schists derived from the granite rock, relatively easy to work. The Bas-Beaujolais begins after the valley of the Nizerand, which flows into the Saône at Villefranche. It is of lower altitude, its soil clay and limestone, richer and deeper. This area used to be known as the Beaujolais-Bâtard, its wines rated below those of the north. The rating is unchanged, but the name is now Beaujolais-Sud, or Beaujolais des Pierres Dorées, from its ochre limestone houses. The third part, the valley of the Saône, has tertiary and quaternary soils. Less rained on and hotter than the hillsides, it is subject to brusque changes of temperature due to the north–south winds, and is unsuitable for viticulture.

There are, of course, local soil variations in the wine-producing villages. In Odenas (Brouilly AC) or Saint-Etienne-la-Varenne (Beaujolais Villages AC) one may find granite, in Juliénas schists, in Frontenas (Beaujolais AC) pebbles, in Theizé (Beaujolais AC) pebbles too, but also sandstone and various limestones. The soil plays its part in the vegetative cycle, sandy granite soils, for instance, delay the opening of the buds.

One vine dominates the region, covering 98 per cent of the vineyard area: the Gamay Beaujolais. P. Galet gives its synonyms: Gamay *Noir à jus blanc*, Petit Gamai, Gamay *rond*, Bourguignon *noir*. It is a productive vine, all its buds being fertile, giving a satisfactory harvest even after spring frosts, for the shoots come a second time. The bunches are compact and cylindrical and subject to grey rot. It is found at a density of between 9,000 and 13,000 plants per hectare. Short pruning is the classic method in the Beaujolais (as described in the chapter on vines and viticulture) with the vine trained to a goblet or fan shape. Each vine has three to five horns, carrying two fruit-bearing eyes per shoot, the maximum permitted total being twelve. Long pruning (Guyot) is permitted for Beaujolais AC, as is a mixed system featuring a long fruit-bearing shoot and one to five shorter canes, each bearing two fertile buds. These tend to speed up the vegetative cycle slightly.

As in the Côte d'Or, research is under way to discover by clonal selection the most suitable types of Gamay for replantations in the Beaujolais. The Sicarex-Beaujolais in Villefranche is responsible, working with the Domaine de L'Espiguette at Le Grau du Roi, and experimental plots are spread around the vineyard area, in Oingt, Légny, Salles, Saint-Étienne, Odenas, Emeringes and at the Domaine de la Chaize. Each clone is examined for its state of health, *millerandage*,[1] regularity, vigour, susceptibility to grey rot, weight of the harvest, number of bunches, total acidity, sugar content, colour of juice, weight and size of the grapes (the smaller the better). The most important element is the sugar content, related to a satisfactory yield. Multiplication of five satisfactory clones of Gamay began in 1977, the object being the eventual renewal of the 40,000 hectares (half of it in the Beaujolais) of Gamay vineyards in France.

The most important root-stock in the Beaujolais is the Vialla, said to be the sole descendant of a Labrusca vine which survived the phylloxera. It has a remarkable affinity with the Gamay, and thrives in lime-free granite soils. Other root-stocks are used in the Bas-Beaujolais, most of which we have already met in the Côte d'Or—the all-purpose 3309C, the lime-resistant SO_4 which is now replacing the 5BB and a new one called 420A, a *Berlandieri* × *Riparia* cross, which is suitable for pebbly granite soils above a certain altitude. It is found above 350 metres on the terraces of Chiroubles, Regnié and Villié-Morgon.

Co-operatives play an important part in the Beaujolais, although they are not as dominant as in the Mâconnais. Seven date back to the period 1929–34: Chiroubles, Liergues, Quincié, Saint-Jean d'Ardières, Fleurie, Gleizé and Chénas, the remaining eleven having been founded between 1954 and 1961: Lachassagne, Sain-Bel, Létra, Saint-Vérand, Saint-Étienne-des-Oullières, Bully, Le Bois d'Oingt, Le Perréon, Saint-Laurent, Juliénas and Theizé. Over the five years preceding 1975, they produced 35 per cent of the AC Beaujolais, 17 per cent of both Beaujolais Villages and the *crus*, according to the INAO in Villefranche. Nearly half the Beaujolais and Beaujolais Villages 1975 released as *Primeur* came from them. They have all increased their capacity substantially since their creation, and ten of them have grouped together to offer their wines in bottle to merchants located in the areas of consumption in France and abroad. If this initiative succeeds, it will dent the traditional Beaujolais distri-

---

[1] The extent to which the berries vary in size.

bution pattern, which has the grower selling his wine, via a *courtier*, to a local *négociant*. At present based at Saint-Jean d'Ardières, this group, the *Producteurs-Distributeurs des Vins du Beaujolais* will soon be occupying large new premises at Quincié.[1]

The tendency for growers to cut out their local merchants is one that can be observed in every vineyard area of France—but I do not see it attaining proportions in the Beaujolais comparable to those in the Côte d'Or. Beaujolais merchants are more agile than the north Burgundians. They work on smaller margins, have less obligation to finance stocks, and provide the important service of making reliable styles of wine available in quantity throughout the year.

Skullduggery certainly takes place (literally tens of thousands of hectolitres of the poor 1975 harvest were unsaleable until they had been restored to health with bone-setter red wine according to the method described in Chapter 8), but the problem is not so acute as in the Côte d'Or. Quaffing wine (more or less alcoholic) can be made most years in the Beaujolais—and quaffing wine (more or less alcoholic) is what the consumer expects.

A well-balanced Beaujolais might be a blend of three wines: something supple and fruity from Saint-Étienne-des-Oullières; a *cuvée* from Marchampt or Beaujeu to bring body and staying power, and a Saint-Julien wine, from the borders of the Beaujolais Villages, to bring fatness. In the early part of the year the merchant may try to ship wines from Le Perréon or Blacé, which make excellent *Primeurs*; if he is exporting, he may draw stocks from Vauxrenard for their staying power, or Emeringes for their colour. If he must keep within a price he will go to the marginal zones to the south and north, particularly the Bâtard-Beaujolais.

A study published in May 1978 by the *Union Interprofessionnelle des Vins du Beaujolais* shows that direct sales between producers and private customers, restaurants or retailers accounted for between 10 and 15 per cent of all Beaujolais wines for the years 1975 to 1977. In top communes like Fleurie or Juliénas where there is an important co-operative, or Moulin-à-Vent where there is a concentration of merchants, direct sales accounted for less than 15 per cent of the *appellation*. However, both Chiroubles and Morgon disposed of over 30 per cent of their harvest directly.

---

[1] Another grouping of growers (on a much smaller scale) is the *Eventail des Crus de Haute-Bourgogne* in Corcelles, specializing in individual producers' wines.

As in the Mâconnais, I have not attempted to visit and describe the most important merchants and estate-bottling growers. Their addresses may be had from the *Union Interprofessionnelle des Vins du Beaujolais*, 210 Boulevard Vermorel, 69400 Villefranche-en-Beaujolais.

The following list gives details of the various names by which good Beaujolais is known. (The figures given for the area under vines were obtained in 1974.)

SAINT-AMOUR   (330 ha. Average harvest: 12,000 hl)
This is a wine which holds up well in bottle. Some tasters detect odours of peach and raspberry on the nose.

JULIÉNAS   (490 ha. Average harvest: 25,000 hl)
The first Beaujolais is said to have been planted on this spot, and the name to hark back to Julius Caesar. The vineyards are high up on hillsides; like Saint-Amour the wine should be solidly built.

CHÉNAS   (260 ha. Average harvest: 12,000 hl)
The wines of this commune have often in the past been used to bolster northern Burgundies. On their own they sometimes lack charm.

Hubert Piat[1] would abolish the *appellation*, for its name is little known, and the styles of its wines too diverse. Part should become Fleurie, part Juliénas, part Saint-Amour and part Moulin-à-Vent—which shows a thoroughly healthy disrespect for the importance of Beaujolais commune names.

MOULIN-À-VENT   (700 ha. Average harvest: 32,000 hl)
Moulin-à-Vent was first mentioned as recently as 1757—and the wine was being exported. Four hogsheads were sold, for despatch to Namur, Belgium, at a price of 112 francs *la botte*.

This is the wine for those who believe in laying down their Beaujolais. In a good year it has a splendid deep colour and powerful fruit.

FLEURIE   (708 ha. Average harvest: 35,000 hl)
Easy to pronounce, attractive to drink yet holding up stoutly in bottle, one of the largest productions of the nine top growths—Fleurie has many advantages.

[1] *Le Beaujolais*, Editions France Empire, Paris, 1977.

CHIROUBLES   (280 ha. Average harvest: 13,000 hl)
This has a scarcity value, being always in demand in France and one of the first communes each year to sell out at grower's level. The style of the wine is transitional between Fleurie and Morgon, according to P. Forgeot. Others find a good Chiroubles the very essence of what Beaujolais is all about.

MORGON   (910 ha. Average harvest: 42,000 hl)
With Brouilly, this is the largest production of the nine growths. The wine is said to have a particular character, deriving from the disintegrating schists on which it grows. Messrs Louis Orizet and Robert Allouin[1] discover a dominating nuance of sherry and wild cherry, decorated with apricot tonalities.

BROUILLY   (1,075 ha. Average harvest: 45,000 hl)
This is the largest *appellation* of the nine growths, and often the best value for money. It has charm and depth and a record number (68) of growers offering wine in bottle.

CÔTE DE BROUILLY   (255 ha. Average harvest: 12,000 hl)
According to Hubert Piat, the wine lacks a certain delicacy, is solid, powerful, perhaps too individual. I have rarely come across it.

BEAUJOLAIS VILLAGES   (approx. 5,300 ha. Average harvest: 25,000 hl)
The wine can be made in thirty-nine communes: Juliénas, Jullié, Emeringes, Chénas, Fleurie, Chiroubles, Lancié, Villié-Morgon, Lantigné, Beaujeu, Regnié, Durette, Cercié, Quincié, Saint-Lager, Odenas, Charentay, Saint-Étienne-la-Varenne, Vaux, Le Perréon, Saint-Étienne-des-Oullières, Blacé, Arbuissonnas, Salles, Saint-Julien, Montmelas, Rivolet, Denicé, Les Ardillats, Marchampt and Vauxrenard in the Rhône *département*, and Leynes, Saint-Amour-Bellevue, La Chapelle-de-Guinchay, Romanèche, Pruzilly, Chânes, Saint-Vérand and Saint-Symphorien d'Ancelles in the *département* of Saône et Loire.

BEAUJOLAIS   (7,200 ha. Average harvest: 350,000 hl red wine and 4,000 hl white)
French writers tell us that basic Beaujolais is *le type parfait du*

[1] In the notes to the excellent map at the back of Louis Orizet's *Mon Beaujolais* (Les Editions de la Grisière, Mâcon, 1976).

vin de carafe, and so it can be. But the formula which appears to correspond to what consumers actually enjoy today is no longer that of 10·5° or 11° light carafe wine. 'Sugar is the besetting sin of the Beaujolais,' writes Pierre-Marie Doutrelant.[1] He goes on: 'Take a Beaujolais Villages coming from a vine which yielded forty hectolitres per hectare; it will have a natural alcoholic degree of 11°–11·5°, and one will round it off with an additional 1° by adding sugar. Perfect. No consumer will complain. The wine will be balanced, and able to travel. On the other hand, take a Beaujolais produced at the rate of a hundred hectolitres per hectare as was common between 1970 and 1974. It will naturally have 8°–9° of alcohol and sugaring will automatically bring it up to 12·5°. Even if the consumer does not notice, this wine will damage his health more than the other.'

Nevertheless, I do not find myself indignant over chaptalization excesses in the Beaujolais to the extent that I am in the Côte d'Or. One ·cannot help admiring what Beaujolais wine-growers and merchants have achieved during their brief history. Starting from misery and abandon they have built the region into one of France's most prosperous. They have made their wines known by opening up their cellars, inviting their customers in, and sending them away happy. More than one rival vineyard area looks on enviously at their success.

[1] *Les Bons Vins et les Autres*, Éditions du Seuil, Paris, 1976.

APPENDIX A

Burgundy Vineyards under Single Ownership

COMMUNE	MONOPOLE VINEYARD	SIZE	OWNER/ DISTRIBUTOR
AUXERRE	Clos de la Chainette (Bourgogne *blanc* and *rosé*)	3 ha.	Hôpital Psychiatrique de l'Yonne
CHABLIS	Chablis *Grand Cru* Moutonne	2⅓ ha.	Domaine A. Long-Depaquit
	Chablis *Grand Cru* Clos Clos des Hospices	2⅖ ha.	J. Moreau et Fils
CHENÔVE	Bourgogne Clos du Chapitre	1½ ha.	Michel Pont
FIXIN	Clos du Meix-Trouhans	2 ha.	Camille Crusserey
	Clos de la Perrière	5 ha.	Domaine de la Perrière
	Clos Napoléon (Aux Cheusots)	1⅘ ha.	Pierre Gelin
	Clos du Chapitre	4¾ ha.	Pierre Gelin
GEVREY-CHAMBERTIN	Les Varoilles	6 ha. ⎫	Domaine des Varoilles/ Naigeon-Chauveau
	Meix des Ouches	1 ha. ⎬	
	Romanée	1 ha. ⎥	
	Clos du Couvent	½ ha. ⎭	
	Clos des Ruchottes-Chambertin	1 ha.	Domaine Rousseau

337

COMMUNE	MONOPOLE VINEYARD	SIZE	OWNER/ DISTRIBUTOR
	Clos de la Justice	2 ha.	Pierre Bourée
	Clos du Fonteny	$\frac{9}{10}$ ha.	Clair-Daü
	Clos Tamisot	$1\frac{1}{2}$ ha.	Pierre Damoy
MOREY-SAINT-DENIS	Clos de la Bussière	$2\frac{1}{2}$ ha.	Domaine Georges Roumier
	Clos de Tart	$7\frac{1}{5}$ ha.	Mommessin
	Clos des Lambrays	9 ha.	Cosson
VOUGEOT	Clos Blanc de Vougeot	3 ha.	Domaine de l'Héritier-Guyot
	Clos de la Perrière	$2\frac{2}{5}$ ha.	Ets. Bertagna
VOSNE-ROMANÉE	La Grand Rue	$1\frac{1}{2}$ ha.	Henry Lamarche
	Clos des Réas	2 ha.	Jean Gros
	Romanée-Conti	$1\frac{4}{5}$ ha.	Domaine de la Romanée-Conti
	La Tâche	6 ha.	Domaine de la Romanée-Conti
	La Romanée	$\frac{4}{5}$ ha.	Abbe Liger-Belair/distrib. Bouchard Père
	Clos Frantin	$\frac{1}{10}$ ha.	Domaine du Clos Frantin/ Bichot
NUITS	Clos de Thorey	$3\frac{1}{2}$ ha.	Moillard
	Clos des Grandes Vignes	2 ha.	Moillard
	Clos des Forêts Saint-Georges	7 ha.	Jules Belin
	Clos de l'Arlot	4 ha.	Jules Belin
	Didiers	1 ha.	Hospices de Nuits
	Didiers Saint-Georges	$2\frac{1}{5}$ ha.	Hospices de Nuits
	Clos de la Maréchale	$9\frac{1}{2}$ ha.	J. Faiveley
	Clos des Perrières	1 ha.	Jouan-Marcillet
	Clos des Corvées	5 ha.	Domaine du Général Gouachon

COMMUNE	MONOPOLE VINEYARD	SIZE	OWNER/ DISTRIBUTOR
	Château Gris (aux Crots)	4 ha.	Lupé-Cholet
	Clos de Lupé (Bourgogne *rouge*)	2 ha.	Lupé-Cholet
	Clos des Porrets Saint-Georges	$3\frac{1}{2}$ ha.	Henri Gouges
	Clos Saint-Marc	$1\frac{2}{5}$ ha.	Distrib. Viénot
CÔTE DE NUITS VILLAGES	Clos des Langres	7 ha.	Domaine de la Juvinière
	Clos du Chapeau	$1\frac{3}{5}$ ha.	Jules Belin
HAUTES CÔTES DE NUITS MAREY-LES-FUSSEY	Clos du Vignon, Bourgogne Hautes Côtes de Nuits	8 ha.	Thévenot-le Brun
LADOIX	Clos les Chagnots	7 ha.	Domaine Les Terres-Vineuses
ALOXE-CORTON	Corton Clos des Meix	$1\frac{1}{5}$ ha.	Daniel Senard
	Corton Clos des Vergennes	2 ha.	Distrib. Moillard
	Corton Clos de la Vigne au Saint	$2\frac{2}{3}$ ha.	Louis Latour
	Corton Clos des Cortons-Faiveley	3 ha.	J. Faiveley
PERNAND-VERGELESSES	Clos de la Croix de Pierre (en Caradeux)	2 ha.	Louis Jadot
	Clos Berthet	2 ha.	P. Dubreuil-Fontaine et Fils
SAVIGNY	Clos la Bataillère (Vergelesses)	$1\frac{1}{5}$ ha.	Albert Morot
CHOREY-LES-BEAUNE	Champ Chevrey	$1\frac{1}{2}$ ha.	Tollot-Beaut
	Château de Chorey	1 ha.	Domaine Germain

COMMUNE	MONOPOLE VINEYARD	SIZE	OWNER/ DISTRIBUTOR
BEAUNE	Clos de l'Ecu	2⅘ ha.	Jaboulet-Vercherre
	Clos de la Féguine (Cras)	1¾ ha.	Jacques Prieur
	Clos des Ursules (Vignes Franches)	2½ ha.	Louis Jadot
	Clos de la Mousse	3⅓ ha.	Bouchard Père et Fils
	La Vigne de l'Enfant Jésus (Grèves)	4 ha.	Bouchard Père et Fils
CÔTE DE BEAUNE	Clos Saint-Landry	1¾ ha.	Bouchard Père et Fils
	Clos des Topes Bizot	4¼ ha.	Machard de Gramont
POMMARD	Clos du Château de la Commaraine	1½ ha.	Jaboulet-Vercherre
	Clos de Cîteaux (Epenots)	3 ha.	Jean Monnier
	Clos des Epeneaux	5½ ha.	Comte Armand
	Clos du Château de Pommard	19½ ha.	Jean-Louis Laplanche
VOLNAY	Clos de la Barre	1 ha.	Distrib. Moillard
	Clos du Verseuil	⅔ ha.	Jean Clerget
	Clos des Santenots	1⅕ ha.	Jacques Prieur
	Clos des Ducs	2 ha.	Marquis d'Angerville
	Clos des Soixante Ouvrées (Caillerets)	2⅔ ha.	Domaine de la Pousse d'Or
	Clos de la Bousse d'Or	2⅓ ha.	Domaine de la Pousse d'Or
	Clos d'Audignac	⅘ ha.	Domaine de la Pousse d'Or
	Clos de la Rougeotte (Fremiets)	1⅔ ha.	Bouchard Père et Fils
	Clos du Villages		B. Delagrange

COMMUNE	MONOPOLE VINEYARD	SIZE	OWNER/ DISTRIBUTOR
MONTHÉLIE	Clos Gauthey	1 ha.	Domaine Darviot
AUXEY-DURESSES	Clos du Val	1 ha.	Jean Prunier
	Clos du Moulin aux Moines	2⅘ ha.	Domaine du Moulin aux Moines/Roland Thévenin
SAINT-ROMAIN	Clos des Ducs	1 ha.	Domaine de la Corgette/Roland Thévenin
	Clos de la Branière	1½ ha.	Domaine de la Corgette/Roland Thévenin
MEURSAULT	Clos de Mazeray	3 ha.	Jacques Prieur
	Clos des Perrières	1 ha.	Domaine Albert Grivault
	Clos Richemont (Cras)	⅔ ha.	Les Héritiers Darnat
	Clos de la Barre	2 ha.	Comtes Lafon
	Clos de la Baronne (red)	2½ ha.	René Manuel/ Labouré-Roi
	Clos de la Velle	1 ha.	Domaine Darviot
	Clos des Grands Charrons		Berthe Morey
BLAGNY	La Genelotte	3 ha.	de Montlivault
PULIGNY-MONTRACHET	Clos du Cailleret	3½ ha.	Jean Chartron
	Clos du Meix	1¾ ha.	Domaine Etienne Sauzet
	Clos de la Mouchère	4 ha.	Henri Boillot
	Clos de la Garenne	1⅕ ha.	Duc de Magenta
CHASSAGNE	Abbaye de Morgeot Clos de la Chapelle	4½ ha.	Duc de Magenta

COMMUNE	MONOPOLE VINEYARD	SIZE	OWNER/ DISTRIBUTOR
	La Cardeuse (Morgeot)	$\frac{3}{4}$ ha.	Marcel Moreau
	Clos du Château de la Maltroie	2 ha.	André Cournut
	Clos Pitois	3 ha.	Joseph Belland
	Clos Saint-Marc		Baudrand et Fils
SANTENAY	Clos de Malte	7 ha.	Joly Père et Fils
RULLY	Les Varots	17 ha.	Renarde/Delorme
	Clos de Bellecroix (red)	7 ha.	Domaine de la Folie
	Le Meix-Guillaume	1 ha.	Ninot-Rigaud
	Clos du Chapitre	2 ha.	Mme Niepce
MERCUREY	Clos Voyen	4 ha.	Jeannin-Naltet
	Clos la Marche	3 ha.	Bouchard Aîné et Fils
	Clos de Myglands	9 ha.	J. Faiveley
	Clos Rond	5 ha.	J. Faiveley
	Les Mauvarennes	15 ha.	J. Faiveley
	Clos Rochette	2 ha.	J. Faiveley
	Clos Dardelin	$2\frac{1}{2}$ ha.	J. Faiveley
	La Framboisière	6 ha.	J. Faiveley
	Clos du Château de Montaigu	2 ha.	Yves de Launay
	Clos Fortoul	$4\frac{1}{2}$ ha.	Bordeaux-Montrieux
	La Mission	2 ha.	Antonin Rodet
	Clos Marcilly		Baudrand et Fils
GIVRY	Clos Saloman	7 ha.	Du Gardin
	Clos Saint-Pierre	2 ha.	Baron Thénard
	Clos de la Barraude		M. Pigneret

TOTAL: 115 vineyards

APPENDIX B

Recent Vintages

I have been fortunate to have access to the descriptions of recent vintages produced by the Beaune brokers Henri Meurgey & Cie and the weather statistics collected by the *Service de la Protection des Végétaux*, and gratefully acknowledge my debt to them. For more detailed information on Burgundy vintages (back to 1753) reference may be made to *The Great Vintage Wine Book* by Michael Broadbent.

1982   Considerable care will be needed in selecting Côte d'Or wines as some red vineyards yielded 75 hl/ha., some whites 80 hl/ha. Much of the best Beaujolais went as Nouveau.

1981   Some exceptional Chablis and white Burgundy, and the Beaujolais was generally successful. Côte d'Or reds seem correct but lacking flesh; they may be slow to evolve.

1980   Disappointing weather in the spring and early summer was followed by a finer August and September, but it rained during the late vintage. There was some rot and not all the grapes were ripe.

1979   A large harvest of generally healthy grapes, the wines having less concentration and staying power than the 1978s. Nuits and Vosne hit by hail. White vineyards yielded particularly abundantly, and prices dropped in Chablis and Mâconnais but held their level in the Côte d'Or. The Beaujolais were fruity and sound.

1978   A late harvest but quality exceptionally good for both red and white throughout the region.

1977   Abundant production, particularly on the Côte de Nuits. The summer had been wet, requiring many treatments against mildew and rot. Low natural degrees, so heavy chaptalization, the result being '*une corpulence assez maigre*' and high acidities.

1976   A good quality vintage from an abundant and healthy harvest. Flowering took place 5–10 June, picking of the whites started generally 4 September and reds 10 September. Red wines deep-coloured stayers, whites generally lacked acidity to balance their richness. Mercurey and Rully badly affected by hail.

1975 From mid-August the initial high hopes for quality were dashed by rain. A small harvest, losses being due to grey rot. Some Côte de Beaune whites were respectable but most red wines browned early.

1974 Average size harvest but short, fruitless tannic wines. Low degrees in the Côte de Nuits.

1973 Record production in the Côte d'Or: 388,745 hl, but wines often below minimum legal natural sugar levels and lacking acidity to boot. Red wines flat and uninteresting, some whites respectable. The law of 1893 which defined the relationship between alcohol and dry extract in wine was much flouted (by the excessive sugaring).

1972 Abundant quantity, particularly on the Côte de Beaune, after a late flowering and not much sun until 10 September. Red wines healthy with good colour, some lacking flesh. Acidities high in red wines and whites.

1971 June was cold and wet, giving shrivelled berries and not many of them. Picking began 18 September, a ripe and healthy harvest. The year marred by heavy hailstorms in Côte de Beaune and to a lesser extent Côte de Nuits. When free of *goût de sec* (the 'mousey' taste produced by hail) both reds and whites are exceptionally good.

1970 A very abundant harvest, low natural degrees on the Côte de Nuits particularly. Whites uneven in quality, reds lacking the fruit and concentration of 1971 or 1969.

1969 The grapes ripened well after a rainy flowering. Reds: very good colour, good fruit and tannin; whites well-balanced.

1968 A few respectable white wines were made, but grey rot was widespread and the red wines were pale, thin and early browners.

1967 A year of irregular quality. Spring frosts reduced the yields, the Côte de Beaune whites and Beaune itself being worst hit. Hail in August and rain in September brought grey rot. The whites were better than the reds.

1966 June was good, July and August poorish, but September put things right. Quite a large yield, wines had character and elegance. A sound vintage.

1965 A small yield of poor wines—some of the reds having a 'yellow-brown colour from the beginning which was most distressing to behold'. High acidity and low sugar content throughout the region.

1964 Abundant yield of powerful aromatic red wines; the whites were rich and luscious.

1963 A large yield of red wines which generally lacked concentration; the whites were better.

1962 Well-balanced fine wines, an excellent year for reds and particularly whites.

Glossary of Wine Terms

CEP: Vine stock.

CÉPAGE: Type of vine.

COURTIER EN VINS: Wine broker.

CHAPTALIZATION: The addition of sugar to grape-must at the moment of wine-making, in order to increase alcoholic content.

CLIMAT: A specific vineyard site.

CLOS: An enclosed plot of land or vineyard (but not all *clos* are, in fact, surrounded by walls).

CRU: See *Grand Cru, Premier Cru*.

CUVÉE: The contents of a vat (*cuve*) or several vats blended together.

DOMAINE: A vineyard estate.

FEUILLETTE: The Chablis barrel, holding 132 litres.

GRAND CRU: Greath Growth—the highest classification in Burgundy for the best individual vineyards.

HECTARE (ha.): Approximately 2½ acres.

HECTOLITRE (hl): One hundred litres, approximately 22 gallons.

HOGSHEAD: See *Pièce*.

LEES: The sediments which fall to the bottom of vat or barrel during and after fermentation (see Racking).

MONOPOLE: The description given by Burgundians to a vineyard under single ownership. Appendix A lists 115 *Monopole* vineyards.

MUST: The grape-juice before and during fermentation, at the end of which it has become wine.

NÉGOCIANT: Wine shipper.

PIÈCE: The Burgundy barrel, holding 223–8 litres (approximately 25 dozen bottles). Mâconnais-Beaujolais barrels hold 212–16 litres.

PREMIER CRU: First Growth. One would expect this description to apply to Burgundy's best vineyards but confusingly it means the second best (see *Grand Cru*).

RACKING: Removing wine from one vat or barrel to another, leaving the lees (q.v.) behind, to be discarded.

RÉCOLTE: The harvest or vintage.

TASTEVIN: A shallow tasting receptacle about $\frac{3}{4}$ in deep by 3 in across, made of silver or baser metal. Its surface is indented with stripes and dimples to catch the light when tasting hazy young wine.

VIGNERON: Wine-grower.

VIN DE GARDE: A wine for keeping, i.e. which requires and will benefit from maturation.

Bibliography
and further reading list

Académie de Dijon, *Géologie de la Côte d'Or*. Centre Régional de Documentation Pédagogique, Dijon, 1967

Agnel, H., *Guide des Plantations de Vignes*. I.T.V., Paris, 1964

Anon. *Détails Historiques et Statistiques sur le département de la Côte d'Or*. Dijon Imprimerie Carion, chez Gaulard-Marin, Nov. 1818

Arlott, John, and Fielden, Christopher, *Burgundy Vines and Wines*. Davis-Poynter, London, 1976

Audin, M., *Le Musée Folklorique de Beaujeu*. Les Editions de Cuvier, Villefranche, 1945

Aulas, Michel, *Anthologie du Beaujolais*. Gougenheim, Lyon

Bastien, Bruno, *Principaux types de grands vins rouges de la Côte d'Or*. Mémoire d'études ENSSAA, Beaune, 1970

Bazin, Jean-François, *Bourgogne de 1975 à 1985*. Informations et Conjoncture, Paris, 1976

Bazin, Jean-François, *Le Vignoble des Hautes Côtes de Nuits et de Beaune*. Les Cahiers de Vergy, 1973

Bazin, Jean-François, *Le Vin de Bourgogne ou L'Ivresse du Succès*. Réproduction de texte de l'enquête parue dans Les Depêches, Dijon, C.I.B., Beaune, 1971

Bernard, Raymond, et al., *Le Vin de Bourgogne*. Editions Montalba, 1976

Bertall, *La Vigne—Voyage autour des vins de France*. Plon, Paris, 1878

Berthelier, Bernard, *L'Evolution et l'Avenir de l'Aligoté*. Fédération Interprofessionnelle des Vins de Bourgogne, Beaune, 1978

Boidron, R., *Le Mâconnais Viticole*. CETA Viticole du Mâconnais, Chambre d'Agriculture de Saône et Loire (undated)

Boidron, R., *La Sélection clonale en Saône et Loire*. L'Exploitant Agricole, 1977

Boidron, R., *Vignes Hautes et Larges*. L'Exploitant Agricole, Saône et Loire, 1978

347

BIBLIOGRAPHY AND FURTHER READING LIST

Bréjoux, Pierre, *Les Vins de Bourgogne*. Société Française d'Editions Vinicoles, Paris, 1967

Bro, Louis, *Chablis*. Paris, 1959

Broadbent, Michael, *The Great Vintage Wine Book*. Mitchell Beazley, London, 1980

Capus, J., *L'Evolution de la Législation sur les Appellations d'Origine*. Louis Larmat, Paris, 1947

Caspar, P., *Le Climat de Dijon et de ses environs*. R.G.L., 1949

Chauvet, Marcel, et Reynier, Alain, *Manuel de Viticulture*. Editions J. B. Baillière, Paris, 1975

Chidgey, Graham, *Guide to the Wines of Burgundy*. Pitman, 1977

Clos-Jouve, Henry, et Benoit, Félix, *Le Beaujolais Secret et Gourmand*. Solarama, 1973

Colombet, Albert, *L'Action Tutélaire du Parlement de Bourgogne vis-à-vis des vignes et des vins de notre province*. Bulletin de la Société d'Archéologie de Beaune, Congrès des Sociétés Savantes, Beaune, 1951

Colombier, Jean, *Les Vins d'Appellation d'Origine Contrôlée* (Application Côte d'Or). Mémoires d'études ENSSAA, Beaune, 1971

Cook, Philip, *A Wine Merchant's Assessment of Burgundy*. Ridley's Wine and Spirit Trade Circular, 1967

Courtépée, M. (Prêtre), et Béguillet, M. (Avocat), *Description Générale et Particulière du Duché de Bourgogne*. 7 vols. 1775–85.

Danguy, M. R., et Aubertin, M. Ch., *Les Grands Vins de Bourgogne, La Côte d'Or*. H. Armand, Dijon, 1892

Delissey, M., *Beaune, ses vins fins et le commerce du vin*. 1961

Denman, James L., *Wine and its Counterfeits*. London, 1876

Derognat, Donnot et Defer-Lagoutte, *Beaujolais Mâconnais-Ecologie, Archéologie et Oenologie*. C.R.D.P., Académie de Lyon, 1975

Des Ombiaux, *Petit Manuel de l'Amateur de Bourgogne*. 1908

Dion, Professeur Roger, *Histoire de la Vigne et du Vin en France des Origines au XIXe Siècle*. Paris, 1959

Doutrelant, P. M., *Les Bons Vins et les autres*. Editions du Seuil, Paris, 1976

Dulau, L., *Géologie de la Côte d'Or*. 1961

Dumay, Raymond, *La Mort du Vin*. Stock, 1976

Durand, E., et Guicherd, J., *La Culture de la Vigne en Côte d'Or*. Arthur Batault, Beaune, 1896

Dutraive, Justin, *Jadis en Beaujolais*. M. Lescuyer et Fils, Lyon, 1976

Editions du Cuvier, *Almanach du Beaujolais*. Jean Guillermet, Villefranche, 1933, 1937, 1941, 1945, 1948, 1955, 1956, 1957, 1958, 1960

Engel, René, *Propos sur l'art du bien boire*. Filiber, Nuits St. Georges, 1971

BIBLIOGRAPHY AND FURTHER READING LIST

Ferré, L., *Traité d'Oenologie Bourguignonne*. I.N.A.O., Paris, 1958

Foillard, L., et David, T., *Le pays et le vin Beaujolais*, J. Guillemet, Villefranche

Forgeot, Pierre, *Guide de l'Amateur de Bourgogne*. Presses Universitaires de France, Paris, 1967

Forgeot, Pierre, *Origines du Vignoble Bourguignon*. Presses Universitaires de France, 1972

Fromageot, L., Marion, Maurice, Colombet, Albert, Perraux, Lucien, *Bulletin de la Société d'Archéologie de Beaune*. 25–7 mai 1951

Gadille, Rolande, *Le Vignoble de la Côte Bourguignonne*. Les Belles Lettres, Publications de l'Université de Dijon, Paris, 1967

Galet, P., *Cépages et vignobles de France*, Tome II. Paul Dehan, Montpellier, 1958

Gardien, Jacques, *Le Vin dans la Chanson Populaire Bourguignonne*. L'Arche d'Or, Dijon, 1967

Ginestet, Bernard, *La Bouillie Bordelaise*. Flammarion, Paris, 1975

Goujon, Pierre, *Le Vignoble de Saône et Loire au XIX Siècle*. Université Lyon II, Lyon, 1973

Grivot, Françoise, *Le Commerce des Vins de Bourgogne*. SABRI, Paris, 1962

Guyou, Aline, et Parel, Jean Luc, *Vigne, Sol, Sous-Sol en Beaujolais*. Mémoire de fins d'étude 5ème Promotion des Elèves Ingénieurs, Institut Supérieur d'Agriculture Rhône Alpes (ISARA), Lyon, 1976

Guyot, J., *Etude des Vignobles de France*. Paris, 1868

Hallgarten, S. F., *German Wines*. Faber and Faber, London, 1976

Jacquemont, Guy, *De la mise en bouteilles obligatoire dans la région de production Bourgogne*. Mémoire d'études ESA Purpan, Toulouse, 1970

Jeffs, Julian, *The Wines of Europe*. Faber and Faber, London, 1971

Johnson, Hugh, *Pocket Book of Wine*. Mitchell Beazley, London, 1977

Johnson, Hugh, *The World Atlas of Wine*. Mitchell Beazley, London, 1971

Jullien, A., *Topographie de tous les vignobles connus*. de Lacroix et Baudry, Paris, 1832

Kempf, Michel, *Rapport de Stage*. Centre de formation permanente pour adultes, Section 'Techniques et Métiers de la Vigne et du Vin', Lycée Agricole de Macon-Davayé, 1977/8

Lagrange, André, *Catalogue du Musée du vin de Bourgogne à Beaune*. G.-P. Maisonneuve et Larose, Paris, 1974

Lavalle, Dr Jean, *Histoire et Statistique de la Vigne et des Grands Vins de la Côte d'Or*. 1855

Leglise, Max, *La Vinification en rouge en Bourgogne—méthode classique et recherches nouvelles*. INRA, Station Oenologique, Beaune

349

BIBLIOGRAPHY AND FURTHER READING LIST

Léglise, Max, *Une Initiation à la Dégustation des Grands Vins*. DIVO, Lausanne, 1976

Léglise, Max, Naudin, R., et Prévost, J., *Essais de traitement de raisins rouges entiers par la vapeur d'eau avant vinification*. Extrait de Progrès Agricole et Viticole, 84 Année Tome CLXVII

Lichine, Alexis, *Encyclopaedia of Wines and Spirits*. Cassell, London, 1967

Marrison, L. W., *Wines and Spirits*. Penguin Books, 1958

Morelot, Dr, *Statistique de la vigne dans le département de la Côte d'Or*, Dijon, Paris, 1831

Morton Shand, P., revised and edited by Cyril Ray, *A Book of French Wines*. Penguin Books, 1968

Moucheron, E. de, *Grands Crus de Bourgogne*

Ordish, Georges, *The Great Wine Blight*. Dent, London, 1972

Orizet, Louis, *Mon Beaujolais*. Editions de la Grisière, Macon, 1976

Pacottet, P., *Viticulture*. Paris, 1905

Perriaux, Lucien, *Histoire de Beaune et du pays beaunois*. Presses Universitaires de France, Paris, 1974

Peynaud, Emile, *Connaissance et Travail du Vin*. Dunod, Paris, 1971

Piat, Hubert, *Le Beaujolais*. Editions France Empire, Paris, 1977

Poulain, R., et Jacquelin, L., *Vignes et Vins de France*. Flammarion, Paris, 1960

Poulet, Père et Fils, *Grand Livre du Vin*. Beaune, 1747

Poupon, Pierre, *Nouvelles Pensées d'un Dégustateur*. Confrérie des Chevaliers du Tastevin, Nuits St. Georges, 1975

Poupon, Pierre, *Plaisirs de la Dégustation*. Presses Universitaires de France, Paris, 1973

Poupon, Pierre, *Toute la Bourgogne, Portrait d'une province*. Presses Universitaires de France, Paris, 1970

Poupon, Pierre, *Vignes et Jours, Carnet d'un Bourguignon*. Jean Dupin, Beaune, 1963

Poupon, Pierre, et Forgeot, Pierre, *Les Vins de Bourgogne*, 8ème Edition. Presses Universitaires de France, Paris, 1977

Quittanson, Charles, et Aulnoyes, François des, *L'Elite des Vins de France*. Centre Nationale de Coordination, Paris, 1969

Quittanson, Charles, et Vanhoutte, R., *La Protection des Appellations d'Origine et le commerce des vins et eaux de vie*. La Journée Vinicole, Montpellier, 1970

Rat, Pierre, *Bourgogne Morvan*. Guides Géologiques Régionaux, Masson et Cie, Paris, 1972

Réal, Antony, *Les Grands Vins, Curiosités Historiques,* 1887

Redding, Cyrus, *A History and Description of Modern Wines*. Whittaker, Treacher & Arnot, London, 1833

Richardot, Jean-Pierre, *Papa Bréchard Vigneron du Beaujolais*. Stock, 1977

Rodier, Camille, *Le Clos de Vougeot*. Librairie L. Venot, Dijon, 1949

Rodier, Camille, *Le Vin de Bourgogne*. L. Damidot, Dijon, 1948

Roncarati, Bruno, *Viva Vino, D.O.C. Wines of Italy*. Wine and Spirit Publications, London, 1976

Rozet, Georges, *La Bourgogne, Tastevin en main*. Horizons de France, Paris, 1949

Saintsbury, George, *Notes on a Cellar-Book*. Macmillan, London, 1927

Siloret, G., *Le Vin*. Hachette, Paris

Simon, André L., *Bottlescrew Days*. Duckworth, London, 1926

Simon, André L., *The History of the Wine Trade in England*, Facsimile Ed. The Holland Press, 1964

Taransaud, Jean, *Le Livre de la Tonnellerie*, La Roue à Livres, Paris, 1976

Union Interprofessionnelle des Vins du Beaujolais, *La Vente Directe, 1975 à 1977*. Villefranche, 1978

Vaughan, Richard, *Valois Burgundy*. Allen Lane, Penguin Books, London, 1975

Vedel, A., Charle, G., Charnay, P., Tourmeau, J., *Essai sur la dégustation des vins*. I.N.A.O., S.E.I.V. Macon, 1972

Wallace, Dr Peigi, *Geology of Wine*. 24th International Geological Congress, Section 6, London, 1972

Warner Allen, H., *A History of Wine*. Faber and Faber, London, 1961

Younger, William, *Gods, Men and Wine*. The Wine and Food Society, Michael Joseph, London, 1966

Yoxall, H. W., *The Wines of Burgundy*. The International Wine and Food Society, Michael Joseph, London, 1968

Index

Page numbers in **bold** refer to the vineyard holdings in Part Two.

367

371